Lin

D0346204

discover

This book should be returned on or before the due date.

the very plainness of her style . . . adds to the tension
Times Literary Supplement

ruth
rendell

A SIGHT FOR SORE EYES

arrow books

Reissued by Arrow Books 2011

4 6 8 10 9 7 5 3

First published in Great Britain in 1998 by Hutchinson

This edition first published in paperback by Arrow Books in 1999

Arrow Books
Random House, 20 Vauxhall Bridge Road,
London SW1V 2SA

www.randomhouse.co.uk

Addresses for companies within The Random House Group Limited can be
found at: www.randomhouse.co.uk/offices.htm

The Random House Group Limited Reg. No. 954009

A CIP catalogue record for this book
is available from the British Library

ISBN 9780099557159

The Random House Group Limited supports The Forest Stewardship
Council® (FSC®), the leading international forest-certification organisation.
Our books carrying the FSC label are printed on FSC®-certified paper.
FSC is the only forest-certification scheme supported by the leading
environmental organisations, including Greenpeace. Our
paper procurement policy can be found at
www.randomhouse.co.uk/environment

MIX
Paper from
responsible sources
FSC
www.fsc.org
FSC® C016897

Printed and bound in Great Britain by Clays Ltd, St Ives PLC

For Don again

For Don again

Chapter 1

They were to hold hands and look at one another. Deeply, into each other's eyes.

'It's not a sitting,' she said, 'it's a standing. Why can't I sit on his knee?'

He laughed. Everything she said amused or delighted him, everything about her captivated him from her dark-red curly hair to her small white feet. The painter's instructions were that he should look at her as if in love and she at him as if enthralled. This was easy, this was to act naturally.

'Don't be silly, Harriet,' said Simon Alpheton. 'The very idea! Have you ever seen a painting by Rembrandt called *The Jewish Bride*?'

They hadn't. Simon described it to them as he began his preliminary sketch. 'It's a very tender painting, it expresses the protective love of the man for his young submissive bride. They're obviously wealthy, they're very richly dressed, but you can see that they're sensitive, thoughtful people and they're in love.'

'Like us. Rich and in love. Do we look like them?'

'Not in the least, and I don't think you'd want to. Ideas of beauty have changed.'

'You could call it "The Red-haired Bride".'

'She's not your bride. I am going to call it "Marc and Harriet in Orcadia Place" – what else? Now would you just stop talking for a bit, Marc?'

The house they stood in front of was described by

1

those who knew about such things as a Georgian cottage and built of the kind of red bricks usually called mellow. But at this time of the year, midsummer, almost all the brickwork was hidden under a dense drapery of Virginia creeper, its leaves green, glossy and quivering in the light breeze. The whole surface of the house seemed to shiver and rustle, a vertical sea of green ruffled into wavelets by the wind.

Simon Alpheton was fond of walls, brick walls, flint walls, walls of wood and walls of stone. When he painted Come Hither outside the studio in Hanging Sword Alley he placed them against a concrete wall stuck all over with posters. As soon as he saw that Marc's house had a wall of living leaves he wanted also to paint that, with Marc and Harriet too, of course. The wall was a shining cascade in many shades of green, Marc was in a dark-blue suit, thin black tie and white shirt, and Harriet was all in red.

When the autumn came those leaves would turn the same colour as her hair and her dress. Then they would gradually bleach to gold, to pale-yellow, fall and make a nuisance of themselves, filling the whole of that hedge-enclosed paved square and the entire backyard to a depth of several inches. The brickwork of the house would once more be revealed and the occasional, probably fake, bit of half-timbering. And in the spring of 1966 pale-green shoots would appear and the leafy cycle begin all over again. Simon thought about that as he drew leaves and hair, and pleated silk.

'Don't do that,' he said, as Marc reached forward to kiss Harriet, at the same time keeping hold of her hand and drawing her towards him. 'Leave her alone for five minutes, can't you?'

'It's hard, man, it's hard.'

'Tenderness is what I want to catch, not lust. Right?'

'My foot's gone to sleep,' said Harriet. 'Can we take a break, Simon?'

'Another five minutes. Don't think about your foot. Look at him and think about how much you love him.'

She looked up at him and he looked down at her. He held her left hand in his right hand and their eyes met in a long gaze, and Simon Alpheton painted them, preserving them in the front garden of Orcadia Cottage, if not for ever, for a very long time.

'Maybe I'll buy it,' Harriet said later, looking with approval at the outline of her face and figure.

'What with?' Marc kissed her. His voice was gentle but his words were not. 'You haven't any money.'

When Simon Alpheton looked back to that day he thought that this was the beginning of the end, the worm in the bud showing its ugly face and writhing body among the flowers.

Chapter 2

One cold Saturday, Jimmy Grex and Eileen Tawton went on a coach trip to Broadstairs. The year was 1966 and it was summer. It was the first time they had ever been on such an outing together. Their usual activities – Eileen called it 'courting' and Jimmy had no name for it – consisted of visits to the White Rose and Lion, and Jimmy occasionally coming round to Eileen's mother's for tea. But the pub came under new management, events were organised for regulars at the weekends and one of these was the Broadstairs trip.

It rained. A sharp north wind roared all the way down the coasts of Suffolk, Essex and Kent before blowing itself out somewhere in the Channel Islands. Jimmy and Eileen sat under a shelter on the front and ate the sandwich lunch they had brought with them. They bought seaside rock and looked through a telescope in a vain effort to see the coast of France. At teatime they resolved on a proper meal and went into Popplewell's restaurant on the seafront.

It was unlicensed, like most restaurants and cafés at that time, and Jimmy was dying for a drink. He had to be content with tea because the pubs didn't open till five-thirty. Even when they had finished their eggs, chips, peas and mushrooms, their apple pie and custard and slices of Dundee cake, they still had half an hour to kill. Jimmy ordered another pot of tea and Eileen went to the Ladies.

This was a tiny, windowless and – as was usual at the time, filthy – concrete-floored cupboard from which a single cubicle opened. A washbasin hung perilously from one wall, but there was no soap, towel, paper towel or, naturally, hand drier. One of the taps dripped. A woman came out of the cubicle and Eileen went in. From in there she heard the tap running and then she heard the outer door close.

Eileen had no intention of washing her hands. She had washed them before she left home that morning and, besides, there were no towels. But she glanced at her face in the bit of chipped mirror, pushed at her hair a little, pursed her lips, and in doing these things could hardly fail to take the shelf below the mirror into her vision. In the middle of it was a diamond ring.

The woman who had been here before her must have taken it off to wash her hands and forgotten it. It just went to show what too much washing led to. Eileen hadn't noticed anything about the woman except that she was middle-aged and in a raincoat. She looked at the ring. She picked it up.

Even to the totally ignorant, to those with no knowledge or appreciation of good jewellery, a fine diamond ring is apparent for what it is. This one was a solitaire with a sapphire in each shoulder. Eileen slipped it on to her right hand, where it fitted as if made for her.

Walking out of there with the ring on her finger wouldn't be a good idea. She put it in her bag. Jimmy was waiting for her, smoking his thirtieth cigarette of the day. He gave her one and they walked along to the Anchor, where he had a pint of bitter and she a half of cider. After a while she opened her bag and showed him the diamond ring.

It occurred to neither of them to take the ring back to the restaurant and hand it to the management or to go to the police. Finding's keeping's. But other ideas were in both their minds. Or, rather, the same idea. Eileen put the ring on again, but this time on to the third finger of her left hand and she held her hand up, showing it to Jimmy. Why should she ever take it off again? This she didn't say aloud, though her thought somehow communicated itself to him.

He bought a second pint of bitter and a packet of crisps and, returning to the table, said, 'May as well keep it on.'

'Shall I?' Her voice was unsteady. She felt the seriousness of the occasion. It was an awesome moment.

'May as well get engaged,' said Jimmy.

Eileen nodded. She didn't smile. Her heart was thudding. 'If that's all right.'

'I've been thinking about it for a bit,' said Jimmy. 'Been thinking of getting you a ring. I didn't reckon on this one turning up. I'm going to have another drink. You want another cider?'

'Why not?' said Eileen. 'Celebrate – why not? And give me another ciggie, will you?'

In fact, Jimmy hadn't thought of an engagement until this moment. He had no intention of getting married. Why should he marry? His mother was there to look after him and his brother, and she was only fifty-eight, there were years of life in her yet. But the discovery of the ring was too good an opportunity to miss. Suppose he'd done nothing and just let Eileen hang on to the ring, and then one day he did decide to get engaged, he'd have to buy her a ring, a new one. Besides, being engaged was just being engaged, it could go on for years, it didn't mean you had to get married tomorrow.

Eileen wasn't in love with Jimmy. If she had thought about it she would probably have said she liked him

6

all right. She liked him better than any other man she knew, but she didn't really know any others. No men ever came into the woolshop where she was assistant to Miss Harvey, the owner, and where she sold double-knit and baby-soft two-ply to an elderly female clientele. She met Jimmy when he and his boss came to paint Miss Harvey's flat upstairs and put in a new sink unit. That had been five years before.

Though she was right-handed, Eileen served customers with her left hand for the next few weeks and held that hand up to her chin a lot and flashed the diamond about to catch the light. It was greatly admired. She and Jimmy went on going to the pub and he continued to come to tea with Mrs Tawton. Eileen had her thirty-fifth birthday. They went on several more outings under the auspices of the White Rose and Lion, either alone or with Mrs Tawton and her friend Gladys.

Sometimes Eileen mentioned marriage, but Jimmy always said 'We only just got engaged' or 'Time enough to think of that in a year or two'. And they'd never be able to afford a place to live. She wasn't moving in with her mother or his. Their relationship was not a sexual one. Although he sometimes kissed her, Jimmy had never suggested anything more and Eileen told herself she wouldn't have agreed if he had, she respected him for not asking. Time enough to think of that in a year or two.

Then Jimmy's mother died. She fell down dead in the street, a laden shopping bag in each hand. Loaves of bread, half-pound packs of butter, packets of biscuits, hunks of Cheddar, oranges, bananas, bacon, two chickens, tins of beans and tins of spaghetti in tomato sauce rolled across the pavement or dropped into the gutter. Betty Grex had suffered a massive stroke.

Her two sons had lived in the house since they were born and neither considered moving out. Now there was no one to look after them, Jimmy decided he had better get married. After all, he had been engaged for five years. The ring, which Eileen wore day in and day out, was there to remind him. She wouldn't be lucky enough to find a *wedding* ring on a shelf in a Ladies but, fortunately, he had the one that came off his dead mother's finger. They married at the Registrar's Office in Burnt Oak.

The Grex home was a small semi-detached house, two up and two down with small bathroom and kitchen, its outside stucco-coated and painted yellow ochre, among rows of such houses near the North Circular Road at Neasden. Because it was on a corner, access to the garden was possible from the street and here, filling most of the small area, Keith Grex kept his car. Or, rather, his series of cars, the current one at the time of his brother's marriage being a Studebaker, red and silver with fins.

Keith was younger than Jimmy and unmarried. Uninterested in women or sex of any kind, a non-reader, no sportsman, he was largely indifferent to everything except drink and cars. Not so much in driving them as in tinkering. Taking them apart and putting them together again. Cleaning and polishing them, admiring them. Before the Studebaker he had had a Pontiac and before that a Dodge.

For use, for going to work, he had a motor bike. When his car was in perfect condition and looking at its best, he would take it out and drive it up the North Circular Road to Brent Cross, up the Hendon Way, down Station Road and back along the Broadway. And when the Studebaker Owners' Club held a rally he and the car always attended. An outing for the car meant taking the engine apart and reassembling it. In the building trade like his brother, he had long ago laid a concrete pad all over the back garden for the car and the motor bike to stand on, leaving only a very small green rectangle, a 'lawn' of grass, dandelions and thistles.

In their mother's lifetime, and earlier in their father's, the brothers Grex had shared a bedroom. There, in the evenings, while Keith worked on his car, Jimmy had attended to his own sexual needs with the assistance of *Penthouse* magazine. Now he was moving out and into what had been Betty Grex's room, another transition must be made. Jimmy, who didn't think much, supposed it could be done with ease. As it happened, it took about a year and was never as satisfactory for Jimmy as his fantasy liaisons with those centre-folds had been. As for Eileen, she accepted. It was all right. It didn't hurt. You didn't get cold or made to feel sick. It was what you did when you were married. Like vacuum cleaning and shopping and cooking and locking the back door at night.

And, of course, having a baby.

Eileen was forty-two. Because of her age she had no idea she could be pregnant. Like many a woman before her, she thought it was the Change. Besides, she didn't know much about sex and still less about reproduction, and she had curious notions picked up from her mother and her aunts. One of these was that in order to be productive ejaculation had to be frequent, lavish and cumulative. In other words, a lot of that stuff had to get inside you before anything resulted. It was rather like the Grecian 2000 lotion Keith put on his greying hair, which only took effect after repeated applications.

In her marriage, applications had been infrequent and were growing rarer. So she didn't believe she was pregnant even when she put on a lot of weight and grew a big stomach. Jimmy, of course, noticed nothing. It was Mrs Chance next door who asked her when she was expecting. Eileen's mother knew at once – she hadn't seen her for two months – and expressed the opinion that the baby would have 'something wrong with it' on account of her daughter's age. Nobody talked about Down's Syndrome then and Agnes Tawton said the child would be a Mongol.

Eileen never went near a doctor, none of them did, and she wasn't going to start now. A common feeling with her was that if you ignored something it would go away, so she ignored her expanding shape while giving in to her food cravings. She developed a passion for doughnuts and for croissants which were just beginning to appear in the shops, and she smoked ferociously, forty or fifty a day.

This was the early seventies when the phrase 'getting in touch with one's body' was current. Eileen wasn't in touch with her body at all, she never looked at it or in the mirror at it and most of its sensations, with the exception of actual pain, she disregarded. But these pains were another thing altogether, Eileen had never known anything like them, they went on and on and got worse and worse, and she couldn't be out of touch with her body any more. Of course, the Grex family had no phone, it wouldn't have occurred to them to have one, so, in the extremity of Eileen's travail, Keith was despatched to the doctor's to get help. He went in the Studebaker which happened to be due for its fortnightly outing.

There was no question of Jimmy going. He said it was all a storm in a teacup. Besides, he had just bought a television set, their first colour one, and he was watching Wimbledon. A doctor came, very angry, almost disbelieving, and found Eileen lying

10

among her broken waters, chain-smoking. A mid-wife came. The Grex family, all of them, were furiously castigated and the midwife turned off the television herself.

The baby, a nine-pound-nine-ounce boy, was born at ten p.m. Contrary to Mrs Tawton's predictions there was nothing wrong with him. Or nothing in the sense she meant. The kind of things that were wrong with him were unresponsive to any tests then and, largely, still are. In any case, it depends on whether you belong in the nature camp or to the nurture school. In the seventies everyone who knew anything at all believed a person's character and temperament derived solely from his early environment and conditioning. Freud ruled OK.

He was a beautiful baby. During his gestation his mother had lived on croissants with butter, whipped-cream doughnuts, salami, streaky bacon, fried eggs, chocolate bars, sausages and chips with everything. She had smoked about ten thousand eight hundred cigarettes and drunk many gallons of Guinness, cider, Babycham and sweet sherry. But he was a beautiful child with smooth, peachy skin, dark-brown silky hair, the features of a baby angel in an Old Master, and perfect fingers and toes.

'What are you going to call him?' said Mrs Tawton after several days.

'He'll have to be called something, won't he?' said Eileen, as if naming the child was expedient, but by no means obligatory.

Neither she nor Jimmy knew any names. Well, they knew their own and Keith's and Mr Chance's next door, he was called Alfred, and their dead fathers' names, but they didn't like any of those. Keith suggested Roger because that was the name of his pal he went drinking with, but Eileen didn't like this Roger, so that was out. Then another neighbour

11

came round with a present for the baby. It was a small white teddy bear with bells on its feet attached to a ribbon you hung inside the roof of the pram.

Both Agnes Tawton and Eileen were quite moved by this gift, said 'Aaah!' and pronounced it sweet.

'Teddy,' said Eileen fondly.

'There you are, there's your name,' said Keith. 'Teddy. Edward for short.' And he laughed at his own joke because no one else did.

12

Chapter 3

No one ever took much notice of him. But none of them took much notice of each other. Each seemed to live in a kind of non-clinical autism, doing their own thing, wrapped up in themselves. With Keith it was his cars, with Jimmy the television. Having sold the stuff for years, Eileen developed an obsession with wool and other yarns, and finding knitting unsatisfactory, took up crochet in a big way. She crocheted for hours on end, turning out quilts and mats and tablecloths and garments.

Teddy slept in his parents' room until he was four. Then he was moved in with his uncle on to a camp-bed. When he was little he was left for hours in a play-pen and his crying was ignored. Both Eileen and Jimmy excelled at ignoring things. There was always abundant food in the house and large meals of the TV-dinner and chip-shop variety were served, so Teddy was amply fed. The television was always on, so there was something to look at. No one ever cuddled him or played with him or talked to him. When he was five, Eileen sent him off to school on his own. The school was only about fifty yards down the street and on the same side, so this was not quite so dangerous and feckless a procedure as it sounds.

He was the tallest and best-looking child in the class. A Teddy should be rotund and sturdy, with a pink-cheeked, smiling face, blue eyes, brown curly hair. Teddy Grex was tall and slender, his skin was olive, his hair very dark, his eyes a clear hazel. He had the kind of tip-tilted nose and rosebud mouth and sweet expression that made childless women want to seize him and crush him to their bosoms.

They would have got short shrift if they had.

Aged seven, he moved his bed out of his uncle's room. Nothing untoward had ever happened to him in that bedroom. There had been no encounters with Keith, not even the verbal kind. They had seldom spoken. If, in later years, Teddy Grex had had dealings with a psychiatrist, even such an expert would not have been able to diagnose Repressed Memory Syndrome.

All Teddy objected to was the lack of privacy and his uncle's terrible snoring, the liquid glugs and bellows that seemed to shake the room and sounded like nothing so much as the water from ten bathtubs roaring down the drain when their plugs have been pulled simultaneously. And the smoke, he minded the smoke. Though he was used to it and had, so to speak, drunk it in with his feeding bottle, in the small bedroom it was worse, the air nearly unbreathable as Keith had his last fag of the day at half-past midnight and his first at six a.m.

He moved the camp-bed himself. Keith was at work, plumbing a new block of flats at Brent Cross. Jimmy was at work, humping bricks on his hod up a ladder in Edgware. Eileen was in the living-room skilfully performing five acts at once, smoking a cigarette, drinking a can of Coke, eating a Crunchie bar, watching television and crocheting a poncho in shades of flame and lime and royal-blue and fuchsia. Teddy dragged the bed downstairs, making a lot of noise about it because he wasn't strong enough yet to lift it. If Eileen heard the bed bumping from stair to stair she gave no sign that she had.

Nobody ever used the dining-room, not even at

Christmas. It was very small, furnished with a Victorian mahogany table, six chairs and a sideboard. There was barely room for anyone to get in there, let alone sit at the table. Everything was thickly coated with dust and if you twitched the floor-length indeterminately coloured velvet curtains, clouds of it billowed out like smoke. But because no one ever went in there the room smelt less of actual smoke than any other part of the house.

Even then, even at seven, Teddy thought the furniture hideous. He studied it curiously, the swollen buboes, with which the legs were ornamented, the brass feet like the claws of a lion with corns. The seats of the chairs were covered in some forerunner of plastic, a black and brown mottled mock-leather. The sideboard was so ugly, with its wooden shelves and pillars with finials, its cubbly-holes and carved panels, its inset strips of mirror and green stained glass, that he thought it might frighten you if you looked at it for long. If you woke up in the half-dark or as it began to get light and saw its walls and spires and caverns looming out of the shadows like the witch's palace in a story.

That was something to be avoided. He drew patterns with his forefinger in the dust on the chairs and wrote both of the rude words he knew on the table surface. Then he stacked four of the chairs, seat to seat and legs to back, heaved up the last pair on to the sideboard to hide its horrors and made himself space for his bed.

Keith noticed, but didn't comment, though he sometimes came into the dining-room, smoked a cigarette and chatted desultorily at, rather than with, Teddy about his car or his intention of going down to the betting shop. Probably neither Eileen nor Jimmy knew where their son slept. Eileen finished the poncho, wore it to go shopping in and started on her most ambitious enterprise to date, a floor-length topcoat in scarlet and black with cape and hood. Jimmy fell off a ladder, hurt his back and gave up work to go on the benefit. He was never to come off it and never to work again. Keith exchanged the Studebaker for a Lincoln convertible in lettuce-green.

People down the street said that Teddy Grex started going next door because he was neglected at home. He wanted, they said, the affection, the hugs and the tenderness a childless woman like Margaret Chance would give him. Conversation, too, someone to take an interest in him and what he was doing at school, maybe a clean house, proper cooked meals. Tongues were always wagging busily about the Grex family, those cars, Jimmy's being unemployed, Eileen's extraordinary garments and her smoking in the street.

But they were wrong. Neglected he might be, though he always had enough to eat and no one ever hit him, but he had no craving for affection. He had never received any, he didn't know what it was. That may have been the reason or he might have been born that way. He was quite self-sufficient. He went next door and spent long hours there because the house was full of beautiful things and because Alfred Chance made beautiful things in his workshop. Teddy, at eight years old, was introduced to beauty.

In the area of garden corresponding to where Keith Grex kept the green Lincoln, Alfred Chance had his workshop. He had built it himself some thirty years before from white bricks and red cedar, and inside he kept his bench and the tools of his trade. Alfred Chance was a joiner and cabinet-maker and sometimes, in special cases, a carver in stone. A tombstone on which he had done the lettering was the first example of his several crafts that Teddy saw.

16

The tombstone was granite, dark-grey and sparkling, the letters deeply incised and black. 'Death the Period and End of Sin,' Teddy read, 'the Horizon and Isthmus between this Life and a Better.' He had, of course, no idea what it meant, but he knew that he liked the work very much. 'It must be hard to get the letters like that,' he said.

Mr Chance nodded.

'I like the letters not being gold.'

'Good boy. Ninety-nine people out of a hundred would have wanted gold. How did you know black was best?'

'I don't know,' said Teddy.

'It seems you have natural taste.'

The workshop smelt of newly planed wood, a sharp, organic scent. A half-finished angel carved from ash, the colour of blonde hair, leant up against the wall. Mr Chance took Teddy into the house and showed him furniture. It was not the first house Teddy had been into apart from the Grex home, for he had been an occasional visitor at his grandmother Tawton's and had once or twice gone to tea with schoolfellows. But it was the first not furnished with late-Victorian hand-downs or G-plan or Parker Knoll.

The Grex house contained no books, but here were full bookcases with glass doors and moulded pilasters, with break-fronts and pediments. A desk in the living-room was a miracle of tiny drawers, an oval table of dark wood as shiny as a mirror was inlaid with leaves and flowers of pale wood equally glossy. A cabinet on shapely legs had painted doors and the design on each door was of fruit spilling out from a sculptured urn.

'A sight for sore eyes, that is,' said Mr Chance.

If there was something incongruous in housing all this splendour in a poky little north-London semi,

Teddy was unaware of it. He was moved and excited by what he saw. But it wasn't his way to show enthusiasm and in saying he liked the lettering he had gone about as far as he ever could. He nodded at each piece of furniture and he put out one finger to stroke very delicately the fruit on the cabinet front.

Mrs Chance asked him if he would like a biscuit.

'No,' said Teddy.

No one had taught him to say thank you. No one missed him while he was next door or even seemed to notice. The Chances took him out. They took him to Madame Tussaud's and Buckingham Palace, to the Natural History Museum and the V and A. They liked his enthusiasm for beautiful things and his interest in everything, and cared very little about his lack of manners. Mr Chance wouldn't allow him to touch a saw or a chisel at first, but he let him be there in the workshop, watching. He let him hold the tools and after a few weeks allowed him to plane a piece of wood cut for the panel in a door. There was no need to ask for silence as Teddy never said much. He never seemed to get bored either, or whine or demand anything. Sometimes Mr Chance would ask him if he liked a carving he had made or a design he had drawn and almost always Teddy would say, 'Yes.'

But occasionally came that cold unequivocal, 'No,' just as it had when he was asked if he would like a biscuit.

Teddy liked to look at Mr Chance's drawings, some of which were framed and hung on the walls inside the house. Others were in a portfolio in the workshop. They were meticulous line drawings, clean and pure, made with an assured hand. Cabinets, tables, bookcases, desks, of course, but occasionally – and Mr Chance had done these for his own amusement – houses. These houses were the kind he

18

would have liked to own if he could have afforded anything better than his semi next door to the Grexes. Craftsmen who make beautiful furniture and produce exquisite lettering and paint designs on tables seldom do make much money. Teddy learnt this by the time he was ten, which was also when Margaret Chance died.

These were the days before mammograms. She felt the lump in her left breast and then she never palpated the place again, hoping that if she pretended it wasn't there it would go away. The cancer spread into her spine and in spite of the radiotherapy she was dead in six months.

Mr Chance made a headstone for her grave out of pink granite from Scotland, and this time Teddy agreed that it would be tasteful and suitable to fill the letters in with silver. But the words 'beloved wife' and a line about meeting again meant nothing to him and he had nothing of comfort to say to Mr Chance, in fact nothing at all to say, he had already almost forgotten Margaret Chance. It was to be some time before Alfred Chance worked again, so Teddy had the workshop to himself, experimenting, learning, taking risks.

No Grex ever went to a doctor. Teddy had never been immunised against anything. When he cut himself in the workshop and Mr Chance took him to the hospital's casualty department in a taxi, practically the first thing they did was give him an anti-tetanus shot. It was the first injection Teddy had ever had, but he was silent and indifferent when the needle went in.

If Jimmy and Eileen noticed they said nothing about it. Keith didn't notice. The only person who did was Agnes Tawton. 'What have you done to your hand?'

'I cut off the top of my finger,' said Teddy casually,

in the deprecating tone of someone admitting to a slight scratch. 'I did it with a chisel.'

Agnes Tawton had dropped in on her way back from the shops and found her grandson alone in the house. She wasn't a sensitive or perceptive woman, or particularly warm-hearted. Nor was she fond of children, but there was something in Teddy's plight that made her uneasy. It struck her that he was often alone, she had never seen him with a chocolate bar or a bag of crisps or a can of Coke, he had no toys. She remembered the play-pen, in which he had so often been coralled like a farm animal. And, making an entirely unusual leap of the imagination, unprece-dented in her life – it tired her out, doing it – she somehow understood that almost any mother of a child who had lost the top of his finger in an accident would have told *her* mother about it, would have been on the phone, maybe in tears. If Eileen, as a child, had hurt herself like that she, Agnes, would have told everyone.

But what was to be done? She couldn't make a fuss, tell Eileen, tell Jimmy, she couldn't stick her neck out like that. It would be *interference* and she never interfered. There was only one solution. In her experience it was always the answer to everything. Money brought you happiness and anyone who said otherwise was a liar. 'How d'you get on for money?' she said to Teddy.

'Money?'

'Do they give you any, you know, pocket money?'

Both of them knew 'they' didn't. Teddy shook his head. He was studying his grandmother's physiog-nomy and wondering how it had happened that she had four chins and no neck. When she bent over to unclip the clasp on her big black handbag the chins became part of her chest like a bulldog's.

She produced a pound from a red leather purse.

'Here you are,' she said. 'That's for the week. You'll get another next week.'

Teddy took it and nodded.

'Say thank you, you little devil.'

'Thanks,' said Teddy.

Agnes had an idea that the occasion demanded she put her arms round Teddy and kiss him. But she never had and it was too late to start. Besides, she sensed that he would push her away or maybe even hit her. Instead she said, 'You'll have to come to my house and fetch it. I can't be running round here at your beck and call.'

Keith was a tall, heavy man who looked like the late David Lloyd George, with that statesman's square face, broad brow, straight nose, wide-set eyes and butterfly-wing eyebrows. He had longish yellow-grey hair and a drooping shaggy moustache. Lloyd George, when young, had been handsome and so had Keith, but the years and food and drink had taken their toll and by now, at fifty-five, he was in a state of serious decay.

There was something about him that suggested a half-melted candle. Or a waxwork left out in the sun. The flesh of his face hung in wattles and dewlaps. It seemed to have waddled down his neck and sagged from his shoulders and chest to settle in stacked masses on his stomach. He wore his trousers or jeans tightly belted under the huge curve of his rotund belly. The melting, or whatever had happened to him, had left his arms and legs thin as sticks. His dyed hair had receded, but was long at the back and he had just begun wearing it in a pony-tail, fastened by a blue rubber band.

By the time Teddy went to the Comprehensive Eileen had become a notorious figure in the street, more like a bag lady with no home to go to than a housewife and mother of an eleven-year-old son. Dressed from head to foot in home-made woollen garments of rainbow colours – literally head to foot, since she crocheted hats and slippers as well as dresses and capes – her long grey hair fanning out from under the stripy cap to well past her shoulders, she strolled to the shops chain-smoking, often returning with only one item in her crocheted string bag. Then she would have to go back again, and sometimes stop to sit down on someone's garden wall, smoking and singing early Come Hither hits until coughing put a stop to it. The coughing maddened her, so she gave up the singing and hurled abuse at passers-by instead.

Jimmy went to the pub, he went to the Benefit Office to sign on and that was about all. He had emphysema, though without benefit of medical attention he didn't know it, wheezed all day and gasped through the night. Eileen and he and Keith all said smoking was good for you because it calmed the nerves. The walls in the Grex house, and particularly the ceilings, were tinted a deep ochre colour, very much the same shade as the stain on Eileen's and Jimmy's and Keith's forefingers. No one ever repainted the house and, of course, no one washed the walls.

At the Comprehensive Teddy did well. He showed particular promise at art and, later on, at the subject called Design Technology. He wanted to learn to draw, but there were no facilities at the school for actually teaching drawing, so Mr Chance taught him. He taught him precision and accuracy and to be *clean*. He made him draw, over and over, circles, and told him the story of Giotto's O, how when the Pope's messenger came to him to collect an example of his work, Giotto produced no elaborate painting but with a flourish of his brush drew a perfect circle on a piece of paper. Teddy never got to draw a perfect circle, but he didn't do badly.

He liked drawing and soon he liked making things in Mr Chance's workshop, simple objects at first, then more complicated pieces and carvings. He took his GCSEs and transferred to a sixth-form college to study for A Levels in Art and Graphic Design and English.

At home, of course, no one took the slightest interest in what he did at school, though his father had begun making noises about its being time for him to leave and earn money. Now Teddy was growing up, all three senior Grexes were beginning to see him with new eyes, as someone who might be of help to them, a member of the household they might use. A runner of errands, a mediator with any representative of the local authority or Gas Board, a breadwinner, even a cook and cleaner. That they had largely ignored his existence up till now weighed nothing with them. They were unaware of any lapse on their part. But, in a small way, scarcely consciously, they began courting Teddy. Eileen put cans of Coke in the fridge for him, having never noticed that he hated all fizzy drinks, and they all took to offering him cigarettes.

Only he was seldom there. Or, if he was, he made his domain in the dining-room. That was where he did his homework and hung up his drawings on the walls the way Mr Chance did. He framed them himself, using Mr Chance's picture-framer's cramp. Jimmy toddled in there one evening, found his son sitting on the camp-bed reading Ruskin's *The Two Paths* and asked him if he didn't think it was time he took his backside down the Job Centre.

'Why don't you take yours down there?' said Teddy, barely looking up.

'Don't you speak to your father like that!'

Teddy thought this undeserving of any reply, but after a while, during which Jimmy shouted a bit and banged his fist on the dusty sideboard, he said, 'I shall never have an employer.'

'What? What the bloody hell is that supposed to mean?'

'You heard,' said Teddy.

Jimmy came at him then with his fists up, but he was too fat and feeble to do much and all that shouting had brought on a hacking cough. It doubled him up and he stood there, in front of his seated son, bent over and heaving, obliged finally to clutch at Teddy for support. In silence Teddy removed the shuddering hands that clutched at his Oxfam-shop sweat-shirt and guided his father out of the room, holding him by the back of his jacket collar, rather as one might grasp a struggling animal by the scruff of the neck.

But even Jimmy and Eileen knew about unemployment. If Teddy left school there would be no work for him to do. He would be obliged to stay at home, occupying the dining-room, a threatening presence. And a very tall and powerful one, for Teddy had grown to six feet one and though slim was well-built and strong, so when the forms came for his university grant they signed them and did so almost with relief. Not that Teddy would be going far or living away from home. He would merely be at college up at the end of the Metropolitan Line, a tube-train ride away.

So fat had Eileen grown that she could no longer wear her engagement ring. By greasing her finger with Vaseline she managed to get it off, but the wedding ring remained, becoming embedded in flesh until only a gleam of gold showed like a sequin fallen among pink cushions. She had begun upon her magnum opus, the crowning of her life's work, a lace

24

counterpane to cover the double bed she shared with Jimmy. The thread she used was pure white but already, after she had been crocheting it only a month, the work had taken on a uniform yellowness, as if it had been dipped in tea.

Keith exchanged the Lincoln for a primrose-coloured Ford Edsel Corsair, dating from the late fifties. Perhaps Americans of the time were not happy with a perpendicular gear shift or perhaps they disliked the shape of its grille, a mouth saying oooh! instead of a shark's grin. Whatever it may have been, the Edsel was a notorious failure from the start, which was possibly why Keith picked his up for only five thousand pounds from a dealer in south London.

Before Keith, in spite of its age, it had had just one owner, had seldom been driven and had clocked up only ten thousand miles. Nevertheless, Keith took the engine to pieces and reassembled it. He worked outside all that long, hot summer and the noise he made met no competition from sawing next door, for Mr Chance died in the July.

He had no descendants and his nearest relative was a cousin. When he died this cousin was the only mourner. It never occurred to Teddy to go to the funeral. His sole concern was that now he would have nowhere to work, for the house would certainly be promptly sold. His worries were somewhat mitigated when he learned Mr Chance had left him all his tools plus a lot of wood, paints and drawing materials. He tried to stuff it all in the dining-room and when he found this impossible, experienced the first real burning rage of his life. He was a cold person, but his anger was hot and fierce, a silent interior boiling that swelled and crimsoned his face, and made veins stand out on his forehead.

It was the horrible junk in the dining-room that should have been put outside to rot in rain and sun.

25

He would have put it there if he could have got it through the narrow french windows. At one point he thought of dismantling those windows, tearing the back of the house apart, kicking out the glass and splintering the wood, but he was cautious as well as angry. They were capable, the lot of them, of fetching the police. How had the furniture ever got in there?

Keith told him. 'It was my grandad's. My dad loved them tables and chairs. And that sideboard, that's a fine piece of craftsmanship. They don't make furniture like that no more.'

'Hopefully,' said Teddy.

'You watch your mouth. What do you know? You show me a piece of furniture that old bugger Chance made that ever come up to that. My dad bought this house – did you know that? He was just a working man, but he wasn't paying no council rents, getting into that trap. He saved. He bought his house and when this furniture come to him and he saw he couldn't get it indoors it near broke his heart. So he had it taken to pieces and put together again *when it was inside*. And who do you think did that?'

'Don't tell me. I can guess.'

'Chance was only too happy to do it for the money. Falling over himself to do it, he was.'

It was the ultimate disillusionment. If Teddy had for a while believed Alfred Chance was different, he did so no longer. People were, as he had long suspected, uniformly vile and rotten, vastly inferior to things. Objects never let you down. They remained the same and could be an endless source of pleasure and satisfaction. There might be people, or a person, of whom that was also true, but he had never, by the age of eighteen, come across any of them.

As for the tools, in the end he had no choice but to keep them in the small area of garden that wasn't

26

occupied by Keith's Edsel. He couldn't use them out
there. He had to keep them on the 'lawn', covered up
under plastic sheeting. If Keith didn't live there or
hadn't had that car he could have built himself a
shed like Mr Chance's.

But Keith did live there, though very soon Eileen
didn't. Eileen came to a bad end. When she was a
child her mother had often told her she would, but
this particular exit was not what she had in mind.

Chapter 4

Being naughty saved Francine's life. She survived because she had misbehaved. Or that was what Julia said. Julia wasn't there, no one was but herself and her mother and, of course, the man, but Julia always knew everything. He came upstairs looking for you, Julia said. Why else would he have gone into one bedroom after another?

The strange thing was that for a long time afterwards Francine could never remember what the naughty thing was that she had done. Been noisy or disobedient or rude? And yet such behaviour wouldn't have been typical of her; she had never been that sort of child. But she must have done something she shouldn't because her mother hadn't been a strict woman but quite easygoing. Making a noise or being difficult about eating bread and butter wouldn't have led to the exasperated voice saying, 'Francine, that was very stupid and careless. You had better go up to your room.'

Perhaps, after all, she had been that sort of child. How would she know? What had happened in the next half-hour had changed her life, made her into a different person, and she had no means of knowing if her character then had been refractory and mischievous or the same as it was now. She hadn't argued with her mother. She had obeyed and gone upstairs and into her bedroom and closed the door. It was about ten to six on a June evening, fine and

28

warm. She hadn't yet learnt to tell the time. Her father said that learning to tell the time was harder for children now than it had once been because while some clocks had hands, others were digital and only had figures. But she knew it was ten to six because her mother had said so just before she sent her to her room.

Her bedroom window was open and for a while she had leant on the window-sill, looking out across the garden into the lane. There were no other houses or gardens to look at, the nearest was a quarter of a mile away. She could see a field and trees and a hedge, and a long way away the church spire. A car had pulled up on the opposite side of the lane and parked on the verge, but she hadn't taken much notice of it, she wasn't interested in cars and afterwards couldn't even remember what colour it was. She hadn't noticed the driver or if there was anyone else in the car.

A butterfly in her bedroom, fluttering against the glass, that she remembered, and how she caught it, holding it between thumb and forefinger, delicately so as not to brush the dust from its wings. It was a red admiral and she had released it out of the open window, seen it fly up into the sky and watched it until it was just a speck in the blue. Then she had come away from the window and lain on her bed, bored by this solitude, wondering how long it would be before her mother came up and opened the door and said, 'All right, Francine, you can come down now.'

Instead, someone rang the doorbell. They weren't expecting anyone and that made it more exciting because a visitor calling, a neighbour, a friend, would almost certainly result in her being fetched downstairs. She got off the bed, went back to the window and looked down. From here it was possible to see someone who came to the door, at any rate to look down on to the top of his head. Once, she had looked down and seen a totally bald top of someone's head, a white, shiny moon. This one wasn't like that, but a good head of hair, brown hair, though she couldn't see any more except his brown shiny shoes.

Her mother answered the door. It must have been her mother because there was no one else to do it and the door closed. She heard it close quite quietly. At first there were no voices, then she heard his voice. Rough, not very loud, but angry, very angry. That surprised her, someone coming to their house and being angry, shouting at her mother. She heard her mother's voice but not what she said, but she spoke calmly, steadily. The man asked her something. Francine pressed her ear to the door. The next thing she heard was her mother crying out, 'No!'

Just that, just a single 'no', and then gunfire. A shot, followed by more shots. She had heard shots on television so she knew what they were. But whether the scream came before the first shot or between the shots or after all the shots were done she could never remember. Something fell to the ground or was turned over, it might have been a piece of furniture, a chair or, more likely, a small table, because there came a slithering sound and a crash, a tinkling of broken glass. Then noises she had never heard before, thuds, a gasping, choking groan, and one she had heard, a whimpering like her friend's puppy made when it was left alone. And after that, one more final shot.

Francine thought of getting out of the window. She went to the window and looked down, but it was too far. Besides, she had to hide, and getting into the front garden wouldn't be hiding. Julia always said she hid because her instinct told her that the man would come upstairs in search of her, intending to shoot her too. But she was sure she hadn't thought like that at the time. If she had had to account for why she hid she would say it was because children always hide instinctively when there is any danger, like animals do.

At the door she had listened, heard something being pulled across the floor. It was the sound a rolled-up rug makes, dragged across carpet. Once, and only once in her short life, she had seen a grown-up cry. It was her mother who had cried when her own mother died. That sound, a grown-up sob, far far worse than a child crying, she heard the man make. It was more frightening than the shots and the dragging sound. She got into the cupboard.

Inside the cupboard her clothes hung on hangers and her shoes stood on the floor. There was also a cardboard box full of toys she had got too old to play with. She pushed her shoes up against the toy box and crouched on the floor. At first it looked as if the cupboard door wouldn't shut from the inside, there was no handle, but she found she could close it by inserting her fingers between the bottom of the door and the carpet. That was an advantage of being only seven, her fingers were very small. If she had been older she wouldn't have been able to do that and the man would have found her when he came into her room. So said Julia.

He did come in. She heard his footsteps on the stairs first. Hers was the door you came to immediately at the top, so he came into her room first. Came in, looked round, left again. She heard him in her parents' bedroom, opening drawers, throwing the contents on to the floor. Throwing the drawers themselves on to the floor. She was icy cold with fright and her teeth were chattering the way they had last year when she had been swimming in that cold sea. Her mother had wrapped her in a big beach

31

towel and then in her father's jacket. There was no one to do that for her now.

She heard him run downstairs. He closed the front door after him very quietly. Like a person does at night when they don't want to wake people who are asleep. Her mother wasn't asleep. She was dead. But at the time she didn't know that, she didn't know what death was, though when she crept downstairs at last and saw her lying there on the hall floor she knew the man had hurt her and that she had been terribly hurt.

She knelt beside her mother, and picked up her hand and moved it about. Strangely, she didn't notice the blood then. That might have been because her mother had dark hair and the carpet was dark red. Later, she remembered that there had been blood because when she took her hand from stroking her mother's hair the palm and the fingers were red, as if painted with a fine brush. And some people who came later, men in uniform, policemen, nurses, one of them said she had been sitting in blood, her school skirt was red with it.

Her father would come home soon. Usually this was at seven or a quarter to seven. She looked at the clock and saw hands pointing at incomprehensible angles. It was only when they pointed straight up or straight to the sides that she had much idea of what the time was. She sat on the floor beside her mother and watched the clock, wondering why you could never see the hands move. But if you looked away for a while and then looked back they had moved.

Her teeth had stopped chattering. Everything had stopped, really. The world. Life. But not time, for when she looked at the clock again, one of the hands had crept up and was pointing straight to the side, the left side. She could tell right from left.

Her father's key in the lock made a scrabbling

noise, a mouse-scratching noise, and then the door opened and he was inside. Standing there, staring, Richard Hill made a sound unlike all the other sounds she had ever heard. She could never have described it, even when she regained the power of speech, it was too dreadful and too different, not a people sound at all, but the roar of an animal alone in the wilderness.

She couldn't talk to him. She could tell him nothing. It wasn't that her voice was small or hoarse or whispery like her mother's had been when she had laryngitis. Her voice wasn't there, the words weren't. When she opened her mouth and moved her lips and her tongue, nothing happened. It was as if she had forgotten how to speak or had never learnt to talk.

Richard Hill held her in his arms and called her his baby, said he was there now, he had come home, he would never leave her. Even at that moment he was able to tell her that all would be well, he would keep her safe for ever. But she couldn't answer him, only turn to his a frozen face and eyes which, he later said, had grown to twice their size.

The psychologists got to work on her. Not Julia, not then. Later on, she understood how careful and caring they had been. The police had, too. No one had pressed her. No one had shown the least impatience with her. The psychologists had given her dolls to play with and in after years she understood this had been in the hope she would act out, in her play, the events of that evening. There was a man doll and a lady doll and a little girl doll.

Francine had never been a doll person.

'She doesn't like dolls,' Richard Hill told them, 'she never has.'

33

But dolls were the recognised tool whereby children revealed themselves and their experiences to psychologists. If they had given her toy rabbits or dogs she might have acted something out with them, but they never did. Sometimes the police came and talked to her. The women officers were the kindest, gentlest people she had ever known, so kind and gentle that they made her suspicious.

She understood why they questioned her. They wanted to catch the man who killed her mother. She couldn't talk to them, she couldn't write much more than her name or read more than simple words, so there was little communication. But it wasn't for years that she found out they had suspected her father. For two days they believed Richard Hill might be responsible for the murder.

He was the dead woman's husband. It was family members who were usually responsible for family murders. The police questioned him and treated him warily. Then he was cleared. Two men, one of them a stranger, came forward and said they had been in the train from Waterloo with him from six o'clock until twenty-five-past.

'I think you know Mr Grainger,' the Detective Inspector said to him. 'You saw him on the train and he has come forward and said he saw you.'

'I asked him how his wife was,' Richard said. 'His wife had been ill.'

'Yes, he has told us that. Unprompted, I may add. He said hallo to you and you asked after his wife. The other man is Mr David Stanark. He knows you by sight.'

'I don't know him.'

Detective Inspector Wallis ignored this. 'He came forward of his own volition to say he was on the train and that he saw you on the train.'

34

Years later, because she asked, Richard told Francine all this. He told Julia what David Stanark had done for him. 'He saved my life.'

'Not your life, darling,' said Julia.

'Well, my liberty then.'

'The reality is that he just saved you from a few days' serious awkwardness, isn't it?'

Julia was always saying what the reality was.

After Richard's life and liberty were saved there came a limbo time. It was a time of silence and stillness. Francine no longer went to school and Richard didn't go to work. They were together all the time, day and night. He moved her bed into his bedroom, he read to her, he never left her. What else could he do for her? He would do anything. For a while, compensating her was his whole life. He bought her a kitten, a white Persian, and for a while that helped her, cuddling the kitten and watching it play so that she was even seen to smile a little. But one day the kitten caught a bird and brought it to her as a gift, laying it at her feet. The dead bird had dark feathers and blood dripped from it, so that she shivered and stared, clenching and unclenching her hands. A good home was found for the kitten, it was the only way.

No one wanted to buy the house, though it was a beautiful place, a 'gentleman's' cottage, nearly three centuries old. Potential buyers hardly seemed to notice the lattice windows or the pretty garden, the green and gold and red Virginia creeper which half veiled its gables or that the house was in the country yet only thirty miles from London. They knew what had happened there and they came to gaze ghoulishly or to ask themselves if they could live with that knowledge. One woman stared at the hall floor as if looking for a blood-stain.

In the end the house was sold for a much lower price than its market value.

Because she couldn't speak, and her reading and writing skills were very limited, Francine could barely communicate with anyone. She couldn't tell her father about the video cassette or write down that she had found it. She could have handed it over to him, but for some reason she didn't do that. Even then, young as she was and mute as she was, she sensed that there was something wrong about that cassette and it would make him unhappy. Perhaps it was because it had been so carefully hidden.

She had been sure the hiding place was her discovery and hers alone, her father didn't know about it and maybe her mother hadn't known either. There was an old cupboard in the wall of the chimney which was called a wig cupboard because in olden times, before he went up to bed, the man of the house took off his wig and put it inside there for the night. Her mother had kept her sewing box in there and a pair of scissors. The floor of the wig cupboard was of wooden boards which looked as if they fitted tightly together, but if you pressed one of them in a certain way it lifted a little, you could get hold of it in your fingers and prise it out. Underneath was a small hollow space.

When first she found it there was nothing inside. She wanted to use the scissors and in reaching for them rested her hand on the secret board and tilted it up.

Her mother had seen her with the scissors and, although she wasn't cross, she hadn't sounded very pleased. 'You are not to use my scissors without asking first, Francine. You aren't old enough to use scissors on your own.'

So was that what she had done and for which she

36

had been sent to her room? Used the scissors without asking?

Perhaps. But she had never in fact used the hollow space for hiding things. She had never raised the board again until the day they moved away. On moving day, collecting up her things, she looked in the wig cupboard, but her mother's sewing box and the scissors were gone. Richard Hill was outside in the front garden with the removal men and there was no one to see her. Francine put her hand into the hollow and found inside a video cassette. Or, rather, the rectangular plastic container of a video cassette.

On the outside were a picture and some large printed letters. She could read the word 'to' but that was all. She put the cassette into the bag that she would be carrying with her with all her special things in it, the things that would not be going in the removal van but coming with her and her father in the car.

They were moving to a house as different as could be from the old one. About two hundred years younger, for one thing. It was a big suburban semi-detached on a wide road in Ealing. Buses ran along the road and cars were always passing. Neighbours were on the left side, neighbours were joined to the house on the right side and more neighbours were all along the street. Their house was number 215. It wasn't the sort of place where a man could come to the door and be let in and kill someone's mother with a gun.

A few days after they had moved into the new house she talked again.

It was about nine months after the murder. She had long unpacked the bag she brought with her and, without looking inside the case, had put the video cassette on to a shelf with some of her books. She and her father were still unpacking things out of the boxes and there, among combs and brushes and hair slides in a tin that had once contained chocolate bicuits, she found the broken pieces of a record, a single of Come Hither's 'Mending Love'.

Richard wept when he saw it. The tears rolled down his face. 'It was her favourite,' he said. 'She loved that tune. We once danced to it.'

And Francine, who hadn't uttered a word for nine months, said quite clearly and with a kind of wonderment, 'I broke it. That's what I did.'

His grief temporarily forgotten, Richard cried out and seized hold of her, put his arms round her, holding her tightly against him. Unwise, probably, frightening to a child, but he couldn't help himself and in the event it didn't stop her speaking again.

'It was on the record player,' she said. 'Mummy said to be careful if I wanted to take it off, but I wasn't careful enough and I dropped it and it broke, and Mummy sent me upstairs. I remember now.'

'Oh, my darling,' said her father, 'my sweetheart, you're talking, you can speak.'

The psychologists came back again with their dolls. The kind, gentle police ladies came back. They showed her hundreds of pictures of cars and played her dozens of tapes of men's voices. In her mind's eye she saw the car parked on the verge, under the overhanging branches, but she saw it like a black-and-white photograph. The car might have been green or red or blue. It looked pale grey to her, as the grass did and the sky. She saw the top of the man's head, brown like rabbit fur, and his brown shiny shoes.

She had the big room at the back of the house where her window gave on to their garden with its summer-house and swing and apple trees, and on to all the gardens next door and behind. She had her own bathroom, called *en suite*, and completely new bedroom furniture. But for a time, while her bedroom was being decorated, she had the small room at the front and several times she had looked down from her window and seen a man standing on the doorstep, seen his shoes and the top of his head, and she had screamed out, 'It's him! It's him!'

Once it was the postman and the other times David Stanark and Peter Norris, who lived next door. Her father grew very upset when that happened and later on she found out that he had told the police and the psychologists that they must stop questioning her. They must give it up. Julia agreed with him. It was bad for her, it would traumatise her. They must close the case.

But they wouldn't do that. Not, at any rate, for years. They would find him, the Detective Inspector said, if it was the last thing they did. They had a theory. The reason for the murder that they had decided on, the man's motive, horrified Richard Hill. It brought him so much shame and guilt that he wished many times that they had never told him.

Chapter 5

A week after the murder David Stanark had come round unasked to see Richard. He presented himself on the doorstep, a good-looking man of about Richard's own age with an anxious expression. He held out his hand and said who he was. 'I was the man on the train, the one you didn't know.'

Usually mild and self-effacing, Richard in his grief and confusion shouted at him, 'I suppose you've come to be thanked? Is that it? You want gratitude?'

David Stanark said, 'May I come in?'

'You don't know what it's like,' Richard said, 'no one does. No one who hasn't been through it knows what it's like to be suspected of murdering the person you –' his voice fell and he turned away before muttering '– love best in the world.'

'I think I can imagine.'

After that David came in and the two men talked. Or, rather, Richard talked and David listened, and when that had gone on for two hours David told Richard that he too had once lost the woman he loved, that she had died violently. But it was to be some months and the friendship firmly established before Richard told him of the load of guilt that weighed on him and the shame that went with it.

Flora Barker, who had been a nurse, came to look after Francine while her father was at work and away on business trips.

Francine went back to school. Or, rather, she went to a new school in the new place and made new friends. She was behind in her school work, but she soon caught up because she was bright. And she liked Flora. In finding her to care for his daughter and as a mother substitute, Richard had chosen wisely. It was one of the few wise decisions he ever made.

Flora was among those women who are an instant hit with children because, as well as being kind and patient and loving, they like children and enjoy their company and talking to them. Such people never talk down to children, they are too simple and too aware of their simplicity, to talk down to anyone, even supposing they knew how to condescend. They never patronise or exercise power or pull their rank.

Flora would say, 'I like these new biscuits, don't you? And they're no dearer than the other lot. Go on, have another one, I'm going to.' Or, 'Let's have the telly on. I tell you what, if you'll watch *EastEnders* with me I'll watch your lion programme with you.'

She was a great one for deals. 'If you'll teach me to do jigsaws I'll teach you to knit. Jigsaws are something I've never got the hang of.'

'But they're easy!'

'So's knitting when you know how. I tell you what, if you'll sing me a song, one of your school songs, I'll make pancakes for our tea.'

Julia Gregson was a very different kettle of fish. It was Flora who referred to her as a kettle of fish, a term Richard disliked. He said it was impertinent. But Julia looked like a fish, Francine said. Not a dead, slimy mackerel or cod of the kind you see on the supermarket counter, but a bright, healthy, swimming fish, a beautiful fish, a Shubunkin perhaps, or a Koi carp. Julia had a high-browed face and a rather long nose, and she was all gold and white and red.

Her skin was gleaming white and her hair gleaming yellow, her wide curved mouth painted scarlet and her nails varnished to match.

It was David Stanark who recommended her. She was a child psychotherapist, or as she put it, a paedopsychiatrician. David suggested Francine see her because Richard sometimes confessed to his friends that his daughter was too quiet, too preoccupied, and that she needed to come out of herself. At first Richard was doubtful. A firm advocate of formal education and plenty of it, he wondered what mind-mending skills a woman could possibly have whose qualifications were a teacher-training certificate and a diploma from a counselling crash course. He had always been deeply disapproving of the legal loophole that allows anyone who wishes to call herself a psychotherapist and set up in practice to do so, without benefit of a medical degree or training in psychiatry. But all that changed when he met Julia.

So confident was her manner, so calming her words and so excellent her timing, that you could scarcely be with her for five minutes without trusting her utterly. Or so it seemed to Richard. Almost without reserve he put Francine into her hands.

Julia had Francine playing with dolls. There was no escaping those dolls, Francine sometimes thought. Here, though, in the pleasant sitting-room overlooking Battersea Park, she was not apparently expected to reveal by her play any hidden knowledge of the crime against her mother, only perhaps show by the dolls' movements and interaction with each other the deep secrets of her childhood. Julia watched her and sometimes she wrote things down. She talked a lot to Francine, but not as Flora did, about the books she was reading and the television programmes she watched, about going shopping and what to cook for dinner, and whether Francine liked this friend more than that friend, and about Flora's own friends.

Julia asked questions. 'Why do you like that, Francine?'

'I just do,' Francine would say.

'Why do you like ice-cream?'

'I don't know. I just like it.'

'What would you like to happen best in the world?'

Francine knew but she wouldn't say.

'If you could have three wishes what would they be?'

Francine's three wishes were for the man not to have come, for her mother not to have died and to live with her mother and her father in the cottage once more. And maybe have Flora living next door. She didn't want to tell Julia that. Julia ought to know it without being told, everyone ought to know it, for it was obvious. But Francine could read now, she was a good reader, and before she came to Julia for this session she had been reading a book in which a character confessed to a fear of pursuit by pirates whose treasure he had unearthed. The story was vividly told and much of it remained in her memory. 'I want to be safe,' she said, quoting directly. 'I don't want them to get me, I don't want them to find me.'

Julia nodded, looked grave and said that was all for now as her father would be coming for her in a moment. Her father did come and he and Julia had a quiet talk in private, while Francine sat in the other room, watching a carefully selected children's video. After a few minutes he took her home in the car. She had been asked enough questions for one day, but he started asking her more. Did she like Julia? Was Julia helping her to feel happier? Was she lonely when he was away?

'I've got Flora,' she said. 'I do like Flora.'

43

Off he went on a trip to Glasgow, Francine went to school and Flora came to the school gates to meet her at home-going time.

'You're not frightened of being outdoors, are you?' Flora said as they walked along.

'No. Why?'

'Daddy said you found being outside a bit scary,' said Flora.

At home and in her room Francine took a book out of her bookshelf. It was a collection of Roald Dahl stories which Flora had given her and which she had not yet read, but was now ready to attempt. Next to it was the video cassette container.

She hadn't looked at that since she put it there over a year ago. Then she hadn't been able to read much, but now she could read anything – anything printed, that is. The big print on the coloured sheet inside the container, the bit that was like a book cover, of which, when she first found it, she had only been able to read 'to', she now saw said 'A Passage to India'. There was a picture, too, of a man in a turban and an old woman outside a cave. Francine opened the container, but there was no video cassette inside.

The small plastic box was full of sheets of paper with writing on them. Not printing but joined-up writing. Francine looked carefully at it, but she couldn't read a word. Grown-ups could read writing, though she sometimes wondered how, and even they probably wouldn't need to much longer. Flora said no one wrote anything any more except shopping lists and notes to the milkman. Everything else was done on computers. But this person had written with a pen on the kind of paper that came in a pad from newsagents' shops and someone at the cottage had put the paper in this box and hidden it. Not herself, and somehow she knew it wasn't her father.

So her mother must have taken the video cassette of *A Passage to India* out of its box, put those papers into it instead and placed the box in the hollow space under the floor of the wig cupboard.

Francine made no further attempts to read the writing. She put the box back on the shelf where it had been before.

There are people in this world with very good brains and astute minds who at the same time have no common sense whatever. Bad judges of character and situation, unable to take the long view, they are both very clever and very unwise. Richard Hill was one of them.

He had murdered his wife and child. Not with a gun, not with malice aforethought and evil intent, but as he saw it, by his own thoughtless vanity. His pride in his own achievement had brought about their deaths.

The Detective Chief Inspector in charge of the case had told him the man's motive and with that telling destroyed what peace of mind Richard had managed to achieve for himself. The crime committed against his wife had been drug-related and, most probably, the result of mistaken identity and dreadful coincidence. He, Richard, was called Dr Hill, though his doctorate was a D.Phil and his home was in Orchard Lane. Another Dr R. Hill, a doctor of medicine, of an Orchard Road some ten miles away, kept considerable sums of money in the house – black money, though the police didn't say that – paid him by certain private patients. The perpetrator, suspected of being a heroin addict, certainly under toxic influence at the time of the murders, confused the two men. He had probably, the Chief Inspector said almost apologetically, found Richard's address in the phone book.

And ever since then Richard had suffered inner agonies of guilt over that 'Dr' before his name in the telephone directory. For there had been no need of it. His profession and his success in it hardly required that all and sundry should know he had a D.Phil. from Oxford. He had had it inserted in the directory through pride. He was proud and vainglorious of this achievement of his and the title it conferred, and because of it, through vaunting it, he had murdered his wife.

One evening, while the two men were having a drink together, he told David Stanark how he felt. David didn't tell him anything comforting. He said not a word about Richard not blaming himself, having nothing to be ashamed of, or that he should put this guilt out of his mind. Richard had rather expected he would say that, had hoped he would. David's, 'It's just something you have to live with, all you can say is it'll get less with time,' disconcerted him.

'So you do think it was my fault? I'm right to feel guilt?'

'Any reasonably responsible human being in your situation would feel guilt,' David said, and he smiled, perhaps to soften harsh words. 'You did lead this man to your house. You did so directly by your action. You call it vanity, a kinder judgement would be that it was evidence of a justifiable pride in your achievement. Whatever it may have been, it resulted in this man killing your wife. But we can't predict what our actions will lead to. Maybe if we could we'd never go out at all, put pen to paper, never even get up in the morning. That's not possible, so the answer is to try always to be very circumspect in what we do.'

'Avoid the Seven Deadly Sins?' said Richard.

But he didn't like it when David nodded and said

46

in a parsonical tone, 'Events like this one show us why Pride is one of them.'

After that a coolness arose between the two men and although they still occasionally saw each other, things were not the same. Their friendship was mended only after both were married and their wives became close. Instead of David Stanark, Richard took his troubles to Julia and her reaction was more to his taste.

She was – at least in her own estimation – a child psychotherapist but, having no sound belief in psychotherapy of any kind, Richard rather thought this wouldn't matter. The two beliefs were balanced side by side in his mind: the one that psychotherapy was rubbish and the other that Julia, because she was good-looking and understanding and calm and confident, must be a good psychotherapist. In fact, as he told himself, she was the only one of her ilk whom he could trust.

Julia had no objection to taking him on as a client. An adult was more challenging than a child. An adult man and an attractive one confessing to you the secrets of his heart, while you sat close together in a warm room at dusk with just one lamp on, was more exciting than watching a child play with dolls. And Richard found that he could say anything to Julia, he could tell her everything. She listened, she never interrupted. She put one elbow on the arm of the sofa and, her head a little on one side, rested her rather small receding chin in the palm of her hand and, with her beautiful fish's lips slightly parted, she listened. Occasionally she nodded, in such a way as to imply that the horrors he admitted to, the weaknesses and follies, were all perfectly understandable. *She* knew, *she* understood and she pardoned.

He told her of the vanity that had led him to call

47

himself Dr Hill in the phone book and how he therefore blamed himself for the death of his wife.

'The first thing you have to understand', she said, 'is that guilt is part of the cumbersome and often dirty baggage we human beings have to carry around with us. Often it doesn't bear much relation to reality, but you'd be a strange man if you didn't have it. Suppose I said you'd have to be a psychopath not to feel guilt? How about that?'

He told her how his wife and he had grown apart in the months before her death, how she had become cold towards him and he had spent more and more time away from his family, furthering his career. Now he blamed himself for that too, for being insensitive to Jennifer's needs, for failing to ask, to talk.

'What would you like best in the world?' said Julia.

He didn't have to think about that. 'To undo it. To go back and do things differently.'

'But the reality is that you can't do that. No one can. If you had three wishes, three reasonable, possible wishes, what would they be?'

'To protect Francine,' he said. 'Have her grow up safe and without trauma. To sleep at night the way I used to.'

'And the third wish?'

Until that moment he hadn't known what a third wish would be. It came to him like a beam of light penetrating a dark room. Disclose it now he couldn't. He could only look at Julia, shake his head and say, 'One day I'll tell you.'

She smiled. She took her hand from under her cheek and laid it on his. 'Time's up, Richard. Shall I see you next week? Same time, same place?'

'Of course.'

Francine came to her next day, brought by Flora.

48

'It's time we talked about that day, Francine,' said Julia.

What was meant by 'that day' Francine knew at once. She had never spoken of it with Julia, though she had with almost everyone else. She would have liked to try and put it away from her, bury it in the past and have it come back only in her dreams. Now Julia said that would be wrong. It must be talked over.

She wasn't a rebellious child, but quiet and sweet, and above all anxious that her father should be happy. She came to Julia without protest because her father wanted her to. But she was desperate not to talk to Julia about that day.

'You think the man will find you, don't you, Francine?'

It had never crossed her mind.

'I know the reason why you don't want to talk about it. It is because you are afraid of the man finding you. Aren't I right?'

Francine was anxious not to cry, but she did,˙ she couldn't help herself.

Julia took her into her arms and held her against her slippery white satin blouse, hugged her long and lovingly and stroked her hair. 'I will never let you come to any harm. Daddy will never let you come to harm. You know that now, don't you?'

Nearly a year was to pass before Richard understood the cause of Julia's sudden decision to retire from practice, sell her house and move. At the time these seemed acts heaven-sent for his own purposes, or beautiful coincidences. One Saturday evening, when he and Francine were alone, when they had had their supper and had just finished listening to a CD of Britten's *Young Person's Guide to the Orchestra*, he said to her, 'Sweetheart, I want to ask you something. It's rather serious.'

'Is it about that day?' she said.

He knew what she meant and he was taken aback. Had he been in danger of forgetting how much the past preyed on her mind? 'No, it's not about that. We've said everything there is to say about that.'

She nodded, then, as if on an afterthought of doubt, shrugged her shoulders.

'What I want to ask you is quite different. It's about the future, not the past, the time to come.' He waited, then said, 'How would you feel if I got married?'

'Married?'

'I'd like to get married. I will never forget your mother, you know that. I will never stop loving her. But I want to be married again, for your sake too. I expect you know who it is?'

'Flora,' she said.

Her guesswork, as wide of the mark as could be, almost angered him. She was only a child. Still, to suppose him likely to marry an overweight frump with permed hair and red hands, a one-time State Enrolled Nurse with a Bristol accent ... 'It's Julia.' He kept his patience. He even smiled, but without looking directly at her. 'I haven't asked her yet. I am asking your permission, Francine. I am saying, my dear little girl, may I marry our good friend Julia?'

A parent who asks a child if he may marry again always intends to do so whatever the answer may be. It just makes things smoother if the answer is yes. Francine didn't know this, but she intuited it. If she had been five years older she would probably have said, I can't stop you, or, Do as you like, it's your life. But she was only nine and she loved the idea of seeing him happy.

Once she had lost the power of speech and

sometimes even now, though she had never confessed to anyone, she was afraid muteness might
come back. One day she would wake up and be
unable to speak. That had never happened and it
wasn't happening now. Her failure to speak this time
was a matter of choice. She looked at him in silence
and nodded.

Chapter 6

All the years of his childhood Teddy had called at his grandmother's once a week for his pocket money. Both of them, by nature or conditioning, had cold temperaments and both were loners. Agnes Tawton had been relieved when her husband died and said so without shame. She no longer had someone living in the house whose wishes might not invariably accord with her own and who had occasionally demanded a modicum of her attention.

She gave little of this to Teddy, but she gave him his pound. Sometimes his visit would pass without a word being exchanged beyond his thanks which she insisted on, which she demanded even before it reached his hand. If he stared at her in silence, his mouth clamped shut, she would snatch the money away and hold it behind her back. 'What do you say?'

'Thank you.'

'Thank you, *Grandma*.'

'Thank you, Grandma.'

Often she didn't ask him in and if she did, offered him nothing to eat or drink. Their conversation, at these times, consisted in her bullying him with questions about his school work and picking his brains as to what went on in the Grex household, and in his monosyllabic if not quite dumb insolence. She was old, in her mid-seventies by the time Teddy was ten, but strong and spry. Though never invited, she occasionally came round to see her daughter, but even if this visit happened at the time Teddy's weekly stipend was due, she would never pass over his pound. He had to call on her for that.

So a relationship of a kind developed between these two apparently unfeeling people. Though each was uninterested in human nature – beyond sharing a general contempt for it – they probably knew each other better than either of them knew anyone else. As Teddy entered his teens and grew tall, and became highly personable, Agnes even softened her attitude towards him, occasionally making a remark that was neither censorious nor hectoring nor derisive. 'Cold out today,' she might say, or, with great satisfaction, 'You're going to be a lot taller than your dad.'

It was therefore strange, beyond ordinary human understanding, that when Teddy was eighteen and off to college, Agnes blew it. She could have given him twice or even three times what he was getting – she could afford it – but instead, because he had his grant, she announced that his weekly pound was to stop. 'You've got more coming in than I have,' she said.

Teddy made no reply, for he had no idea of his grandmother's income.

'Won't bother with me any more now, will you?' This was uttered in a tone of triumph.

'Probably not.'

'Suit yourself,' said Agnes.

When Keith asked why the house smelt of acetone Eileen knew for sure she shared her late father's disability. It was on her breath and perhaps coming out of her pores, but Jimmy hadn't noticed it. For a long time she had suspected. Knowing Tom Tawton's symptoms, she finally recognised what her constant raging thirst, dry skin and weariness must mean. She had been coping with thirst by drinking lager, pouring it down alternately with cans of Diet Coke. Her eyes weren't what they had been either, but she had coped with that by buying herself glasses at Boots.

Some degree of eyesight was essential if she was to continue with and finish the white lace counterpane. The time had come when ignoring things and pretending they weren't there was no longer going to work. She would have to do something. None of the men in the household showed any more interest in the state of her health after Keith had commented on the acetone smell. She would have been surprised if they had.

In spite of the lager she had lost weight, for she had no appetite. 'I reckon I could get my ring on again,' she said to Jimmy as they were watching 'Allo, 'Allo one evening. 'You look at my finger.'

But Jimmy didn't. He dodged round the hand she thrust in front of him, a hand so dry and the skin so flaky that it looked as if it had been dipped in a bag of flour. He leant in the other direction, peered at the screen and laughed throatily.

Dressed in a red and grey crocheted skirt and jumper with a crocheted red cape and crocheted yellow peaked cap, Eileen set off to get the bus to her mother's. On the way she passed the doctor's surgery, newly renamed the medical centre, and she noticed it, she actually paused outside it, and read on the notice board the times at which patients could attend and directions for making appointments. But she passed on. She still remembered, after nineteen years, the fuss there had been over her failure to seek medical attention before and when Teddy was born, the contemptuous GP and the tight-lipped midwife. And she thought of what they would do if she went in there. Her knowledge of this was culled from

54

television. She imagined the tests, the nagging, the humiliation, the adjurations to stop smoking.

At the bus-stop she lit a cigarette. A woman who was also waiting fanned the smoke away with her hand and Eileen relieved her feelings by giving her a mouthful of abuse. By the time she got to her mother's she was very tired, not least because during the journey she had twice had to seek out public lavatories to cope with her lavish urination.

When she heard what Eileen intended, Agnes made a feeble attempt to argue her out of it. But along with any warmth or real interest in the fate of others, she lacked persuasive powers. She wasn't sufficiently involved. 'You'll upset your insides,' she said.

'It's not my insides, is it? It's my leg I'm going to do it to.'

'Your dad's stuff will have gone off. It's been there five years.'

But she couldn't stop Eileen going into the bathroom for the syringe and the ampoule. Eileen had watched her father do this so often that she knew exactly what it involved. Tom Tawton had left ample supplies of the stuff behind and Agnes had thrown out none of it, as the NHS practice nurse had instructed her to do. Eileen thought she could take some of it back with her and buy her own syringe.

Searching through the medicine cabinet, she found a container labelled Tolbutamide. Remembering that this had once been prescribed for her father to take by mouth before his treatment had become intravenous, she swallowed a couple of capsules in water from the cold tap. It couldn't do any harm. Injecting herself was more of a challenge, but she had seen it done so she could do it.

Afterwards, she went back to her mother and said she'd make them a cup of tea. She was going to stop taking sugar in her tea. 'It'll be a wrench,' she said, 'but I have to think of my health,' and then, because she had heard the phrase somewhere, or something like it, 'I owe it to Jimmy to think of my health.'

In the kitchen, while the kettle was boiling, she had to sit down. She sat, felt her head swim, her vision blacken, her body quake, she slid to the floor and collapsed in a coma. Her mother, weary with waiting for her tea, fell asleep and failed to find her till five hours had passed.

Home from college for the Easter break, Teddy found that the house was deserted by day. Jimmy had neglected to inform the authorities of his wife's death and continued to draw the full retirement pension for a married couple to which he had previously been entitled since he became sixty-five. At much the same time the law had changed and pubs stayed open all day. Jimmy went to the pub at ten in the morning and stayed there until six or seven in the evening.

Always a hard worker Keith, who had been drawing his pension for a year longer, still worked as a plumber as well, mostly for money in the back pocket. He was a serious earner, was Keith, having, for instance, made enough in the past year to take himself away on holiday to Lanzarote and build a carport on the concrete pad to shelter the Edsel from the elements. A good plumber, who will come whenever he is called on, when the tank in the loft leaks, when the lavatory cistern won't stop filling, is always in demand. So the house was empty and for the first time in his life Teddy had it to himself.

He could have asked friends round, but he had no friends. Alfred Chance had been the nearest to a friend he ever had. Girls at college fancied him and made their feelings plain, but he repulsed them. He was a loner and he liked to think of himself as such. At first, when he was alone in the house, he explored and searched it in a way he had never had the opportunity to do before.

It was very dirty and, because there was so much wool about and so many woollen garments, infested with moths. Woodworm were devouring the living-room furniture and from the television table had bored into the skirting board. Teddy closed his eyes and thought of the house as being eaten up by insects, boring and drilling and chewing, and he almost fancied he could hear their depredations as a range of steady hummings and buzzings on various different notes.

Spiders were in the bath and silverfish wriggled across the floors. Ladybirds were concentrated in crimson clusters on the dirty curtains. From a distance they looked like scabs on skin. He went into Keith's room, not because there was anything in there he specially wanted to see or to check on, but rather in wonderment and fascinated disgust. An obscure pleasure was what he felt in simply contemplating the bed which was never made and on which the sheets were never changed. Since Eileen's death there was no one to do the washing and a heap of soiled clothes lay in one corner. Keith would wait until he had just one pair of trousers and one ragged T-shirt left and then he would put the pile of clothes into a bin-liner and take it down to the launderette.

The room smelt of stale cigarette smoke, sweat, blue cheese and the dry, bitter, yellow stink of unwashed bedlinen. Normal-sized ashtrays weren't big enough for Keith and he used an old Pyrex casserole in which to deposit his ash and stub out his fag ends. It stood on the floor beside the bed. Teddy squatted down and looked underneath. From his childhood he remembered that Keith kept drink under there. He still did, a half-bottle of vodka, a whole one of gin, three cans of lager, still in their quadruple plastic collar.

Keith stuck memos to himself on pink and blue Post-its all over the window-panes and the front of the tallboy. They had phone numbers of clients on them and addresses of sanitary goods suppliers. And on one wall were pinned photographs (cut out of library books) of Keith's heroes: Karl Benz and Gottlieb Daimler, originators of the motor vehicle, and of Ferdinand Porsche standing beside his People's Car in Hitler's Germany. Their prim, serious faces and spotless dress made a ludicrous contrast with the squalor of the room.

Next door, Jimmy now slept alone. The bed was a larger version of his brother's. Jimmy had had a nose-bleed over one of the pillows; to judge by the colour and texture of the stain, some weeks before. It may have been this which attracted the flies, a dozen or so of which danced and bobbed against the closed window while a bluebottle, as big as a bee, zoomed frenziedly in diagonals across the room. Teddy looked inside the wardrobe. His mother's clothes smelt of old sheep. The tracks made by moth grubs already showed on the lumpy woollen surfaces and moth cocoons, greyish-white like mildew, nestled between the stitches.

It was the colours she had used which fascinated and repelled Teddy. He knew something about colour and had been taught more. He knew, for instance, that what may look beautiful in nature, a primrose against dark-green ivy leaves, a blue butterfly on a pink rose, is less aesthetically acceptable in art or in textiles. Eileen had put lime-green next to scarlet and ochre beside purple, turquoise vied with peach and crimson jostled powder-blue. These conjunctions of colours hurt his eyes and made anger well up once more inside him.

He moved to the dressing-table and stood there for a while, his hands pressing down on its glass-topped surface, his eyes closed. His back was to the bed now, but it was present in his mind. In here they must have, occasionally must have, at least once must have, since he was born five years after they were married perhaps often must have, had sex. From what people had said at school he knew that everyone finds the idea of their parents having sex unimaginable, but in the case of his it was more unimaginable than usual. It made him shudder. He had slept in here till he was four, he vaguely remembered it, so perhaps they had done it in his presence.

He kept his eyes shut. At twenty he was a virgin and not ashamed to be. If anyone had asked he would have admitted it proudly. He had read somewhere, in a newspaper probably, that 'saving oneself', preserving a state of virginity, was becoming fashionable. For once he didn't mind being a follower of fashion. As for saving himself for something or someone, the idea of marriage was ludicrous; marriage was this bedroom, those people, the smoke and the moths and the dining-room furniture. But he could imagine keeping himself pure and intact for – what? A creature as fair and untouched as himself.

Turning round sharply, he opened his eyes and stared at his reflection. The fly-spotted mirror was losing its silvering in a kind of greenish ulceration round the edges, but this only served to throw his beauty into a starker relief. His likeness to his uncle Keith he had never observed and this was just as well; he would have repudiated it with fury. He saw only a face and figure he never tired of admiring, that square jaw, those eyes and cheek-bones, that perfect nose and mouth, that black silk hair and the slim, strong body, hips and pelvis too narrow, it seemed, to contain all that was inside them.

Yet it was scarcely vanity. There was no idea in his mind of improving on his looks or dressing for them or *using* them. He simply derived pleasure from the contemplation of himself as he did from looking at any object of beauty. He would no more want to flaunt himself or thrust himself upon anyone than he would want to set up a beloved piece of sculpture in the front garden or invite people in to look at a treasured painting on his wall. He was his. He was the only person he cared for as much as he cared for things.

The flawlessness was marred only by the damage to his left hand. He had got into the habit of holding his hand with the little finger curled round and tucked into the palm. These days, or in circumstances where parents felt some responsibility for a child, they would have found that bit of finger and taken it with them to Accident and Emergency, and it would have been invisibly stitched on again. This lack of care, of interest, was another reason for hating them. He lowered his eyes and contemplated the clutter on the dressing-table. Nothing had been moved, nothing had been dusted, since his mother died. The place was kept as it had always been, as a shrine might be, but out of indifference, not devotion.

An old Mason-Pearson hairbrush, its stiff black bristles clogged with Eileen's equally wiry but greying hair, a scent bottle in which the perfume had grown yellow and viscid with age, a comb whose teeth were gummed together with dark-grey grease, a cardboard box that had once held Terry's All Gold chocolates, a glass ashtray containing pins, hairgrips, scraps of cottonwool, a dead fly, the top of a ballpoint pen and, horribly, a piece of broken fingernail. And all this sitting on a greyed and stained crocheted lace mat, rumpled in the middle and curled at its fringed edges, like an island in a dusty sea after a nuclear explosion.

Teddy nearly swung out his arm to sweep it all on to the floor. His father wouldn't notice, wouldn't see anything amiss for years, for ever. Something stopped him doing that, simple curiosity as to what was inside the box. If it was still what had originally been there he imagined them coated in mould, the ghosts of chocolates, pale phantom cubes and hemispheres and shell-shapes.

But the chocolates had long been eaten. This box was where Eileen had kept her jewellery. Teddy had never seen her wear any of it, ropes of pearls with peeling surfaces, a green glass necklace, a scottie dog brooch, a copper bracelet for keeping rheumatism at bay – it said so, engraved on it – a necklace apparently woven out of plastic-covered thread. Then he saw what it actually was. So you could crochet jewellery too.

He tipped out the lot. Right at the bottom, like an orchid planted in a bed of thistles, was a ring.

Just as his mother had done, all those years ago, in the Ladies at Broadstairs, he saw its worth. Not its probable value, as she had done, but its beauty. He laid it in the palm of his hand and turned it this way and that for the diamond to catch the light. The diamond was large and deeply glowing and richly flashing, with rainbows skimming its facets and rainbows cast from it to dance up and down the dirty wall. Inside the setting of the diamond and the sparkling shoulders, the ring was clogged with the same kind of epidermal detritus as Eileen's comb. He curled his lip in disgust at the dark grease caking the gold band and delicately fashioned sockets. Where had it come from? Had she ever worn it?

It ought to be cleaned, he would find out how you cleaned a diamond ring. But first, after these explorations, he would have a bath.

The neighbours, abandoning slanderous gossip and unkind judgements as people do when tragedy strikes, said that Jimmy's not lasting long after his wife's death went to show what a devoted couple they were. They couldn't live without each other. Not that Jimmy had died, but he had been taken to the hospital in an ambulance after suffering a heart attack in the pub.

He had been standing at the bar with a pint of draught Guinness in front of him, talking to anyone who would listen about race relations in north London. Or, more precisely, about the conduct of the newsagent of Indian extraction, though born in Bradford, who had sold out of copies of the *Sun* before Jimmy managed to visit his shop. 'So I said to Paki the blackie,' said Jimmy, using the witty sobriquet he believed was his own invention, 'I said to him, you're not in Cal-bloody-cutta now, you know, you're not among the snake-charmers and the cow-buggerers no more, and he went – well, not white, not that, do me a favour – no, he went the colour of the curry he has with his fuckin' chips and ...'

Pain cut off whatever Jimmy had intended to say next. He clutched the upper part of his left arm with his right hand, an action which seemed firstly to pull him forward, then double him up, and to release a low groan from his slackening mouth. The groan rose to a throaty howl as Jimmy buckled at the knees and collapsed, sprawling, to the floor.

Though existing for a long time without a telephone, the Grexes had acquired one ten years before, largely for Keith's plumbing business. Keith was on the phone, talking to a woman who had water coming through her bathroom ceiling, when a policeman came to the door. Keith was in a dilemma, whether to go to the aid of the bathroom woman or get down the hospital. He came into the dining-room where Teddy was sitting on his bed, drawing a design for a footstool. 'The whole family's breaking up,' he moaned. 'You'd best get down there and see your dad, you can come on the back of the bike with me and I'll drop you off on my way to Cricklewood.'

'No, thanks,' said Teddy. 'I'm busy.'

The footstool would be beautiful, a creation of simple lines and smooth, gleaming surfaces. He closed his eyes, imagining a future life from which all ugliness was banished.

Chapter 7

Back at college a few days later, Teddy attended a
lecture on the Joyden School. It was given by a
visiting professor and he wasn't obliged or even
expected to attend. 'Fine art' had no part in his
course, but he admired the work of Michael Joyden,
Rosalind Smith and Simon Alpheton, samples of
which he had seen reproduced in a Sunday supplement, and he wanted to hear what Professor Mills
had to say about it.

As always spotlessly clean, with newly washed
hair and scrubbed fingernails, Teddy was dressed in
his usual immaculate near-rags. He had no money
for clothes and shopped, when he had to, at Oxfam
and the Sue Ryder shop. His mother had always
dressed him from these establishments, he was used
to it and took no interest in what he wore. On this
day he had on blue jeans, like everyone else in the
lecture hall of the Potter Building, a snowy though
shabby T-shirt and a dark-blue sweat-shirt that had
been bought new from C & A by the Sue Ryder
donor twelve years before.

The girl who sat down next to him gave him one of
those appraising looks he was accustomed to. She
was pretty enough. He took virtually no interest in
people's characteristics or attitudes or opinions, but
he always noticed whether they were good-looking
or the reverse. This one had a bright, sharp-featured
face and a neat little body, but to use a phrase of his

grandmother's, she looked shop-soiled. As if, he thought with an inner shudder, she had been through too many grubby hands and tumbled on too many beds as smelly as Keith's.

'Hi,' she said.

He nodded at her.

'I haven't seen you here before.'

He raised his swallow's-wing eyebrows.

'I'd remember you, believe me,' she said flirtatiously. 'There are some people you don't forget.'

'Is that so?' It was an interrogatory he often used and it meant very little. He forgot everyone except those he was obliged to be with in daily proximity. 'Tell me something.'

She was smiling now. 'Anything!'

'How would you clean a ring?'

'*What?*'

'How would you clean a diamond ring?'

'For God's sake, I don't know.' She gave him a resentful glance, but seemed to be considering the question. She shrugged. 'My gran puts hers in gin. Leaves it in a glass of gin overnight.'

The lecturer was coming on to the podium.

'Right,' he said. 'Thanks.'

Teddy had wondered how Professor Mills would show examples of the paintings and not, he hoped, by sticking reproductions up on a board. To his relief he saw that slides were to be used. The lights in the auditorium were dimmed a little and the first picture appeared on the screen. It was Michael Joyden's *Come Hither Blues* and Teddy hadn't seen it before. The pop group with whom Joyden and Alpheton had been friends, and whose music they had loved, appeared on the canvas in swirls of colour and flashes of light, so that strangely you could almost hear the picture.

The girl muttered something about not being able

to see to make notes. Teddy ignored her. Professor Mills talked about Joyden and Smith and the influence of the Fauvists, their bold style and use of brilliant colour. While Rosalind Smith demonstrated this influence perhaps more than any other member of the Joyden School, Alpheton owed more to Bonnard, Vallotton and Vuillard than to Matisse and Rouault. Some called his work retrograde, but the lecturer claimed for it a striking modernity comparable at least to Hockney or Freud.

Teddy barely knew who most of these people were. Lucien Freud he knew, but thought his work ugly, no matter how good it might be. He had seen a reproduction of one of Alpheton's paintings on a flier put through the Neasden letter-box and now here it was again, as large as life up on the screen: *Music in Hanging Sword Alley*.

Come Hither again, this time the four musicians leaned languidly against a concrete wall of the building where the recording studio was, their instruments at their feet. Marc Syre, the lead guitarist, had his mouth wide open, his head hanging backwards and his long hair streaming down his back. The date of the painting, Professor Mills said, was 1965.

'My mum's got all their old singles,' whispered the girl. 'She was a Come Hither groupie – can you believe it?'

Teddy shrugged. He wasn't interested in music of any kind. All those people were probably dead by now, anyway. People recorded in paint, that was another thing. Like this next one, Alpheton's masterpiece, the most famous of the Joyden School, the one that was in the Tate, the one that was in all books of modern art and found its way into superior calendars. Until now Teddy had only seen it in that

Sunday magazine, but it was really on its account that he had come to this lecture.

Marc and Harriet in Orcadia Place. The two young people were in a sunlit garden or courtyard in front of what looked like a tree. But a tree without trunk or branches, more a curtain of leaves. All this was mere background to the man and the woman who stood a little apart, joined to each other by his extended right hand, her left, the fingertips lightly linked. He was dark, bearded, long-haired, dressed in dark blue, she a red-haired beauty, with a russet curling mane, the precise same shade as her long Regency dress. Their eyes were concentrated on each other with, it seemed, a tender love and yearning. Passion informed the painting so that after all these years and in spite of the million eyes that had looked on it and the thousand commentaries made on it, this couple's love remained fresh and eternally enduring.

'Marc Syre, as your parents no doubt could tell you,' said Professor Mills, 'was a member of Come Hither and as such made himself a fortune which enabled him, as early as nineteen sixty-five, the date of this work, to occupy this house in St John's Wood and enjoy this *rus in urbe*. Believe me, there is a Georgian house behind all those ivy or vine leaves, or whatever they are. Harriet Oxenholme was what we should call today his live-in girlfriend.

'But we need not concern ourselves unduly with these people, who are important only insofar as Simon Alpheton was their friend and they became, by a most happy chance for subsequent generations, his subjects. What we must look at is Alpheton's arresting use of colour, his subtle handling of light and his curious ability to convey with extreme economy powerful emotion and, indeed, sexual passion. He had in mind, of course, as template or exemplar, Rembrandt's *The Jewish Bride*, but before

67

we discuss that, let us first look at the play of light and shade . . .'

Teddy decided to take himself down to the Tate Gallery and confront the real thing. He thought about leaves and carving leaves, something like what Grinling Gibbons did, but modern, leaves for today. A picture frame of leaves or a mirror – yes, why not make a mirror?

When the lecture was over and the lights went up again the girl next to him looked at the notes she had struggled to make. 'Would you call that picture erotic?' she asked him.

'Mills did.'

'Did he? Then I will. I'm Kelly. What's your name?'

'Keith,' said Teddy.

'What happened to your finger, Keith?'

He said gravely, 'My uncle bit it off.'

This time she didn't believe. She giggled. 'Would you feel like coming out for a drink, Keith?'

'I've got a tutorial,' said Teddy.

He got up and walked away without a backward glance. Why had he lied instead of just saying no? He'd say it next time. Of course he hadn't a tutorial and he had no essay to write. No one seemed to care in his course whether you ever wrote anything or not. He was going home to perform a task, or begin to perform a task, he had for several years longed to do. His uncle would be out, putting in a power shower in a flat in Golders Green and afterwards visiting Jimmy in hospital. Keith, who had never shown much affection for his brother in the past, or indeed for anyone, had become a faithful visitor at Jimmy's bedside. So no one would be at home to see or to hear.

The Edsel, a delicate pale-yellow and spotless, its engine several times rebuilt, stood on the extended concrete pad under the new carport with its four metal posts and its gleaming roof of corrugated polytetrafluoroethylene. It was – or seemed – the largest of any cars Keith had had, too large to be parked horizontally across the garden, its bonnet and grid like a pursed mouth facing the back fence, its huge finned boot with high tail-lights close up against the french windows. Next to it, underneath where the motor bike stood when Keith was at home, was a long slick of oil. The carport, designed to shelter a big car, had taken up even more of the space than the original pad and Teddy's tool collection was crowded up into a corner, in the right angle where two fences met.

He lifted up the plastic sheeting and shook off the water which the previous night's rain had left in its folds. Underneath, from a box and then from their newspaper wrappings, he took a saw, a hacksaw, chisels of varying sizes and a hammer. Mr Chance had owned nothing so crude as an axe, but they had one Grandma Grex had used in distant wood-chopping days. Teddy found it, damp and blunt, among the welter of mould-coated rubbish under the sink.

He carried his tools into the dining-room and began. It was five o'clock when he started and by seven-thirty he had sawn the legs off all the chairs and the arms off the carvers, sawn off their backs and prised out the seat cushions. He didn't want to stop to eat, so he sharpened the axe on Mr Chance's whetstone and started chopping. Within half an hour he had reduced the six chairs to firewood. That was when the people next door banged on the wall. They banged a few times and then the phone started ringing. Teddy guessed it was them, a yuppie couple who had bought Mr Chance's house and thought themselves a cut above the rest of the people in the street. He ignored the banging and the phone, but his axe work was done for the time being and he began sawing up the sideboard.

The man next door came round and rang the bell when Teddy started chopping again at nine. Teddy let him ring a few times and then he went to the door with Kenneth Clark's *Civilisation* in his hand, open at the chapter called 'Grandeur and Obedience'.

'Look, what's going on? What is this?'

'My uncle's making a coffin,' said Teddy. 'He's got a deadline.'

The neighbour was one of those who blush when they think they've been told a lie or are being sent up, but don't know how to handle it. 'What deadline?' he said.

'Ten p.m.' said Teddy. 'Nearly over. Good-night.'

He shut the door hard and gave it a kick. Saying sorry wasn't a habit of his. Before going back to his dismemberment of the furniture he went upstairs, found the gin bottle under Keith's bed and poured an inch of it into the egg-cup he had taken up with him. Into it went the diamond ring. Teddy put the egg-cup under his own bed. He chopped up the sideboard in double-quick time, stacked a woodpile four feet high and was in the kitchen eating a large can of baked beans on three rounds of toast when Keith came in at twenty-five to eleven.

'You're eating late,' said Keith.

Teddy didn't reply.

Keith set down his two plastic carriers, full of bottles and beer cans, lit a cigarette with a match and dropped the match on the floor. 'Don't you want to know how your dad is?'

'What do you think?' said Teddy.

'You watch your mouth. You haven't been near your dad since he went in there and that's all of two fuckin' months. Poor old sod's on his way out and you don't give a fourpenny fuck.'

70

'How about you watching your mouth?' said Teddy. 'Or *washing* it out? With like cyanide.'

He went into the dining-room and banged the door. But he started laughing when he was inside. That night he slept like a log. Or like a Grex, they were all heavy sleepers, though he was sometimes the exception. The following evening he sawed the legs off the table and chopped them up, but not the table top. Late in the day, but not too late, he saw what a fine piece of mahogany it was. He took it carefully apart and stacked the boards against the wall.

The chopped wood made a pile to occupy a space roughly the size the sideboard had been. The only way to get rid of it that came to mind was to take three or four pieces with him in a plastic carrier every time he left the house. Rather like someone disposing of a body, half a leg one day, a hand another, finally the head.

Fortunately – he had never thought of it as being *fortunate* before – the place was awash with plastic bags. They filled the kitchen drawers and flopped out when you opened the cupboard under the sink. Keith got them from the Safeway when he bought his booze and he never took used ones back. Recycling in any shape or form had no place in his life-style. When Teddy went to get the tube to college he'd take some of those bits of leg with him in a bag and put them in a waste bin.

As Kelly's grandma had predicted, the gin had cleaned the ring. Lumps of grey waxy substance, one with a hair embedded in it, floated on the surface of the liquid in the egg-cup. Teddy sniffed it with a shudder. He was preserving another virginity, that of never letting alcohol pass his lips.

The ring sparkled in the morning light. Teddy wondered whose it had been before it came on to his mother's hand. Grandma Grex's? Surely not. More likely it was stolen, but he doubted if his father had ever had the courage to steal anything. Perhaps he was wrong and the ring was worthless, perhaps it had come out of a Christmas cracker.

He questioned if something so beautiful could be valueless. One day he would find a woman and give it to her.

Chapter 8

Soon after Richard and Julia were married the police asked Richard if he would let Francine attend an identity parade.

'She only saw his shoes and the top of his head,' Richard protested.

'If you think about it,' Detective Inspector Wallis said, 'I'm sure you'll agree that no one looking down from above ever just sees the top of someone's head and his shoes. There's going to be a lot more than that. His hands, for instance, the shape and size of him, his ears, his shoulders.'

Julia thought the project very wrong. Francine, in her opinion, was disturbed enough already, a frightened, traumatised child. This might send her over the edge. It was their first disagreement, hers and Richard's. Richard won it, but that was the last struggle with Julia he was ever to win. She sighed and looked sad, saying, 'I hope we aren't talking about irreparable damage to Francine's already fragile personality.'

They both went with her to the police station in Surrey where the identity parade was held. Because of the peculiar nature of the view Francine had had of the man on the doorstep, she was placed in a room where she could look down on the eight men in the line-up. The glass in the window was one-way so that she could see them but they could not see her. Or so the police told Richard.

It looked like normal glass to Julia. 'They would say that, darling,' she said, 'to set our minds at rest.'

In any case, Francine was unable to pick out the man. She could pick out four, she said the tops of their heads all looked like the top of the head she had seen, but no particular one. What happened to the men in the line-up none of them was told, but no one was arrested.

'But he's seen her, hasn't he?' said Julia.

'That was the point of the one-way glass,' Richard said, 'so that he couldn't see her.'

Julia, who was nothing if not illogical, said, 'It doesn't matter, though, does it, if he saw her or not? The reality is that he knows who she is and he knows she's the only witness the police have.'

'You're presupposing that he was one of those eight men.'

'Well, of course he was, Richard. He wouldn't have been there if he wasn't.'

What motivated Julia towards her subsequent actions? Later on, this was a question Francine asked herself. At the beginning she was too young to ask. Richard didn't ask. He didn't question at all, for he recognised that Julia had a genuine fear for Francine's safety and believed that Francine herself was afraid. In embarking on her system of the protection and cocooning and insulating of Francine, she was only obeying her conscience and her knowledge of psychology.

That she might be carrying out her safeguarding programme for other reasons, because she was herself childless and likely to remain so, or because she had lost her means of livelihood and profession, or because she had abandoned all other areas in which to exercise power, occurred only to her stepdaughter, and that not for another ten years.

But at that time what principally troubled Francine was the departure of Flora. She might have stayed, at least as an occasional visitor or helper, or been invited to be a sitter while Richard and Julia went out in the evenings. But Richard and Julia never went out in the evenings, they never went out together. Julia thought it harmful for Francine to be in the house without either one of them. So Flora left and Francine cried.

'You can come and see me,' Flora said. 'I'm not far away. You get Mrs Hill to bring you.'

But somehow Julia never had the time. She was too busy looking after Francine. Privately, she told Richard it was better for Francine to make a clean break with Flora. 'On a practical level,' she said, 'you wouldn't want your daughter picking up that accent.'

It was at about this time, after Flora had gone, when Francine was nearly nine and had tried and failed to spot the man in the identity parade, that Richard read a letter to Julia from a former client's solicitor. He read it by mistake, confessed and apologised, but still, quite humbly and contritely, wanted to know what it meant.

'It means that a very vindictive, and I must say unbalanced, man has finally won his victory over me. He has succeeded in putting me out of practice and no doubt his triumph is complete.'

The explanation which followed made Richard nearly as indignant as his wife. This man's son had been Julia's client. He was a boy of ten. A tragedy had nearly ensued when, after coming home from a session with Julia, the boy had tried, and luckily failed, to hang himself. The father threatened to bring an action against Julia, was set to do so, being certain he could show evidence of damage to his son's mind directly caused by her, but had finally been persuaded to settle on payment by Julia of two thousand pounds and her promise to retire from all psychotherapeutic work.

'You should have fought it,' Richard said.

'I know. I hadn't the strength. I hadn't the courage, Richard. I was all alone – then.'

She said nothing about the eminent psychiatrists who had been willing to give evidence in court. She gave no hint of the boy's testimony to his father's solicitor of the terrors, agoraphobia and recurring nightmares her questionings and suggestions had allegedly induced in him.

'I'll still be able to make use of all my knowledge,' she said quite gaily. 'There are others to benefit from it. You and Francine. Would you think me melodramatic if I said I intend to devote my life to Francine?'

All children need to be looked after and at first it was only that Francine was looked after more thoroughly than most. For instance, there was the matter of her father and her stepmother never leaving her with anyone else, there was the business of Julia vetting her school friends for their suitability and there was the baby monitor. This transmitted from her bedroom to Julia's and Richard's bedroom any sounds that might indicate she was having a nightmare or even a disturbed night. Her reading matter was scrutinised by Julia and the small amount of homework she did, the occasional essays she was expected to write, studied for evidence of a disturbed psyche. Flora had left her considerable privacy. With the coming of Julia she had none.

It was Julia's discovery of the video cassette box that prompted Francine's drastic action. Remarkably for her, Julia didn't look inside the box, only at the wording and illustration on its cover. '*A Passage to India* is a wonderful book, Francine, and I believe a very good film was made from it,' said Julia, 'but I don't think you're quite old enough for either yet. It's best to postpone these things until you can understand them.'

'I don't want to watch it,' Francine said, 'I just want to have it,' and she put out her hand for the box.

'Shall I take it downstairs and put it with the others? Then we'll know it's safe.'

'It's safe here,' said Francine as firmly as she could, but was quite surprised just the same when Julia's scarlet-tipped fingers relinquished the box and Julia gave one of her bright, colourful smiles, red lips, white teeth, the prominent blue eyes of an ornamental fish.

Of course, it was not true, what she had said. The box and its contents were far from safe. While she was at school there was nothing to stop Julia coming in here and taking it and looking inside. Julia, certainly, could read that writing.

But now, perhaps, so could Francine.

A curious reluctance to look at those sheets of paper took hold of her. The idea of them frightened her. Not as an illustration in her book of *Grimm's Fairy Tales* frightened her, so that, knowing precisely where it came in the fat volume, between page 102 and page 104, she carefully turned three pages at once when she looked into that particular story. Not like that, for she felt only a kind of distaste, a sense of wishing to avoid the contents of the cassette case in the way she wanted to avoid eating anything flavoured with ginger.

It happened that she was reading a child's book of Greek myths and one of the myths described was of Pandora and how when she opened a certain precious box she released into the world a swarm of evil things. Francine didn't believe that she would let out anything similar if she opened her box, but even at ten years old she could see the analogy. Still, that same day she lifted the lid of the box and took out the now yellowing sheets of paper. And for the first time she understood that what she was looking at were letters.

On the top sheet was no address, but there was a date, a day in March some three and a half years before. She read the way the letter started: 'My darling.' It was no longer difficult for her to read this handwriting, but it was still impossible to do so. For some reason, and she had no idea what, she was too frightened to read on. Her eyes refused to focus on the forward-sloping letters. She saw a blur of darkish stripes on a pale ochre background, and then she put the pages back into the box and closed the lid as hard as she could, pressing it down as if it hadn't clicked into place at once.

The house had no fireplace. She was never alone in the street where there were rubbish bins. It was only at school that she was away from Julia's loving, watchful eye. She took the video cassette box to school with her in the navy-blue, yellow-trimmed backpack all the pupils of this select preparatory school carried with them, and at morning break took the letters out of the box, put them into her blazer pocket and went out into the playground. Everyone else was also out in the playground, which was really a garden with lawns and play areas and a sandpit and a mini-zoo, and Holly, who was Francine's best friend, called out to her to come and see the new baby guinea-pigs.

On her way Francine had to pass one of the crimson-painted bins with swing-lid tops which were set about this part of the gardens to teach pupils the virtues of tidy litter disposal. Francine swung up a lid as she passed and pushed the letters quickly in under it. Holly was still calling her and now she waved back and ran over to look at the little curled-up blind things and their fat mother who was coloured like a tortoiseshell cat.

But next morning, when Julia dropped her off at the school gates – it was only with difficulty that Francine had stopped Julia accompanying her all the way into the class-room – she had to pass that red bin with its swing lid. With a hasty look over her shoulder, to check that Julia was moving off, she lifted it up and looked inside. The bin was empty and someone had put a fresh liner inside.

Sometimes Richard thought Julia too watchful. Francine had no chance to be independent or private or to develop without supervision. But he hardly knew what to believe or what to think. Perhaps the child *was* in danger. The man who had killed his wife was still at large and maybe he lived in fear of what Francine might one day remember, and remembering, tell. And apart from that there was the possibility of damage to her mind or her psychic self or whatever the term was. In the light of present-day thinking it was almost unbelievable that the things that had happened to Francine could leave any child unscathed.

She must be damaged, even if the scarring was unapparent to him. He might be unable to see it, but that need not mean it wasn't there. He was torn in two by half-belief and dread of further self-blame, in no mood to argue with Julia or attempt to dissuade her from her excessive vigilance. Suppose he were to call off this watchdog and then find that all her warnings had been well-founded? He thought of the story of Cassandra whose predictions were doomed to be disbelieved, yet who had been right.

So when the time came for Francine to change

schools, the grant-aided former grammar school where the neighbours' daughters went and that she herself favoured was rejected in favour of Julia's choice, a very select, very expensive private girls' school called the Champlaine. Holly de Marnay was going there and it was from Holly's mother that Julia gleaned all the knowledge she had about it. The Champlaine was housed in a Georgian mansion on the edge of Wimbledon Common, a long way from where the Hills lived, but it had an exemplary record of pupils going on to the best of further education. In the previous year just under ninety-five per cent of the sixth form had entered university, twelve to Oxford or Cambridge.

Classes were small, academic qualifications of teachers high. Among the students – never called pupils – were an earl's granddaughter and a Thai princess. Lacrosse was played, but soccer too. The Champlaine had a large heated swimming pool, squash courts and both hard and grass courts for tennis. Its new science lab was reputed to have cost three million pounds. Fees, therefore, were extremely high and paying them would involve considerable sacrifice on the Hills' part. Julia didn't protest. If it meant no foreign holidays, no second car and few new clothes, she accepted this as the price which must be paid for Francine's safety.

Though boarding was favoured by the Champlaine authorities, she was not allowed to board. Julia would never have a quiet moment. There had been a recent story in the newspaper of a man getting into a school dormitory and raping a girl. If he could rape he could kill. So Francine became a day girl and thus a member of a slightly disfavoured minority. From certain in-jokes, cult behaviour, secret societies and private rituals she was excluded. It might have been less marked if the pupils had not known her past history and the events in the house in Orchard Lane. But they did know. Julia had insisted that the Headmistress – mysteriously known here as the Chief Executive – told the entire school and staff at an assembly before Francine arrived.

'For her own protection,' Julia explained to Richard. 'If they know they will be vigilant on her behalf. They will help to protect her.'

Richard doubted if teenagers thought or behaved like that, but Julia must know. She had been a teacher before she became a psychotherapist.

'There is less to worry about when she's in the classroom,' said Julia. 'I'm thinking of when she's outside in the grounds. Her friends can operate surveillance.'

Francine had many friends, other day girls. It was to be a long while before she was allowed to go to their houses, but Julia allowed them to come to the Hills, once they had been carefully vetted by her. She would ring up a girl's mother and suggest they meet for lunch, then grill the woman as to her family, her husband's – and occasionally her own – profession, the number of her children, and her attitude towards crime and punishment, this to include what she thought of prisons and whether she favoured the re-introduction of capital punishment.

The women didn't seem to mind too much. Julia never revealed her motives and these parents of Champlaine pupils thought she was interested in their ancestry or their claims to belong to an upper class and particular political persuasion. The result of it all was that Francine was allowed to ask one or two friends round and occasionally have them stay the night. But she was never to go out with a friend and the friend's family or on school trips. The Champlaine took the fourth form to Lake Lucerne one year and the fifth form to Copenhagen the next without her. National Theatre visits happened, but in Julia's company, not her schoolfellows'.

Francine was at an age to rebel and rebel she did – a little. Why was she guarded like this? What was the point? She even said, 'I'd rather have someone attack me than be kept in prison.'

The occasion was a proposed visit to the ballet with two school friends and the mother of one of them. Julia had uttered an unhesitating no. To the West End in the evening by public transport? All right, Miranda's mother would be with them and Francine would stay the night at Miranda's and phone when she got there, but suppose . . .

'You have to realise you're in a special position, Francine.'

'I'm never allowed to forget it.'

'Do you think I like it?' said Julia. 'Do you think it's for my pleasure?'

'I didn't say that. But I don't think I'm at risk – I mean, who am I at risk from?'

Then Julia did what she had promised Richard she would never do. She told Francine her theory.

Francine turned white and began to shiver. 'But I didn't see him. I didn't see anything.'

'Francine, you have nothing to worry about if you behave sensibly, if you let us look after you.'

'Can't we somehow let him know I didn't see him? Can't we – I don't know – put it in the papers, make the police tell him?'

'Now you're being silly.'

Why did she do it? Julia, that is. Why? Her own explanation for her vigilance she believed. The man thought Francine could identify him, therefore he pursued Francine. If she hadn't believed that and continued to do what she did she would either have been an evil woman or a fool. Julia was neither. She was no wicked stepmother. At first, and for a long while, she had confidence in that theory of hers, but after a time her motives blurred and her aims became confused.

For instance, she seldom asked herself what use she would be as a protector, how she, a not particularly athletic woman of nearly fifty, could defend Francine or convince a potential attacker she was a force to be reckoned with. She never carried a weapon or would have dreamt of doing so. By night she slept and Richard slept while Francine was alone in her bedroom, which an intruder might surely have entered as easily, or more easily, than a school dormitory.

The baby monitor was long gone. (Francine, who put up with a lot, who was both gentle and stoical, had protested finally about that and demanded its banishment.) Julia, moreover, had no real knowledge of what happened while Francine was at school. She hoped, she trusted, but she didn't know whether Francine went out in her lunch-time or what she did during free periods or even if she sometimes played truant. Many did – even the earl's granddaughter.

All this Julia was vaguely aware of and aware, too, that the time was coming when either Francine must be shut up, institutionalised like some helplessly handicapped girl, or else set free into the world. But it was over just this question that what good sense she had left, and what common sense, collapsed. Francine was her charge, over whom she fancied she had absolute power. She had saved her, preserved her through childhood and adolescence to the approach of womanhood, and she could not relinquish her.

And during those years she had sacrificed herself for Francine. No one had asked her to do so – Richard had merely asked her to marry him – she had done it entirely of her own volition. But it had been a sacrifice. There had been time, when she was first married, to have a child of her own, she was young enough, but that would have meant in part deserting Francine. She could have pursued one of her two careers – but that would have meant neglecting Francine. Day in, day out, during term time, she had driven Francine the ten miles through heavy traffic to school and the ten miles back and the ten miles to fetch her and the ten miles back. Not once had she been out with her husband in the evening unless they had Francine with them.

Her marriage, too, she had sacrificed. She had spoilt it for Francine's sake. For things were never the same again between them after Richard found out that she had broken her promise and told his daughter. It was farcical, that theory of hers, but Francine was only fifteen years old and to lay such a burden on a child who had surely suffered enough, who had suffered a lifetime's agony before she was eight, that he thought indefensible. Julia he saw with new eyes, as predatory and overweeningly possessive, and as spiteful, too. For what other motive could she have had for telling Francine but malice? The girl had wanted a little freedom, had been, if not rude, a little too direct, and Julia had lashed back with a tale calculated to terrify.

'Malice?' she said. 'Malice? I *love* Francine. All I want is to make it possible for her to live as happy a life as she can in an imperfect world.'

'You are going to have to rethink your whole attitude,' he said in a sombre tone. 'You are going to have to understand that she is growing up and will inevitably grow away.'

Julia saw it very differently. To Francine she had devoted herself and how could she now wrench herself away or even pave the way for so doing? Besides, there was another aspect to be considered.

84

She couldn't relinquish Francine now, give her up and see her make closer friends and take up other interests more important than her, Julia. With her sacrifice and her self-denial, she had *bought* her stepdaughter, she had paid a price for her and made her hers. Francine was her stepdaughter, but she was also her possession, a girl she had created out of a frightened child.

In a way Francine was more her child than if she had given birth to her. And she would fight to keep her.

Chapter 9

One night after his brother had been to see him, had sat by his bed for an hour while they both watched the ward television, Jimmy Grex died. The last of his viable arteries closed up, the substance which lined it finally thickened so that the thread-breadth passage shrank to hair's-breadth, to nothing, and Jimmy, gasping, in agony, fighting for blood, breath and oxygen, passed out of life. He was sixty-seven.

The neighbours said he hadn't wanted to live after his wife died. His brother registered the death, summoned undertakers, fixed up the funeral and invited a chosen few home for a beer, whisky and crisps after the cremation. His son attended, though virtually silently, surveying the place that was now his, not thinking much of it, but gratified by the possession of property, any property.

After everyone had gone, Teddy said to Keith, 'I'm not evicting you, you needn't think that. I know this has been your home all your life. But I'd like you to think about being gone by, say, Christmas.'

It was October. Teddy's final year at the University of Eastcote had just begun. They were in the living-room, among the heavy crowded furniture, with its throws of coloured crochet, an antimacassar over the back of an armchair, a shawl draped across the settee. Lilies, a wreath of them, brought unexpectedly by someone, lay wilting in the dust on the coffee table. Keith, heavily sedated with Chivas Regal, but recovering fast and absolutely on the ball, favoured Teddy with a slow smile. His drooping jowls and the long, now grey, moustache, gave him the look of a benign walrus. His eyes remained sharp, the eyebrows flaring in Mephistophelean arcs.

'This house belongs to me,' he said. 'To me. It's mine. You needn't look like that. Well, I mean, you can if you like. It's all one to me. My dad left me this house. My mum had a life interest and when she died it reverted to me. That's the term, "reverted". OK?'

'You're lying,' Teddy said. He didn't know what else to say.

'Let me explain. I don't fuckin' see why I should, but I will. I might as well. Your dad, God rest his soul, poor sod, your dad wasn't my dad's son. My mum was carrying when he took up with her. Well, you can guess the rest. He was OK about it, but as for getting the house, well, you've got to draw the line, right?'

'I don't believe it,' said Teddy.

'Too bad. That's your problem. I got the deeds in the bank and that's more proof than anything you believe in. However . . .' Keith repeated the word which he seemed to like the sound of. 'However, I'm less of a bastard than what you are. Surprise, surprise. And since you're my nephew, or my half-nephew, not much doubt about that, I'm not turning you out the way you'd have got shot of me. You'd have kicked me out at Christmas, but as far as I'm concerned you can stop here so long as you're up at that fuckin' college. How about that?'

Keith wasn't averse to further explanations. His father had told him the facts of Jimmy's paternity when Jimmy was twenty-three and he was twenty-one. Grex senior was a magnanimous man and had brought up the elder son as his own. Property, though, and the inheritance of property, was another matter. The house that he had saved for and for years had a mortgage on must go to his own natural son.

'I might make a will and leave it to someone else in the family,' said Keith. 'I reckon I've got a bunch of cousins somewhere. Or I might leave it to you. If you behave yourself. Show a bit of respect. Clean the place, bring me up a morning cuppa.' He started laughing at his own wit.

'Why was I never told?'

'Why wasn't you what? Do me a favour. Your mum and dad was alive, you want to remember that. I let them live here and now I'm letting you. You're fuckin' lucky if you did but know it. A lot of men in my position'd expect you to pay rent.'

Teddy walked out, slamming the door behind him. He went into the dining-room and sat down on the floor by the woodpile. He had intended, if not tonight, tomorrow, to begin clearing out the living-room and his parents' bedroom. Maybe get someone in to clear it, a second-hand furniture dealer who might give him something for the bedroom suite and the battered sofa. That was not now possible, might never be possible.

He felt overwhelmed by ugliness. Everything in the house was ugly with the exception of one or two objects in this room and these, his own drawings in their pale wooden frames, his row of books between the bookends he had carved now seemed to him pathetic. His tools weren't ugly, the workbench where the sideboard had been, the two planes, the rack of saws, the hammers and the drills, but they were simply utilitarian. The smell seemed more than usually pervasive, penetrating even here. It was too cold to open the windows. The house was a hideous dump, but he had thought it was his, it was all he had. Only he didn't have it. Keith did, Keith who was one of the ugliest things in it, whose bloated body and soggy face, begrimed hands and broken, yellowing teeth, offended him every time he saw him.

For a little while he seriously considered leaving. But where could he go? At his university it was possible to live in one of the two overcrowded halls of residence, but not in one's third year. There was no way he could afford to rent even a single room. His grant was inadequate for just the bare living and travelling. It occurred to him – as a matter of interest, he didn't care that much – that never in his life had he bought a new garment or had one bought for him. He'd never been abroad or to a London theatre or into any restaurant more up-market than the Burger King.

His plan, scarcely formed, taken for granted, had been to sell the house. Clear it out, do it up, paint the outside and sell it. It was probably worth about as little as any thirties-vintage semi anywhere in London, but it would still fetch thousands and thousands, maybe as much as forty thousand pounds.

But it was Keith's.

Teddy kept the ring in the pocket of his only other jacket, the zipper one that hung on a hook on the inside of the door. He held it in the palm of his hand and looked at it. He still hadn't had it valued. If he tried to sell it the jeweller would think he had stolen it. He could try pawning it. Teddy knew very little about pawning things but pawnshops existed, he had seen them, and he had an idea a pawnbroker would give him approximately half what the ring was worth. That would be a way of getting it valued. He wasn't going to sell it.

He would never sell it. Money wasn't all that much of a serious problem, anyway. He could manage, he always had. While Keith continued to provide some of their food he wouldn't starve. And he could go on making things and learning to make things, and finish his course and get his degree.

He had to make something for his degree submission, some artefact that would be a sample or demonstration of his particular skills. Most of the others would produce a coffee table or a desk and there was someone who was a gifted wood carver, who Teddy knew would be making a mermaid for a ship's figurehead. His talent was in inlaid work, but he also fancied himself as an artist in painted furniture. He would make a mirror. His would have a frame of pale wood, sycamore or the darker walnut, inlaid with holly and yew, painted blue and grey and gold.

If only it didn't have to be here, in this place where everything his eye alighted on was a deformity or a vulgar affront. Outside the window even the Edsel was covered up in plastic under its four-legged plastic-roofed shelter. Keith's motor bike had a black bin-liner over its handlebars and another covering its saddle. The place was a storehouse for plastic bags, there was even one drifting about on the concrete, where greyish blades of grass struggled up through the cracks. Another had plastered itself up against the chain-link fencing, its corners poking through into next door as if it were trying to escape. Teddy drew the curtains.

Keith was asleep in the living-room. He had been drinking more since his brother died, you could say he was drinking for two, Jimmy's share as well as his own. Quite often he didn't go to bed, but came back from whatever job he had been doing, covered up the bike with the bin-liners and moved directly into the living-room with his two plastic bags, one containing the smaller and more portable of his plumber's tools, the other his preferred Chivas Regal and Guinness for the evening. The television went on, Keith uncapped his first can or bottle and lit his first cigarette for some hours. His customers refused to let him smoke in their houses.

When he saw Teddy looking, he offered an explanation. 'I'm not leaving no drink in this place while I'm out working. I wouldn't trust you round my Chivas further than I could fuckin' throw you.'

Teddy made no answer. What was there to say? He never touched alcohol and Keith knew it as well as he did himself. For some reason Keith, who in days gone by had behaved rather better to him than his parents had, since their departure had become abusive, foul-mouthed and unremittingly surly. Teddy didn't care. He made no conjectures either as to whether this happened because Keith had in fact loved his brother and missed him or was disturbed by having no one to look after him and, occasionally, to talk to. It was nothing to him. He watched Keith, sometimes from the open doorway, and especially when the whisky and the Guinness had done their work, not out of interest or sympathy or pity, but with a kind of fascinated disgust.

Often he stood there for ten or fifteen minutes, just looking. Not only at Keith but at Keith's surroundings, absorbing the dreadful room, the curtains coming off their hooks and pinned together with some clip or clamp from Keith's tool bag, the dust so thick that it grew off surfaces like fur, the never-emptied ashtrays, the saucers, tin lids, glass jars full of ash and fag-ends, the sagging broken furniture and square of carpet on which the seemingly floral pattern was in fact made by drink stains, mud brown on sewage grey, the discarded lampshade and bare bulb hanging from a knotted lead, until his eyes finally fixed themselves on Keith himself.

His snoring was worse now than sixteen years ago.

He trumpeted, he snorted, and every few minutes jolted and jumped as if jabbed with an electric probe. Then the rhythmic snoring was re-established, regular, long drawn-out, rattling through Keith's nasal passages and expelled in a kind of juddering whistle. Once – but once only – he came fully to his senses and sitting up yelled, 'What are you fuckin' lookin' at?'

It never happened again. Keith was too stunned and bludgeoned by his favoured mixture. He lay with his mouth wide open, his arms hanging over the arms of the chair and his big round belly, covered by a moth-eaten green wool sweater, reared up like some grassy hill in which speculators have dug holes. He never used a glass but drank straight from the can. The whisky he poured into a yoghurt pot, though where it came from Teddy didn't know. Crazy to imagine anyone living here ever eating yoghurt. Usually one plastic bag lay on his knees, a couple of others on the floor beside him. Quite often he didn't even bother to take the whisky out of the bag it had been bought in, but pouring it out, lifted bottle and enveloping bag together.

It might be midnight, but the television would still be on. Keith would be there all night. If he needed to pee he would never make it up the stairs to the bathroom but would stagger out into the front garden. Teddy often smelt it. The yuppies next door thought it was cats. Keith snorted and gave one of his violent galvanic starts. By coincidence the characters in the Accident and Emergency sitcom on the television were on the point of administering heart-stimulating shocks to a patient on a trolley. Teddy switched it off and went to bed.

Chapter 10

The painting was two years old, already much acclaimed, and bought for a large sum, when Marc Syre threw Harriet Oxenholme out of the house.

She had asked him once too often if he still loved her. His self-control, of which he had never had much, snapped. He fetched her such a swipe to the head that she fell over and lay sprawled on the badly stained carpet under the broken chandelier. Then he took hold of her by the hair, that massy, thick, curly red hair, and tried to drag her out of the room. But a hank of hair came away in his hand, so he dragged her by the shoulders instead.

For once no other members of Come Hither were in the house, nor was their road manager, nor any of the groupies Marc was in the habit of bringing home for a night or just for a quickie on the drawing-room sofa. Harriet and Marc had been alone which was why, harking back to their passion and exclusivity which seemed so recent yet at the time so eternal, she had asked the fatal question.

He hadn't knocked her unconscious, but she gave up the struggle. She let him drag her out of the house, it was easier than walking. Outside the front door she got up because she didn't fancy being bumped down the stone steps. He gave her a push and she staggered, though she didn't lose her footing. When he had gone back into the house and slammed the door she sat down on the paving stones and rubbed her head where the hair had come out. There was blood on her fingers, he had wounded her.

It was autumn and the dense tapestry of leaves had changed from green to pale-yellow and bronze touched with dark-red. When a window upstairs was roughly flung open broken tendrils and torn foliage fluttered down. Marc started throwing out her clothes. She had to duck not to be hit by a flying boot. The red dress, *the* dress, came floating down like a great crimson butterfly or a snippet of that Virginia creeper, airily and as if it were enjoying itself. Then came a cardboard box.

She got up and shouted at him, 'Give me a suitcase, you bastard! I'm not carrying my stuff in a bloody box.'

She didn't think he would. She started putting her clothes in the box which had once held bottles of Babycham. When had he ever had Babycham, for God's sake? The suitcase came flying out with its lid flapping open, to fall slam bang right on top of the single rose bush. She seized it in her arms, scratching herself on thorns.

It was the dawn of the age of cheesecloth and she was always in the forefront of fashion, so there was a lot of it, limp, pale stuff, as feeble as she felt. She stuffed it into the suitcase and blood got on it from her fingers, streaking it with tie-dye patterns. Tears ran down her cheeks and she began to wail.

The window went up again and there he was with a big pink-and-white china bowl balanced on the sill. Those Victorian jug-and-bowl sets were all the rage, so of course she'd had to have one. Marc had bought it for her like everything else and now he was going to empty its contents on to her head. She struggled to her feet, whimpering, dragging the suitcase behind her, and she was at the gate when the water came down in a cascade. The bowl followed, hitting the paving with such a crash that the people opposite came out into their front garden.

Harriet didn't look at them. They had complained to the police in the past about Marc's goings-on and probably would again. It wasn't her problem. She had problems enough, what with no money and nowhere to go. Her parents lived in Shropshire, in the manor house of a village near the Long Mynd, and were what her mother called 'gentlefolks'. They hadn't exactly shown Harriet the door, but after she had been expelled from her public school and had taken to following Come Hither everywhere, camping in her sleeping bag on the doorstep of the recording studio in Hanging Sword Alley, then moving in with Marc, telling the newspapers how much she adored Marc, after all that they had more or less made it plain she wasn't welcome in Colling Magna. Even *Marc and Harriet in Orcadia Place* being the Royal Academy's picture of the year hadn't changed their attitude.

At that time Harriet hadn't cared whether they wanted to see her or not. It was rather a relief that they didn't, for it saved a lot of trouble. Now, though, they would have been useful. Colling Manor would have been somewhere to go to where they had to take you in. But what was the use of even thinking about it when she hadn't got the train fare or the coach fare? She hadn't any money at all and hadn't the energy to hitch. The only thing to do was get down to Camden Town and throw herself on the mercy of some friends of hers who lived in a squat in Wilmot Place.

It was hard to tell if they were pleased to see her or fed up with her or what. They were all high on something most of the time anyway, and this made them dreamy and spaced-out, walking about slowly like very old zombies or staring into corners as if seeing things sitting there that no one else could see. Terry and John, who had renamed themselves Storm and Anther, offered her a spare mattress in a room already occupied by Anther himself and a woman called Zither, but told her it could only be for a few nights. They were keeping the space for Storm's guru, who was soon to join them from his ashram in Hartlepool.

Harriet had to lug the suitcase upstairs herself. But she hadn't really expected things to be otherwise. The mattress, naturally, was on the floor and she sat down on it. The only other furniture in the room was a second mattress, also on the floor, which Anther shared with Zither. An Indian bedspread served as a window curtain. On one wall was pinned a large sheet of paper on which someone had written in a curious script and red paint: *Fourteen Manvantaras and one Krita make one Kalpa*. Harriet started to cry again, she couldn't help it.

She had had nothing to eat since breakfast, or what passed for breakfast, at midday, and now she was very hungry. Storm and Anther and Zither might share their food with her and they might not. Come to that, they might not be going to eat at all. She would very much have liked a drink. Along with a lot of other indulgences, she had got into the habit of drinking with Marc, but anything like that was out of the question here unless you were talking about maté or Boldo tea and Harriet wasn't.

She could go on the streets, but she didn't know how to start. Did you just dress up and stand about until someone came up and asked you if you would? She might get beaten up by someone's pimp or by a client. Sooner or later it was going to have to be Colling Manor via the M1 in a lorry, but even then she'd have to have something to eat on the way. In gathering up the stuff Marc had thrown out of the window she hadn't looked closely at what she was putting into the case, she'd been too upset. There was always the possibility he had thrown out something she could sell. He'd never given her much in the way of jewellery, the only item worth anything being a gold bracelet and that was probably still in the drawer at Orcadia Place. She undid the case despondently and lifted the lid.

Cheesecloth. How had she ever come to accumulate so much of it? Shirts and tops and waistcoats and pants as if the original long dress and jacket had got together and had cubs. A creamy, crumpled, pallid mass, streaked with blood, that she never wanted to see again, her boots and a couple of pairs of shoes, a bunch of bruised red leaves that had somehow got mixed up with it. And under it all the dress she had worn when Simon Alpheton painted her, its finely pleated silk the exact same colour as her hair. No bracelet, no watch. Marc had paid a fortune for the red dress, which was appropriate, really, since the person who designed it was someone called Fortuny, and it hadn't even been new. She remembered now, Simon had got him to buy it, had even found it for her and for his picture.

If someone had bought it second-hand maybe someone else would buy it third-hand. There were a few places she knew, she'd try them in the morning. The suitcase was empty now, but for the zipped-up compartment at the back and she hadn't opened that to put anything in there. It was Marc's case, not hers, and it was just possible he had left something in that compartment. A half-empty packet of cigarettes from the last time he used the case? She was dying for a cigarette.

Harriet undid the zip. She gave a little squeak. The

compartment was full of money. It wasn't fastened in wads but loose banknotes. She felt quite faint: weak and as if her head was rising out of her neck on a long stalk. After she had closed her eyes and counted to ten and opened them again and the notes were still there, she began counting again, the money this time.

There were still pound notes in those days. Oncers. Most of the notes were pounds, but some were fives and a few were tens. Harriet counted. She forgot she was hungry and longing for a cigarette. She had never in all her life enjoyed counting anything so much and she was quite sorry when it came to an end. But not sorry about the sum. Two thousand and nine pounds.

Her euphoria lasted about an hour. Downstairs she found Anther and Zither in the kitchen baking hashish cakes. They offered her one, but she shook her head. She didn't want anything at the moment that might change her consciousness, she liked it the way it was. 'I'm going up the road,' she said. 'Can I get you anything?'

For answer they turned on her their strange spaced-out smiles but when she came back with two carriers full of purchases they each accepted a cigarette and a glass (a cracked cup) of wine. Harriet said she would be gone in the morning.

'That's OK,' said Anther. 'The holy rishi won't be here till Thursday.'

'I have to find a place of my own,' said Harriet.

Her face felt sore where Marc had hit her and when she looked in the smeary mirror in the bathroom – it was a long time since she had been in a bathroom as squalid as this one and she had forgotten they existed – she saw her cheek that had at first been bright pink was turning the colour of the Virginia creeper leaves. She went back to the room with her wine bottle and the chocolate she had bought. Her happiness was quickly being replaced by apprehension. Why was that money there?

There were two possibilities, as far as she could see. One was that Marc hadn't wanted to leave her destitute and had put it there on purpose. He kept money all over the house, in drawers, under the bed, it was just the way he was, a crazy eccentric. Maybe he'd snatched up a bundle of cash and stuffed it into that compartment as a farewell gift. But in that case wouldn't he have put the bracelet in too? And would he have speeded her parting by chucking a bowl of water at her?

No, she couldn't see it as a final uncharacteristically generous gesture on Marc's part. A more likely explanation was that he had put the notes in there the last time he went anywhere – to Spain it might have been, a month before – and simply forgotten about them. It could even be that the case was one of his 'banks' along with the drawers and the top of the wardrobe. No doubt it had slipped his mind, but he would soon realise. He would know she'd got his two grand and he'd come after it. Or his heavies would. Other musicians had minders, but Marc had heavies, she'd met one of them and he was aptly named, the biggest man she'd ever seen in her life.

She had better disappear.

The room Harriet found was in Notting Hill in the neighbourhood of Ladbroke Grove, known as 'the Grove' to its denizens, and the landlady waived references when Harriet produced a hundred pounds' deposit. She didn't see how anyone could find her there, but she was nervous whenever she went out. And she was lonely.

All her friends were Marc's friends too. She had always liked Simon Alpheton, had quite *fancied*

Simon, but she held back from getting in touch with him. He knew Marc, he might tell Marc, and then Marc would come like a shot after the swiftly dwindling two thousand pounds. Apprehensive she might be while out in the street, but she had still managed to spend. Buying things comforted her. She always felt more cheerful and less lonely when she came back to Chesterton Road with, for instance, a pair of boots, a floor cushion, a couple of the newest records in the charts, *Vogue* magazine and *Forum* and *Cosmo*, gold nail varnish and an Indian dress. She even bought a wig, with vague ideas of disguise in mind, but she had so much hair of her own that she couldn't get it on.

Never, since she was fifteen, had she gone so long without sex. Celibacy lasted two months until her landlady had the house painted. The man who was doing it appeared at her window one day on top of his ladder. Otto Neuling was the son of a German ex-prisoner of war and an English blonde, he was tall and well-built, with the colouring of Siegfried and the features of Paul Newman. He was younger than Harriet, just eighteen to her twenty-four, and he was to be the first in a long line of young lovers who belonged in the rough-trade genre as well as the youth category.

After a heavy flirtation conducted at the window, Harriet invited him to step over the sill and come into the room.

Otto had never heard of Simon Alpheton or *Marc and Harriet in Orcadia Place*, was inarticulate, of limited intelligence and very virile. That suited Harriet fine. Sometimes she went drinking with him in the Sun in Splendour and once to Clacton on the back of his Honda. It would never occur to Marc, she thought, to look for her in Otto's company.

When there was just under five hundred pounds

left of Marc's money Harriet, wearing the red dress and carrying a Biba bag full of newly bought finery, was walking home along Holland Park Avenue. The only economy she practised was to stop taking taxis. The man approaching her with a dog on a lead was the kind to whom she never gave a second glance: old, certainly getting on for forty, with receding hair and glasses. She noticed the dog because it was an Irish setter with a coat the same colour as her hair. But neither was interesting enough to distract her from her favourite pastime of studying her own reflection in the shop fronts that she passed.

He spoke to her. She had never seen him before, but he spoke her name. 'Harriet.'

He said it in a tone of pleased satisfaction. She was wary. 'And how is Marc?' he said.

If she had had a better understanding of human nature she would have detected a kind of serendipity in his manner, as of someone who has happily made an unexpected discovery. His smile should have told her and his raised eyebrows. As it was Harriet, the solipsist, immediately thought this man had been set on her, might even be a private detective or some kind of bailiff, sent to recover the money. She said shrilly, 'What do you want?'

'Please,' he said. 'I'm sorry. But you are Harriet, aren't you? Alpheton's Harriet in Orcadia Place? I would have known you anywhere.'

'Is that all?' she said and breathed again.

'I've been in love with that picture for three years. Maybe I should say I've been in love with the girl in that picture.'

You've got a bit of a bloody nerve, thought Harriet. She didn't say it aloud. She looked at him, properly this time, and with renewed interest. He wasn't too bad. Quite tall and he hadn't got a belly, in spite of his age. Nice hands, reasonable teeth and a *lovely* dog. She stroked the dog's silky red head. 'What's his name?'

'O'Hara.'

'You're sure Marc didn't send you?'

He burst out laughing. 'I don't even know who he is – a pop singer, right?'

'He's very famous,' she said indignantly.

'I'm sure. I only know him from the picture, but then I'm not very with it. I'll tell you what, why don't we go and have a cup of tea?'

'I'd rather have a drink,' said Harriet.

The Prince of Wales had just opened for the evening. They both had Tequila Sunrises, which he told the barman how to make. A bowl of water was put on the floor for O'Hara. He told her his name was Franklin Merton and he lived in Campden Hill Square. That made Harriet prick up her ears and she asked if he had a flat there. No, a house, he said, and what about her? She couldn't think of anything to say, there wasn't anything, she was just Harriet Oxenholme who had been painted by Alpheton.

'A lily of the field?'

She didn't know what he meant and thought him a little mad. But rich. She never asked people what they did for a living because this wasn't something that much concerned her and when he said that he looked after people and made sure they were safe, she thought disappointedly that he must be a social worker.

'I'm in insurance,' he said.

'Oh.'

'And I'm married.'

'Right.'

She gave him an innocent, carefree smile. How could his being married interest or trouble her? Marriages, anyway, as far as she could tell, were made to be broken. But he was rich and she, in only a few weeks, was due to be poor again.

'You look wonderful in your Fortuny dress,' he said. 'If I just pop home first with the dog, will you have dinner with me?'

She detected a curious coldness in his strained smile, but she didn't, then, see it as sinister.

Chapter 11

It was always there. The other girls she knew, her friends, Miranda and Isabel and Holly, also had memories of the eighth year of their lives to look back on, memories which would be everlastingly recalled. The puppy her parents had given her for her birthday, in Miranda's case; in Holly's, falling off her pony and breaking her leg; for Isabel it was her brother being born. She, Francine, had her memory too: the murder of her mother.

Why did you remember some details and not others? Had anyone ever explained that satisfactorily? Why did you – and you clearly did – falsify memory?

All the circumstances of being sent to her room and waiting there, bored and fretful, remained with her. The butterfly she had caught and put outside the window. Red admirals were a common sort of butterfly, perhaps the commonest British kind, and motifs and logos of it were used everywhere. Probably most people didn't notice the red admiral on the cereal packet, the book cover, the bubble bath. She did. She'd even seen one on a T-shirt. The ring at the doorbell she remembered and getting inside the cupboard and pulling the door closed with her small seven-year-old fingers.

But not the cry of 'No!' and the screaming. She only knew about it because Julia said she had told it to the police. Julia kept her memories alive. She had no recollection of finding her mother, of sitting with her, getting her blood on herself, waiting there till her father came. Julia said it was better for her to confront what had happened, so Julia reminded her. Otherwise all that would completely have gone from her mind.

Julia said, had been saying for years, that the man would think she had seen him. She had seen him, the top of his head and the tips of his toes. Her father had told her, it must have been about a hundred times by now, that the man wasn't looking for her, that it was all nonsense and a complete fabrication that he had ever hunted for her. As a heroin addict, he was probably dead, anyway. It was another Dr Hill's house he had thought he was in, not theirs.

Francine wasn't afraid of the man and never really had been. She didn't want to know who he was or where he was or what had happened to him. There was a cliché often uttered about finding out the cause of someone's death: 'That won't bring them back.' She thought of it often, that knowing who the man was, catching him, punishing him, removing him from being a danger to others, wouldn't bring her mother back.

Julia's psychotherapy technique had been to ask her clients how they would use three wishes. She had asked Francine that once and she had asked Richard once, but since giving up her profession she had never asked it again. If she had asked, Francine would have said that the first would be have that day not happen and, if that wasn't possible, to be made to forget it; the second to go up to Oxford; the third she was too polite and too kind to say.

Except to herself. For her third wish was for Julia to go away. She didn't wish her any harm. The last thing she wanted was for her to die, of death she had

105

seen enough, but maybe to meet a really nice, good-looking, wealthy man and go off with him.

It was Holly's suggestion. Anything to do with sex usually came from Holly. 'She's fat and she's old, but she's still quite good-looking,' said Holly. 'Some old man might fancy her.'

'She's not fat,' said Francine.

'Oh, come on. She's a size sixteen. At least. A big fat fish. She used to be a goldfish, but now she's a dolphin. And one day she'll be a whale.'

'Dolphins and whales aren't fishes, Holly.'

'Marine creatures, then. She's a big fat marine creature.'

The only way to deal with Julia was to agree with her, acquiesce, and quietly do your own thing. Insofar as you could. Anything else, anything in the nature of an argument or a discussion, wore you out. You might be sixteen to her forty-nine, but you still got worn-out first. Francine had reached a point where she didn't really speak to Julia much, just said yes and no and thank you and smiled.

This didn't stop Julia saying, and saying with variations quite often, 'Now, Francine, what is the matter with you? What have I done? If I've done something to upset you I would really like to know what it is.'

'You haven't done anything, Julia,' Francine always said.

'Because if I have it's better to have these things out in the open, to confront them and talk them through, you know.'

'But there's nothing, Julia.'

'You're very young, you know, not much more than a child. Well, you're a child to me and yet you often seem old beyond your years. You act like an old woman. Are you aware of that?'

Francine didn't answer. If she acted like a young

one, would Julia like it any better? Like Miranda, who boasted that her new boyfriend was the fourth one she'd slept with? Or Kate, who kept a pack of Ecstasy tablets in her desk as she, Francine, kept Smarties? She felt in lots of ways much older than her contemporaries. She had suffered more than they, had lost more, had seen things that she knew most people would never see in a whole lifetime, had dreams so bad that she could tell no one about them, had been set apart by fate.

Which of them, for instance, if she saw a red admiral would see the long red streak on its black velvet wings as a splash of blood, flown there from a murdered woman's wound? Only she of all the school had shivered, been momentarily struck dumb, frozen and staring, when shown by a visiting police lecturer, a kindly, quiet man, the pistol he was issued with in occasional emergency situations.

Her voice had soon come back. But she was afraid of a reversion to that loss of the power of speech which had afflicted her for so many months after the murder. For years she was afraid, when she woke up in the mornings, of having no voice, of being unable to utter a word, and the first thing she did was to speak to herself aloud. To say her own name and the day and date. 'Francine, it's Thursday, June the fourteenth.'

She no longer did it, but she still dreamed of loss of voice. In one dream, a very recent one, she was in a museum and, entering an inner gallery, found herself in a hall of weapons, arrows, javelins, harpoons, pikes, cudgels, carbines, hand grenades. She hadn't known she knew of such things, still less what they were called, but she awoke moaning, stuffing the sheet into her mouth to keep the sounds from her father.

Would she always do this? Was this her fate?

It must have been her father, working on Julia, whose efforts led to the order of release. School was too far away for her to go there and come home by public transport, and it was reasonable for Julia to continue taking and fetching her by car. Most of the girls were brought to school by car. But most were allowed to go home with another girl after school if they wanted to, perhaps stay overnight in another girl's home. Francine never had been, but now that changed. She might go, in their company and supervised, to Holly's house or Miranda's or Isabel's. They might come to her. She was freed from another constraint and allowed to go out with them – so long as she was home before dark.

Julia was the ideal mother. She kept the house exquisitely and she was always buying Francine little presents: a new kind of honeycomb soap from Neal's Yard, boxes of notelets, Calvin Klein perfume, paperback books, CDs. Francine had clean sheets put on her bed every other day and clean towels in her bathroom. Her favourite food was always prepared for her. She was wakened in the mornings well in advance of the time she was due to get up and last thing at night a hot drink was made for her.

Julia and she had many long interviews and serious talks. It was a great trust, Julia said, as Francine learned to be responsible for herself. It must happen slowly and gradually. She made Francine feel as if it was she who had committed a crime and was being let out on parole.

'There isn't anyone waiting out there to harm me, Julia,' Francine said gently. 'You know there isn't. Perhaps there was once, but not now.'

'I am not saying there is,' said Julia. 'I no longer believe that, the danger of that is past. It's of you, not him, that I'm afraid.'

'What do you mean?' She hated this.

Julia explained. Her stepdaughter, in her view, was innocent, naive, fragile, incapable of taking care of herself, the reverse of streetwise. Her history and one terrible experience had made her so. Julia didn't say, perhaps she didn't know, that her fear of one particular man had been replaced by her fear of many, those men she read about in newspapers and saw on television, who mugged women or abducted them or raped them. But she lectured Francine on the habits and desires of strange men, on not lying to one's parents, on punctuality, keeping one's word and choosing one's friends carefully. 'Evil communications corrupt good manners,' she said, quoting the Apostle Paul.

For Christmas, among other presents, she had given Francine a mobile phone. Young people, she believed, loved things like that, anything that demanded a little technological expertise, this button to press, then that one, this antenna to pull out, these numbers to juggle with. The idea, of course, was that the girl should use it to phone home to give them some idea of where she was and especially if there was a chance of her being delayed. She would love possessing something so grown-up that would give her a chance to behave responsibly. Julia said she saw the ownership of the mobile phone as the next essential step in Francine's slow metamorphosis.

Francine thanked her politely and said that some time or other she would read the instructions that came with it. If she did, she never used the phone. Challenged, she said she couldn't get on with it, she was baffled by it. She was sorry because it had been a present and she didn't want to hurt Julia's feelings when she had been so thoughtful. Would Julia perhaps like to use it herself?

One day in February, when she had been out with Holly, she got home an hour later than she had said.

It was still only six in the evening, but nevertheless she was an hour late. Of course she had not been given a key to the door, Julia would never have agreed to that, and she had to ring the bell. Trembling, her mouth working, Julia pulled her inside and struck her.

It wasn't a hard blow. If you have never in your life hit anyone across the face, when you come to do it your effort will be ineffectual, a glancing smack that can be easily dodged. Francine dodged, but not enough, and Julia's hand caught the side of her neck. Holding her hand to the place where she had been struck, Francine stared in breathless silence at her now-weeping stepmother. The tears gushed down Julia's face and she moaned.

'I won't tell my father,' Francine said.

Not 'dad' or 'daddy' but 'my father'. It was the first time.

'I'm sorry, I'm sorry,' sobbed Julia. 'I don't know what came over me. I've been so frightened, I was nearly out of my mind.'

You *are* out of it was what Francine would have liked to say, but she never said things like that to anyone. 'You mustn't do violent things to me,' she said. 'Or say violent things. Please.'

And then she went upstairs to her room, but when Richard came home she came down again and asked him for a key to the front door.

'I thought you had one,' he said untruthfully, glancing at his wife.

Julia said, 'You should have asked. Why didn't you ask?'

'Of course you must have a key,' Richard said. 'You can have my spare one and I'll have another cut.'

Francine went to a disco with Miranda, but she didn't like it much. All those teenage years when

110

others had gradually been indoctrinated into the enjoyment of noise she had lived in unnatural quiet. The disco was too much for her and the club where she went with Holly and Holly's male cousin she found boring. At home she was accustomed, had been for ages, to drinking wine with meals and she thought alcoholic lemonade, not to mention Bacardi and blackcurrant, revolting. The cousin, though, she liked, or thought she did until, while they were dancing, he put his hands all over her.

Richard was proud of Francine when she was offered a place at Oxford consequent upon her securing satisfactory A Levels. Of course she would do well. He had been told several times she was the brightest girl of her year. And he marvelled that her intellect was unaffected by what had happened to her. Every aspect of his beautiful, clever daughter seemed untouched by it. Several years had passed since either of them had made reference to the murder of her mother. Francine was learning to forget, had perhaps already forgotten. When he looked at her he saw a happy, well-adjusted girl, not particularly vivacious perhaps, rather quiet and contained. But that was her nature. He wouldn't have liked a bouncing hoyden – he used the old-fashioned word to himself – like Miranda, or Holly, that sly little flirt with her sidelong glances.

Much of Francine's contentment and adjustment to normal life must be due to Julia. He could see that now. Protecting and sheltering her had been the wisest thing. Possibly, at one time, she had gone too far, but that was over now. Francine had the key to the door. Francine had gradually been brought out into the world and was behaving impeccably in it. If there was anything he could be certain of it was that his daughter would firmly say no to any drugs that

111

were offered her and to any importunate young man and – it went without saying – to any behaviour at all on the wrong side of the law.

For this he had Julia to thank. Unfortunately, he had ceased to like her very much, certainly to love her. But he must be grateful. He could see now that Julia had known best. Julia had been Francine's guiding star. So that when Francine said something to him that might be construed as indirect criticism of Julia he was taken aback. They were alone. Julia occasionally went out by herself these days just as he occasionally did, though they had never yet left Francine at home alone. She had gone to some reunion at her old college.

Francine was curled up in an armchair, reading a novel. But when he glanced at her he saw that she wasn't reading, but had lifted her eyes and was staring across the room. He looked away and looked again a few minutes afterwards and she had still not returned to her book. Before he could ask her what was wrong, she said in a clipped, forced voice, 'I *will* go to university, won't I?'

That was unexpected. 'Of course you will. Why do you ask?'

She didn't reply. 'Julia won't stop me?'

'Julia loves you, Francine. She wants what's best for you. She always has.'

Francine said no more for a while and Richard was troubled. Whenever his daughter showed unease his guilt, these days dormant, came to life. If he had not out of his vanity directed that entry to be put into the telephone book, if he had appeared as plain Hill, R., if he had not been a slave to pride, his dear wife Jennifer, whom he was sure he would have adored to this day, would still be alive, his daughter would have grown up a normal, happy girl and as for Julia . . . 'What is it?' he said.

112

Francine's large dark eyes were a little too bright. 'If I'm never allowed to go out alone and I'm never here in the house alone and I always have to be home before dark, how am I going to go up to Oxford where I'll have to be on my own?' She added, 'I'm only asking. If it sounds sarcastic I don't mean it to.'

Julia was – the word that came into his head was 'grooming' – was training her up for that. Gradually. Getting her used to life and the world out there and social usage. Or was she? Was she really?

'How am I going to *live* alone? Because that's what I'll be doing, won't I? How am I going to be allowed to look after myself with no one to watch over me the way Julia does?'

A memory came to him of reading about people who had been accompanied to their universities by parents or guardians or selected companions. It was a nightmare idea – or was it? He said tentatively, 'You know, you could take a year out.'

It was Julia's suggestion. She had made it to him the evening before. 'Let her go up to Oxford in October twelvemonth, let her take a gap year. They're all doing it, it's the fashionable thing.'

'What and loaf about at home here? Doing what?'

Julia hadn't replied. 'And when her year is up I was thinking, well, I was wondering – could we possibly move to Oxford so that we'd still all be together?'

'And what am I supposed to do every day? Commute?'

But after a moment's thought Richard had agreed to the first part of Julia's proposal. Francine should take a year out. If she wanted to. She hadn't replied. He put it to her again.

'Holly is going to do that,' Francine said thoughtfully.

Richard had never thought he would bless that little hussy Holly for anything. He smiled.

Chapter 12

When he had taken the last bagful of wood out with him and the dining-room was empty Teddy cleaned it. He took down the curtains and threw them into his parents' bedroom. He swept the floor and washed the french windows. Many of his drawings were already up on the walls and now he added to them another design in a frame he had made from the mahogany from the dining-table. The rest of it had been transformed into a low circular table. The thick polish and dirt-encrusted surface planed away, he had left the wood its natural shade of a warm golden russet and inlaid the border with ebony and maple, pieces of which he had picked up at college when no one was looking. This table, his bed and the books between the bookends were the room's sole furnishings, but the rest of it was filled up with his workbench and his tools.

Keith hadn't been into the dining-room since the day the policeman had come and told him Jimmy had been taken to hospital. What brought him in now Teddy didn't really know. Possibly, having returned from his last call-out of the evening via Oddbins, he had been made suspicious by the light behind the french windows. Undimmed by the thick velvet curtains, it must have streamed out across the concrete, a floodlighting to meet Keith as he wobbled in on the motor bike.

Teddy switched off the light. The back garden

went pitch dark, as Keith had turned off the motor-bike lights when he came through the gate and there were no lights on next door. The yuppies, Teddy was pretty sure, were out. He heard Keith stumble as he blundered to the back door. Once he was inside, Teddy turned his light on again and returned to his drawing. It was January and the mirror he was designing had to be finished and submitted by the last day of April.

Keith didn't knock. It wouldn't have occurred to him to do so. Teddy heard how he opened the door. He turned the handle, then stepped back and aimed a mighty kick at the door. It flew open and its handle hit the wall behind. He stood there, breathing heavily from the effort. The bags he let fall on to the floor as if their weight was finally too much for him. Whatever he might have come to say, he didn't say it. His mouth fell open. 'What's happened to the furniture?'

'What furniture?' said Teddy.

'Don't you fuckin' give me what furniture. My dad's table and chairs and sideboard as was in here. What you done with it? Old Chance had to take that to pieces and put it together again to get it in here.'

'Then it can't have got out, can it?'

Keith picked up his bags and retreated to the kitchen. While there he must have taken a swig of whisky. He came back, wiping his mouth with the back of his hand. 'If you've sold that furniture I'll have the law on you. That was mine, like everything else in this house.'

'It's got legs,' said Teddy, 'so it can walk, can't it? What else are legs for? It squeezed through the doorways and walked out in the street and got on a bus and now it's living in a second-hand shop in Edgware.'

Keith put up his fists and came at him the way

Jimmy had done all those years ago. Teddy stood up. He was about three inches taller than Keith, as well as a couple of lifetimes younger. 'Don't try that,' he said.

After a while he heard Keith go into the front room. The television came on, some gangster film, all crashes and gunshots and the choking cries of the dying. He listened, heard the top of a can peeled off. Keith's evening of gradual befuddlement had begun.

The mirror was to have some sort of geometric inlay on its frame. Teddy hadn't made up his mind what kind. Crosses, maybe, but not circles and crosses. He didn't want it looking like the Oxo building. Triangles perhaps, simple triangles, in pale wood lightly stained. Sycamore or holly would take a pale-yellow and a green stain. On the other hand parallel lines of inlay, all kept very light in colour, apricot, gold, beige, olive, might be the best. He drew designs, found Alfred Chance's box of water-colours.

Keith's return was unexpected. He hesitated outside Teddy's door, perhaps summoning up the energy for his kick. The door flew open hard enough for the handle to hit the wall again. Keith had an open can of Guinness in his hand. 'I want you out of here,' he said.

Teddy put down his paintbrush. 'You what?'

'You heard. If you'd toed the line a bit, if you'd kept your nose clean, I might have let you hang on till the summer. But oh, no, not you, you're destroying my home, breaking the place up, you're a fuckin' menace, you are, and you've got to go. Right? Savvy?'

'Who's going to put me out? You?'

'Me,' said Keith, 'and the law if that's what it takes.' And in a movement like a fist punching he threw half the contents of his drink can across Teddy's painting. A pool of brown liquid with a scud

117

of foam on it flooded across the delicately coloured-in drawing of the mirror frame.

No sound came from Teddy and scarcely any movement. He had been staring at Keith before the Guinness was thrown and he continued to stare, impassively, steadily. And Keith must have been more unnerved by this cold passivity than he would have been by any violent reaction, for his own gaze fell and, taking a defiant swig of what remained in the can, he turned and left the room.

Teddy went out to the kitchen to find a rag. The cloth in a bowl under the sink had probably been crocheted by his mother. He looked at it without sentimental feelings or indeed any feelings at all except to notice, so to speak, her trademark, mistakes in the stitches and a bright-red border. It served its purpose, that is for mopping-up operations, but of course the drawing was ruined. Teddy wiped down his table, dried it on kitchen roll, wiped the floor, screwed up the drawing and dropped it into his waste-paper basket.

When he had taken the cloth back he went to listen outside the front-room door. The television sound had been turned down. He heard the top peeled off another can and something that might have been the cap of the Chivas bottle unscrewed. Was it at this point that he decided or an hour later? Afterwards, he couldn't have said. Best, probably, not to think too much about it. Act, don't think.

His room smelt of Guinness, heady, yeasty. Should he do another drawing or not? It was the pleasantest way he knew of passing the time. For half an hour or more he drew designs, but this time not colouring them in from his paintbox. Then he put the new drawings into a cardboard folder and the pencil into its box, gave the table another polish and stood by the french windows.

The night was very dark, the hopeless blackness of midwinter when the sun, or what there was of it, had set at four and there had been no natural light for hours. He heard the yuppies next door come home. He could hear the click of their light switches, the one in the room next to this making quite a sharp crack. He switched off his own light. For a moment or two it was like being inside a black bag. Then objects outside began to take shape. Street lights were on, though not near at hand; light from next door made a yellowish glow on the air and yellow bars between the palings of the fence.

He could see the outline of the carport, the tail of the Edsel immediately outside the windows, like a spacecraft that has landed too near for comfort. Light coming from somewhere made a pale streak on the bin-liners covering the bike. The sky was a very dark reddish purple. Next door they were switching off lights, they were going to bed. Their stairs creaked as they went up. He hadn't got a watch, had never had one, but he guessed the time at past midnight, nearer twelve-thirty.

Out in the hall he had to feel his way, for all was in darkness. The line of dim light under the front-room door was a guide to him. He listened. He opened the door very quietly and stepped inside. On the bright but muted television a fat comedian was telling jokes deemed unsuitable for transmission at an earlier hour. Keith lay back in his armchair, his eyes closed, his mouth open. As if to acknowledge Teddy's arrival he suddenly emitted a rich, bubbling, liquid snore.

The stub of the last cigarette he had smoked had failed to make it to the ashtray but had burnt itself out on the table top. A grey furry caterpillar it looked like in the dimness. The whole table top was scored with grub-shaped burn marks as if someone had been attempting poker work. Teddy came closer, blew at the ash caterpillar and watched it disappear in a pale cloud. Keith didn't stir. He had drunk three cans of Guinness and, if that whisky bottle had been full when he came in, getting on for half of it.

Now to find another, suitable, plastic bag. There were so many names for the stuff, he knew them all because he hated them and what they stood for: polythene, polyethylene, polypropylene, polyester, polystyrene, polyvinyl. Polythene was the one needed here. There was plenty of it in the room, green and yellow and white and red bags discarded by Keith, dropped on to the floor, or thrust one inside the other, ten or eleven of them, to make a poly-cushion.

One of these, the innermost, he pulled out. It was a biggish yellow bag with a single seam and it came from Selfridges. How had the likes of Keith ever acquired a Selfridges bag? It was impossible that he had ever been into the store. One of his customers must have given it to him because his own had come apart or because he had something to carry home with him. The polythene was smooth, slippery and thick, what might be called an up-market grade-one *superior* plastic. Instead of holes cut in each side it had a stout band of the same plastic threaded through its top rather as cord passes through the waistband of track-suit pants. But this band protruded from two openings to form handles which, pulled on, would draw the top of the bag tight. It was just what he wanted, Teddy thought, it was ideal.

Then he stopped thinking and acted. He acted mindlessly. First he turned off the television and stood in the dark, listening to the quietness. Traffic on the North Circular Road made a distant hum beyond the silence. He took off the clip that fastened

120

the curtains together, parted them and let in the light from a street lamp that wasn't outside but up on the corner of the side-road. Keith made a gurgling noise, not quite a snore. He moved his head to the left, then back to its former position.

Teddy picked up the yellow bag in both hands, holding it open. He disliked touching Keith but he had to, his hands coming into contact only with hair and briefly with a woollen pullover as, taking a deep breath, he pulled the bag over Keith's head.

A certain amount of struggling was to be expected, but Keith didn't struggle. He was too far gone for that. Teddy drew the band on the bag as tightly as he could without breaking the plastic. He didn't leave the room, not then, but he turned his back.

He stood in the window, looking out at the street he had seen from this window all his life, the long straight roadway, its surface painted yellow on black from the street lamps, the squat stucco houses, each with a mean little shelf over its front door instead of a porch, the chain-link fencing and behind it, where gardens should be, his neighbours' transport, aged cars, re-sprayed vans, motor bikes, push-bikes, and in one, next to a caravan, a boat with its hull uppermost.

Teddy felt his usual loathing of it, a hatred that was always fresh; familiarity never taught him indifference. For a moment or two he almost forgot Keith and what was happening to Keith. Give mankind half a chance and it would make anything it came in contact with, anything it touched, ugly. His parents and Keith had been worse; they had found something ugly and made it uglier.

Outside, a cat ran across the street, squeezed through a gate and, safe now, sauntered up to the doorstep where it sat down and began washing itself. A beautiful creature, large, slender, pale – he couldn't tell what colour – elegantly detached. People had bred dogs into grotesque shapes, hideous joke creatures, presumably to have something to laugh at, but they couldn't do that with cats, cats were always the same shape. He wondered why they couldn't and was sure it wasn't for want of trying. They would be bound to do their best in the pursuit of ugliness. The cat got up on to a window-sill, slithered in through an open fanlight.

Teddy went back to his room. He dared not put on a light, so he sat in the dark. He didn't think about Keith, it was quite easy not to, but about his mirror and what he was going to do when he left college, how he was going to live. By making furniture? He doubted if you could earn a living at it. By doing it and doing something else as well?

He would make a start tomorrow, he would advertise. Whatever it would cost he would get the money somehow. He got up and felt in the pocket of the jacket that hung on the door. Even in the dark a faint glitter came from the diamond. The ring was like a talisman. He held it tightly in his hand and felt the stone dig into his mutilated finger. The money for advertising must be found, but not by selling the ring.

After what he calculated was half an hour he returned to the front room, loosened the band on the yellow plastic bag and lifted it off Keith's head. The blue rubber band came off his pony-tail at the same time. It was too dark to see much and he didn't want to see. But he had to feel. He felt for pulses on Keith's neck and wrists and, bracing himself, thrusting his hand under pullover and shirt, palpated with his finger where Keith's heart must be. There was nothing. The blood had ceased to circulate. Keith was dead.

*

122

The french windows couldn't be fully opened since the coming of the Edsel. Its tail wasn't much more than two feet from the back of the house. Teddy unlatched the windows and pushed them ajar. The boot of the Edsel, like a grinning mouth with upturned corners, was locked. He hadn't thought of that. It meant feeling in Keith's pockets and fumbling through Keith's clothes once more, but it had to be done.

No keys, but quite a lot of money. He didn't look closely at the money, only enough to be aware that many of the notes were reddish-brown and purple, not green. His hands were shaking, his whole body now. He hadn't shaken when he killed Keith, but the possession of this money was making him shake. What did that say about human beings? Confirmed what he had always believed since he could reason, he told himself in a sudden gush of self-dislike, that they were low, degraded and devoted to materialism.

He went upstairs. The keys must be somewhere. They must be somewhere in Keith's bedroom. With mounting distaste, he hunted through Keith's clothes, the clean, or cleaner, ones in the cupboard, the dirty pile on the floor. Through jacket pockets and trouser pockets and leathers and old canvas bags and the welter of rubbish in the tallboy's drawers. He looked under the bed and in the bed, under the pillows, lifted up the grey and greasy square of carpet. At least the shaking had stopped. The urgency of his hunt had somehow allayed that trembling.

Back in the front room, avoiding the eyes of dead Keith – how and when had his eyes come open? – Teddy investigated the toolbag, the drinks bags, then turned his attention to the furniture. There were no drawers in here, only shelves made to contain books,

but holding instead the clutter and debris character-
istic of this household. But no keys, and none either
on the table tier under the television set. The kitchen
next, an obvious place. Why hadn't he thought of it?

Was nothing useful or worth preserving kept in
this place? Even as he searched he marvelled at the
minds of those who filled drawers and cupboards,
jars and vases and even a teapot – unused since the
invention of the teabag – with pins and paper-clips
and elastic bands and safety-pins and hairclips and
screws and drawing-pins and tissues and hair comb-
ings, with broken pencils and bits of biscuit and
throat pastilles and nail-files and copper coins and
shoelaces and aspirins. And even keys, but not *the*
keys. He opened the cupboard over the sink and a
bunch of plastic bags fell out.

The keys must be in Keith's bedroom. They *must*
be there and somehow he had missed them. The
kitchen clock, the only one in the house, told him the
time was just after one-thirty. Hours must pass
before it grew light, six, seven hours, but still the
swift passing of time troubled him. Suppose he never
found those keys?

Once more into Keith's bedroom. He had looked
under the carpet before, but this time he rolled it up.
Black beetles scurried away in all directions. Teddy
kicked at the full Pyrex casserole, and ash and
cigarette stubs scattered everywhere. He went
through the drawers again, he looked inside Keith's
boots, his smelly trainers, his one pair of good shoes.
Teddy's temper was always slow to burst into flames
from its steady smouldering, but now it did. The
austere faces of the originators of the motor car,
gazing so sternly at the window, suddenly enraged
him and he tore the magazine cut-outs off the wall.
Ferdinand Porsche's portrait was the last to be
ripped down and it came away more easily than the

others. Necessarily so, since behind it was a hole in the wall, gouged out of the plaster. And in the hole were car keys on a key-ring from which a doll was suspended, a tiny, pink, naked woman.

Teddy didn't speculate for long as to what Keith's motives might have been in thus concealing his car keys. No doubt he had suspected Teddy of going joy-riding in his absence, even though he couldn't drive and had often expressed his loathing of the Edsel. He took the keys and went downstairs. His room was freezing cold because he had left the french windows open. Aware that putting any lights on would be a mistake, he stood shivering, accustoming his eyes to the dark. Then he unlocked the car boot and raised the lid. Ample room inside, as he had supposed.

Keith was heavy. Was it possible people were heavier dead than alive? Perhaps. He had heard or read somewhere that you were supposed to close the eyes of the dead, had actually seen it done in some television film. But he couldn't bring himself to lay his fingers on Keith's eyes. Soon he would no longer have to see them. He dragged the body through the house in the dark, Keith's quite long hair, released from its band, sweeping the floor. At the french windows he had a momentary fear that he wouldn't be strong enough to lift Keith off the floor and hump him up and into the boot. But the events of the evening were teaching him something. He was learning that if you need to do a thing badly enough, a task demanding physical strength, if you *must* do it, within reason you can.

Keith must have weighed seventeen or eighteen stone. Teddy's heart felt as if it would burst and his arms come out of their sockets as he struggled to lift him. A harness to put on Keith would help, but he knew there was no rope in the house. Drawing deep

125

breaths, he looked up at the windows next door. All was in darkness, all was silent. Yet some faint gleam of light – there is always somewhere, somehow, a sliver of light – touched the shiny slippery plastic that covered the motor bike.

Teddy had never bothered to examine it before, had merely glanced at it with distaste. Now he approached it, his eyes growing accustomed to the darkness. It was not a sheet but a bag, a huge bag of plastic that must have been several millimetres thick and measured a good two and a half metres by two.

He lifted it off the bike and brought it in through the french windows, careful to avoid making any sort of slithering noise. Keith's body could be rolled comparatively easily into it. Then Teddy got a purchase on the top of the bag and heaved and hauled it over the rim of the Edsel's boot. Once bag and body were inside it occurred to him that it would be a hygienic and perhaps wise measure to seal it as best he could. Was there any adhesive tape in the house? He didn't think so.

Then he remembered Keith's bag of tools, his plumber's equipment. Inside it he found a roll of heavy black tape. He had no idea what it might be used for, possibly for binding round the joints in pipes, but it would suit his purpose. He drew together the open end of the bag and bound it round and round, twenty times round, with the black tape. It was done. He had made no noise while carrying out this disposal of Keith's body and now he closed the boot lid quietly and locked it.

Somewhere, in the distance, the sound borne on the crisp, icy air, a clock struck two. He had lived in that house all the twenty-one years of his life and never heard that clock before. Perhaps his awareness had never been so great nor his senses so sharpened. He went inside and closed the french windows.

Chapter 13

He had a bath. It was the first thing he did after what he had done. If he had gone straight to bed after handling Keith's body he couldn't have slept. As it was, he woke and sat up some time in the small hours, long before it was light, and still half asleep, still in a dream he had forgotten was happening, saw the sideboard up against the wall in the shadows, its finials and sugarstick columns and clouded glass and gargoyle-like carvings. He saw it as a building, as the sinister mansion of his childhood imaginings, its crenellations as towers, its finials as spires and its green glass as windows, but quivering there in the gloom. And he shouted out in horror before full wakefulness and sanity returned and nothing could any longer be seen in the deep darkness. The sideboard was gone and the room empty of all but his bed and his tools and his table.

Memory came back then and what he had done to Keith. The body lay no more than five or six feet from his pillow, albeit enclosed in thick plastic and binding tape and in the metal casket of the Edsel's boot. He couldn't see it, he could see nothing. Had he done that, had he really done that? He thought of getting up and going to look in the front room, then in Keith's bedroom. Instead he stood at the window, staring at a lamp in a side-street, a lamp which shed no light as far away as this beyond a distant glow. The garden, the carport, the fences, were a dense

127

darkness, the sky a dark reddish-brown. He realised suddenly how cold he was, he was shivering, and he went back to bed, huddling the blankets and the quilt tightly round him.

Next day was Saturday. He had thought he wouldn't sleep, but he slept late, awakened by the bright sunlight of a clear blue-skied winter's noon. Or perhaps by the phone. He went to answer it, wondering what he would do if it were the police, alerted by the yuppies next door. But it was someone for Keith, a woman who couldn't turn off her hot tap and who wanted a plumber urgently.

'Mr Grex has retired,' Teddy said. It was true in a way.

'Retired?'

'That's right. We all come to it in the end, even workaholics like Mr Grex.' He was – incredibly after last night – enjoying this. 'He's gone to live in a cottage in Liphook.'

Not surprisingly, the customer wasn't interested. 'Well, can you come?'

'Afraid not,' said Teddy. 'I'm a craftsman. I suggest you consult the Yellow Pages.'

After he put the phone down he started laughing. He felt immeasurably, incredibly, better than he had done at that small-hours waking. The story would do for everyone who phoned for Keith. Was there such a place as Liphook? He didn't really know, the name had come to him out of the air, but he had better find out. Almost immediately the phone rang again, and again he gave his version of Keith's departure from plumbing and from north London.

There was going to be a lot of this. Old customers and potential clients would probably call round, too. But there was no chance of anyone guessing what had happened to Keith or where he was now. Troubles lay ahead, he could see that. For instance, could he leave the body there indefinitely? Could he take over the house and go on living in it as if it were his? Perhaps it *was* his now. And where was the money to come from to pay for everything?

In Keith's bedroom he found a dog-eared, much-thumbed map of the British Isles. Keith must have used it when he went on those car rallies. He looked for Liphook and finally spotted it in Hampshire not far from Midhurst. Fortuitously, he had found quite a suitable place for Keith to have retired to. He imagined the squat little bungalow with pantiled roof or even one of those cottages that had started life as railway carriages. Knowing Keith, the latter would be his choice. It would stand on a raft of concrete bordered by walls of breeze blocks with a garage of corrugated asbestos for the Edsel ... Only the Edsel was here, with Keith inside it.

Teddy abandoned fantasies and began on the room. He tore all the Post-its off the window-panes and the tallboy. He filled three plastic bags with Keith's clothes, two with his empty bottles and cans and three more with his car magazines and cigarette cartons. The six pairs of boots went into a cardboard crate which had held the magazines. Not until the room was empty of all but Keith's newly stripped bed, tallboy and single chair, and the bags and box were out on the doorstep to await Monday morning's refuse collection, did he turn his attention to the money he had taken off Keith's body.

He counted it. Five hundred and sixty-five pounds. His hands were shaking again. He clenched his fists and breathed deeply until the shaking stopped. Some of that money he would spend on advertising, on offering his services as a joiner and cabinet-maker. He had no idea how to do it, but he could learn.

The tail of the Edsel with its flaring fins seemed

closer to his windows than it had done in the past. It occurred to him then that he would have to learn to drive. Money would have to be spent on driving lessons. Some time, and not too far distantly, he must be able to drive this car away.

He dreamed again that night, but not of the sideboard-turned-mansion this time. This dream was of the thing occupying the Edsel's boot six feet away from his sleeping brain, of its gradual metamorphosis over the weeks and months into a waxen effigy, a skeleton, a bag of dust; until, having driven the monstrous pale-yellow car out of London and through Surrey and Sussex in the direction of Liphook, he parked and opened the boot and found inside the bags a tiny shrivelled thing like a dried-up insect, which he picked up between forefinger and thumb and threw into the ditch.

By the middle of February Teddy had begun work on the mirror. He had decided on sycamore rather than walnut because the colour and the grain were so beautiful, its pattern like multitudinous strands of wavy blonde hair. He worked meticulously and quite slowly, cutting the triangles for his inlay accurately to a fraction of a millimetre, aiming at perfection. And he worked in peace and quiet and fresh air. The smell of smoke had disappeared from everywhere but the front room. Keith's tallboy he had brought down here, sanded down the greasy cigarette-burned surface and, having lightly stained the mahogany, french-polished it.

When he had filled more bags and boxes for the refuse collection, this time from his parents' bedroom, he went down the road to the newsagent's. The glass case beside the door contained no advertisements of the kind he was looking for, so he bought two newspapers the newsagent recommended, the *Ham and High* and the *Neasden Times*.

The *Ham and High* had what he wanted. The 'Services' section of the small ads was divided into specific sections: Building and Decorating, Chimney Sweeps, Gardening and Landscaping, Health and Beauty. Under Household Clearance a company offered 'Large, small clearances, clothes, oddments, anything, good prices paid'. 'Rubbish disposal' was also on offer, but no mention was made of payment – except from the customer. In the next column a driving school offered lessons for 'competitive fees' with 'rapid test passing' guaranteed. 'Rapid', Teddy thought, could mean anything, six weeks or two years. But he called the house clearance number and the driving school number in the hope that money received from one would pay for the other.

Next he came to some unexpected services. 'Articles for sale' occupied a lot of space and so did 'Massage'. Carpenters were on offer in plenty, he counted twelve advertisements. Shelving systems and wardrobes were what they offered, as well as fitting kitchens and replacing doors. Someone calling himself a cabinet-maker specialised in desks and one ad was from a pair of women joiners.

Teddy couldn't see the advantage of having a woman build one's cupboards and the ad made him feel obscurely uneasy. But the rest cheered him up. People obviously did do this and must make a living at it or they wouldn't go on advertising, would they? He was sure he could do a better job than most of them.

Time enough to compose his own advertisement when the mirror was finished. Perhaps in May. Maybe he would describe himself as an expert, as one of these joiners did, and put in the qualification he would have by that time. Would he also put

131

'friendly and reliable service'? In his case, 'thorough and dependable' might be better.

Meanwhile, he had enough money to get by on. He folded the *Ham and High* carefully and put it in the top drawer of the refurbished tallboy.

'Max and Mex House Clearances' took away the main bedroom furniture and gave him fifty pounds for it. He had expected at least a hundred and he protested, but the house clearers said it wouldn't fetch that and what about their profit? They quoted the *Ham and High* and said they weren't really in the business of *rubbish* disposal.

To have rid himself of the front-room furniture would have been risky, for his grandmother still came round, if rarely. Probably the last time had been before Christmas. It was as well he had kept it, for she turned up the day after 'Max and Mex' had been.

Without much interest in the thought processes of others and having none in their emotions, he had never asked himself how Agnes Tawton must have reacted to surviving a husband, an only daughter and her son-in-law; to having no one in the world but him. After all, he had no one but her. He didn't ask now, only felt a vague disquiet as she surveyed the clean and tidy front room, the neat, scrubbed kitchen.

'Keith's been busy,' she said.

It was the only solution she could conceive of, that Keith, having been made uncomfortable by the disorder all these years, had tidied up once his brother and sister-in-law were gone. She trotted through the rooms, looking curiously about her. An armchair seat cushion was lifted up and its interior scrutinised for cigarette ash and dirty tissues. She ran a twisted arthritic finger along the lintel of the back door, seemed nonplussed that her hand came away clean. 'I reckon he'll put you out now,' she said. 'He's got the right. This house was never your dad's. I don't suppose you knew that.'

'Sorry to disappoint you, but as a matter of fact I did.'

'I don't know what you mean, disappoint. It's nothing to do with me.'

'Shame,' said Teddy. 'I was counting on finding a corner for myself under your roof.'

Agnes's reply was lost in the shrill pealing of the doorbell. Teddy had been anticipating the arrival of the driving instructor for the past ten minutes. He opened the door and let the man in. Now to get rid of Agnes.

She had made her way into his room and was standing at the french windows, looking out. Teddy had only ever had one children's book, a collection of anthropomorphic animal stories and she had given it to him. He thought she looked like an illustration from that book, a toad in hat and coat, for instance, or a housewife mole. She turned round, asked him if he was going to introduce her and, when he didn't, held out her hand and said, 'I'm Mrs Tawton, I'm his grandma.'

'Pleased to meet you,' said the driving instructor. 'Call me Damon.' Then he saw the Edsel. 'That belong to you?' he said to Teddy.

'It's his uncle's,' said Agnes.

'D'you mind if I go out and take a closer look?'

Teddy minded very much, but he could hardly say so. They all went outside by way of the back door, Agnes, though about half a century Damon's senior, tripping along faster than he. The March day was no warmer than January had been. An icy wind struck their faces and Agnes was obliged to keep a grip on her sugarloaf-shaped red hat.

'Keith not on his bike then,' she said.

133

It was one of those remarks that, though merely pointing out what must be obvious to all, seem loaded with menace. Teddy felt the bike as a threat to himself. If Keith had gone to work, as his grandmother must believe, the bike would be with him. If he had retired, as all his erstwhile customers believed, the bike would be with him or have been sold; it would certainly not be in this garden.

But Agnes answered her own speculations. 'Too cold for him,' she said and, with an edge of spite, 'He's past tearing about on them things at his age.'

Teddy wondered if learning to drive a car also taught you to drive a motor bike. He didn't feel he could ask. Damon was gazing with adoration at the Edsel and had moved too close to it for Teddy's comfort. He had actually laid one hand on the boot lid.

'That is a beauty. That is a vehicle as would do a ton and twenty when it was new,' he said. 'Maybe would today, the little darling. You can see it's been kept in lovely condition.' It was as if he were talking about a horse, Teddy thought. 'Mind you, with its fuel consumption in the low teens, it's not for everyone.'

'A poor man's car, would you say?' said Teddy.

'Come again?'

'Owning it would keep you poor.'

'Oh, yes. Very good. You got it.'

Was there a smell? No, there was nothing. It had been very cold and must be as icy as a fridge inside there. He thought he saw Agnes's nose twitching like a rabbit's. He said, 'Shall we get going, then?'

Damon offered Agnes a lift home. She declined it. She wasn't going in any car driven by her grandson, she said, not when he'd never been at the wheel before. It didn't do to have your bones broken at her age.

Teddy got into the driving-school car and when Damon had finished telling him about switching on the ignition and moving the gear shift from neutral into first, he asked if getting his licence would also entitle him to ride a motor bike. Damon said no it wouldn't, no group D types, whatever that meant, and began enumerating all the varieties of vehicle Teddy would be able to drive, including invalid carriages and heavy goods vehicles up to a certain tonnage. Teddy turned on the ignition, let in the clutch and stalled the engine.

By the middle of April he had finished the mirror and submitted it. He was in love with it, it was so beautiful and so flawless, as he tended to fall in love with objects, ornaments, pictures, *Marc and Harriet in Orcadia Place*, for instance, and the diamond ring. After he had packed it with the greatest care in bubble wrap and polystyrene – another of his bugbears among plastics but essential here – it was a wrench to let it go. After it had been exhibited at the Eastcote College degree show, would he ever be able to bring himself to sell it? To part with it?

He willingly sold Keith's motor bike. A friend of the yuppies came round one day, said he had seen the old Enfield from a window next door and Megsie said the man that owned it had retired and moved away, and the bike might be for sale.

'Megsie?'

'Next door,' said the friend, surprised. 'Megsie and Nige. *You* know.'

He hadn't, but he did now. How did they know? How did this Megsie know? Somehow or other the news must have filtered through from one of Keith's customers to whom he had told this story. Luckily, he had kept the registration certificate for the bike that he had found, before throwing out Keith's few papers. Then he had to name a sum. It was necessary to pretend that Keith had asked him to sell the bike and therefore had suggested a possible price. The Enfield was as old as the hills. Though Keith had changed cars three times in Teddy's lifetime, he had always ridden the same bike.

Firmly, as if he knew what he was doing, Teddy asked a hundred pounds. As soon as the words were out of his mouth he knew he had underestimated. Megsie's friend was all smiles and eagerness. The Enfield probably had some sort of vintage value, but it was too late now and Teddy had a great sense of relief in just seeing it go. It had been a hideous object, an offence to the eye, as in his estimation all motor bikes were.

If only he could as easily rid himself of the Edsel! The end of April was warm. Feeling the increasing heat of the sun and watching the temperature rise, he grew more and more anxious about the contents of the Edsel's boot. By day he dared not spend much time hovering over the big yellow car, but in the night, when the street was in darkness and Megsie and Nige had turned out their bedroom light, he opened the french windows and put his face close up against those flaring fins.

His sense of smell was very good, but he couldn't tell if he was smelling something or imagining a smell. Keith used to say the Ford Edsel was a very well-built car and the way this boot closed must be like a hermetic seal. The air was fresh and the night cool. There was a smell, but it was of diesel mingling with the scent of flowering trees, cherries and prunuses, one of which grew in every garden but the Grexes'. He closed the windows and slept until disturbed by that recurring dream of the wooden mansion that shimmered out of the darkness, more crenellated and turreted and battlemented than before. No longer doll's-house size, but big enough to push aside the walls of his room, it had lost also its immobility and seemed to tremble and swell, its façade and towers shivering like an image under water.

When the great door under the central arch opened and someone or something came out he woke up, crying out. Whoever had emerged he couldn't see, hadn't wanted to see, it was just a tiny indistinct shape. He lay still, breathing deeply, savouring his return to reality and hoping his cry had not reached Megsie and Nige next door.

He took his driving test in June and passed. Once he had his licence he considered phoning Damon at the driving school and asking for one more lesson – this time at the wheel of the Edsel.

But there were terrible drawbacks to this plan. The smell, if smell there was, might not be discernible in the garden, but could permeate the interior of the car. Particularly if moving it shifted the body in the boot. Or if neither he nor Damon could get the car back again into the narrow garden, if it had to be left in the street. It was an enormous car and certainly Damon had never driven anything in its class. And what if – the worst possibility this, but real enough – they were involved in some minor accident. This could happen through no fault of his or Damon's, but simply by someone driving too fast behind them and going into the back of the Edsel. It hardly bore contemplating.

Over and above all this was his reluctance to phone Damon, or anyone, to place himself in something close to a making-friends situation. One thing would lead to another, the Edsel-driving experiment to a drink in some pub, to coming back here or even an invitation to Damon's place. That was how it went, or how he thought it went, and he didn't need it. He didn't want a friend moving into his life, discovering things. He would have to take the Edsel out on his own. One day, but not yet. And then he must think of how to rid himself of the car as well as its contents, be free of this pale-yellow mobile coffin.

Damon had called the Edsel a beauty and over the fence the other day Nige had said it was 'a lovely job'. But to Teddy it was hideous, as ugly as the sideboard had been and even uglier than that, for the sideboard had been made of wood, a natural substance, and the Edsel was a confection of tortured metal, painted an offensive colour. The colour of puke, he thought, tormenting himself, the colour of contaminated water, of certain alcoholic drinks, of piss. He longed to be rid of it, but longed almost as much to discover the condition of what lay under that boot lid.

It was sealed in plastic. But the plastic had seams in it, it wasn't airtight. Would that make a difference? Would there be a smell or only if the binding tape were loosened? How bad would it be? He didn't know, he had no idea. Like meat on which flies have crawled? Like the inside of their dustbin used to be before Keith's death? What did a dead body smell like?

But more than that, more than anything, he was afraid to look inside. He was afraid of what he might see. Reality would not be like the dream he had had, the one where he opened the boot and found only a shrivelled grey doll.

Chapter 14

In the first flush of love Franklin Merton had bought Harriet one present after another. A lot of jewellery, that went without saying, and an ocelot coat. The wearing of furs was soon to provoke hatred on the streets, but not in the early seventies. He would have bought her *Marc and Harriet in Orcadia Place*, but he couldn't afford it. Rich as he was by anyone's standards, by that time the painting was beyond his means.

Instead he bought the house. Orcadia Cottage was its name, but it was known to the Post Office as 7a Orcadia Place. Marc Syre had not owned but rented it and now it had come on to the market.

'A curious world we live in,' said Franklin to his love, 'where one can afford a house but not a picture of a house. That must tell us some profound truth. But what, I wonder?'

'Oh, I don't know, Frankie, how should I know? I hope it'll be all right.'

What Harriet had meant was, if you buy it will Marc find out where I am? She didn't say this aloud, for Franklin knew nothing of the two thousand pounds. But as it turned out, by some bizarre coincidence, if coincidence it was, on the day Franklin completed the purchase of Orcadia Cottage Marc Syre died. Already full of heroin, he sucked some LSD according to his custom on a lump of sugar and, reacting uncharacteristically, jumped to his death off Beachy Head.

Harriet would have gone to the funeral if she had been able to find out where it was taking place. It would have been a way of getting her picture in the papers. She could get into the papers now without risking her life. Simon Alpheton went, was on the front page of the *Daily Mail*, and the Tate Gallery bought *Marc and Harriet in Orcadia Place* for an undisclosed sum.

As to the house, Franklin said he had bought it for her. He must have meant for her to live in, for it was kept in his name. He furnished it with the eighteenth-century furniture he was particularly fond of, taking a very long time about it, to get it quite right. Harriet was not consulted. Harriet was not married either. Anthea Merton refused to divorce Franklin and made him wait five years, after which her consent was not required.

People said 'Ooh!' and 'Aah!' at the sight of Franklin's house. Because of the high wall between it and the pavement it was almost invisible from the street, but passers-by peered between the bars of the wrought-iron gate set under its brick arch. They saw the pastel-grey front door and the bay trees on the shallow stone steps, the little medallion after Della Robbia peeping out between the green or yellow or red fronds of creeper and they saw the flowers that were everywhere from March till October, filling the border and cascading from the window-boxes and spilling over the rims of the round stone tubs.

Franklin saw to the flowers. He was a great gardener. The Virginia creeper made a glorious backcloth in spring and summer for the red impatiens, the orange begonias and the purple petunias, and in autumn for the white chrysanthemums. He planted scyllas and specie tulips and Star of Bethlehem in the majolica pots and a daphne in the round bed where Marc Syre's suitcase had come down. Harriet took very little notice. Gardening wasn't among her interests. Harriet was interested in very little except Harriet and her appearance, and a certain kind of young man.

She had accepted the house and moved into it because it was a house and somewhere to live, and be safe and looked after, but she had no sentimental feelings for it. Its beauty had never much struck her when she was living in it with Marc Syre and it didn't later. It was her own that was her principal concern and, ever since she was fourteen, a long time ago now, she had looked into every mirror that she passed. The mirrors in Orcadia Cottage had reflected her own adoring image at her a dozen times a day and the mirrors in Chesterton Road and through the twenty-three years of her marriage a different set of mirrors in Orcadia Cottage did the same just as often.

Franklin commented on her habit before he left for work that morning when he caught her sitting up in the four-poster bed they still shared and gazing at herself in the dressing-table glass. The wondrous hair, dyed now, still fanned out to frame her small white face in a cloud of crimson froth. 'Why are you always looking at yourself?' said Franklin irritably. Nearing seventy now, he was rather shrunken and dried-up, though spry as ever. 'What on earth is the point at your age?'

'I'm not always looking at myself,' said Harriet, who thought this kind of defence would make people believe themselves mistaken. 'I don't look at myself any more than anyone else does. *You* look at *your*self.'

'Only to shave. I suppose you like what you see.' He laughed a little, as if this were odd enough to provoke mirth. 'I suppose you must do. How extraordinary.'

'Oh, shut up,' said Harriet.

She had liked him once, for a year or two. From that moment when they met in Holland Park Avenue the idea of all the money he must have had dazzled her. But love had never come into it. By the time she and he had lived in Orcadia Cottage for five years Harriet no longer had the slightest interest in marrying him. She had done so because what else was there to do? He was her meal ticket and landlord and clothes voucher and replacer, endlessly, in series, of the money she had brought away in the suitcase with her from this very house. Sometimes she thought he had never forgiven her, not for taking him from Anthea, but for the consequent separation from O'Hara.

Franklin came back into the bedroom with her coffee and the newspapers, *The Times*, the *Daily Telegraph*, the *Financial Times* and the *Ham and High*. He put the coffee cup on the bedside cabinet and the papers on the bed in front of her. This was typical of him, to insult her, then placate her. Not that she was a reader of newspapers, more a dipper-into a particular section of them, but he didn't know that. Or did he know and not care?

She watched him. All their married life, all their life together, before going to bed at night he had taken all the contents out of his trouser pockets and laid them on her dressing-table: invariably a large white handkerchief, house keys and car keys, his cheque-book folded in the middle and his loose change, and occasionally a train ticket or a business card. She hated this litter deposited there among her silver hairbrushes, her flagon of Eau d'Issy and her ear-rings hanging on their silver-branched ear-ring tree.

142

He had other maddening habits. Before sitting down in an armchair or on the sofa he threw all the cushions on to the floor. Yet he had bought the cushions himself and insisted on their being there. Picking them up again was left to her. She watched him putting all that stuff back into his pockets. They bulged and eventually sagged, ruining his expensive Huntsman suits.

She looked away and directed her gaze to the 'Services' columns of the *Ham and High*.

It began with Otto Neuling. He was the first of them. And perhaps it was because Marc Syre had cured her of love, or being rejected by him had cured her. Marc had been demanding, exigent, critical and, no matter how she had obeyed him and done her best to please him, he had still had other girls, dozens of them, hundreds probably, anyone he wanted. Otto had demanded nothing except sex and when they went out on his bike her paying her share, just going Dutch, really. And he never had enough of sex, he never got tired and had, she was sure, been faithful while it lasted.

She gave him up when Franklin came along. Nothing else was feasible. Otto disappeared and for a few years he wasn't replaced. She knew what she wanted: another Otto, another strong, virile, vigorous, insatiable young working man, without much in the way of brains. After all, and she had never been slow to admit it, she hadn't much in the way of brains herself. Franklin wasn't sexy. Franklin wasn't much to look at and he had a lot of brains. He was intelligent and all his friends were intelligent and, as far as sex went, Harriet wouldn't have given them a second glance.

He expected her to do everything in the household, even the house*work*. Once they were married, that is. Before they were married she was still his goddess, up on her pedestal, the icon of *Orcadia Place*, to whom tributes were almost daily brought and for whom endless sacrifices were made. Then, after their little hole-in-the-corner wedding – Harriet in the Fortuny dress and a black hat – he changed. He even said so, in a quotation from something or other. 'Men are April when they woo and December when they wed.' He smiled, presumably to soften the brutality.

Anthea's alimony was costing him a fortune. And keeping up the Campden Hill Square house. Or so he said. The least Harriet could do was the cleaning and the laundry, and see to sending for electricians and plumbers and decorators and roofers and carpenters when the services of such artisans were required.

'You don't keep a bitch and bark yourself,' said Franklin.

'Pity I'm not an Irish setter,' said Harriet and had the satisfaction of seeing him wince.

Cooking, which she would quite have enjoyed, he wouldn't allow her to do. Franklin said she couldn't cook and she wasn't hygienic, he wasn't in the business of getting food poisoning. Salmonella and listeria were unheard-of in those days, but that was what he meant. They ate out. They went to restaurants on a daily basis long before anyone else in London did and became trendsetters.

He usually laughed or smiled pleasantly whenever he made a particularly nasty remark. Smiling made it all right. As when he said, 'I intend to take separate holidays from you. I shall go away on my own in the spring and the autumn. You can do as you like.'

And when he said, 'I didn't want to get married, you know. I married you because I'm a man of honour and you were my mistress. Some would say my views are out of date, but I dispute that. The apparent change is only superficial. I reasoned that no one would want my leavings so, for your sake, the decent thing was to make an honest woman of you.'

That was what did it. Next day, or soon after, they had a new carpet fitted in his study. The carpet fitter was fat and sixty and his assistant skinny and sixteen, and wouldn't do at all. But the door had to come off and couldn't be put back until a quarter of an inch had been planed off its base. A suitable carpenter was named by the carpet fitter and his phone number supplied. He came two days later.

He might have been Otto's brother or his clone. His name was Lennie and he was about twenty. Harriet knew that you were supposed to give a workman cups of tea, but tea went nowhere when it came to helping a man lose his head and his inhibitions. After the door was back on its hinges she made dry martinis for herself and Lennie. Not only had he never before tasted a dry martini, he hadn't tried gin either. Its effect, combined with Harriet's winning ways, was startling and after half an hour and two more martinis they were in bed.

Lennie came back several times a week for a couple of months. Then one day he asked her in a rather resentful tone if she realised he went without his lunch in order to come and see her.

But what finished things was when she said, 'Why is it only working-class men are called Lennie and never, ever, anyone else?'

For a while she was without a lover. Just as she was starting to feel restless Franklin did something to solve her difficulty. He bought a computer. Not quite a prototype but almost. Anthea had remarried and he no longer had to be even moderately careful of what he spent. The computer was big and unwieldy and took up most of his desktop, and he needed a new double point inserted in the wall as outlets for the power it required. 'You'll have to find an electrician,' said Franklin.

'How?'

'I don't know. Running the household is your business. Try the one we had before.'

The one they had before had moved or was dead. At any rate, dialling his number resulted in the unobtainable signal. Harriet looked in the paper. Among the small ads she found a man who offered his services under the line, 'Stephen will do any electrical work, big or small.' She called the number and Stephen came, even younger than Lennie, darker, thinner, but otherwise just as satisfactory.

In the years that passed, the eighties and early nineties, a stream of young working men came to Orcadia Cottage. Not at Franklin's request, of course, there is a limit to the number of electrical points that are required, door bases that need planing and tap washers replacing. Harriet became very blasé and brazen about the whole thing, simply inventing a task for the man she had summoned – the shower head dripped, there was a smell of gas – and after a while scarcely bothering even with that.

Of course, it didn't always work. The handsomest young man ever to arrive on the Orcadia Cottage doorstep, a television engineer, was gay, and a likely-sounding electrician astounded Harriet by turning out to be a woman. Not everyone who responded to her phone calls was attractive to her, but on the whole they were what she wanted and apparently she was what they wanted. In recent years she had had more refusals than she was used to and she couldn't understand why. It accounted for her scrutinising herself even more closely in mirrors – though she could hardly give that reason to Franklin.

After all, she was only a little over fifty. People

said she looked ten years younger. She had kept her figure. Any possessor of her hair colour was fortunate because everyone thought it was dyed anyway, so when you did start dyeing it no one noticed. Harriet ran her fingers through it and took a good long look at herself in the mirror. If she turned her head and looked upwards yearningly, if she extended one white arm, if she parted her lips and gazed at some unseen other face, she was Harriet in Orcadia Place again, unchanged, no different.

Back to the *Ham and High*. How about a landscape gardener? Not a very good idea. He might be middle-class, he might be a woman. Besides, anyone summoned to look at this garden, so exquisitely maintained by Franklin, would think its owner mad to want to change it. Double glazing? Impossible on the Orcadia Cottage windows. Perhaps she should try the Yellow Pages instead. But there was something so *official* and respectable about that. The small ads were best and had seldom failed her.

How about 'Hardwood floors laid to your specification, pine, cherry or oak finish, incredibly low prices'? Calling the number would fetch someone called Zak. Harriet liked the sound of it. She dialled the number. Zak seemed short of work, sounded eager and said he would come that day at noon sharp. His accent told her he was eminently suitable, the timbre of his voice that he was young.

Sometimes she wondered if Franklin did much the same thing. Well, not the *same* thing, but had a girlfriend or a series of girlfriends. Those separate holidays he insisted on taking, for instance. The huge sums of money he spent. When she had a young man like this Zak calling and then the guarantee of his dropping in twice a week for weeks, she didn't care about Franklin. He could have a woman if he liked, it was nothing to her. But when she was alone or her latest invitation had met with no success, she cared. She wondered who it could be, if it was someone they knew, a so-called friend. And she would review the members of their circle, his business acquaintances, that relative of Simon Alpheton's who had been to dinner once or twice, the woman from the flats in the mews called Mildred Something he always stopped to gossip with.

After a while she got up. She stripped the bed, fetched clean sheets from the airing cupboard. Before she had her bath and washed her hair and dressed she would run the vacuum cleaner around, dust a little, pick some of Franklin's flowers for the vases. She would see to it that there was ice and put the gin bottle and the glasses in the fridge. Harriet had never become lackadaisical about things like this. Her young men deserved a good time too, the best kind of time she could give them, it was only fair. Besides, she liked to see their cautious wonderment as they cast covert glances around the house, climbed the stairs, came in here.

For them it must be the experience of a lifetime, something to look back on when they were married and living in a council tower block in Hounslow.

Chapter 15

Julia had a great many friends. Women, of course. It was her opinion that a married woman's men friends should be her husband's friends, encountered only in his company. So for her David and Susan Stanark were 'our' friends. Hers were women contemporaries gathered up along life's highway, but mostly in the early stages of the march. She even still retained one that she had been at school with.

This was Laura, a PR consultant, almost her precise contemporary, having been born in the same month of the same year as herself, but two days before. Rosemary she had found an instant rapport with on her first day at teacher training college. Noele, the buyer for a prestigious dress shop, had been her first husband's sister-in-law; Jocelyn, the civil servant in the Home Office she had met at Noele's wedding and, as Julia herself put it, they had immediately 'clicked'. Della, the most recent acquisition, was the aunt of Francine's friend Isabel and had no job. Had she belonged to a less elevated social stratum she would have been called a housewife.

All these women were or had been married and all but Noele and Susan had children. Julia lunched with them and held long telephone conversations with them. Occasionally one of them would come to lunch with her at home. She spent evenings with one or other of them, always providing, of course, that Richard was at home to be with Francine.

149

Many of their discussions concerned the difficulties of bringing up children, especially when those children became adolescents. This was a stage of life they had all entered in the past few years or were about to enter, being of that sort of age, the late forties. And although Julia was not a mother but a mere stepmother, they tended to defer to her opinion. She was, after all, or had been, a psychotherapist specialising in children's problems. Perhaps, too, they felt some generosity was owed to Julia who had, and often told them she had, given up her own chance of children to devote herself to Francine.

This stepdaughter they all knew to be a profoundly difficult child. They hadn't personally seen any evidence of this, but they knew from their experience with their own children that the young can be perfectly charming to visitors, while monsters of rudeness and recalcitrance at home alone with their parents. Francine, Julia told them, could of course be excused, they mustn't think she was blaming her, it wasn't her fault, but she was a *damaged* girl. It was Julia's mission to lead her painstakingly towards the possibility of a normal life one day – the possibility only.

'The reality is', Julia said to Susan, 'that I am the only one who can keep her from shutting herself up in her own room from morning till night. That is what she would do at the weekends if she had her way. She has to be prevented from *disappearing into herself*.'

And to Jocelyn she said, 'Responsibility is something she simply can't handle. I mean, for instance, she has her own front-door key, of course she has, but she hardly ever uses it. She expects me to be there waiting in the hall to open the door for her. It's for reassurance, I know that, it's a facet of her total dependence on me.'

Noele, the childless one, received different explanations. 'The way to teach independence, contrary to popular belief, is not to load the subject with tasks too challenging for her fragile capabilties, but to build infinitesimally, day by day, a structure of confidence.'

'How on earth?' said Noele.

'One way of crafting this structure is by requiring a series of small duties from the subject, then increasing and enlarging them until whole areas of responsibility can be assumed and a routine of life-management established.'

'If you say so,' said Noele. 'The new designers-for-less range is coming in this week so if you're interested you want to pop in on Thursday.'

Taking a year off was what Julia had aimed for, but now it had been decided on there loomed before her a new anxiety. While Francine was at school she had been taken care of for a large part of every day and when she came home there was homework to be done and friends to visit or be visited under supervision. Now she would be free, at liberty, idle. But what if she wanted to work? Take a job? The idea of that was far worse.

'Holly's got a job,' Francine said. 'Starting in August. She's doing some work for an MP, it's not paid, of course, that's how she got it. This MP has a surgery where she sees constituents and Holly will be working there.'

'Doing what, for heaven's sake?' said Julia.

Francine admitted that she didn't know. 'I'd like to do something like that.'

'No, you wouldn't, my dear. You think you would, but you wouldn't. Not keeping office hours and meeting those sort of people, the kind you've never come across. You're totally unfitted for anything like that.'

'I'd like some sort of job. I can't just stay at home here.'

'Why can't you?' said Julia. 'I do.'

Because I'm eighteen years old, thought Francine, and that means I'm young but I'm also, officially, an adult. You're fifty. It's different for you. She didn't say this aloud because she shrank from anything like rudeness.

'I should have thought', said Julia, 'that you had enough on your mind with your A Levels coming up without thinking about jobs.'

Francine returned to the book she was reading. It was Chekhov's *Letters* and she was enjoying it but for a while she stared unseeing at the page. Yet she had plans for a future if she could only be allowed to carry them out. Everyone at school had known about those events in her early life, they knew what had happened, though no one ever mentioned it. Francine was determined that no one she might encounter in the next stage of her life should know anything about it. She would only tell if she was asked. And another part of the plan was to break away, not so much from her father as from Julia. Yet she sensed that once school and exams were over and she was at home, Julia would want to spend long hours with her, take her about, accompany her to museums and libraries, cinemas and theatres, have her meals with her, talk exhaustively to her.

Holly had been very ready with advice. 'Legally, you're an adult. You can vote. Actually, you've been old enough to get married for two years. Not that I suppose you want to.'

'Of course I don't want to get married,' Francine said.

'Everybody knows what your wicked stepmother does, you know. Everybody can see and everybody's sorry for you. But you'll have to assert yourself. I mean, all you have to do is say, I'm going to do this or that or whatever, and you can't stop me, and just do it. Stay out all night if you want. You're an adult. You can do as you like.'

'You say, all I have to do,' said Francine, 'as if it's easy, as if anyone can do anything.'

'They can.'

'She's not wicked, you know. She means well, she wants what she thinks is best for me. Only what she wants isn't what I want.'

At the moment it was less important because of her A Levels. Julia or no, she had to stay at home and work for them. For a few months she would be no different from her friends, for whom all going out in the evenings had ceased. They were as much prisoners in their rooms as she. At last she was the same as other girls.

She hadn't calculated its effect on Julia. She hadn't anticipated – how could she? – the view Julia would take of her stepdaughter's sudden abandonment of the mild rebelliousness she had recently shown. All she saw was Julia's apparent satisfaction and the new pleasure she took in her, Francine's, society. Julia must be happy, Francine thought, as her father was, that she was working so hard for her A Levels.

And Julia was happy, but not because Francine was studying. She was an astute woman in her way, had a very good idea of Francine's high intelligence quotient and knew that she was a natural scholar who loved application to books for its own sake. You might say she was a person who couldn't help studying.

'I'm told that these days it's the girls who work harder for examinations than the boys,' said Richard. 'It's going to be a woman's world.'

Julia gave one of her sad smiles. From being statuesque, she had become a big, heavy woman, solid and massive. Her face and arms and bosom were whiter than ever. Skin thins with age, but Julia's seemed to have grown thicker and more opaque, her hair, bleached now, more golden and her fingernails redder and longer. But in spite of being so large and colourful, sadness suited her and she reminded Richard of a statue he had seen somewhere of Niobe weeping for her dead children.

'I fear it will never be Francine's world,' she said.

'Of course it will.' The flights of fancy that he indulged in brought colour into his face. 'I see her one day as – as mistress of a women's college or as a government minister or – well, something distinguished.'

Julia said nothing for a moment, then, 'I do love her, you know, I love her as if she were my own.'

'I know,' he said.

'It is just that we see these things so differently. It's rather odd but, you know, my dear, you're living in a pre-Freudian world, I might almost say a pre-psychology world. You sent Francine to me while I was in practice – and thank God you did because that was how we met – but I honestly believe that you thought it was like sending someone with an abscess to the doctor. All he has to do is lance the thing and a cure is immediately effected. The mind isn't a sore finger. The emotions aren't so easily mended.'

'I might agree with you if I saw any of these signs of trauma in Francine, but I don't. She seems to me eminently normal. Maybe a little quiet and bookish, but that's about it.'

Julia smiled and patted his hand. 'One day she will be normal. I shall see to that. Leave it to me. She wants a job while she's taking her gap year. Did you know?'

'A job?'

'That tiresome little Holly has something fixed up

154

for herself and naturally Francine wants something similar. The reality is that they're very imitative at that age. Shall I ask around and see what I can come up with?'

'Do you think you can?'

'Something close to home,' said Julia thoughtfully, 'something undemanding. The pity is that ladies don't have companions any more. I frankly doubt if Francine is fit to look after children.'

'Fit?' said Richard.

'I really mean "up to". But we'll see. I am afraid working in a nursing home might lead to too many horrible sights. But leave it to me.'

He did. He had a new job and travelling was an essential part of it. Nothing must be allowed to take priority over this projected four days in Zurich and, later in the month, a conference in Frankfurt. Why should there be anything to upset his plans? Julia, as always, was loving and concerned and attentive to Francine, and Francine was – he nearly said it – 'obedient'. Even 'compliant' wouldn't be the word. She was just being her sweet, gentle self. Working, concentrating, intent on getting the best possible A-Level passes.

Richard's trip to Switzerland passed uneventfully. On the way home, in the plane to Heathrow, he was struck by a sudden alarm that on reaching the house he would find a frightening chaos, Francine a resentful, weeping prisoner, Julia an adamant wardress, the two of them hurling reproach at one another. Not that there had ever been anything like that, not so far as he knew, and he surely did know. He was imagining things. Sometimes he hated his own imagination, yet even as he thought that, leaning his head against the seat back and closing his

155

eyes, he let himself indulge in the fantasy he increasingly had and increasingly enjoyed.

Jennifer was alive. The man had never got into the house and killed her, for the entry in the telephone directory read simply, as his current entry did: Hill, R. He was not a vain man, subject to the sin of Pride, but modest and simple, and it wouldn't have occurred to him to call himself Doctor just because he possessed a D.Phil. So Jennifer was alive today and they were still living down there in the cottage in the lovely semi-countryside of Surrey, Jennifer older, of course, but rather more beautiful in her maturity, and perhaps there had been another child.

Why not? They had sometimes talked of it, or they had up until that last year when she had changed towards him. But he would have changed her back and there might have been another little girl, a child playing with toys while Francine sat studying for A Levels. In her own old home with her own mother, with no ugly past.

He came into the cottage and took Jennifer in his arms and kissed her. Once or twice, though this obscurely shamed him, he had made love to Jennifer in this fantasy, with real excitement and, curiously enough, real satisfaction. But now he only kissed her and kissed Francine, and as they talked the small dream child came running in and called, 'Daddy, Daddy' and put out her arms . . .

The seat-belt sign came on and the instruction to place seats in the upright position, and in ten minutes they had landed. His fear came back in the car as he was on the M4, but when he let himself into the house – the home of his second, less idyllic marriage – he found that all was well.

Julia was full of news. Her friend Felicia in Australia was coming over for a holiday, her friend Rosemary and her husband had won a substantial sum on the Lottery, her friend Noele was opening a shop selling nearly new designer clothes. Julia had more women friends than he could keep up with. He asked about Francine, but before Julia could answer his daughter appeared in the doorway, smiling, with a textbook in her hand.

'You smell of the lamp,' he said.

She thought quickly. 'Because I've been burning the midnight oil? Well, I have, I've been working so hard I can't see straight.' She came to him and kissed him. 'Have you had a good trip?'

'Pretty well what I expected.'

'I'm going to need that gap year,' she said, and he had the not entirely welcome idea that she was saying it to please him and to please Julia. 'I'm worn out. I'm never going to want to see a book again after June.'

'We should all take a holiday, Richard,' said Julia. 'Can we do that? In August, say. You're due for a month off, aren't you? Could we take a month?'

'Maybe. We'll see.'

'And go somewhere quiet and secluded, away from everything. That's what Francine would like.'

Holly showed Francine her body piercing, a ring in her navel, a stud at the base of her spine. Francine knew about Miranda's tattoo and Isabel's diamond nose stud, but this shocked her, though she concealed her amazement.

'I wanted my nipples done but the guy wouldn't. Do you know why not? He said it was my accent. Not with that posh voice, my love, he said, I'll have Daddy on my doorstep. It makes me *spit*. It's that naff school we go to, it's as bad as Eton. I'm going to change the way I speak, I'm going to get Estuary English tapes and learn to talk like other people.'

'It was a man who did it?' Francine said.

'Why not? It's a man who's going to see it. Well, he has seen it and the reaction was deeply satisfying, I'm telling you.'

Holly's new boyfriend was called Christopher and she was out with him every night, in spite of exams. If he wasn't fazed about the Finals he was in the throes of at Eastcote College she certainly wasn't going to get steamed up about a piddling thing like A Levels.

'I'd like to meet him,' Francine said.

'You know, sometimes you sound like your wicked stepmother. You really do. A hundred years old and well past everything.'

'Because I said I'd like to meet Christopher?'

'Because of your tone and your words. Oh, don't look like that. I'm sorry. I'll tell you what, when Eastcote puts on its degree show you can come along with me and we'll meet Chris there and his twin brother who's been doing Fine Art and who's got a painting in the exhibition. He looks just like Chris and he's bound to fancy you and – wouldn't it be great, France, if you and me were going about with *twins*?'

Francine shook her head. 'Imagine Julia.'

'If I didn't know her I couldn't imagine her,' said Holly. 'You'd have to be a – a Balzac to imagine her.'

'Which reminds me I ought to work. I've got French tomorrow morning.'

Francine experienced no traumas over her exams. She encountered no surprise questions and nothing much to alarm her. But when she had done the last exam and all was finished she was surprised to find Julia waiting for her outside school with the car. Julia explained that she had been to see the Chief Executive with a request which, she said, she knew would gladden Francine's heart.

'To whisk you out of school now those A Levels

are done with and carry you off on holiday. And she was perfectly charming about it. Absolutely no point, she said, in trolling in here for another two weeks until the official end of term.'

And no school-leaving parties, no idling about the grounds with one's friends, no freedom to swim in the pool whenever one chose and play tennis and make plans for future reunions. 'Where are we going?' Francine asked.

'Wait till you hear. A lovely little island in the Outer Hebrides. There's nothing there but the sea-birds and the beaches and the mountains and the heather.'

I won't go, she thought of saying. Julia can't drag me out of the house by force, any more than she can keep me a prisoner inside it. When they got home she found that Julia had already packed her suitcase. All their luggage was standing in the hall. Julia had arranged with Noele to keep an eye on the house, cancelled the milk and the papers. And no time was to be wasted. They would be flying to Glasgow that evening, meeting her father at Heathrow.

Before they left she tried to phone Holly, but there was no reply and when she tried Miranda she got the answering service.

Chapter 16

He hardly ever got letters. His post was mostly services bills and junk mail. The envelope he picked up from the doormat was buff-coloured with University of Eastcote and the college's eagle crest in red in the upper left-hand corner. He couldn't expect to be informed of his degree yet, it was too soon and wouldn't, anyway, come like this. Opening it suspiciously, he stared for a while without understanding. Then he did, then he realised.

It hadn't crossed his mind. Of course he knew that Eastcote annually awarded a prize to the producer of the best piece of craft work submitted for the BA degree in Ornamental Art. He knew it, but hadn't connected it with himself. And here, now, he was being told that he had won the Honoria Carter Black prize for his mirror. It brought with it an award of one hundred pounds.

The money was nothing – though he could do with *any* money – but the prize was prestigious, something to be immensely proud of. Teddy had never before won anything. He had not even won praise or encouragement. His school had been so committed to establishing equality that the staff only told a pupil he or she had done well if they could tell every other member of the class the same thing. Non-competitiveness was the watchword. As to his family, his grandmother thought praising a child encouraged him to show off; his parents hadn't thought about it at all.

A strange thing was happening to him. And this, too, was new. He was feeling what all who have a sudden success experience, a desire to tell someone about it. He had never before wanted to tell anyone anything, but now telling himself wasn't enough. That inner exchange which was his version of conversation seemed inadequate. But there was no one to tell.

Mr Chance was long dead. He made a face at the idea of going round to his grandmother's. What would he say and what would she? Damon he had never phoned again after his driving test was behind him. Megsie had put her head over the fence and invited him to Nige's birthday barbecue, but he had said he was busy. And he had sat indoors on that hot Saturday afternoon, watching Mr Chance's workshop used as a summer-house, his garden filled with smoke and the smell of burnt burgers and sausages, wondering what they were all saying about the car next door, maybe looking at it and speculating. But he had never regretted not accepting the invitation. He couldn't *be* with people, just as he couldn't now, to save his life, tell his news to Megsie and Nige.

His satisfaction must be from the prize alone and from himself alone knowing about it. Still, he soon found that others knew, everyone who mattered, for when he went along to the Chenil Gallery in the King's Road where the Eastcote Graduation Exhibition was being set up he was congratulated by all sorts of people. The Dean of Studies happened to be there and the Head of the Ornamental Art Department as well as a great many graduands, none of whom had taken much notice of him before. It was the first time anyone had ever shaken hands with him and he found it a novel, not altogether pleasant, experience. He didn't really know how to comport himself, but shifted about, muttering his thanks and longing to get to his mirror which he could see in the distance out of the corner of his eye.

A woman whose function he didn't know and whom he had never seen before told him it was to have a section of the wall space to itself. Winners of the Honoria Carter Black prize always did have their own stand in pride of place. They thought of hanging it just here where the light was good – what did he think?

He didn't think, he didn't know. 'I guess it's OK,' he said.

'Why don't you come back the day before the Private View and see if you like it?' She smiled. He was so handsome and so shy, and so talented. 'Then there would be time to change it round.'

'No, it'll be OK,' said Teddy and he went off to find someone to tell him when and where he would get the money.

Winning the prize stimulated him to phone the newspaper with his advertisement. While he'd still got some money left to pay for it. The fifty pounds from 'Max and Mex' was gone and not much remained of the sum he had taken off Keith's body, though, apart from buying himself a watch, he had been as frugal as possible. In drafting his small ad he would have liked to find some way of putting in 'winner of the Honoria Carter Black prize' but people might not know what that was and it would raise the price of insertion. In the end he simply wrote: *Joiner and cabinet-maker. BA in Ornamental Art, will make or fit fine furniture to your specification. Reasonable charges*, and he added his phone number. Then he thought that putting *young* before *joiner* and *newly starting out* after *art* would make it sound more appealing. He asked for the paragraph to go in three weeks running.

With no positive idea of where he was going or even why he was going, he screwed up his nerve and took the Edsel out. First he checked there was petrol in the tank. It was nearly full. Petrol was something he couldn't afford, but he certainly couldn't afford to run out of it and have to abandon the car somewhere. The Edsel, he remembered Damon saying, had a heavy fuel consumption. He wouldn't take it far. Maybe only round the block.

Handling it was very different from driving Damon's VW Golf. The engine stalled. The car juddered and sprang about like some lively young and very large animal – a cheetah maybe. Teddy kept his head, told himself to keep cool. It was a matter of getting the hang of it and very soon he did, reversing the Edsel and, finally, learning control, manoeuvring it through the wide-open double gates into the quiet street. It was early on Sunday morning.

He did what he had promised himself and drove it round the block. Twice he had stalled the engine, but twice started it again without difficulty. He came back to the open gates, the empty garden and the carport and, much more confident now, took it out again. This time he stopped and parked it, bought a Sunday paper, started it up again with no difficulty. A man carrying a carton of milk turned round to watch him pass, a woman with a dog stared at the great pale-yellow, glittering, fish-like torpedo-like *thing*. The purring many-finned projectile with its silver eyes and pursed codfish mouth. It was no longer polished and gleaming, for no one had laid a sponge or duster on it in five months, so when Teddy got back for the second time without mishap he set about cleaning it.

Leaving the car dirty would, he thought, eventually attract attention to it. Besides, he wanted to be near it legitimately for a while, with a reason for close-up contact. He fetched a sponge, two buckets of water, cloths from the kitchen. Without a hose, cleaning the Edsel took a very long time, particularly as it was not in Teddy's nature to do a less than thorough job.

He couldn't smell any smell. And if he couldn't no one could. Plastic had its advantages and this car its uses, if only as a coffin. He felt he had taken a big step. He had taken it out and brought it back, he could drive it. What he must do now was find somewhere, think up somewhere, he could take it and dump it and Keith's body. Some pond or reservoir – the sea? This was flagrant fantasy and he knew it. He wouldn't be capable of driving a car into a pond and sinking the car and getting out of it alive. Besides, where was there such a place he could use without being detected? Brent Reservoir? Impossible. Unthinkable. Probably he would have to dump the body and then, one day, sell the car. Sell it back perhaps to the firm in south London Keith had bought it from.

Lift that body out again? If you can kill it and put it there you can lift it out, he told himself, rubbing hard at the Edsel's pastel-lemon bodywork with a duster. You got it in, you can get it out. Nige had come out into the garden next door with a woman who was probably his mother. They gave him approving smiles. Teddy had noted, with disdain, that people always enjoy the sight of manual work being done, particularly when it is unpleasant.

'You can come and do mine when you've finished with that,' the woman called out.

'Fancy a coffee?' said Nige.

Teddy said thanks, but he was busy. He finished

the Edsel, locked it and went indoors where he settled down to read the paper he had bought. An article about the kind of people who murder other people told him that psychopaths often begin their career by killing a member of their own family. Did that mean he was a psychopath? He started thinking about Keith's body again, how to dispose of it.

In spite of saying he was satisfied with the arrangements for displaying his mirror he went back to the gallery. But on the day of the Private View itself. There is a limit to the indifference one can feel to the opinions of others and though Teddy's scorn threshold was very low, he found he very much wanted to see the look on visitors' faces when they contemplated the mirror, their admiration and perhaps their longing to possess it.

He arrived just in time for the Chancellor's speech. The Vice-Chancellor was an academic, but the Chancellor was a television actor who had achieved fame through appearing in a detective series. He spoke in a very actorly way, not saying anything of note, but with impeccable timing and in a Royal Shakespeare Company accent so beautiful that it didn't matter what he said. Teddy was surprised to see so many people. He positioned himself near but not absolutely beside his mirror, preparing for reactions.

Then he saw her. She was just a human being among other human beings, a species he disliked. So for a moment he hardly believed her human. Not as the man next to her was, the twin of that guy who was Kelly's boyfriend's friend, and the girl with him, normal ugly people. She was an angel or a wax effigy, a statue or an illusion. Her pale oval face, the dark shining eyes, the full red mouth, formed just one more object of beauty among all these artefacts on show. The most perfect of them, the best, the one that should have won the prize, but still an object.

He closed his eyes, mentally shook himself. Was he crazy? This was just a girl. He looked again. She was looking at him. Their eyes met. Never had there been such eyes, never in his experience, so large and depthless and clear and sweet. That word 'sweet' he used to himself and again thought he was losing his mind. He had never used it before except to describe a taste or, as everyone did here, in the college slang meaning of 'good'. She put up her hand to smooth back the black hair that fell across her white forehead, her comma eyebrow, and then she smiled at him. He tried to smile back and was just about succeeding when the crowd shifted, faces moved in front of hers – pig faces, ape faces, misshapen, unfinished, the twin man, the frizz-haired girl – and she was lost.

He pushed his way through the crowd. They were drinking now, wine and water and fruit juice. A girl he shouldered past spilt orange juice all over her dress and she shouted angrily at him. Teddy took no notice. He found the woman who had arranged the show and asked her, 'Who's that?'

'I beg your pardon?'

'That girl with the long black hair in the white dress.'

'My dear boy, I don't know. Just a guest.'

Kelly would tell him. He looked for her, saw the twin's twin and the twin's friend, but not Kelly. Teddy had never had much to do with these people, had long ago cold-shouldered their pleasantries and their overtures of friendship. They disliked him now, but he couldn't help that. Presumably they would still speak to him if he spoke to them. 'Who's that with your brother?'

The twin hesitated. He shrugged, said, not very warmly, 'You mean his girlfriend? Holly?'

'The one with the long black hair.'

'Don't know who that is. Friend of Holly's maybe. Why?'

Teddy was now completely nonplussed. He didn't know what one did in a situation like this. Come to that, he didn't know what he wanted. To look, he supposed. To be near and to look and to marvel. He remembered his grandmother and Damon meeting by the french windows, and what Agnes had said and done. 'I want someone to introduce me.'

The twin shook his head like someone who has seen everything bizarre this world can offer, but who can still be surprised. 'You really are something else, Grex. I don't know why I don't just tell you to piss off. Come on, then.'

They found the three people standing in front of Teddy's mirror. Teddy's internal organs shifted and moved about, and some of them seemed to turn over. He had never before felt anything like it. Perhaps he made a sound, a gasp or a grunt, for the girl turned round and he experienced again the full frontal effect of those eyes, those softly parted red lips, that skin as white as a lily. And this time he saw the whole of her, slender, long-legged, her waist the span of the stems of a bunch of flowers, her wrists and ankles narrow as a child's.

The twin was saying, 'Holly, James, this is the guy who made it. The prize winner. He's called Grex, can't remember what comes before Grex.'

She said – she, the only she who counted – 'It's on the card, Christopher.' She looked at him. 'Is that right? Teddy?'

'Yes.'

'Your mirror is utterly gorgeous.'

It wasn't she who said it but the Holly girl, that

167

big-breasted, green-eyed frizz-head, her voice unbe-
lievably loud and upper-class after *hers*. Teddy just
nodded. He wanted *her* to say it, but she only smiled.

Holly said, 'Have you won thousands and thousands of pounds?' Luckily, she didn't wait for an
answer. 'What are you going to do with your mirror?
Sell it? Give it to your mum?'

They were all looking at him. Their faces, curious,
teasing, malicious, confirmed him in his misan-
thropy. Except hers, which was shy, reserved, those
eyes no longer meeting his. A little white hand like a
flower held her glass of sparkling water. He knew
everyone's name but hers, the only one he wanted to
know. Along the crown of her bowed head, bisecting
the silky blackness, the parting ran like a narrow
white road. He imagined laying on it a wreath of
pale flowers.

He drew a deep breath. 'I shall give it to my
woman.'

He said it violently, quelling any possible amused
response. There was none, but a vague uneasiness.

The Holly girl pursed up her thick lips. 'What do
you mean, your woman? That's a very peculiar way
of putting it. Do you mean your girlfriend?'

'My woman,' he said firmly and added, 'when
she's mine.' His voice entered a deeper range. 'To see
her face in,' he said and he turned away with an
unfamiliar sensation of the blood rushing up to his
face and neck. Then and only then, when he was
yards away, swallowed by the crowd, he remembered that he had been told everyone's name but
hers.

It couldn't be left like that. She was gone. He could
no longer see her. Come to me, he asked her silently,
come away from them and to me. How did one
manage these things? He had no experience, no
guidelines, no knowledge. He turned back, pushing

his way past the table that stood beneath his mirror, past Kelly's painting, James's wrought iron, searching the crowd for her, frustrated by bodies, legs, arms, heads, buttocks, bulk, getting in the way. And then suddenly she was in front of him.

Alone, if you could be alone in this crowd, Holly and the twins somewhere else. He and she were alone, facing each other in this swell and press of people, an island of him and her in a sea of humanity. *So shows a snowy dove trooping with crows, As yonder lady o'er her fellows shows.* It was what he felt if he didn't know the words. He didn't know the words in which to put his question either, so he said it straight out. 'What's your name?'

She put up her hand, but not quite to her lips. 'Francine. Francine Hill.'

What did you ask next? Phone number, of course. He asked, she answered, he repeated it over and over, imprinting it on his mind.

'My friends are waiting for me,' she said gently, almost apologetically.

She could go now, he didn't care. It was too much for him, anyway, it was killing him. Her eyes were eating him up, so that he felt faint, sick. 'Goodbye,' he said.

'Did you mean that? About giving the mirror to – someone?'

'Yes.'

'Oh. Well, goodbye.'

By the time he got home half the number had gone from his mind. He had had nothing to write with or write on and his head was spinning. He didn't know if the last part was double nine three two or double three two nine, but he remembered the exchange number. The phone book had Hill, R., and nine two double three. What to do with it now he had found it

169

he didn't know. He lay on his bed, still the same camp-bed his parents had consigned him to when he was four, and thought about her.

The most beautiful thing he had ever seen. The perfect object made flesh. Better than anything a man could make or shape or paint. He imagined having her here with him, in this room, but it was unimaginable, this was no place for her, it would be like the diamond ring mixed up among his parents' rubbish. 'Francine,' he said aloud, 'Francine.' He had never heard the name before but it was beautiful, like her. Francine.

If he had money and a beautiful place to live he would like to build a plinth for her and drape it in white and seat her on it in a white-and-gold chair. He would put the diamond ring on her finger and tiny white orchids from a florist's shop in her hair and dress her. A dress like Marc Syre's Harriet wore in Orcadia Place, a floor-length tunic of fine pleats, but white, not red, the purest white of her skin and the orchids. And she should look at her face in his mirror and worship it as he would, as he did.

Francine.

The evening sun glinted on the fins of the Edsel and suddenly, as clouds parted, made a blinding flash there so that it hurt the eyes to look. It was as if flames licked along the boot lid and seared the rear windscreen. He buried his head in the pillow. Francine.

Chapter 17

'Well, my dear, you have a job!'

Julia said it with one of her bright and somehow conspiratorial smiles, hands clasped, shoulders hunched. She might have been talking to a child whose parents have made a compromise with its bad behaviour. If you must be naughty, let us direct your naughtiness into useful channels. Francine returned the smile, not very enthusiastically.

'In Noele's shop. You'll be helping Noele sell her gorgeous nearly new designer clothes. Three days a week, she won't need you more than that, and the marvellous thing is she's going to pay you. Not very much, but she will pay you. Now I think you said Holly isn't getting paid, so you can pull rank over her. So what do you say?'

Francine remembered from childhood that when the grown-ups asked you what do you say, they meant, 'Why haven't you said thank you?' She resisted doing that now. Why would she want to have an ascendancy over Holly? She nodded, said, 'All right, Julia, I'll try it. I expect I can do it.' It would get her out of the house, she thought.

'Of course you can do it. Standing on your head. And I expect Noele will let you have all sorts of lovely things at a discount.'

Francine didn't want second-hand Jean Muir and Caroline Charles designed for forty-five-year-olds but she didn't say so. Imagining herself serving customers at Noele's standing on her head with her hair trailing along the floor and her feet waving in the air made her smile. Julia took this for pleasure and even excitement.

'And the beauty of it', she said to Richard, 'is that she'll only be a stone's throw from home. I mean, right up at this end of the High Street. If I look out of the front upstairs window at the side I could almost see her going in at Noele's door.'

Richard nodded. At least Francine would have a job, she would have an occupation for her gap year. He could tolerate Julia, even revive fondness for her, when he saw her only for two or three days at a stretch. And he could teach himself to be easy in Francine's company when he had presents to bring her home and questions to ask her about her activities, things to tell her about places she had never visited. No longer seeing her on a regular basis, he was distanced from her, able to convince himself she was learning what all people of her age must learn, to grow away from the family home and adjust herself to the outside world.

For Julia as guardian and guide he had no misgivings. Or none he wanted to bring to the forefront of his mind. In her care, as he told himself over and over, Francine could come to no harm, Francine would be the safest girl in London. He had begun planning for the move to Oxford. Now he could work from home while in this country, now he spent so much time travelling to and from Heathrow, Oxford would be just as convenient a place to live in as Ealing. More convenient. Francine would be safe and Julia would be pleased.

But safe from what? When that question arose in his mind he quelled it. If he told himself often enough that Julia knew best, he could stop worrying. About anything.

Clothes held little interest for Francine. This may have been because they interested Julia very much and since Francine was twelve she had been trying to dress her in jumpers and skirts with pearls and pretty cotton frocks. But Francine had her own dress allowance from her father and, when she was allowed out with Holly or Miranda or Isabel, spent it on jeans and leather and old army greatcoats and Doc Martens. Like the others did. She had two black dresses and a white dress – the one she had worn at the Private View – and bits and pieces that had taken her fancy, odd-shaped little jackets and skinny tops and miniskirts. That was the extent of her wardrobe.

Noele looked her up and down rather grimly when she arrived for work in jeans and an endangered-species T-shirt with leopards on it, and suggested she change into 'something from the Moschino rack'. Willing to compromise a little, Francine looked for plain black trousers, but nothing she found fitted. 'I'm afraid they're miles too big, Noele.'

The proprietor of New Departures was herself a scrawny, taut-bodied woman, a hook-nosed white-blonde, brimming with nervous energy. She said rather unpleasantly, 'I hope you're not going to take an insensitive attitude towards our clients.' Noele had clients, not customers. 'Normal-sized women don't feel very happy having adolescents flaunt their size-six bums at them, you know.'

As it happened, Francine had little opportunity to flaunt anything, for most visitors to the shop were received and fêted by Noele, who did all the showing and persuading herself. Francine spent most of her time in the workroom. There she received garments brought to be sold and her function was to examine them for flaws and wear. The slightest blemish disqualified a dress or suit for

New Departures. If anything seemed perfect to Francine Noele had to be summoned to fix the price. Even though the garment had to have been dry-cleaned and still in its plastic bag, this was always very low, allowing Noele to make an enormous profit of something like two hundred per cent.

Occasionally, if the hem of a dress or skirt was coming down it would have to be repaired. Noele was appalled when Francine said she couldn't sew. 'What on earth did they teach you at that expensive school of yours?'

'Maths and French and English literature and history,' said Francine. She said it politely, though her patience was tried, and she smiled.

'There is no need to be sarcastic,' said Noele.

When she arrived at the shop in the mornings she looked back at the window from which Julia watched her. Julia's face she couldn't see, it was too far away, only the movement of the curtain. And when she left Noele's at five she saw the curtain move again. Julia was on the watch for her and would be waiting.

Julia asked Francine how she had got on at work in much the same way as a mother questions a child newly started at primary school. Francine must be tired, on her feet all day, she would want an early night. It would be unwise to go out in the evenings during the week and, in fact, said Julia with a certain triumph, none of Francine's so-called friends had phoned to make arrangements to meet her. 'I am afraid you must be prepared for some of those people to drop you now you've left school and aren't seeing them on a daily basis. It's the way of the world, Francine.'

'It's down to me to phone them just as much as for them to phone me.'

Julia's smile was sympathetic, a little rueful. 'I wonder if they think themselves a cut above you socially? I wouldn't be surprised. School is a great leveller and when it's past ...'

Outwardly, Julia seemed serene. She showed nothing of her inner anxiety. If Richard were at home she would have told him everything, but Richard was in Brussels till the weekend. It had begun with the phone call. A voice, a young man's, with an accent Julia dubbed Brent Cross, had asked to speak to Francine. With no preliminaries, no pretence at courtesy, more abrupt than one could imagine. 'I want to talk to Francine.'

'Who is that?' Julia said in her icicle tone, long drawn-out and cold.

'Can I talk to her?'

'My stepdaughter is not available,' said Julia and put down the phone.

Probably there was no connection between that call and the car. Their street, of course, was always full of cars, parked cars and passing cars – what street is not? But this was a bright-scarlet sports car with no top, or with a soft top that folded down, a two-seater and very speedy. It sped along the street with its radio blaring. Down the street it cruised at ten in the morning and up again at eleven. Back it came at four in the afternoon, rock music throbbing from its open windows and roof, but it had disappeared by the time Francine returned home.

The phone call wasn't repeated and the car didn't come back. Julia might have thought no more of it, but for the appearance of the man. Again, she had no reason to connect him with the phone call. He might have been the driver of the red car, for that driver too had been young and dark, but of that she couldn't be sure. She first saw him on the opposite side of the road at about midday.

Almost directly opposite the house was a bus-stop with a shelter. He was sitting in the shelter, reading a book. Or pretending to read a book. Julia happened to be looking out of the window when he arrived and sat down in the middle of the seat.

It had occurred to her, ten minutes before, that she had no idea what Francine did about lunch on these working days. She could ask her, or Noele, but it might be just as satisfactory to observe the shop door from her window. It was possible Francine went out alone and ate in some café. Anything could happen to her, she might meet anyone.

She didn't see Francine, but she saw the young man. And in that sight Julia's world turned over. In the past she had thought of men in connection with Francine, but only *the* man and other vaguely conceived psychopaths who might want to harm her physically. Now a terrible thing occurred to her, that Francine sooner or later might attract a man and be attracted by him.

In her eyes Francine wasn't attractive. She was too thin and too dark, too unlike Julia's own ideal of beauty. And she was too young – or so Julia had thought. Now she realised that Francine was by no means too young, she was eighteen, an age which many people would call too *old* to have a first boyfriend.

Hot tides of pain and panic surged through Julia. She broke out into a sweat. Francine as a young woman with a *lover* was a prospect she knew she couldn't face. Even contemplating it made her feel sick. And the horrible thing was that Francine was probably highly sexed. Damaged or disturbed people often were. 'It will destroy her,' said Julia aloud into the empty room.

'I will lose her,' she whispered to herself.

The young man on the seat looked dangerous. He

176

was too handsome and too casual. As if he cared about nothing except getting what he wanted. Julia stared at him, willing him to go away, to prove her wrong.

Two more people came to the bus-stop. One of them sat down and a third looked as if she would like to, but the man wasn't going to shift along, not he. He sprawled over half the seat with his right leg crossed over his left above the knee. Julia thought of going over there and speaking to him. She would go up to him and tell him off, ask him why he hadn't the courtesy to let an old lady sit down. She was considering doing this when the bus came. The other three people got on it, but he didn't. He remained where he was.

Julia hated that. It frightened her. But what could she do? He had a perfect right to sit there if he wished and as long as he wished. She kept returning to the window throughout the day, but by four he was gone. There was no reason to suppose a link between the phone call, the red sports car and the young man in the shelter, but she did suppose one. She supposed, too, a link with Francine and longed for Friday when Richard would come home.

On the following afternoon he was back. Julia felt sick with apprehension. He was sitting there reading, occasionally glancing at the house. At last, half an hour before Francine was due to leave New Departures, she went across the road and accosted him. He looked up and fixed on her dark, cold, expressionless eyes.

'What exactly do you think you're doing here?'

'Sitting,' he said. 'Reading.'

'I can see you're sitting and reading, I'm not blind. Why are you doing it here? You're not waiting for a bus, I've watched you. Haven't you got a home to go to?'

The stare he fixed on her was unnerving. She had the strange incongruous impression that he was an actor and one who has mastered the art of timing. He was not afraid to be silent, to create a long enduring pause. At last he said, 'Go away.'

Julia couldn't handle it. She said, with bluster, 'If you're still here in half an hour I'm calling the police.'

Walking home, Francine saw no one, heard nothing. She was deep in thought. If she stuck Noele's for another month that was about all she was going to manage. Yet she had to stick it, for if she told her father how much she hated New Departures and how bored she was, Julia would say that went to prove what she always said, that Francine wasn't fit to be in the outside world and couldn't cope with even a little part-time job.

Now she wished she hadn't acquiesced in that gap-year plan. It was really only because Holly was taking a year out, she had somehow thought she would be with Holly and they would do things together and enjoy themselves, while in fact Holly was so busy working for her MP and going about with Christopher that they hardly spoke and seldom saw each other. Thanks to her own weakness and impulsiveness she had fallen into Julia's trap and was due to pass another year of her life in tedium and near-imprisonment.

She refused to look up in the direction of that window, from which Julia would certainly be gazing, smiling and probably waving, and even stayed on the other side of the wide street. She didn't want to tease Julia, she had never done that, though she had been tempted, but she wasn't above walking along behind the row of parked vans and delivery trucks that would conceal her from Julia's view. Eventually, of course, she must cross the street and she decided to do so on the pedestrian crossing, a few yards along from the bus-stop.

There was someone waiting for a bus. She wasn't sure afterwards if she recognised him first or he her. Perhaps recognition was simultaneous.

'Hi,' he said.

'Oh, hi, hallo.'

'Do you . . .' he tried and then he tried again, 'do you remember me?'

'You're the mirror maker.'

'Yes.'

He stood looking at her.

She couldn't recall anyone looking at her so intensely before. It was as if he were studying her, *learning* her, to store up for future use. 'Do you', she said tentatively, 'live round here?'

He shook his head. 'I came to see you. I've seen where you work and I've been waiting here to see you.'

'Have you?' She felt the blood come up into her face. The heat of it embarrassed her.

'That woman in your house is staring at us out of the window,' he said. 'She came out and asked me why I was here.'

'Why are you?'

'I told her to go away. Can I come in with you for a bit?'

Her horror must have shown. He stared intensely at her, not smiling, his face hard with concentration. Then, in that moment, the bus came. If he realised she didn't know, but she knew at once that the bus would cut them off from Julia's view. A man got off it, then an old woman, taking her time.

'If I write down my number,' he said, 'will you give me a phone?'

Before she knew what he was doing he had taken

her left hand in his and turned back the sleeve of her cardigan. It was then that she noticed the mutilation of his little finger, how it had been cut off at the first joint. He began to write in ballpoint on her wrist. She held her hand stiffly for him, extending the fingers. It was a phone number he wrote.

'I can't,' she said. 'I really can't.'

'Please. I want you to.'

The bus started. She ran across the road behind it, avoiding a swerving bicycle. He might still be there, but she refused to look back. She pulled her cardigan sleeve right down over the ballpoint writing and half-way across her hand. Julia opened the front door just before she got there, a favourite trick of hers.

For a moment Francine thought Julia was going to seize her by the arm and pull her into the house. It was just the impression she got from her stepmother's stance and extended hand. But Julia restrained herself, stepping back and quickly pushing the door shut behind Francine. 'Who were you talking to?'

It would be easy to lie and say it was a stranger who had asked her the time or which bus went to Chiswick. 'Someone I met at that Private View I went to.'

'Do you mean he picked you up, Francine? Is that what you're saying?'

'No, Julia, I'm not saying that. I was introduced to him.'

'Do you know he has twice been hanging about out there, spying on this house? He came driving down here in a red sports car. I went over to speak to him and he was extremely rude. Your father will be horrified.'

Francine went upstairs to her room. She looked out of the window at the bus shelter but of course he was long gone. Almost any one of her friends would know what to do in this situation, but she didn't.

And although she was sure they would be very free with advice she didn't want to ask them. She must ask herself. Did she like him? Did she want to know him better? He was young and good-looking, and she thought he was clever and she liked the way he talked.

She shut her eyes and put her head in her hands and thought that if he touched her, put his arm round her, held her hand, put his mouth on her mouth, she wouldn't hate it. When he took hold of her hand to write on her wrist she hadn't minded. She had even felt a kind of strange little thrill as his skin touched hers. But phone him? Use that number and phone him? She turned back her sleeve and contemplated the number. Wash it off, forget it. She was saying this to herself when Julia's voice came up the stairs.

'Francine?'

This always happened when Julia had been harsh or dictatorial. She would hector, then ten minutes later cajole.

'Francine?'

'What is it?' Francine opened her door, put her head over the banisters.

'I've made tea, dear. I thought we might have an early meal and go to the cinema. Would you like that?'

Francine used the phrase she never used to anyone else and which she disliked, but which best expressed her feelings. 'I don't mind.'

She went into the bathroom and washed her hands and wrists, but first she wrote down the phone number. She wrote it in three separate places to be on the safe side.

181

Chapter 18

Teddy's ability to concentrate, usually so good, had been badly shaken this past week. The sight of the girl Francine at close quarters was responsible for that. He had never before felt like this. Why couldn't he get her out of his head? Why did he see her face when he shut his eyes and look for her in every young dark-haired girl he passed? He didn't even know what he wanted from her except to have her with him and look at her all the time. Every time the phone rang he jumped and something knocked at his chest wall.

He had got into the habit of snatching up the receiver and speaking into it breathlessly. That was what he had done when the woman phoned. His disappointment was correspondingly stunning, like a heavy blow to the back of his knees. He sat down. The voice was shrill and ringing with an upper-class accent. She said she had read his advertisement and wanted some joinery done. A cupboard and shelves to be built into an alcove. Would he come and see her? She was Harriet Oxenholme and she lived at 7a Orcadia Place, NW8.

He ought to have been delighted, but all he felt was, maybe he'd get some money out of it. The name ought to have rung bells, but the only name that meant anything or affected him at all was Francine Hill's. He shut his eyes and pictured himself as he had been, holding her white hand in his, writing his phone number on her white wrist. Her hand had been soft and warm and dry. The skin felt like silk. Why hadn't she phoned him?

He remembered how he had half forgotten her number. It hadn't been written down and he had had to hold it in his head. But he had looked up her father in the phone book and found the number. Perhaps she had washed his number off her wrist or that woman who had come and questioned him had taken hold of her by force and washed it off. He never found it hard to imagine violence.

Go back to that bus shelter and try again? The idea was humiliating, he wouldn't do that, he would never show himself to that woman again. He could go to that shop she worked at and ask her to go out with him. How did you ask? Just said, will you come out for a drink, presumably, or, we could go for a walk. She might say no.

And should he take the Edsel? Should he go down to St John's Wood in the Edsel? Maybe not. It was a reckless act, however you looked at it, taking the Edsel anywhere. All that was needed to put an end to everything was a minor accident, even a flat tyre. Better get the tube, go down on the Jubilee Line.

The phone rang as he was leaving. His heart jumped. It was just after one. Somehow he thought that if she phoned it would be from that shop and at her lunch-time. But it wasn't her, it was a woman with water coming through her kitchen ceiling who had been given Keith's number.

'He's retired and gone to live in Liphook,' said Teddy.

A girl got into the tube train who looked a lot like Francine, but a cheap, shabby version of her. Like a poor reproduction of a great painting, Teddy thought, or chipboard with a veneer made to resemble oak. This girl had bitten nails and a spot in the middle of her right cheek and bony knees. Really, it was only her hair that was like Francine's and her dark eyes. Francine was perfect. You could take Francine's clothes off and train a powerful arc lamp on her and search her all over and find no flaw, no mark. One day he would do that.

He got out at St John's Wood, walked down Grove End Road and across Alma Gardens. Orcadia Place was hidden away where you would least expect a street of houses to be, off the end of Melina Place. He stood still for a moment, for he hadn't known such places as this existed in London. It was like somewhere in the country, a corner of a country town, or a picture in a book of photographs of a country town. And it was quite quiet. Traffic could be heard only distantly and like the humming of bees. Orcadia Cottage was an invisible house, nothing of it to be seen behind the tall barrier of many varieties of leaves, feathery and pointed, shiny dark-green and tender pale-green, bronzed gold and pastel-yellow. He opened the iron gate and went in.

Flowers everywhere, he didn't know the names. He only knew roses and of those there were plenty, pink and red and white, heavily scented. Window-boxes and baskets spilled out pink and purple trumpet flowers and blue daisies and long sprays of silver leaves. They blossomed against a backcloth, a rippling layered canopy, of glossy leaves, green but touched with bronze. Most of the front of the house was covered by this foliage, like a drapery or a dense but faintly trembling screen.

Where had he seen it before, that wall of leaves? The picture, of course, the painting that must be a picture of this very house. Orcadia Place. He must have been very preoccupied not to have caught on before. He went closer, peering, touching the layers of leaves and the red-gold tendrils that crept across and clung to the brickwork, stroking with one finger the pale-grey door, examining the glass that was like no other glass he had ever seen, but more like solidified clear green water.

She opened the door before he could ring the bell. Another woman who had been watching for him. What got into them? This one looked as she sounded on the phone, showy, shrill, too old to dress like that. Her eyes went all over him, like groping hands.

'Come in, Teddy,' she said, as if she had known him for years. 'It's so hot, I expect you'd like a drink.'

Harriet Oxenholme, she had said on the phone. The bell that should have rung, but hadn't because of his disturbed concentration, pealed now. The red hair was the same and maybe the nose, but it couldn't be . . . He wasn't going to stick his neck out, anyway, and look a fool when she didn't know what he was talking about. Besides, by the time he had taken two steps into the hall he was overcome by something much more important to him, his surroundings, this house.

It was far and away the most beautiful place he had ever seen. The proportions of this hall, this room into which she took him, the windows, the walls, the carpets, the flowers, the furniture, the paintings, all of it dazzled him. The only place he had ever been in remotely like it was the V and A where the Chances had once taken him, the only place where one could hope, he had thought, to see chairs like these and rugs like this and vases like that. He stared about him, turning this way and that, his eyes going up to the ceiling and down towards the long windows that led into the courtyard at the back.

People lived here. This woman lived here. And was real, an ordinary middle-aged, long-nosed woman with dyed red hair. Only perfection should be here, only perfect loveliness was fit for it, to be

185

ensconced in this matching beauty. Only Francine. In her white dress, in that creamy brocade chair, her white hand on its white-and-gold arm.

'What will you drink?' the Harriet woman was saying. 'I've a glorious Chardonnay on ice, deliciously cold, unless of course you'd fancy something stronger?'

Teddy shook himself, came back to earth. Why was she offering him drink? For a moment it had gone out of his head why he was there. He felt as if he had been in a dream, the kind where you go to a place to perform some task and there are people there who treat you as if you've come to do something quite different. 'You'd better show me where you want this cupboard,' he said.

'Do let's have a drink first.'

He nodded, gave in. 'Water, then.'

Her disappointment was obvious. He couldn't understand it. In the unlikely event of his inviting someone in for a drink he would be very pleased if they drank water and saved him expense. Money probably didn't mean much to her, she must have lots of it. He took the glass of water absently, not looking at her, she was the least attractive thing in the place, far and away the least. She had poured herself an enormous glass of wine and was eyeing him in a peculiar way over the top of it. He said abruptly, 'Could I have a look over this house? See the rest of it, I mean?'

'You want to go over the house?' Her tone suggested that this was the most bizarre request he could have made.

'Yes. Is that all right?'

She nodded. 'It's a rather unexpected request.'

Because she didn't see him as an educated craftsman but a common working-class labourer? He turned cold eyes on her and she said hastily, 'Of

186

course I'll take you over the house, I'll be delighted. This is the dining-room,' she said, 'and that's the alcove I want the cupboard in.'

Teddy stared at the picture above the sideboard. It was a still life, or almost a still life, for present as well as the oranges and the piece of cheese on the dark table was a white mouse. You could see from its expression the mouse's longing for the cheese and see, too, its fear and wariness. 'Is that a Simon Alpheton?'

He had surprised her. She had set him down as an ignorant working boy, he could tell. Like the mouse, she was confused, but perhaps also like the mouse, if it ever got beyond the confines of the painting or had existence outside it, she moved closer.

She laid her hand on his arm, on the bit where his sleeve ended and she could touch skin. 'Do you know Alpheton's work?'

'Some of it.'

'Then you must have recognised me. *Marc and Harriet in Orcadia Place.*'

'I recognised the house,' he said. 'You were that Harriet?'

'I don't think you know that painting as well as you say.' She withdrew her hand. 'I wish you'd have that drink.'

'I don't drink. What's in there?' He pointed to a door at the end of the passage beside the staircase.

'Stairs down to the cellar. It's never used.'

'I want to see everything.'

She opened the door, said impatiently, 'It used to be a coal-hole, they delivered coal from outside. Right? There's nothing to see.'

He looked down the stairs into half-dark. She didn't switch on the light. He saw a cavern, a stone floor, a bolted door. He turned away. 'I'll measure the alcove,' he said, 'and if you give me some idea of what you want I'll do some drawings. It won't take long, only about a week.'

She didn't feel capable of stopping him a second time. He measured and stood back and took another measurement, looked at the doors on the china cabinet, the panelling on the walls, nodded, put his measuring tape away.

Her touching him he hadn't liked. He would have liked to take hold of that brown, wrinkled, red-nailed hand and throw it back at its owner. But he wanted this job. He followed her up the stairs to the first floor, pausing on the way to look at pictures and out of a pretty bow window. Only two bedrooms and two bathrooms up here. He had expected more, but the main bedroom was very big and spread out, with a huge, glorious four-poster in it, a bed draped in creamy white silk and hung with veils of white gauze, and with a picture inside its roof of nymphs and gods, and a white bull with a wreath of flowers on its horns.

You could sit up in that bed and look at yourself in the curved and curlicued mirror on the white dressing-table. Francine could do that. Everyone else would be overcome and diminished by this house, but not Francine. For her it would be a fit setting and he imagined her naked in the bed, dressed in nothing but her own long black hair and the ring he would put on her finger. He had never seen a naked girl, but he had seen paintings. She would be better than the paintings.

Another attempt was made to make him drink once they were downstairs again and the hand returned to his arm. He slid away from it in a serpentine movement, got up and walked purposefully out into the hall, promising the drawings within the week. The postman dropped a card through the letter-box at that moment. Teddy bent down, picked it up and handed it to her, careful to keep his fingers from touching hers as he did so.

Once out in the street he was overcome with an unfamiliar feeling: envy. He wanted that house and the things in it. The sensations he had were shared by many of the young, poor and beautiful: how unfair it was that they should be denied benefits which the old and ugly enjoyed.

In imagination his own home suffered by the comparison. It would look worse than ever now. On the way back he bought paint, matt and gloss, in ivory and coffee, and set about decorating the place. He couldn't bring Francine here, not the way it was. The irony of it struck him when the phone rang and it was someone else answering his advertisement, not asking him to make fine furniture, but to do just what he was doing at home and paint her house. Paint one room, rather. He was affronted and on the point of saying no, telling her to go to hell, but then he thought of the money, he could ask good money and he had to find employment.

All evening and all next day he worked on the walls in his room and the living-room, washing them down prior to starting with the paint roller. It soothed him, cleaning away dirt and stains, making a bare scrubbed surface. Francine didn't phone. He was beginning to give up hope. That night, instead of the sideboard dream, he dreamed he was cleaning up the world, getting rid of the ugliness. He had a machine like a giant vacuum cleaner that mowed down motor bikes and chain-link fencing and plastic sheeting, and sucked them into its insides. It ploughed into petrol stations and the shop fronts of discount stores, breaking them up and swallowing the harsh blues and reds and yellows and chrome. He was going to try it on people, sucking in the old and the ugly and the young and ugly, the deformed mob, but just as he directed his machine on to a skinny old man getting out of a car he woke up.

The woman who had called was a Mrs Trent. She was not in the least like Harriet Oxenholme and her house in Brondesbury Park was very different from Orcadia Cottage. Teddy looked around her poky living-room, stuffed with a fat and shiny pink brocade three-piece suite and varnished mock-walnut veneer, and gave her as estimate the first sum that came into his head. He must have set it too low, for she accepted with alacrity. When could he start? Wednesday, he said.

He went down to the Chenil Gallery to enquire if anyone had asked about buying his mirror. No one had. He didn't really want to sell it, but he might if someone offered the asking price of eight hundred pounds. It was quite a distance to St John's Wood from there, but on the other hand it was on his way, so he got out of the tube train and walked over to Orcadia Place. Just to look. That first time he hadn't noticed the medallion of the two cherubs with folded wings or the row of blue and green tiles under the eaves and he couldn't remember the falcon heads on the gateposts.

No one else phoned. He looked up New Departures in the phone book and wrote down the number on the paper where he had written her home number. All that weekend, while he painted the walls and cleaned the Edsel and made his drawings, he thought about Francine. Not about what she felt or thought or was doing or might feel about him, not about her relationship with the fat, fair-haired woman who had scolded him, but solely about the way she looked and smelt and sounded. He seated her on battlements and on a white pedestal and found himself drawing, instead of designs for a

190

cupboard, her face. He had made seven drawings before he got it right and was satisfied.

Chapter 19

Noele talked to her like a Victorian householder whose housemaid has followers. Francine had read enough novels of the period to recognise the attitude and the tone. She listened in silence, but not meekly. A young man had come into New Departures on the previous day, the Tuesday, and asked for her, spoken in a vulgar accent and insolent tone as if he had the right to go where he pleased and do as he liked, and told Noele to give her a message. Who did he think he was? Who did she, Francine, think she was? It was out of the question for her to carry on some kind of intrigue in Noele's establishment.

'What was the message?' said Francine.

Noele laughed unpleasantly. 'I've passed it on to Julia. You can ask her.'

Francine didn't. She asked her father. He was in London for the whole week and when he got home that evening she asked him if he had a message for her. Julia was in the kitchen, cooking dinner.

Richard frowned. 'Do you know this boy, Francine?'

'Of course I do.' She said it sharply for her. The abruptness was sufficiently out of character for her father to look up, concerned. 'He's a friend of Holly's boyfriend – well, someone he knows. They were at university together. Holly's boyfriend introduced us.'

192

'Us?' said Richard. The word hung ominously in the air.

'He introduced him to me.'

'I must say I'm surprised. He sounds a rough customer. Julia says he is very badly spoken. Do you like him?'

'What was the message?' Francine said again.

'Oh, something about you phoning him.' Richard looked unhappy. 'He said you have his number. Do you, Francine?'

She didn't answer. She might have if Julia hadn't come in. Francine recognised the dress she was wearing, a pale-blue crêpe Jean Muir that had hung on Noele's rack since first she went to work there. Painfully and slowly, she had sewn new buttons on it herself. Julia, in it, was a clashing of primary colours, blue, yellow, red.

'Noele won't let him into the shop again,' Julia said, 'you can be sure of that. You have to ring the bell to get in and if she sees him she just won't open the door. She has promised me that.'

Two old witches was the expression which came into Francine's mind. It was Holly's description and it shocked her because she seldom thought in such crude terms. 'I'm not enjoying working in that shop,' she said.

Julia made no reply. 'Your dinner's on the table.'

'Give it a little longer, Francine,' Richard said pleadingly. 'Give it a chance. You've only been there a month.'

'Yes, this world would soon grind to a standstill if everyone gave up a job the moment conditions weren't quite perfect. Come and have your dinner.'

Richard recognised the feeling he had for what it was and didn't much like it or himself. He was jealous. Jealous of a cocky young man with a lower-class accent who had been to one of those colleges

193

that these days were called universities. Possessiveness, it was also called, the fear of losing his precious daughter. But it made him look at Julia with new eyes. Julia was right, Julia knew and understood. She would keep his daughter safe for him, close to him, she would put on the full armour of guardianship and go forth against the enemy with banners flying.

Once he had loved Julia and he would again. Being away from her so much refreshed him and reawakened his feeling for her. They had both recognised that whatever had gone before in Francine's life, she had now reached that most difficult of all ages. Vigilance such as had never yet been attempted was called for. Maybe they could even think of living in Oxford now, selling the house and moving by Christmas . . .

Jennifer used to have an uncanny way of reading his thoughts. He would be about to comment on something that came into his head quite unconnected with their prior conversation and before he could get the words out she had uttered the very thing he had been about to say. Julia had never done that, but now she did. Its effect was to endear her to him.

'I was wondering, darling, if I should think of going up to Oxford and doing a bit of house hunting. Of course I'd take Francine with me. On one of her days off.'

'I was having much the same thought myself,' said Richard, and from sitting some distance from her he moved to place himself beside her on the sofa.

'I think it a very good idea for her to have some say in the choice of her new home. It's all part of this gradual assumption of responsibility I'm recommending for her. After all, she will be living there just as much as we will, both during her three years at the university and afterwards. And I think as near the centre of the city as possible, don't you? We won't want to be at a distance from her and she won't want a lot of travelling.'

'You might go while I'm in Frankfurt.'

He took her hand and held it.

If Noele hadn't made that fuss and Julia been so dictatorial and her father asked all those questions, and Holly on the phone tried to promote James's interest while claiming to have forgotten who the mirror maker was, Francine might not have given much more thought to Teddy Grex. He might have quietly slid from her mind, perhaps to be relegated to her memory merely as the first boy who ever admired her.

But the opposition of all these people made her think about him. Their dislike aroused her sympathy. It was outrageous to condemn someone because he didn't speak like you did; awful to ostracise someone for walking into a shop and asking a question. She remembered the odd things he said, like how he would give the mirror to his woman to see her face in. And how he had waited in the bus shelter for her, waited for hours just to see her.

He began to fill her thoughts. That mutilated little finger on his left hand, how had that happened? And how could he do such a daring thing as push up her sleeve and write on her wrist? She remembered the feel of his skin on hers and it made her shiver, but not unpleasantly. In the shop one afternoon it occurred to her out of nothing, out of the blue, that he was very good-looking. Up until that moment it had hardly struck her. She was in the workroom, ironing that most difficult of all things to iron, a white cotton shirt, when the shop bell rang. The bell was always replied to by Noele's buzzer that operated the door, but this time there was no answering buzz. No one had been let in.

Of course she couldn't be sure and she wasn't going to ask, but she thought it was Teddy who had come to the door. He had come and been sent away. It was then that she felt the first flutter of fear: that they would keep repulsing him until he got tired of trying and gave up. He would think they acted on her behalf and that she wanted to be rid of him as they did.

Maybe he would be in the bus shelter, waiting for her, like that first time. He wasn't and she felt a pang, as if she had lost something she valued. Holly phoned – the first time for a long while – to say she and Christopher were going clubbing and James was coming and would Francine like to join them. Her father would have let her go, provided he had known who she was going with and where, and he did know these people and approved of them, but her father had gone away that afternoon. If she made all kinds of promises to Julia permission would probably be given, but as she thought of those promises – to take taxis, to phone home, to stay with the others whatever happened, to be in by midnight, poor Cinderella that she was – she couldn't be bothered. Besides, she didn't really know James and wasn't sure whether she liked him or not.

Did she like Teddy? Some knowledge beyond her age and her experience whispered to her that if she had plenty to occupy her mind, lots of friends and interests and work, she would forget Teddy overnight. But she hadn't got those things, she had only an emptiness which he could fill. Already, without seeing him again or hearing his voice, she had dropped his surname in her thoughts and was calling him Teddy. Already, she was having silent one-sided conversations with him, telling him how she felt, how unfair things were for him and her – for

196

'us' – and forming an alliance with him against the world.

Although she knew Julia very well by now, Francine hadn't really believed that this idea of buying a house in Oxford would carry weight with her father. But it had. It did. Estate agents' specifications and brochures had begun to arrive and she was expected to give her opinion on this house and that.

In one way it seemed a good thing, for it meant that she would get to Oxford. They were serious about her going up to Oxford, they weren't humouring her or preparing the ground to tell her it was unwise or impractical or anything like that. She would get there. But in another way it was alarming. Julia would be an even nearer presence than she had been when she was at school, far nearer, on her doorstep if she had her way. If she prevailed and could obtain it – Francine knew this from the situations of these houses – she would buy a house opposite the college gates. The porter's lodge, thought Francine bitterly, if only it were for sale.

They had their day out in Oxford, viewing houses. Francine was repeatedly asked for her views and her preferences.

'It is just as important that you should like the place as that we should, Francine. You must say. This is one of those serious decisions in life people aren't usually called on to make at your sort of age. That's why we think it would be so good for you to confront it.'

Francine confronted it, but Julia's reply always was that the houses she liked were too far outside the city, too inaccessible. 'I for one am not going to live in Woodstock,' said Julia. 'But never mind. We'll call it a day. Maybe we should come back tomorrow.'

With the morning post came Francine's A-Level

197

results. Three passes to A. It was impossible to have done better. Holly had two As and a B and, jubilant herself, was gracious and lavish with her congratulations. Francine wanted to phone her father in Frankfurt and fetched him out of a meeting to speak to him, a move which made Julia click her tongue and call her hysterical. 'You really are the centre of your own little universe,' she said, but she said it abstractedly.

Also with the post had come a letter for her from a family member with the news that David Stanark was dead. He had hanged himself. If there had been anything in the papers about it Julia hadn't seen it. The letter said David's wife Susan had left him two months ago, he had been deeply depressed and threatened suicide, but no one had believed him. Julia felt very upset. She felt guilty, too, because she hadn't been in touch with Susan for a long while and, being Julia, she had this conviction that if only she had and could have talked to her and talked to David, appointed herself, in fact, their marriage-guidance counsellor, the entire tragedy could have been avoided.

Hanging oneself was such a dreadful way to do it. Why not pills and drink or even a car exhaust? It must have been, thought Julia in her psychological way, that he had so much self-hatred that he wanted to punish himself right up to the moment of death. But that final moment, that point at which the rope broke the hyoid or whatever it did – Julia didn't quite know what it did but the whole thing was hideous. She longed to tell Richard, to discuss it with him, but Richard was in Frankfurt.

Francine went off to New Departures. She had just two more weeks to work there before the crisis came. She could never be sure whether the trouble was her appearance or her moral character. To please Noele and not cause trouble with Julia she had steadily played down her looks and dressed more and more like someone middle-aged. She put up her hair in a knot, wore loose Dockers instead of jeans and although she had lately enjoyed enhancing her eyes with a little shadow and mascara, left it off. Noele still wasn't satisfied, but seemed unable to find further ways in which Francine might uglify herself.

A customer, angry when the waistband of an Armani trouser-suit she was trying on refused to meet round her middle, turned on Francine and accused her of anorexia. 'You obviously starve yourself,' she shouted, struggling with the tight trousers.

'I'm only eighteen and I'm naturally thin,' Francine said. She spoke coolly but gently, there was no indignation in her voice, but the customer, and then Noele, accused her of outrageous rudeness.

'How dare you imply that you're more attractive than one of my clients?'

Francine could think of a lot of answers to that, but she uttered none of them aloud. In silence she went to the workroom and fetched her jacket which hung on a hook behind the door.

'Where do you think you're going?'

'It was nice of you to take me on, Noele, but I obviously don't suit. And . . .' Francine drew a deep breath '. . . I'm afraid this place doesn't suit me. I won't take any money for this week. Goodbye.'

Noele flung open the door and called after her down the street, 'Julia will have your guts for garters, you little bitch!'

Strange that a woman like that could call Teddy vulgar. Francine ran all the way home, enjoying something she supposed must be freedom. Freedom! She had never had much of it. Julia opened the front door just before she got there. Noele must have been on the phone seconds after she uttered her abuse.

A fresh torrent began. Francine was ungrateful, lazy, egocentric, rebellious and immature. It was a blessing she was taking a year off as she was obviously unfitted to take part in the life of a great university, no matter how brilliant her A Levels. Her father would be so bitterly disappointed that she, Julia, dreaded having to tell him what had happened. And now she thought the best thing would be for Francine to go up to her room and spend the rest of the day there.

Francine sat down in an armchair. She said very calmly, 'Don't be silly, Julia.'

Julia stared. She put both hands up to her face, as if making a protective armour for it against a rain of projectiles.

'I am eighteen years old, I'm not a child. Of course I'm not going to my room till I'm ready.'

Julia's answer, a vain one, was to attempt a phone call to Frankfurt. Richard was out and all she got was the hotel's answering machine. She moaned something about Francine breaking her heart and her father's, and destroying her life. As if she wasn't upset enough with one of her best friends hanging himself, she said, and went out of the room and banged the door.

For form's sake Francine remained in her chair for ten minutes. Then, having listened for a moment to Julia's smothered weeping behind the kitchen door, she went upstairs to her room and found the mobile phone Julia had given her. It took a little while and a little studying of the instructions to learn how to use it, but after a moment or two she mastered its intricacies. Then she punched out Teddy Grex's number and waited. But there was no reply.

Chapter 20

A fumbling among the things on her dressing-table woke Harriet rather than any untoward sound from elsewhere in the house. In the half-dark she made out the figure of Franklin. He was holding the pole with a hook on one end that opened the fanlight.

'What's the matter?'

'Quiet,' he said. 'There's someone downstairs.'

The first time he said that to her in the middle of the night she had shrieked in fear. That was twenty years before. There hadn't been anyone downstairs on that occasion nor on the next or the next and, no doubt, there wasn't now. Franklin heard sounds that no one else did, he had the sort of tinnitus that was less a ringing in the ears than a buzzing and bumping. He also failed to hear sounds that others heard. Silly old man. She repeated the words scornfully to herself. Silly old man, silly old fool.

He had put on his camel-hair dressing-gown and tied the cord round his middle. He opened the bedroom door stealthily, pole in hand. Once, on a similar occasion, she had put on a light, which had made him grimace and punch the air and stamp in dumb show until he got darkness again. She heard the stairs creak as he went down them. No other sound until he gave his usual challenge, uttered in commanding officer tones. 'Don't move. Stay where you are. I am armed.'

After that, when he got no response – and he never

201

had got a response – he put on the lights. She switched on the bedroom lamps.

'I suppose you realise', she said when he came back again, 'that any burglar worth his salt could overpower you in two seconds. You're an old man.'

'I've no doubt you'd prefer me to cower under the bed while the intruder raped you,' said Franklin with a knowing grin.

She lay awake for a while. On the bedside cabinet beside her was the envelope containing Teddy Grex's drawings and his covering letter. She would phone him in the morning and ask him to come back and talk about the project. Of course there wasn't really a project, Franklin would have a fit if he thought some youth from Neasden intended building a cabinet in one of his Georgian alcoves and the whole thing wasn't feasible. None of that mattered because Harriet wasn't serious about it, the only one who was being Teddy Grex. Harriet would give him one more chance to understand her true intention and, if he didn't, give him and his drawings their marching orders.

But, perhaps because it was the middle of the night and things always look different at night, more hopeless and depressing, she told herself that she had made a mistake about Teddy Grex. It wouldn't be the first time. Her overtures had a failure rate of about one in four, for although she had entertained over the years young construction workers in such numbers that, banded together, they could by their combined efforts (as she sometimes thought with a giggle) have built and fitted up a hundred-acre housing estate, there had always been some who turned her down. There had always been one or two, or three or four, who rejected her because they were shy or newly married or gay or even faithful to a wife or girlfriend. It was possible, too, that some simply didn't find her attractive.

Into one of these categories it was likely that Teddy Grex came. If it was so it couldn't be helped. She slept after a while and woke to find Franklin standing by the bed with a piece of broken glass in his hand. The disturbance in the night had apparently been caused by someone in the mews throwing a stone over the wall and breaking one of the rear windows. Since the window was barred there had been no danger, only nuisance.

'Why show me?' said Harriet. 'I'm not going to mend it.'

'Perhaps I'm going to cut your throat.' Franklin laughed merrily to show he wasn't serious. 'You will have to find a glazier.'

'A what?'

'A man who fits glass into window frames.'

That was an idea. Failing Teddy Grex, a glazier. She contemplated herself in the mirror and felt quite pleased with what she saw. Phone Teddy, go to the hairdresser, maybe buy something new to wear in St John's Wood High Street. There wouldn't be time to go down to the West End or Knightsbridge. If Teddy agreed to come at, say, two, she could phone for a glazier at one-thirty. That way their visits wouldn't clash.

Franklin brought her tea and the newspapers. She had a sudden urge to ask him if he had been faithful to her, but what was the use of such a question? You either got a lie in response or the same enquiry cast back at you. She looked at herself in the mirror. Maybe there would be a glazier advertising in the *Ham and High*, she thought, watching herself opening the paper. Franklin got in her way, returning to his pockets handkerchief, keys, small change and folded cheque-book. She dodged round his head and back to see how white her skin was and how red her hair.

'Why are you always looking at yourself?' he said as if he had never asked before.

'I don't look at myself any more than anyone else.'

Franklin laughed. 'I'm off on my hols next week, may I remind you. So I'll want my stuff back from the dry-cleaners. You ought to have fetched it yesterday, I don't know why you didn't.'

'Are you going alone, Frankie?'

'Why do you ask? I never ask you.'

She pouted at her reflection. 'One of these days,' she said, 'you might come back and find me gone.'

'True.' He didn't really think it was true. 'And you might come back and find me gone.'

'What would you do if I just walked out?'

Franklin grinned. As is the case with many thin men when they grow old, his smile made a death's head of his bony face. 'Don't forget to phone a glazier,' he said.

Instead, when he had gone, Harriet phoned Teddy Grex. Two o'clock would suit him. What had she thought of the drawings? Harriet had scarcely looked at the drawings, but she said she would rather not give her opinion over the phone. That was what they would talk about when he came.

The hairdresser put a fresh application of Tropical Mahogany on to her hair, chatting the while about her grey roots which in places had become white roots. Harriet was relieved to see them all covered up in purple paste. In the shop next door she bought a pair of white palazzo pants and a white, pink and jade-green top, which she kept on, carrying the clothes she had been wearing home in the shop's bag.

Today there were no glaziers advertising in the *Ham and High*, but she found a great number in the

Yellow Pages, finally choosing one whose first name was Kevin. Kevins were usually a good bet, being mostly under thirty. This Kevin wasn't at home, so Harriet left a message on his answering machine which suited her very well. It would have been awkward if he had said he would come along immediately.

Her earlier feelings were aroused when she saw Teddy Grex once more in the flesh. A little thrill of excitement, the kind she used to feel when she was young, ran through her. He looked her up and down, but his expression was impossible to read. She liked to think he was attracted and admiring.

But again he refused a drink. The main thing was to look at the drawings together, he said, and decide on what she wanted. Harriet had left them upstairs on purpose. There had been some idea underlying this of getting him to follow her into the bedroom, but he let her go alone, his manner, she thought, growing colder and more distant by the minute. When she came down again he was standing by the broken window, looking out at the paved area, the back of the garage and the gate into the mews. 'How did that happen?' He indicated the broken pane.

'Someone must have thrown a stone in the night.'

He nodded. 'You want to get that boarded up.'

He didn't say why or offer to do it. She stood close beside him, pretending to examine the window. He bent down to pick up something from the floor. It was a pebble that long ago and on some distant beach the sea had worn smooth. Their heads brushed as she bent down and he straightened up. If anything could have told Harriet she was wasting her time his movement of recoil did. He sprang away, the stone clutched in his fist as if he meant to hurl it at her.

Flushing, for she was not totally thick-skinned, she sat down at the dining-table and spread out the drawings listlessly. Even someone less observant than Harriet, or less inclined to take an interest in people other than as sex objects, would have noticed Teddy's eyes light up at the sight of his own work and something that was almost adoration alter the whole expression of his face. But the adoration was plainly not for her and, besides, she was already humiliated and sore. She said suddenly, 'I don't really think so. These aren't what I want.'

The look he turned on her was not a nice one. Contempt was in it and a savage dislike. 'What?'

'I said this stuff isn't what I want.'

'It's what you asked for.'

'I can't help that. It still isn't what I had in mind. It's all *wrong*.' She was half enjoying herself now. 'These designs just aren't very good,' she said. 'I do know about these things. You've only to look around this house to see that. Your designs – well, they aren't up to the standard of the house.'

It was his turn to flush, but he didn't. He turned very pale and his long fingers, perfect but for one that was mutilated and deformed, closed into fists. He got up. Somehow she knew he wasn't going to speak another word to her and she was surprised when he did. His tone was brittle and icy. 'Can I go out the back way? I've left my car in the mews.'

'Go any way you like,' she said. 'It's all the same to me.'

She watched his departure as if she suspected him of stealing something on his way out. Not that there was anything to steal out of that little paved yard but a stone pot with a juniper in it and the white wrought-iron garden furniture, most of it too heavy to lift. He opened the gate, gave her a sullen look over his shoulder and went out into the mews, closing the gate behind him.

Harriet waited until she heard his car engine start

up. Then she went down to the gate and bolted it. The back of the house was even more thickly covered with that creeper than the front, its leaves reddening now. How many leaves would there be on this one plant? Millions – well, hundreds of thousands. Eleven Manvantaras and one Krita make one Kalpa, she repeated to herself. Thinking in this way wasn't like her. What did it matter how many leaves there were? She went into the house and to the nearest mirror to study her image.

Franklin had once told her, in their early days, catching her staring at herself, how no one ever sees themselves in a mirror as they really are. They always pout a little or raise the corners of their mouths or lift their chins, pull in their bellies, straighten their shoulders, open wide their eyes or soften their expressions to wistful idiocy. That was why it was absurd to look at oneself in the glass except to check quickly for neatness and make sure one's flies or skirt zip were not unfastened.

But she had gone on looking in spite of these remarks of his and as she looked now, she did all the things he had cited and more besides, half closing her eyes so that the lines about her mouth were blurred and putting up one hand to hide the parallel ridges that ran horizontally across her neck. In those conditions it was a pleasing picture that she saw, a woman absurdly young for fifty-odd, and while she was admiring herself the phone rang.

It was Kevin the glazier. Could he come tomorrow mid-morning? Gladly, Harriet said he could. He sounded about nineteen.

Chapter 21

They went to a pub. It was the nearest one to where Francine lived, a red-brick thirties roadhouse on a crossroads that looked huge from the outside but was quite small within, packed with fruit machines, smoky and noisy. He drank water and she drank orange juice.

He talked to her about the pub, how ugly it was, what an offence that such places could have been built, could still endure. They should be pulled down, all such places should be demolished, everything that was as hideous as this and things half-way as hideous should be flattened, bulldozed, razed to the ground. Only beautiful things should be allowed to exist so that everywhere one looked one's eye was pleased and one's senses satisfied.

She listened and nodded because he talked well and seemed to know about these things. And somehow she understood, if he didn't, that this was his way of courting her and that his praise of beautiful things was a displacement of his admiration for her.

'I wish I lived somewhere beautiful,' she said, 'but I don't. Do you?'

He didn't want her to see it – ever. He shook his head. A surge of anger rose in him as he thought how he had nowhere to take her that was fit for her, nowhere he wouldn't be deeply ashamed of.

'I did once,' she said and she thought of the

cottage whose prettiness was spoilt for her by what had happened there. 'Do you live at home?'

Where else could one live? Where one lived was home, wasn't it?

'With your parents, I mean?'

'My parents are dead.'

'I'm sorry,' she said. 'I know what that's like. My mother's dead.'

She would never tell him how her mother had died, she would never tell him about hiding in the cupboard and hearing the man come and the shot. Her friendship with him, if friendship it turned out to be, she would keep clear of that. She began talking instead of the year she was taking out before going to university, of the job she had had and of possible future jobs. He listened, he didn't ask. She had no means of knowing that it was her voice he listened to, the tone and timbre of it, her beautiful Champlaine School accent like an actress in a play on television, not her words or her meaning.

'I told her I was going out with a girlfriend,' she said. 'I said I was with my friend Holly. You remember my friend Holly?'

'Do I?'

'At the exhibition.'

'Yes,' he said, 'yes,' and added, 'She's a dog.'

Francine was shocked. 'She's not, she's very good-looking. Everyone says so. She's very attractive to men.'

'Seeing you with her', he said, and his voice was serious and intense, 'was like a – a princess and a toad!'

She laughed at that and after a moment he laughed too, a grim laugh as if he didn't express his feelings this way very often. They soon walked back, but on the way went into a little park and sat on a seat. It was a mild evening, not yet autumnal. Because he was silent and seemed to be waiting for her to speak she remembered why she had made that phone call to him in the first place. Because she needed someone to confide in and someone who was not one of those impatient school friends, someone new, someone who – and the word came strangely into her head – would treasure her. So, sitting beside him on this park bench in the dusk, she talked to him about the way Julia imprisoned her and acted the vigilante, watched her every movement and tried to worm her way into her heart and soul. And how she was afraid Julia and her father would finally close in upon her, find some way of confining her to indoors and prevent her going up to Oxford.

He didn't interrupt. He listened and sometimes he nodded. She expected solutions of the kind Holly and Miranda offered and she dreaded them, but he produced no answers. He was like what psychotherapists should be, listeners, receivers, absorbing everything the better to understand. Real ones, not the Julias of this world. When they walked on he took her hand and held it. No one, she felt, had ever performed for her such a much-needed gesture at precisely the right time.

If he had kissed her before they parted she would have been afraid and perhaps shocked. He didn't, but only said as if there could be no doubt about it, as if it were arranged and scheduled by some higher authority or by fate, 'I'll see you tomorrow then.'

'Where?' she asked him.

'Here. Right where we are now. Under these trees. At seven.'

Julia was waiting just inside the door. It swung open seconds before she reached it. There is always something ominous and almost sinister about a door opening before one has rung a bell or inserted a key in the lock. It suggests reproaches to come. And

210

reproaches there were. Julia said in a high voice, 'How did you get home? I didn't hear a taxi.'

'I walked.'

'Do you mean you walked from the tube station, Francine? You mustn't do that. Not after dark. You *know* that. I thought you were learning to be more responsible. If you haven't enough money on you for a taxi you only have to ask the driver to wait while you fetch me and I will pay him.'

Francine went up to her room.

Mrs Trent chose a sickly pale-green and a muddy ochre-yellow for her rooms. Teddy didn't like applying it to the walls, but he had to. It was his first lesson in understanding that if you work for other people for money you must do as they ask. Who pays the piper calls the tune.

He thought as he worked. Harriet Oxenholme had almost vanished from his mind except, occasionally, as a source of wonderment. That she could be the Harriet of Alpheton's painting still astounded him. A cause of greater concern was that he had left his drawings behind in her house. If he had been able to afford it he would have made photo-copies of those designs, but he couldn't and he hadn't. He wanted them back and he wanted to go to the house again.

Presumably, she lived there alone. No mention had been made of any other occupant. A kind of day-dream began to unfold in which he took Francine to Orcadia Cottage and the place was empty but for them. Harriet had gone away and left it to them. Francine was in the bedroom in that bed and he came up to her ... Teddy could hardly bear to pursue this fantasy, for all his strong young man's need and desire, so long unacknowledged, overcame him. His body became too much for him, the physical was all, and his mind nothing but a red heat and light.

He cooled himself, breathing deeply. This possession of Orcadia Cottage was something he mustn't think about, it was useless to dwell on the impossible. He must think about *using* the place, he must ask himself if the solution which occurred to him was a practicable one.

Home again, instead of relaxing he cleaned the house. In his eyes it still looked horrible. But where could he bring her if not here? If he had a car it would be easier, but with that thought he put away the vacuum cleaner and stationed himself at the french windows. The high, finned rump of the Edsel gleamed a deeper gold in the sunset light. Even if it were not burdened with its cargo of Keith he couldn't imagine her in it, her exquisite refinement in its vulgarity. The only future for the Edsel was to sell it and perhaps buy something less offensive with the money.

First the contents of the boot must go. His eyes fixed on the car, he thought how afraid he would be to open that boot. He admitted it to himself, he would be afraid. Six months had passed, seven, since that night. What had happened in that time? Decay, certainly, but what was decay? He remembered his grandmother approving cremation when his mother died, saying something about that way you wouldn't be eaten by worms. Were there worms in that plastic bag, or some kind of liquefaction or what? He felt the hairs rise on the back of his neck. He couldn't open that boot; yet he would have to open it.

An idea came to him of years passing, of the Edsel standing there for years on end, the boot never opened, of himself everlastingly watching over it until a decade or two had gone, and then one day lifting the lid to find a bagful of dry grey bones. It

212

was another version of his dream. He knew it could never be, he could never tie himself to this place for a lifetime. And what of her? What of bringing her here with *that* a few feet away from his bed?

He went out to meet her under the trees and took her to another pub. She wanted to know all about him, his childhood, his parents, his friends, the people he knew. Telling the truth about Jimmy and Eileen was impossible, but invention was beyond him. Instead, he told her about Keith and his cars, and the great car-makers who were his idols. She wanted to know where his uncle was now and he said, retired to Liphook, he had bought a bungalow in Liphook.

'And left his car behind? Won't he come back and fetch it?'

That nearly made Teddy shudder. Grey, bony Keith, in a stage of decay, lumbering in through the gates to drive away his car . . .

'I know Liphook quite well,' she said. 'My mother came from there. I've got relations there.'

A shadow seemed to pass across her face and he was glad of it, not interested in knowing the cause, only pleased that she wasn't pursuing the Liphook connection. He gazed in silence at her, the folded lips like a red flower, the big dark eyes, the black hair which, parted in the centre, fell in two smooth curtains on either side of her face. He might have taken her hand, but he was afraid to do it in case the touch of her was too much for him and he pulled her to him, seized her, there in front of these indifferent drinkers.

'About the mirror,' he said. 'The exhibition's over. Will you come with me to fetch it?'

'I won't be able to tomorrow or the next day, I'm sure I won't.'

'I'm talking about Saturday.'

'All right.' She thought for a moment, then said, like a much younger girl than she was, 'And then can I come and see your house and the crazy car?'

There was no help for it. He had to be alone with her and where else was there? He had to be alone with her and somehow make her want him as much as he wanted her. How to do that he seemed to have no idea. But standing with her under the trees, where they had parted last night and met this evening, he understood something that made things simple. When you are young and the other person is young and you are both good to look at, words are of no account, nor does cleverness or experience matter. Nothing more is necessary than to look. All you need do is look, then long, then touch. And what follows is an electric charge that brings you together into a desire each to be engulfed by the other, perhaps, even, to *be* the other.

Their kiss was a natural part of this. Kissing her, he didn't want to stop, he wanted to go on to a complete possession and without words he knew she felt the same. A tide seemed to break over them, a wave that threatened to drown them. It was he who broke apart, pushed her away and held her at arms' length, gasping while she gasped.

He stared into her eyes and she into his. They were both breathing like people who have run a race. He put his hands to her face, cupped it and murmured his goodbyes. Then he ran. He ran down the street towards the tube station as if fleeing something, as if instead of embracing a girl who wanted his kiss as much as he wanted to give it he had committed some violent assault and was escaping the consequences.

They had made no arrangements for Saturday. While he was wondering what to do she phoned him. Her father would be home at the weekend and had told her on the phone he wanted to take her and her stepmother on a visit to some friends in the country, but she had said she couldn't, she had this engagement with Isabel. Her stepmother had tried to persuade her to cancel, but she wouldn't, she had told her father she was too old to tag along on outings with him and Julia.

It was a world of which Teddy knew nothing. These people were beyond his comprehension. He asked Francine to meet him at the Tate Gallery and then he went off to Mrs Trent's to paint her living-room pale-green. His own house – he thought of it as his own, though without pride – was as clean as could be, everything neat, washed and scrubbed, the windows sparkling. But could he bring her there? He must. She should come for one visit while the Edsel and its boot contents stood outside those windows, but only one. After that, as soon as possible, he would do what had to be done. Then, and only then, the place would be truly clean and he free.

Chapter 22

The young man with the horrible voice was sitting in the bus shelter. He was there again, in spite of having been warned off by her and by Noele. Julia watched him from the window. She had to be sure he was the right one. By that, of course, she meant the *wrong* one, everything about him was wrong, his voice, his appearance, his manner, his insolence. But was he the one who phoned Francine, talked to Francine and called at Noele's?

If he had a car, why was he waiting in a bus shelter? That was easy, he wasn't waiting for a bus, but for Francine. He would have parked that car somewhere. Julia put on her coat and ran across the road, having to stop in the middle for cars going the other way to pass and hear a driver swear at her.

By this time the young man was standing up, pretending to read the bus timetable on the shelter wall. Julia sat down on the seat and studied him. She wanted to make sure she would know him again. His black hair was curly, which she hadn't noticed that first time, and his eyes were brown. Probably he was Asian or half Asian. The fact that he talked cockney meant nothing. No doubt he had been born here. He was dressed in a suit, dark blue with a pinstripe, and he had a white open-necked shirt on. A ridiculous combination, Julia thought.

She would have liked to ask him his name, but she

216

lacked the nerve. There was hardly anything Julia would not have done to save Francine and protect her from harm. Still, going up to a stranger and asking who he was daunted her. If the time came when she had to she would, but not now.

A complete picture of him imprinted on her memory, Julia walked round the corner into the street which turned off this main road just past the pedestrian crossing. She was looking for the young man's red sports car and she had to walk quite a long way before she found it. The street climbed up a fairly steep gradient and she climbed with it and on top of the hill she found a red sports car parked. It didn't surprise her, she had known it would be somewhere.

There was no one about. As is usually the case the street was populated with cars, not people. She walked round the car, looking in at the windows. On the dashboard shelf lay a brochure, a railway time-table and on top of them an envelope with an enclosure. The name typed on the envelope was Mr Jonathan Nicholson and the address was Fulham, SW6.

Julia returned home well-satisfied with her detec-tive work, but otherwise deeply troubled. She acknowledged to herself that Francine had won a great victory that day she left Noele's and for the first time, when told to go to her room, disobeyed. Since then she had gone out when she pleased, her only concession to authority that she still came home reasonably early. How had it happened? How had she allowed it to happen?

As surely as she knew her own name and where and who she was, Julia knew that through this freedom Francine had snatched for herself she would come to grief. It would be the ruin of her. She would be destroyed and if not die, eventually be confined in a psychiatric ward. Julia would do anything to avoid that.

Francine was up in her room. If only she, Julia, could just go up there and lock the door. Francine, after all, had her own bathroom, she wouldn't be put to any undue suffering. She could use the bathroom and get water. Julia imagined having a new door fitted to Francine's room with a window and a hatch in it. She had seen such arrangements in programmes about prisons on television. The hatch door could be opened and closed only from the outside. The aperture would be big enough for Francine's meals to be passed through. You read stories about people being shut up in their rooms by anxious parents and such incarcerations enduring for years. Julia had read them and thought such things outrageous, but now she was less sure.

The phone rang. It was her friend Laura who had won the Lottery. She and her husband were setting up a business on the proceeds, an hotel and restaurant, and hoped to open in a month's time. If Julia was still looking for a job for Francine, there might be an opening for a good-looking well-spoken girl as a receptionist. Julia thought of the people Francine would meet in such a situation, of how attractive she would have to make herself to the male guests, and she said a decisive no, trying to keep the shudder out of her voice.

She found herself pacing the floor. It happened a lot these days. The only benefit derived from it might be a weight loss but Julia was not losing weight, rather the reverse. She paced, not because she wanted to but because she couldn't keep still. Her restlessness wore her out. She often wished she smoked or had recourse to some other prop to the nerves.

After a while Francine came downstairs, wearing her black leather jacket and with her hair tied back. Julia asked her where she was going and Francine said, 'To the shops.'

Even a few months ago that could never have happened. Julia went upstairs and watched her departure from the bedroom window. She expected her to cross the road to where Jonathan Nicholson was waiting, but Nicholson had gone and the bus shelter was empty. Francine had remained on this side and was walking in the direction of the High Street. Julia left the window and went into Francine's bedroom. She had once been an honourable woman, but now had no compunction about searching Francine's room and prying into her things.

The mobile phone was there, on charge, plugged into a socket by Francine's bed. Bitterly, Julia saw that this object, which had been bought and bestowed to ensure the girl's safety and to keep tabs on her, now had its backlash. Because of it Francine could make private phone calls in secret. Julia opened drawers, looking for she hardly knew what. She found an address book and scrutinised it but, strangely perhaps, jibbed at looking inside Francine's engagement diary. A hot wash of shame flooded over her at the thought.

She went into Francine's bathroom, noticing how clean and neat it was. And this, obscurely, added to her discomfiture. But she opened the cabinet over the basin to see what was inside. Although she possessed a diaphragm, Julia had never taken oral contraceptives and didn't know what the pill looked like. The only item in the cabinet that might possibly be the pill turned out to be paracetamol. She had heard there were some brazen girls, that Holly, she was sure, who actually carried condoms about with them for their boyfriends' use, but those she would have recognised and there was none in Francine's room.

She closed the door behind her, found that she was shaking all over and going downstairs again, clinging to the banisters, poured herself a tot of brandy. This was almost unprecedented. Julia didn't drink. The brandy burned her throat and filled her head with fire. Food provided greater comfort. She went to the fridge and stuffed into her mouth a slice of cheesecake, a piece of pizza and some potato salad, devouring it in gulps as if speedy eating would lessen the quantity and its effects. She sat down on the chair in the hall, the one by the telephone. There, racked by the burning sensation of heartburn, she wrung her hands and moved her head from side to side.

Francine came back after she had been sitting there for about an hour. 'Is something wrong?' she said.

Julia stared at her and at the small gold studs in her ears. 'You've had your ears pierced!'

'That's right.' Francine smiled. 'About time, don't you think? My friends had it done when they were twelve.'

'I suppose you realise you'll get AIDS?'

'No, I won't, Julia. They use a fresh needle from a sterile pack.'

'I don't know what your father will say.'

Francine went upstairs. Still sitting in the hall, Julia wondered what she would do if Francine came down again and accused her of searching her room. Of course she would justify herself, she could do that, she had every right when it was a question of Francine's protection. But Francine didn't come and eventually Julia began to think that she should get

220

lunch for the two of them. She was as hungry as if she hadn't eaten that pizza and that cheesecake.

She pottered about in the kitchen, making a salad, cutting bread and almost cutting herself. Two o'clock had come and gone before it was on the table. Julia called upstairs in a tremulous voice and Francine appeared, looking calm and happy. She began talking about Holly, who was moving out of her parents' house and into a flat which she would share with another girl, and about Isabel's trip to Thailand.

Julia said, 'What are you trying to say, Francine?'

Francine looked at her in bewilderment.

'If you are hinting in a roundabout way that you should be allowed to do those things I wish you wouldn't, I wish you'd come straight out with it. I hate this deviousness. You've become very underhand lately, did you know that?'

Instead of getting up from the table and leaving the room, Francine forced herself to stay there and speak gently. 'Julia, I was making conversation, that's all. I thought it was interesting.'

'Please don't feel you have to make conversation with me.'

'All right. Let's leave it, shall we?'

They separated for the afternoon. Music could be distantly heard from Francine's room, Oasis and then Elton John. The sound of Richard's key in the lock brought Julia rushing out into the hall. He closed the front door behind him and she threw herself into his arms, crying and sobbing, beside herself with inexplicable grief.

Teddy was waiting for her on the steps of the Tate Gallery. She had wondered how to greet him, what she should do and what he would do. Would he kiss her? Embrace her? The memory of that long passionate kiss came back to her with a strange unfamiliar thrill of excitement. He surely wouldn't kiss her like that now.

She walked up the steps towards him. He smiled, held out his hand, took hers and pulled her to him. They stood close for a moment, looking into each other's faces. Then, 'Come on,' he said. 'I want to show you a picture.'

Marc and Harriet in Orcadia Place. She read it aloud from the description on the wall. 'Simon Alpheton,' she said. 'Didn't he paint a picture of a pop group?'

'They were called Come Hither,' said Teddy. 'The painting's called *Hanging Sword Alley.*'

She looked away, said in a troubled voice, 'My mother had a CD of Come Hither,' and then, 'No, it wasn't a CD, not then, it was a record. I broke it. I didn't mean to, but she was awfully upset. "Mending Love", it's called.'

He didn't see the tears in her eyes. He wasn't interested. No kind of music meant anything to him. 'What do you think of it?' he said, directing her attention once more to the girl in the red Fortuny dress, the boy in the blue suit, the house behind in its glowing cloak of green.

'I don't know anything about painting.'

He began explaining, recalling what Professor Mills had said, talking about its accuracy, its breadth of construction and Alpheton's treatment of light and shade.

For her there was only one thing to be noticed. 'You can see they were in love,' she said.

He made no reply. For a few more minutes he continued to gaze at the painting. Then, 'I wanted to show it to you,' he said. 'I've been to that house. With all the leaves. We'll go now. We'll go and fetch my mirror.'

Someone had packed it very carefully and boxed it in hardboard. She expected him to have a taxi to take them and the mirror to his house, she was used to taxis, but they took the bus to Sloane Square station and then the tube. He wouldn't let her help him with the mirror. She could see by the ease with which he carried it that he was very strong.

'My dad and my stepmother have gone out for the day to friends,' she said. 'I wouldn't go. I wanted to be with you.'

'It's a dump I live in. I'm warning you, so don't be surprised.'

But it wasn't a dump. It was the cleanest, neatest place she had ever been in. Everywhere was painted in soft, pale colours, the windows shone, the floors, of plain wooden boards, had been stained and waxed. Of furniture there was very little, most of it being in the downstairs front room, where clean faded cotton curtains hung at the window. Teddy's drawings, in black frames or frames of natural wood, hung on the walls, designs for the mirror, designs for a table, line-and-wash representations of great houses, pastels of statuary. On the table, spread out, portrait drawings.

'You are very clever,' she said. 'Those drawings are me, aren't they?'

'Yes.'

'No one ever drew me before.'

She went into his own room where his bed was and the coffee table he had made and his bookends, where his tools were and where the flaring rump of the Edsel pressed up against the window.

'Can we go outside and look at it?'

'If you like.'

She didn't find the car ugly. Her enthusiasm for it seemed to him to open a gulf between them. The pouting mask that was its bonnet made her laugh. She walked round the car, admiring its size and its colour, but when she laid her hand on the boot lid he couldn't restrain himself.

'Don't touch it!'

He had spoken so roughly that she pulled her hand away as if the yellow metal had burnt her. 'I'm sorry, I didn't mean ...'

'It's dirty,' he said. 'I don't want you to get dirt on you.'

While she was looking at the rest of the house he unpacked the mirror. She came downstairs and went into the front room and there it was, propped on a chair. He said, 'It's for you.'

'Oh, no, I couldn't!'

'I want you to have it. You must have it.'

He put his arm round her and led her to the mirror. She remembered what he had said about giving it to his woman for her to see her face in. A deep blush spread across her cheeks and up to her forehead. She looked at the blush in the mirror, at her fiery face, her shining eyes, and then she turned to him.

He kissed her, the way he had under the trees. He pulled her down on to the settee. Her body felt weak and a wave of heat came over her as if it were a hot summer's day.

'I've never done this before,' he said.

'Nor have I.'

He took the white dress off her. He pulled her underclothes off as if he disliked them, as if they were too functional. She covered her breasts with one arm, laid her other hand across her pubic hair, then seeming to realise the absurdity of it, pulled her hands away and showed him. He was trembling, she could actually see him shake. She wrapped him in her arms and lay down with him.

'You must show me how to do it right,' he whispered.

'But I don't know myself.'

Then she found she did know.

'Like this – is that right? And this? Tell me.'

'Yes, oh, yes . . .'

'And if I kiss you there, is that all right? And do this?'

But she was becoming aware, without knowing what rightness would be, that this wasn't right. His hands had been eager and his mouth urgent, but there should be more to it than the tender touch of fingers and the warm probing of a tongue. She knew very well what there should be and it wasn't this limp shrinking of the flesh, the yielding of his body into apathy. Her own warm wetness – unexpected this, no one had told her of this – dried and cooled. He muttered something. She thought he had said, 'I can't.'

'It doesn't matter.' Only it did, rather a lot. She found herself supplying excuses for him, not knowing that these were the kind woman's reassurances uttered since time immemorial. 'You're tired, it's been a strain. I know it has for me too. All this hiding and tension, and having to be secret. It will be different next time.'

Richard and Julia cancelled their lunch engagement. They had planned to drive down with Francine into Surrey to visit Roger and Amy Taylor. Roger Taylor, Richard and Jennifer had all been at university together, but Roger had married much later than his friends, not until after Jennifer's death, and Jennifer had never known his wife. She, however, had joined the number of Julia's women friends. Julia had been looking forward to seeing Amy, though she hadn't, in her own words, 'much time' for Roger, but even the prospect of half a day with her friend couldn't be

225

contemplated when it was a question of Francine's safety.

'We shall be back here before she is,' Richard said. 'She has a key. You know what they're like at that age, she'll only come in and go straight up to her room. She may as well do that on her own, she doesn't need us there.'

But Julia put forward all sorts of arguments against this. Suppose 'something happened' to Francine, her friends or the police or the hospital wouldn't know where to find her parents. Then there was the danger of this boy. Julia had told her husband all about this boy, how she had seen him several times waiting for Francine in the bus shelter, and how she had found his car with his name and address on an envelope on the dashboard shelf.

'Why was he waiting for a bus if he has a car?' said Richard.

'I've told you. He wasn't waiting for a bus. He was waiting for Francine.'

'You actually saw him meet Francine? You saw her get in his car? Is that what you're saying?'

Julia shook her head in exasperation. 'I am afraid I think it quite possible Francine may bring him here while we are out.'

'What are you suggesting, Julia?'

'She's human, isn't she? She's young.'

'Not Francine,' said Richard. 'She wouldn't do anything like that.' But he phoned Amy Taylor and cancelled their visit, wincing when she was abrupt with him and when she asked why he couldn't have let her know sooner. 'You don't really believe Francine would – well, have relations with this boy, do you? Anyway, I thought she had gone out for the day with Isabel What'shername. Hasn't she?'

'I don't know,' Julia said tightly. 'Why ask me? She never speaks to me.'

226

'Julia, Francine couldn't handle anything like that. She may be old in some ways, but in others she's very young for her age. You don't really think she would let him ...?'

'Fuck her?' It was an expression Julia had never in her life used before. She had barely heard it used except on the television. But she uttered it in a vicious snap and saw her husband gasp. 'Why not?' she said. 'She's unstable, we've always known that. People like her, traumatised people, they've no moral sense and they're over-sexed, it's a well-known fact. Of course she'd let him ...'

'For God's sake, don't use that word again!'

They spent a miserable day. There was very little food in the fridge, Julia had eaten it all, so since she refused to leave the house, Richard had to go shopping. He came back and attempted to watch Rugby Union on television, but Julia came in and switched off the set, saying that he was heartless to amuse himself like this when she was beside herself with anxiety. Pacing had become habitual with her, but he had never before seen her pace. It taught him that this nervous habit is one of the most irritating and upsetting one human being can contemplate in another. He shut himself in their bedroom and lay on the bed to get away from it and he longed for Tuesday when he was due to get on a mid-morning flight to Frankfurt.

It wasn't late when Francine came home. She was probably the only girl from her class at school who arrived home by ten that Saturday night.

She hadn't wanted to come. She hadn't wanted to leave Teddy and would have loved above all things to have stayed the night with him. He wanted that too. In both their minds was the same thought. If she stayed it would be all right, she would be receptive

227

again, he would make love to her. But the difference was that he couldn't understand that she had to go and tried physically to hold her back.

'I have to,' she said. 'I know you don't understand and I don't know how to make you. It's just a fact. I have to go home.'

'I'll come all the way with you. I'll bring the mirror.'

Then she had to explain that she couldn't take the mirror. Not even if she had a taxi all the way. The mirror was something she couldn't explain to Julia and her father. Julia was capable of breaking it. He understood that, she saw a kind of shadow cross his face at the prospect.

'You keep it for me. I'll see it when I come to see you.'

She phoned for a taxi. It amazed him that she had that kind of money. While they waited for it he ironed her white dress for her, for he said he couldn't bear to see her in anything creased. On the front-garden path, watched from an upstairs window by the neighbours he called yuppies, he kissed her so long and so intensely that the cab driver shouted at them to give over as he hadn't got all night.

Francine sat shivering in the back of the cab. So much had happened that she felt almost as Julia constantly forecast she must feel, that life could swiftly overpower her. Almost, but not quite. And when she was home and had paid the driver, she found herself walking quite calmly up to the front door and letting herself into the house as serenely as if she had really made love and had triumphed and been gloriously satisfied.

It was Julia who disturbed her equilibrium by rushing out into the hall and throwing her arms round her, burying a tear-drenched face in Francine's shoulder. 'Oh God, oh God, you're home! Thank God you're home.'

For a moment Francine was afraid. Some chord from the past had been struck. 'It's not Dad, is it? Something hasn't happened to Dad?'

A voice that was both weary and cheerful – perhaps a forced cheerfulness – greeted her from the living-room. 'I'm in here, darling. I'm fine.'

Had he ever called her darling before? She couldn't remember. But when she looked into Julia's wet, crumpled face she didn't like what she saw there. Many times before in her thoughts, and once or twice to Holly and Miranda, she had lightly called Julia mad. Now she knew that in saying it she hadn't known, until this moment, what madness was.

Chapter 23

In his dream the mirror ceased to be a mirror and became a framed portrait. By some curious chemical or magical process, because Francine had looked into it so many times, her image was imprinted and fixed inside the glass, it was now a picture of her. His own face wasn't reflected back at him. He looked at hers and worshipped.

But that was the good dream. In the bad dream she laid her small white hand on the boot lid of the Edsel and the substance of which it was made, the gleaming lemon-coloured metal surface, melted and dissolved like soft butter. Her hand passed through and reached down, down, into grey decay and wet vile putrefaction ... Teddy awoke, shouting so loudly that when, later, he went outside to the dustbin, Megsie put her head over the fence and asked him what was going on. She and Nige had heard this awful scream in the night, they'd thought someone was being murdered.

'Not this time,' said Teddy.

'Don't you make a habit of it, will you? It was touch and go Nige and me didn't call nine nine nine.'

Francine had been to the house four times and every time he thought of what was in that boot and of her proximity to it, of her beauty and perfection, and of that horror. The time had come to do something. She wasn't coming over until the afternoon. At ten in the morning he went up to Orcadia Place.

The house looked different. For a moment he couldn't decide in what respect. Then he understood that autumn had come. The leaves that canopied the house, back and front, were changing colour, from green to a gingery gold or to a reddish purple. The creeping tendrils were the soft, delicate pink of a rose. Without knowing anything about gardens or gardening or plants, he realised that there had been frosts and he saw that Harriet Oxenholme (or her gardener) had cut down the flowers or uprooted them, that the earth in the tubs was fresh and the earth in the borders turned and newly planted. A lover of order and neatness, he almost preferred this spruce look to the wild abundance of blossom.

He rang the bell. The first thing he noticed when she opened the door was the two suitcases standing in the hall, a blue one and a black one, each with an airline's label attached to its handle.

She frowned at him. 'I thought you were someone else. What do you want?'

'My drawings,' he said. 'I left them here.'

She was dressed, in his grandmother's phrase, 'up to the nines'. The long silvery grey skirt and fine silver knitted top would have looked good on Francine. It had been designed for someone under twenty-five and the low boat-shaped neckline, which would have shown off the tops of Francine's smooth white breasts, showed her brown, scrawny, freckled chest. Her fingernails were painted silver and there was some kind of sparkling greasy substance on her mouth. Teddy looked a little away and repeated what he had said. 'I left my drawings here. Can I come in?'

'What drawings?' she said.

'The designs for the cupboard you said you wanted.'

'My God, you don't suppose I kept them?'

He said hoarsely, 'You burnt my drawings?'

'Of course I didn't burn them. What century are you living in? I put them out for recycling.'

He had counted on getting into the house and on doing what he had done before, departing by the back way and leaving the back gate unbolted. That was impossible now. And she had destroyed his drawings! He would have liked to kill her. But his eye fell once more on the two suitcases. She was going away. And soon, by the look of it. He said no more, but turned away, refusing to look back even though he could tell she was still there, she hadn't closed the door.

A van had drawn up outside. On the side of it was lettered: G. Short, Water Softener Maintenance. A man of about Teddy's age, tall, dark-skinned, got out of the driver's cab. Teddy ignored him. He made his way round to the mews at the back and tried the gate. Of course it was bolted on the inside.

But she was going away. If not today, tomorrow. If not tomorrow, soon.

Rooting among Keith's papers, he found on a brochure the name, address and phone number of a dealer in Balham from whom Keith had bought the Edsel. The company was called Miracle Motors. It was probably too much to hope that they would buy it back for the same sort of money. But would they buy it at all?

He phoned them. Rather to his surprise they said that they would like to see the car and when could he bring it. Not today, he thought, and not tomorrow. How about Friday? They said Friday would be fine and he managed to tell them the Edsel was in excellent condition just as they rang off.

Before he drove it to Miracle Motors he ought to

clean it, wash, wax and polish it, and buff up the chrome. He walked out into the garden and examined the Edsel for possible scars and scratches, but there was none. It was in as perfect condition, its bodywork as glossy and unmarked, as on that day in 1957 when it had come off the Ford assembly line, a ton and a half of pristine metal and glass that, though forty years old, seemed to have been endowed with the secret of eternal youth. He thought it strange that something so sleek and cared-for, so carefully designed and lovingly made, should also be so ugly.

Bending over the boot, his hands resting on those gull's-wing tail-lights, he tried to detect if there was any smell. And when he brought his face close to the rim of the boot lid where it met the bodywork a slight whiff of something distantly horrible came to his nostrils. He thought 'distantly' because it seemed far away, no more than a hint of horror, yet it wasn't distant, it was only inches from him. He sniffed again and there was nothing, he had imagined it.

The idea of Francine in the car's vicinity disgusted him. He had even suggested they meet somewhere near where she lived, go to a park, go to the cinema, have a meal. But she had wanted to come to him, be alone with him. And as for him, he could hardly bear the prospect of being with her yet unable to touch her. She must come and this time he must succeed in making love to her, this time there must be no ignominious failure. It was the presence of the Edsel that enfeebled his flesh, he was sure of it, for nothing else could account for failure when desire was so great.

All he could do was keep her out of his room where the Edsel's rear end filled the lower half of the windows. It reminded him of something he had once seen on television, in a wildlife programme: a huge ape turning its back on an enemy and rearing up its rump in a gesture of derisive contempt.

Sometimes he felt that about the Edsel, that because of its size and its colour, and its dreadful contents, it was mocking him.

Even Megsie, looking at it one day from the bottom of her garden, had commented with a giggle, 'That Elgin's got a sort of face, hasn't it?'

'Edsel,' said Teddy.

A pursed mouth, wide-set eyes, sideburns ... He shut his own eyes and turned his back on the car before opening them again. She probably wondered why he didn't use the Edsel, come to Neasden tube station in it to meet her for instance, instead of going down there on foot. There was no explanation he could think of. She would have to wonder, very likely she wouldn't ask. The Edsel would soon be gone, out of the way, forgotten, and maybe he'd get enough money to buy a small modern car, something with elegant lines in a quiet, dark colour ...

He saw her before she saw him. She came out of the station rather tentatively, almost shyly, looking for him. Jeans today and a blue shirt. He was disappointed. Not deeply disappointed, but simply taken aback because he thought of her always in dresses, totally feminine, delicate, a princess.

Concealed in a doorway, he watched her. She stopped still and waited for him. His eyes took in the exquisite modelling of her head, its shape enhanced rather than hidden by water-straight fine black hair that lay on it like a veil, the slight angularity of her shoulders, the narrow span of her waist, the slender length of her legs and the arch of her insteps. The idea came to him that he would like to keep her with him always to look at, never let her out of his sight, touch her but not speak to her, undress her and dress her again in fine linen or a Fortuny dress that was not red like Harriet Oxenholme's but pure white.

She had been looking, with a touch of bewilderment, in his direction. When she turned aside he came out from his hiding-place and called her name. 'Francine!'

Her smile and the flush that came to her cheeks transformed her face. Briefly, he thought that he liked her better snow-pale and grave. He put his arms round her and kissed her mouth, the kiss beginning lightly but becoming intense, deep, searching.

She broke away first, but unwillingly and only to say, 'Can we go to your house?'

'Where else?'

'It was just that you said something about the cinema or having a meal.'

'I've got food in,' he said, 'and I've got wine for you. Let's go.'

Dilip Rao stayed so long at Orcadia Cottage that Harriet became apprehensive. Franklin had signified his intention to come home early. He had a few last-minute tasks to perform before driving himself to the airport. Dilip was virile and ardent and only twenty, and seemed to see no reason why he and Harriet shouldn't remain in the four-poster till the following morning. He didn't listen while she explained and eventually she had to get up, pull the covers off him and dump his clothes on his naked body. He left at twenty-past four and Franklin came home at half-past.

While he made those phone calls that were apparently essential before he could leave the country, hurling cushions on to the floor before perching on the sofa arm, Harriet sat in the kitchen. She brought herself round from a sex and alcohol daze with a strong cup of tea. Dozing earlier, she had fallen into a premonitory dream, not rare with her but still upsetting. These omens were nearly always fruitless, the events they forecast, death, disaster, loss of income, crippling or fatal disease, seldom if ever came to pass, but still they left behind them a feeling of disquiet. She couldn't get out of her head the whispering voice that had uttered 'Last time, last time', though whether it had referred to some previous occasion or to a final instance she couldn't tell.

But it left her wondering if it could have meant she had entertained a young lover for the last time or had sex for the last time or would shortly be seeing – saying goodbye to – Franklin for the last time. There was always the possibility of his not coming back from one of these holidays of his, of his remaining with the woman who had been his companion. If there was a woman – how was she to know?

She was suddenly stricken with a sense of loneliness. Once Franklin came back she would be taking her own holiday, her second of the year, they always took two holidays each, but still the fortnight ahead stretched very emptily. Dilip would come back, of course, would probably not even wait to be invited, but Harriet was not at all sure she wanted to see Dilip again.

Franklin came into the kitchen to ask her if she had seen the going of his luggage strap.

'It's in your wardrobe. On the top shelf. Frankie, why don't I come with you?'

'Because we take separate holidays,' he said. 'Always have, always will.'

'You mean you don't want me.'

'Go up and get that luggage strap for me, will you?'

Harriet went.

After he had brought the car round, put his suitcases into the boot and driven away, she picked up the cushions and started phoning people, acquaintances, the few they called their friends. For a long time now she had noticed that in a marriage or a partnership, when the woman goes away offers flood in to entertain the man and have him to dinner. Things are very different when the one left behind is the woman. No one invites her anywhere and she is lucky not to be ignored completely.

Although she had long ago lost touch with Storm and Anther and Zither, she knew where to find them. They had reverted to their true names, become respectable and set up a company doing market research. Storm had married Zither and Anther had the top flat in their house in Brondesbury. Fourteen Manvantaras and one Krita make one Kalpa, Harriet thought to herself as she listened to the dialling tone. Then Zither's voice came on, saying they had all gone to Hanoi, which Harriet guessed was their idea of a joke, meaning merely that they were down at the pub or possibly in Bournemouth.

Simon Alpheton came into her head. She had looked up and her eye alighted on his painting, the still life which that little bugger Teddy Grex had admired. The oranges and the cheese, and the white mouse looking at it so longingly. Simon lived in Fulham and probably alone. Harriet had read about his divorce in the papers. It was an 0181 number she had for him in her book. If you lived in London you *had* to have an 0171 number, Harriet had long decided, anything else meant you lived in the sticks, an 0181 number was as bad as not having a W in your postcode. But Simon was different, Simon was the exception.

A certain amount of courage had to be plucked up before she phoned him. I am his Jewish Bride, she told herself, his red-headed lady in Orcadia Place, rich and loved. 'Maybe I'll buy it,' she had said while he was painting, and Marc had said, 'What with?' She took a deep breath and dialled the number.

Simon Alpheton sounded genuinely pleased to hear from her. She reminded herself that he was something she hadn't often come across in her life, a nice guy. He asked her to have dinner with him on the following night.

'I've got something for you,' Teddy said.

'You've already given me something,' said Francine. 'You've given me the mirror.'

'You sit there and look in the mirror and I'll go and fetch it and put it on you.'

It was several weeks since he had looked at the ring. Now he saw that it was even more beautiful than he remembered. It was beautiful enough for her. He held it in his left hand, in his fist, and went downstairs to her.

It was past dusk and he had the lights on, but only a single lamp in the front room. She wasn't facing the mirror, as he had instructed her, but had her back to it. He felt a little spark of irritation, a feeling similar to what he had had when he saw those jeans and that shirt. At least she wasn't wearing them now but was wrapped, as he had wrapped her, in the dozen metres of stone-coloured silk he had bought to make curtains out of.

'Turn round,' he said.

She obeyed him, but smiling. He didn't want her to smile.

'Gaze at yourself,' he said. 'There isn't anything in the world better worth looking at. No, don't smile!'

He stood behind her, put his arms over her shoulders, took her hand and set the ring on it. Her

238

third finger was too little for its circumference. She would have to wear it on the middle finger.

'It's beautiful,' she said. 'I can't take it.'

'Yes, you can. You must. I've been saving it for you. I've been saving it for years.'

'But you haven't known me for years!'

'I've known you were somewhere, my perfect woman, waiting for my ring.'

He laid his hands on her shoulders, tucking in his damaged little finger so as not to spoil the image. She looked at the ring, then at herself in the glass, then up at him. He kissed her.

'I can't take it.'

'Then I won't let you go. I'll keep you here.'

'But it's an *engagement* ring.'

'It's a lover's ring,' he said, and then she said she would take it and wear it.

It was time for her to go home. He unwrapped the silk and let it fall in a pale shining heap on the floor. The awful clothes she intended to wear offended him. He would have liked to keep her naked, a living statue, for him to adore. But she put on the jeans and the shirt and a wool cardigan, the same one that she had worn when he folded back the sleeve and wrote his phone number on her wrist. He lifted her hand and admired the ring.

It was dark now, after nine, and he wouldn't let her go on the tube alone.

'Couldn't you take me in your car?'

'I hate it,' he said. 'I never use it. I'm going to get rid of it and buy a small one.'

So he went with her on the tube down to Bond Street and changed with her on to the Central Line and left her only when they were under the trees near her house. All the way, in the trains, he kept his arm round her, holding her close, and holding too the hand that wore the ring.

Chapter 24

Midnight was past by the time he got back. He tidied up the house, washed her wineglass and the plates and cups they had used, put the rest of the wine back into the fridge. It was careless of him to have left that silk lying in a heap on the front-room floor. The result would be creases he might have difficulty in eradicating. He folded the silk once and then once again and hung it over the banisters.

Lying in bed he thought about Francine as she had been, seated in front of his mirror, swathed in stiff silk, her reflected face looking gravely back at her real face. She must easily be the most beautiful girl in the world. A sight for sore eyes. Alfred Chance had once used that expression and it had stuck in his mind. About an object, though, not a person. It meant that looking at beauty took away pain and hurt, and made you better. Francine made him better and his eyes were sore when they couldn't feast on her.

He had never seen anyone to touch her. But there must be changes made, in his life and hers and the way they were together, and in the places they lived in. For one thing, he wanted her with him all the time. And dressed the way he wanted her to be, not in that hideous denim, that blue cotton, those boots. He began to think, not of Alpheton now and the Joyden School, but of Gustav Klimt and the women he painted in glittering gowns of lamé and sequins or velvet and fur, the jewels that hung in heavy ropes round their necks or supported swathes of their hair. He would like to dress Francine like a Klimt woman and decorate her with necklaces and bracelets and collars of pearls. And live with her somewhere beautiful, a fit setting for her.

On that thought he fell asleep and slept late next morning. He was up and counting what remained of the advance payment he had had from Mrs Trent before he remembered that today was the day. Today, or this evening, was when he was going to do it. But still he counted the money and found that he had something under a hundred pounds left.

There had been no more replies to his advertisement and he had decided not to re-insert it. He couldn't afford to advertise – or, for that matter, not to advertise. The Edsel, what he got for the Edsel, was his only hope. Surely prices must have risen in all the years since Keith had bought the car. Might it now be worth as much as ten thousand pounds?

He filled a bucket with hot water, got his sponges and cloths and brushes, and went outside to clean it. Nige, who never went out to work these days but did it all from home on a computer and a modem and e-mail and things like that, put his head over the fence. Megsie had told him she'd seen Teddy's girlfriend and she was a real looker and next time she came round would Teddy like to bring her in for a drink? Teddy said, maybe. He thought Nige would go indoors again, but he didn't. A white cane garden chair was brought out of Mr Chance's workshop that they called the 'pavilion' and Nige sat down in it, enjoying the Indian Summer.

Teddy was polishing the windscreen when a tap on the french window made him jump. His grandmother was standing in his room, looking out, wearing her red sugarloaf hat and with a heavy bag of shopping on either side of her. He hated her having a key, but she had had one since his mother died. For all he knew she had taken it off his mother's body, she was capable of that. He knew no way to get it from her. She opened the french window and came out. 'Keith not back yet, then?' she said.

'He's not coming back.'

'You'd think he'd want his car. What does he get about in? Relies on that motor bike, does he?'

'No, he doesn't,' came Nige's voice. 'He got Teddy here to sell that to one of our chums.'

'Who asked you to put your spoke in,' said Agnes under her breath. But Teddy thought she gave him a funny look. They went into the house together and Agnes insisted on going all over it, admiring the decorating he'd done since she was last there. She looked at the stone-coloured silk hanging over the banisters and said there was a good chance her pal Gladys would run up a pair of curtains for him in exchange for him painting her outside toilet.

On the arm of a chair in the front room she found a fine black hair, a good eighteen inches long. For someone in her eighties she had miraculous eyesight. 'Who's been here, then?'

'My girlfriend,' said Teddy and, liking the sound of it, said it again. 'My girlfriend.'

For some reason that struck Agnes as uproarious and she started laughing. 'You take her about in that car, do you?' she said.

'I'm driving it down to Keith in Liphook tomorrow,' said Teddy coldly.

'Right,' said Agnes. 'I thought something must account for you cleaning it. You're not famous for doing things for other people unless there's anything in it for you. He paying you, is he?'

Teddy got rid of her as soon as he could and

242

returned to polishing the Edsel. At lunch-time Megsie came home, bringing four other yuppies with her, and they all stood about in the garden drinking Buck's Fizzes and calling over the fence every five minutes for him to join them. ('Leave that old Edwin, why don't you?' as Megsie put it.) Cleaning the car thoroughly took Teddy all of three hours and he still, naturally, had done nothing about the interior of the boot.

In the afternoon Francine phoned him on her mobile. They had made no arrangement to see each other that day, but they would meet again on Friday. He hadn't much to say to her, the things his head was full of were not for her to hear and the things she had to tell him, about her stepmother and some job her stepmother didn't want her to take, didn't interest him. But he loved the sound of her voice. He could have listened to it all day even if it had been speaking a foreign language.

If he got a sizeable sum for the Edsel maybe he could find a place for them with the money. Rent a flat in some nice place, a flat with gorgeous rooms in it like the ones in Orcadia Place. He imagined a drawing-room with glass doors giving on to an Italian garden, surrounded by evergreen trees with dark-green pointed leaves, tubs on the paving stones full of lilies and cypresses. A stone seat, a round pond with goldfish, bronze dolphins whose spouting mouths made a fountain. Francine would sit on the seat in her white Fortuny dress, trailing one hand in the clear water . . .

At seven in the evening he phoned Harriet Oxen-holme. The answering machine replied, Harriet's voice uttering a bare sentence, none of your detailed or facetious stuff, but simply repeating the number and saying, 'Would you like to leave a message?'

He would not. He was satisfied that she had gone

away. It was necessary to wait till it was dark, but not till the midnight hours. One terrible difficulty remained and one uncertainty. Should he open that boot and look inside before he left? Or wait until he was up in the mews behind Orcadia Place? He understood now that in some half-unconscious part of his mind, some subliminal region, he had been asking himself that question all day. Under the fantasies of Francine and the Italian garden, under the plans for selling the Edsel and finding a place for him and her to live, had lain that question.

If he opened the boot lid here, there was always the possibility of Nige and Megsie looking out of an upstairs window and seeing the contents. Perhaps, of course, seeing no more than the plastic bag, a grey shiny *thing* tied up with masking tape. But would a smell be released? That was what he had to think of, the chance of a smell. If Nige and Megsie would only go out, he would be safe to do it, but he knew they weren't going out. Throughout the course of the afternoon, the Buck's Fizz drinking, the comments on the Indian Summer and eventually the alfresco eating of deep-pan pizzas, he had several times heard them say they intended to put their feet up and watch their *Trainspotting* video. He dared not open that boot with them only yards away.

But to go to Orcadia Place without knowing what he would find when he eventually opened it? His imagination, always powerful, pictured for him a sodden mass, something like the contents of a drain he had once seen when walking past roadworks, grey, wet, like mud yet full of sticks and stones. There might be powerful acids in a body that could eat through plastic. It was eight months now since Keith had died.

In the end he made a decision and at ten, when their lights showed him that Nige and Megsie were in their front room, watching their video, he got into the driver's seat of the Edsel and turned on the ignition. He had to make several attempts before the engine would fire and he realised that cars had batteries and batteries could go flat. Still, it was all right. He reversed out of the carport, turned and emerged through the double gates into the street.

A nasty moment was when the curtains parted in the front-room window next door and Megsie waved to him. He waved back, making a sort of salute. Not for the first time he wondered what it was those two wanted of him, why did they seem to like him when he had repulsed every overture they made?

The night was dark and moonless, but bright up here with white and yellow chemical light. He drove down one of the roads that border Gladstone Park and there, with open space and shady trees on one side and houses fairly distant on the other, he parked and got out of the car. No one was about. Most of the houses were well lit but some only had lights on in upstairs rooms. He walked to the back of the car and stood looking at the boot lid.

In those moments he was there he asked himself if even now it might be possible just to ditch the Edsel, drive it somewhere out in the country and dump it in a wood or on the edge of a field. Who would know whose car it was or whose the body in its boot was? But it wasn't as easy as that. Megsie and Nige would know. His grandmother would. Miracle Motors would. The police would enquire of the car dealers, of all London dealers in that kind of car, if not of the others. And, anyway, if he dumped the car he wouldn't be able to sell it and get his five, or maybe ten, thousand pounds.

He put the key into the boot lock and turned it. His hand rested for a little while on the chrome clasp of the boot lid just above the number plate. Then he opened it quickly. He shut his eyes, lifted the lid and opened his eyes.

Nothing was changed.

Inside the boot it looked exactly the same as it had when he closed the lid eight months before. As far as he could tell in the not very strong light. He had been consciously not breathing in, or, rather, breathing only through his mouth. Now he drew the air in through his nostrils. There was no smell, nothing. He began to feel sick, nauseous, even though there was no smell. He bent over a little, approached nearer, and then there came to him, as if from a far-distant charnel house, borne on a gust of wind, a faint dreadful breath.

Quickly he closed the lid. He locked it. He got back into the car and drove off towards the Edgware Road. The Edsel attracted a lot of curious or admiring glances while he was stopped at lights. Someone crossing the road behind him, weaving his way through the cars, slapped the boot lid with the flat of his hand. A shudder ran through Teddy.

From Hall Road he turned into the mews. Here the street lamps were the old-fashioned kind, up-ended lanterns on black-painted iron posts, and there were only two of them. As far as he could tell, all the garage doors were shut and all the gates. Two cars only were parked. It was Saturday night and people were either out or had gone to their places in the country.

He parked the Edsel with its rear end up against the double doors of the Orcadia Cottage garage. Climbing over the gate or the wall to unbolt the gate would be easy, but he dared not take the risk. It was one thing to be seen pulling a bag of something out of a car boot and moving it in through an open gateway, quite another to be caught in the burglar act of climbing a wall. Still, the unlikelihood of his

246

being seen at all gave him confidence. No windows overlooked this part of the mews, the flats were over garages a good fifty yards away. The only people likely to see anything would be drivers of cars coming home or the drivers of these two parked cars, come to fetch them.

Carrying Keith's toolbag, a torch and a walking stick that had been his grandfather's, he walked round to the front of the house and let himself into the front garden by the wrought-iron gate in the wall. Once inside, he or anything he did couldn't be seen from the street. Unfortunately, it was impossible to get from this front garden into the back yard without passing through the house. He had been almost sure of this last time he was there and now it was confirmed.

Inside the enclosed garden it was quite dark. No lights were on in the house. The myriad leaves that covered it hung still and dark, but each, it seemed, with a tiny surface gleam. He looked up to see if any windows were open on the upper floor, when a light coming on in the porch over his head gave him a fright. All the leaves suddenly became acid-green. He waited for the sound of running feet, the door to be thrown open, but there was nothing. Then he understood that the light had been on a time-switch. Another had come on inside one of the downstairs front rooms.

Did she have an alarm system? He thought he remembered a keypad on the hall wall. She was scatty enough to have one and not use it. She was feather-brained enough not to have turned the key in the higher of the two locks on the door. The light was a help to him. It would ensure he made very little noise. He closed his eyes, remembering the layout of the door on the hall side, the shape of the square-headed knob whereby the door was opened, the position of the letter-box and, above all, that there was no second interior box covering its opening on the inside.

Slowly and very carefully, he inserted the walking stick, hook end first, through the letter-box. When it and his forearm were fully pushed through, he bent his arm round and felt with the hook for the knob. The hook tapped against the woodwork, then caught on the knob. He pulled the walking stick towards him, the lock clicked and the door came open. Dropping the stick on the floor inside, he picked up the toolbag and went in.

As he had thought, the suitcases were gone. She was gone. The place was very silent and quite warm. She was the kind of person rich enough to leave the central heating on while she was away. Now what to do first? Unbolt that gate or explore the cellar?

Well-off as he must be, Simon Alpheton didn't throw his money about when it came to choosing a restaurant. He never had, Harriet remembered. Still, she had supposed that the acquisition of wealth would have changed his habits. La Ruchetta sounded all right, though she had never heard of it before, and the Old Brompton Road was all right, so long as the place you were going to was at the eastern end of it. The further her taxi took her westwards the more Harriet's misgivings increased. The driver set her down in Earl's Court outside a poky Italian restaurant between a betting shop and a tapas bar, its window full of fishing nets and packets of dried pasta.

Simon, who was already there, said it was his favourite place. In the days when he was poor he had lived just round the corner. Harriet thought he looked awful, his hair quite white and down on his shoulders, his belly spreading expansively above the top of his jeans. Jeans! She was wearing a black and white striped silk dress and jacket, the skirt of the dress four inches above her knees and the jacket lapels very wide and thickly encrusted with red and black bead embroidery.

But she could see they thought a lot of him at La Ruchetta. The proprietor came up to their table and made him a sort of bow and called him 'Maestro'. People at the other tables nudged each other and stared. Simon's picture had been in the paper the previous week. He had done a big interview for *The Times* on the occasion of his new exhibition.

'Must be ten years,' he said to Harriet, without telling her she hadn't changed or looked younger than ever, or anything like that. 'How's Franklin?'

'Gone to San Sebastian on his hols,' said Harriet.

Whatever might have been the rejoinder to that was lost when a gushing woman holding an album came up to Simon and asked if she could have his autograph for her daughter who was at the Chelsea College of Art. Simon signed and smiled at her and was very gracious. They both ordered the risotto and then the veal, and Harriet had to admit it was very good. The Frascati was very good and so was the Chianti. She was beginning to wonder what would have happened if she'd rung Simon in those distant days after Marc and before Otto and if she'd married him instead of Franklin, when Simon suddenly remarked that he had something to tell her. That was why he had responded to her phone call by asking her here. He wanted to try something out on her.

Before he could say whatever it was there came into the restaurant and approached their table the most beautiful young man Harriet had seen for years. He was tall and slender and dark, with the features of Michelangelo's David and the smile of Tom Cruise, and he put Otto, Zak and Dilip, not to mention Teddy Grex, in the shade. A wild idea rushed into Harriet's head that Simon was doing her some kind of long-deferred favour, was for some reason of gratitude or simple generosity producing this boy for her. Disillusionment replaced it. Simon put out his hand and the way he squeezed the other's hand and looked into his dark eyes left no room for doubt.

'I am going to out myself, Harriet. This coming week. I'm actually holding a press conference – can you believe it? I really want to know what you think, about the wisdom of that, I mean. Not the wisdom of our relationship, I'm not in any doubt about that. Oh, by the way, this is Nathan.'

'But you're not gay!' said Harriet.

'Well, no, I wasn't. Or I thought I wasn't. People change with time.' He looked at Nathan again and said fondly, 'Look at him, he's enough to turn Casanova gay!'

They had some champagne. Harriet felt chagrined, though she hardly knew why, for she didn't want Simon herself and she knew from experience the hopelessness of making overtures to such as Nathan.

'So am I making a wise move?' Simon asked her.

She wanted to say that she didn't know and she didn't care. Instead that strange mantra or text she had first come across nearly thirty years before rose to her lips and she uttered it aloud. 'Fourteen Manvantaras and one Krita make one Kalpa.'

'Does that mean yes or no?' Simon asked.

'It means do as you like,' she said.

He could tell he had upset her, but without knowing how could only say that he would stick to his decision. Harriet said rather spitefully that at least it would be something to read about in the papers and she looked forward to seeing what the gossip columnists made of it. A deep loneliness engulfed her, a sense of being left out of everything, and the prospect of the solitary homeward journey, the solitary homecoming, filled her with dread.

She realised that she had anticipated something very different for the evening and when she was in the taxi that Simon had had the restaurant call for her she understood, in a rare moment of insight, that she had been looking for a friendship. Perhaps, more accurately, for the renewal of friendship, for someone to like and who would like her, as against someone to lust after.

In the dim back seat of the cab she confronted her future and knew that the encounters with the Zaks and the Dilips must in the nature of things soon end. This year or next year and probably – she clenched her hands – with some instance of gross humiliation. That was when friends would be needed, but she had no friends beyond those social acquaintances of Franklin's, beyond the always unavailable Anthers and Zithers of this world. An abyss seemed to open before her, the vacant hollow of the years ahead.

In this mood of despair she let herself into Orcadia Cottage and went straight upstairs. A frightening feeling was replacing her loneliness, a sensation that she had no idea of what to do, no notion of how to pass the time, the night, there was absolutely nothing she wanted to do. Not eat, drink, watch television, read, listen to her phone messages, if any, not even go out again – where could she go? Not go to bed, not sleep, not even induce sleep with a sleeping pill.

But she walked into her bedroom, took off her coat and threw it on the bed. Close up against the mirror she looked into her own face before turning sharply away. Far from weakening her, despair made her feel full of a wretched energy so that now she longed to do something active, even violent, attack a punchbag, kick at something soft and yielding. Or break

251

the mirror and see her face and her body and the whole room crack and shiver and collapse.

If she had been inclined to such things she would have gone running. Run around the block, stopped somewhere and worked out the way she had once seen a man exercise in Regent's Park, doing step aerobics up and down one of the seats. But she wasn't and she couldn't. She stretched out her arms, raised them above her head, thought of screaming.

Then she heard it. The door that opened on to the top of the cellar stairs. Someone had come into the house by that door and closed it behind him, very nearly slammed it.

It must be Franklin. Only Franklin had a key. For some reason he had come back. His woman had failed to be there to meet him. No one else, no intruder, would move with such confidence, make so much noise. Yet he never went near the cellar or the cellar stairs. She might almost have said he didn't know the cellar was there.

An undefined anger filled her, rushing through her veins, heating her face. What was he doing? Why was he here? Knowing her to be out, guessing she would go out the moment he was gone, he was putting into action some plan that involved the cellar, that involved deceiving her. He must be hiding something there, and hiding it from her. Or even setting some sort of trap for her. That would be like him, she thought, envisaging his rictus grin and hearing his teasing voice.

She looked for the pole with the hook that opened the fanlight and found it in the landing cupboard. It amused her to think of hitting him with it, striking him, perhaps mortally, and explaining afterwards that she thought he was a burglar, had been frightened out of her wits. She started down the stairs.

The time-switch had caused the porch light to

252

come on and should have done the same by the light in the dining-room. Inexplicably, it hadn't. But the light at the head of the cellar stairs had come on through human agency. The door at the head of the cellar stairs, which was never opened, which hadn't been touched for years, was open now. She forgot her anger in her desire to frighten him, simply to give him a shock. She wouldn't hit him – well, that depended on what he was doing.

She took one step down, looked down and spoke Franklin's phrase in Franklin's menacing tone. The commanding officer bidding reluctant troops go over the top.

He had gone outside by the kitchen door, having turned off the dining-room light on his way.

The courtyard that separated the house from the mews was an oblong, its entire area paved in natural limestone. On each side was a narrow border planted with a number of small silver-leaved shrubs. Teddy had not looked at it properly on his previous visit, then noticing only the manhole cover. This was roughly in the centre of the courtyard, though rather nearer to the gate than the house. Now he saw that the wall which separated the area from the road on one side, the wall which divided it from the garden next door and the wall at the mews end were made of what looked, in the dim, hazardous light, like yellow brick. The height of all these walls had recently been increased and the new brickwork was a slightly different shade.

A garden table and four chairs, cast iron painted white, stood in one of the corners at the house end and in the opposite corner was a large marble urn with a pointed tree growing in it. Something he hadn't noticed last time was that the back of the house, like the front, was covered in those same luxuriant all-conquering leaves. More than the front, in fact, for here not a scrap of brickwork was visible and if those pinkish tendrils crept across the surface, leaves concealed them also. Only the windows, shining black rectangles, peered out, eye-like, and the barred glass doors.

The two lamps in the mews gave enough light to show all this, but to show it in dark monochrome, black and charcoal and grey and flickers of silver on the leaves. He drew back the bolts on the gate. Then he tried to lift the cover off the manhole. This was of some sort of metal incised with the maker's name, Paulson and Grieve, Ironsmiths of Stoke, inside a laurel wreath. He pulled at the metal ring embedded in its centre but to no effect and he soon realised that no failure of his own strength was the problem but rather that something on the other side, probably a bolt, was holding the manhole cover in place. He would have to go down into the cellar from the inside.

First he checked the Edsel and the mews. No one was about. The two parked cars were still there. Distantly, he could hear traffic in Maida Vale, crossing the hump over the canal. He went back into the house, opened the door at the top of the cellar steps and pressed the light switch.

Nothing happened. By the light from the top of the stairs he could make out an unshaded bulb hanging from the ceiling. It pleased him that it didn't work, that the bulb was used up and had never been replaced, for it confirmed what she had said about never going into the cellar.

He could tell that he was not quite tall enough to reach that bulb hanging on its six inches of lead. From a table lamp in the dining-room he undid a hundred-watt bulb, took it down into the cellar and

254

changed it for the defunct one. The light came on at once and showed him what he had come to see.

The rest of the house was very clean, almost up to his own standard. Down here, if not exactly dirty, it was dusty and untended. Spiders' webs hung from the ceiling and clustered in its corners. The place was empty, no more than ten feet square, its floor of rough concrete, its walls plastered and painted white. Or they had been painted white long ago, but that white had cracked and faded to grey. In the wall to the right, the one at the rear end of the house, was a door, bolted at the bottom, composed of rough wooden boards from which the white paint was peeling, and in the lower half of which was a hatch. In the days when coal was delivered from outside to fill the hole, Teddy supposed, the hatch would be raised from the inside and coal pour through. A job for some servant with bucket or scuttle. The mess it must have caused, the filth, made him shudder.

He drew back the bolt. The space he stepped into was perhaps half the area of the cellar proper and consisted of a cuboid chamber about eight feet deep. No coal remained, but the floor was black with coal-dust and a bitter carbon smell hung in the close air. He switched on his torch and its beam sent a spider scuttling away into a dark corner. At the top of the chamber the torch showed him the inside of the manhole cover. As he had expected, it was secured in place by a heavy steel bolt.

Teddy was tall enough to reach it with his fingertips, but it would have taken a man of six feet six to be able to get sufficient purchase for the task of sliding back the bolt. He needed something to stand on and also, in case of need, a spanner and a wrench for the bolt.

For a moment he forgot where he had left Keith's toolbag. Had he taken it outside? He came up the cellar stairs again, carefully brushing coal-dust off his shoes before entering the hall. The idea of dirtying this exquisite place was very distasteful to him. The door into the hall was one of those that slam shut at the least pressure.

Then he remembered. He had left the toolbag just inside the back door when he went out to unbolt the gate. Now to find a pair of steps or failing that – and it almost certainly would be failing that – a chair or stool.

Nothing suitable in the kitchen. He doubted if he could have brought himself to stand on one of those beautiful gilded chairs from the dining-room. A cast-iron chair from the courtyard would do. He fetched one of these. It was heavy, it must weight twenty-five pounds. Carrying the chair and with the toolbag in his other hand, he returned the way he had come to hear a woman's shrill voice say, 'Don't move. Stay right where you are. I am armed,' and end with an hysterical giggle.

Chapter 25

For a moment he doubted it was a real voice. It must be coming from the radio or the television. Or the device that set lights to go on after a cunning delay could be programmed to switch on a tape. He thought that, but he came on, out into the hall, stepping softly on the thick carpet. The silence and then the sound of an indrawn breath told him it was a real woman who had spoken. It was she, Harriet.

He saw her. She was wearing shoes with heels of an extravagant height, shoes for a teenage model on a catwalk, stiletto heels four inches high. At the top of the stairs she stood, looking down, her back to him, wobbling on those spiky heels, some sort of stick or staff in her hand. It was immediately clear that she thought he was down there. Wherever she had been in the house, and perhaps she had been here when he first entered it, she had heard the cellar door close and believed it had closed behind him as he went down the stairs.

He stood absolutely still. The Edsel was in the mews, the gate unbolted. If she summoned help, if she called the police, he would be taken away, the car taken. He closed his hands tightly round the leg of the chair he held, the handle of the toolbag.

She said, 'Come out, you fool. What the hell are you doing?'

Adrenalin poured into his blood. He felt it zing in his head. She knew who it was, she was insulting him again. He drew in his breath and let it out in a roar, 'Turn round!'

Never before had he seen anyone jump. Heard of it happening, yes, but never seen it. The start galvanised her, he could have sworn her feet left the ground. She spun to face him, cried out, 'You!' and at that he threw the toolbag at her.

He hurled it with his left hand and the chair with his right. The bag caught her in the chest, the chair across her legs. She fell backwards and turned over and over, somersaulting down the cellar stairs, her hands grappling with the empty air. A wailing cry came from her and the pole she was holding flew out of her hand, wheeling in an arc out of his sight. He heard the clatter as it fell to the floor and the softer smash of her body.

That it was a body and not the living woman, injured but alive, he hardly knew until he went down there. He even had a momentary anxiety – what to do if she *was* alive. But she had struck her head a violent blow on the floor, rather as if she had dived from a height into the sea, unaware that the water was shallow and the bottom unyielding rock.

His first thought after that was a strange one. He need not touch her now. If anything were to stop him killing it would be the necessity of touching your victim first. Two people had died at his hands without his touching them. He smiled, the idea was so peculiar and so unexpected.

He picked up the chair. Paint had chipped off it, but otherwise it was intact. Nothing had happened to the toolbag except that a screwdriver and a pair of pincers had fallen out of it. He looked at the body dispassionately, the dark-red blood on her dark-red hair, the waxen white of her face under the make-up. What had brought her home? It looked as if she had been away for just two nights. Two big suitcases for two nights away? Maybe, for a woman like that. Probably that was where she had been when he first opened the front door, upstairs at the back out of earshot, unpacking those two cases.

Satisfied with his solution, he carried the chair into the coal-hole, got up on to it and, using the pincers, wrenched back the bolt. It felt as if it had been rammed into that position years before and never touched since. The steadiness of his hands pleased him. He was almost unshaken. So much the better. He pushed against the manhole cover and it rose quite easily.

He went upstairs again and into the hall, looked about him and, seeing her handbag on the small table just inside the front door, put it in the toolbag. To be on the safe side in case a cleaner or someone else with a key came into the house. He returned to the backyard, opened the gate and went out into the mews.

One of the parked cars had gone. Most likely, it had belonged to someone visiting friends in a flat or house higher up the mews. He knew very little about dinner-parties or any social calls, come to that, but he calculated that this was about the right time to be leaving a place you had visited on a Saturday night.

Now for the grand secret. Who used to say that? He had surprised himself with the words that rose unbidden in his mind. His grandmother perhaps, or his long-dead grandfather. Now for the grand secret. A sight for sore eyes. Or a sight to damage healthy eyes? He lifted the Edsel's boot lid, shut his eyes, opened them. With both hands he gripped the top of the big plastic bag that was Keith's shroud, grasped it just below where the masking tape secured it and lifted it.

A smell there was, but not a strong, terrible, fetid

259

odour, nothing like that. If the plastic were to be punctured, it would be a different story, he knew that. To tear it would be fatal, a disaster. He heaved the bag and its contents over the lip of the boot and down on to the flagstones. When it was out, no longer in that boot but on the ground, and the bag was still intact, he knew the worst was over.

He dragged it through the gateway and up to the manhole. Then he went back to close the boot lid and shut the gate. The presence of a man and a woman in the mews, appearing it seemed from nowhere, suddenly materialising, gave him a shock. They were walking in the direction of the remaining parked car.

How much had they seen? Probably nothing. He was sure they hadn't been anywhere in the vicinity while he was dragging that bag. And their behaviour seemed to confirm this, for as he unlocked his car the man called out to him, 'Lovely night!'

Teddy nodded. He never knew how to answer remarks like that.

'Good-night, then.'

'Good-night,' said Teddy.

He closed the boot lid. He tried to behave as a householder would who lived in a place like this. Check the interior of the garage, make sure the car was all right – there was no car, which didn't surprise him – examine the stack of bricks in there which must be left over from raising the height of the walls. Retreat through the gateway with a confident tread, born of years of practice of going in and out of here at midnight. But he was unable to resist looking over his shoulder as the car passed. The woman in the passenger seat rewarded him with a friendly wave.

The gate shut and bolted, he raised the manhole cover, lifted it out and laid it on the flagstones. His principal worry now was that the bag might split as he lowered it down through that aperture. Still, it was hardly the end of the world if it did, only it would be – unpleasant. The end of the world had been averted and the worst of everything was past.

He shoved and heaved the bag to the manhole. The dead-body hole, he thought. He pushed it through, feet end first, holding on to the head-and-shoulders end. Letting go wasn't an option until he could feel the feet end at least graze the stone floor down there. Holding on, breathing deeply, he hung over the edge, his arms stretched to a sense of bursting, until he felt the weight lessen, the tension slacken. The bottom of the bag was on the ground.

He let go and there was a slithering, shuddering thump. For a brief second he thought he was going with it, but he managed to keep a grip on the flagstones with the muscles of his chest and thighs. He had left the iron chair down there and the bag fell across it and subsided, as if the body in its slippery shroud had sat down. He shivered.

A strong press-up brought him to his feet. He replaced the manhole cover, checked that everything in the backyard was as he had found it and went back into the house.

A sheet or a tablecloth, something like that was what he needed. Upstairs, in a cupboard on the landing outside the bedroom she had taken him into, he found both in abundance. The clean, crisply ironed white sheets pleased him. He would like linen like that for his own bed, his and Francine's, fresh on every day. And why not? The work needed to ensure that was nothing compared with the benefits.

A blanket might be better for his purpose, though. There were several, blue and white, fluffy, spotless, on the bottom shelf. He pulled out a blue one and descended into the cellar once more. There was no more blood, it had stopped flowing, as he thought he

261

had heard it did when you were dead. Unfortunately, quite a lot of blood had got on to the floor. No doubt it would also stain this lovely clean blanket. But he had no choice. He laid the blanket on the ground and rolled Harriet's body up in it, not a difficult task, she must have been less than half Keith's weight.

At this point an idea came to him, a wonderful plan. It was simple and beautiful, it solved everything. Rather than put Harriet's body in the coal-hole with Keith's he would bring Keith's out here. Thus, the coal-hole would be empty, a safety measure in case anyone ever lifted the manhole cover, and as for the cellar ... Could he? He was sure he could. The thought made him smile, then laugh out loud. His laughter echoed in that subterranean place.

First he pulled out the iron chair. He kept his eyes shut while he did it, but he couldn't shut his ears to the squelching sound of the body sliding to the floor. This was the last time he would ever drag it, though, this was the end. There had been some considerable disturbance of those contents and anyone would have been able to smell it now. He stood and smelt it. Horrible, really. How disgusting human beings were, in life, in dying and in death ...

He closed the coal-hole door and fastened the bolts. Harriet's blood made an almost black sticky patch on the cellar floor. He considered fetching water and scrubbing brush and cleaning it up, it was very much in his nature to clean up after himself whatever might be the task he had performed, but finally he decided against it. He was dirty enough already. As it was, he felt begrimed from all the energy he had expended and from coal-dust and spiders' webs. He could smell himself, a powerful oniony stink. It was more distasteful than if he had smelt it on somebody else.

Why not do what he longed to do? He was alone, everything was done, the Edsel awaited him, his car, a strange car that attracted curious glances, but only a car and one that could now bear the scrutiny of any authority. So why not go upstairs and have a bath?

He had a choice. A bathroom *en suite* with her bedroom, another opening out from the landing. Hers had a claw-footed tub standing on a tiled dais, the other a sunken bath of blue-green marble, and that was the one he chose, filling it with steaming, foaming water into which he poured a stream of orange-scented essence. He used a loofah to scrub himself – it was the first of its kind he had ever seen – and soap that smelt like a basket of citrus fruits. The towel was pale orange, fluffy on one side and velvety on the other. When he was dry he dried the bath and rubbed a facecloth over the taps to polish them.

When he had noted the time, ten-past one, and checked that her handbag contained a key to the house, he left by the front door and walked round to the mews where the Edsel was waiting.

Chapter 26

There was much more in that small quilted leather handbag than a key to the house. The bunch of credit cards might be of use to him. He would have to think about it. But he also found in the wallet nearly a hundred pounds in notes and a small leather-bound address book, as well as the usual women's stuff, pressed powder, lipstick, a phial of perfume.

The handbag itself he tried to imagine Francine using, but the image he conjured up was all wrong. High heels went with it and a mincing step, red nails and slave bracelets. Shuddering, he put the handbag in his waste bin. The day gone by and the night seemed like a dream to him now, and so surreal was the memory of it, so bizarre the events, that he had to go outside as soon as he woke up and check that the Edsel's boot really was empty.

It looked innocent and ordinary – if anything about the Edsel was ordinary – a clean, empty space that seemed as if it had never held anything more sinister than a suitcase. Of the thing that had been inside it for nearly eight months there was no sign or hint. Any smell there was had gone with Keith into the cellar.

Inside that garage, he remembered, had been a stack of bricks. To someone who knew about these things it was clear what had happened. The rear wall had been considered too low and at some point, recently, a further two feet had been built on to it.

The calculations had allowed for more bricks than were needed and hence the pile in the garage. He would need some ready-mixed cement and maybe a flagstone. Stone, he knew, was very expensive but perhaps there was an alternative . . .

He closed the boot lid, stepped back and viewed the car. Would it help to clean it once more before he took it to Miracle Motors?

Megsie appeared suddenly on the far side of the fence, seeming to materialise as if she had sprung from a trapdoor in the ground. 'I've never seen you open that boot before,' she remarked conversationally. 'I said to Nige, I've never seen him open that boot before, and he said, neither have I, never.'

'I'm selling it for Keith,' Teddy said, more expansively than usual. 'He said to sell it if I can get a good price.'

'You'd think he'd got something in there he doesn't want us to see, I said. And Nige said, yeah, maybe he's got drugs in there with a street value of untold millions. Funny the things you think of, isn't it? Many's the time I've cursed that Esme, taking up the whole garden, but I don't know, I reckon I'll miss it when it's gone.'

'Edsel,' said Teddy, more as a matter of form than because he thought she would learn.

If cleaning the car meant doing it under her eyes he decided against it. Whatever happened, he had a busy day ahead of him. The phone rang and he was sure it must be Francine. There had been some talk of his going with her to look at that Holly's new flat, and then he and she and Holly and some guy called Christopher going out somewhere. He hated the whole idea, but he would do it if that was what she wanted. It wasn't Francine on the phone but a man in Highgate who had come upon Teddy's old advertisement, had noted it down at the time or kept the paper or something, and wanted to know if he could have an estimate for a couple of built-in wardrobes. Having long ago decided to turn nothing down with the exception of rough labouring, Teddy told Mr Habgood of Shepherds Hill that he would be along at three in the afternoon.

The man he saw at Miracle Motors wasn't the one he had talked to on the phone. This was the manager, or perhaps the managing director, and when Teddy said he had practically had a promise of a sale he pursed his lips and began shaking his head from side to side in a discouraging way.

Then the one he had talked to came out and behaved very differently from what Teddy had expected. 'Now if it was part exchange,' he said, 'that would be a whole different ball game.'

The manager stopped shaking his head and started nodding it. 'Then we could be talking a couple of K, right, Mick?'

'Two thousand pounds?' said Teddy, aghast.

'That's about the size of it.'

'And I'd have to buy another car from you?'

They looked amused. Then Mick said quite sharply, 'Frankly, I'm surprised Mr Grex wants to sell. Or maybe what I mean is I'm surprised he didn't come himself if that's what he wants. Where's he got to, anyway?'

'He's living in Liphook,' said Teddy.

'Is that right? He's down there and you're up here with his car?'

Both men looked him up and down. They looked at him in the way people in their forties and fifties do look at young men, with a mixture of contempt and envy and suspicion. A layabout, they were very likely thinking, a drawer of benefit and probably a fiddler of benefit, on the fringes of crime.

'If we're talking about a straight purchase,' said

the manager and, from having exhausted his gaze on Teddy, turned at last to eye the Edsel, 'a grand is the kind of area that'd be realistic.'

Appalled, he thought of the ten thousand he had had in mind. But to be rid of the thing, for it no longer to be the first object he saw when he woke up in the morning, no longer to fill his garden and press its rear against his windows. Even its colour was becoming his most hated colour, that insipid pastel-yellow . . .

'Would you give me a thousand for it, then?'

'I take it you've got the vehicle registration document with you, the MOT and a valid certificate of insurance?'

He had never even heard of these things. What was the MOT?

He dared not ask.

'I'll tell you what, you get Mr Grex to come in here and have a word with us himself. Frankly, I'd rather do business with Mr Grex in person. Liphook's not at the end of the world. You take that motor away for the time being and maybe if Mr Grex puts in a personal appearance we can come to a more satisfactory arrangement for all.'

Teddy said nothing. He walked towards the Edsel.

'You tell him Wally says all the best,' the manager called after him.

Mr Habgood lived in one of those sixties townhouses without a single cupboard. He had just moved there from a Victorian villa that was amply supplied with storage space. Teddy looked at the bedrooms, measured up, lost his enthusiasm when the client said chipboard would do for the doors, he didn't want any fancy stuff, not a lot of expense, but again he felt that he could barely afford to turn down anything of this nature.

'That's quite a vehicle you've got there,' Habgood said, showing him out. 'You must be in a fair way of doing, getting your hands on a nice job like that at your age. Drinks juice, I bet.'

Teddy was almost too angry to speak. But he told himself that if Habgood believed him successful he would be likely and willing to pay more and he resolved to ask double what he had first intended.

On the way home he stopped at a DIY centre and bought ready-mixed concrete. It was a strange sensation using the Edsel's boot for a legitimate purpose, actually putting something into that space which had been for so long a forbidden area.

Petrol was the next requirement. As he served himself he watched the car drinking juice. With its ugly fish mouth and its cocked-up tail, it had something animal-like about it and it was easy to imagine it greedily slurping up the oil that sustained it. He wouldn't have been surprised to see a yellow tongue pop out of its mouth. Thank God for the money in the handbag. But it brought him almost physical pain to see so much of it vanish into the service station's till.

He was experiencing that sensation of hopelessness that follows when we plan to be rid of an encumbrance, are positive it will vanish if certain steps are faithfully followed, anticipate the relief that will result from its disappearance, only to find ourselves back in the situation as before, the position that has always been. It can't be done. The best-laid plans have failed. The thing, whatever it may be, the rash of pimples on one's face, a plague of flies, the next-door neighbour's night-long hi-fi, is still there.

So it was for Teddy. Deep humiliation was what he felt as he drove the Edsel back through the gates and under the hated carport. His shame was exacerbated by his remembering, at exactly that moment, that he had told Nige and Megsie he was selling the car. Yet here it was, back where it had always been. For a while he tried manoeuvring it backwards and forwards in an attempt to find a new position for it, but all he could achieve was to leave a couple of yards instead of a couple of feet between its tail and his window.

He was so preoccupied with the Edsel and his money problem that a curious, even terrible, thing happened to him. When Francine phoned a few seconds passed by before he knew who it was. It simply failed to register. Her voice spoke to him and she spoke her name and he could almost have asked, who?

Then he collected himself. She, his woman, the wearer of his ring, she who saw herself in his mirror, came back to him. But it was with actual relief that he heard her say she couldn't come over that evening, she really couldn't. Her father had gone away again, would be away for a week, and her stepmother – here Francine hesitated, searching for the right term – was 'in a nervous state', she had begged her not to go out and had made wild threats.

This was all beyond Teddy's comprehension. He made no effort to understand. If she wanted to stay at home with that crazy woman, that was all right with him; as it happened he needed no distractions this evening. A flicker of anxiety was teasing him now, the remote possibility of someone else entering Orcadia Cottage and opening that cellar door . . . Naturally, he said none of this to Francine, merely that he would see her the next day.

'Then can we go and see Holly's place? And go out with her and Christopher? We could go to the cinema. I can't go to a club because Julia will fuss – well, she'll fuss anyway, but if I'm out late she'll go mad.'

For the sake of peace and to keep her happy, he agreed. If it had been left to him he would have stayed at home with her or, maybe, if they had to go out, taken her for an afternoon at the V and A.

'You are a dear,' she said. 'You're so good to me.'

'I'll see you tomorrow then,' he said.

It was a funny thing, but unless he could see her she was scarcely there. Asleep, gazed at appreciatively, she was more real than this disembodied distant voice. He felt suddenly angry and resentful, he didn't know why, it must be the prospect of the company of Holly and Christopher. Again the notion of someone coming into the house came to him. But who could? There was no one, Harriet had lived alone. In the unlikely event of a cleaning woman arriving, the dirty state of the cellar was evidence that she never went down there.

But the sooner he was back there the better. He got the Edsel out again. By the time he reached Orcadia Place it was growing dark, the gleaming damp dusk of a London autumn evening. Lamps shone like beads of amber against the far backdrop of a hazier chemical light on Grove End Road. The sky was reddish-purple, an ugly colour. This time he was seen as he drew up at the garage doors. But there was no element in it of being caught out. A woman with two small fluffy dogs on leads smiled at him, or smiled at the car which she evidently recognised. Probably she thought he was a mechanic returning it after a thousand-mile service.

Now he was well-supplied with keys, he could enter the house by the back door. Carrying his toolbag, he paused inside the kitchen and listened. Somehow he thought that if anyone had been there, even if someone had been and gone, he would know, he would sense it. But all was emptiness and silence. Nothing was disturbed, not even the air in the place.

He opened the cellar door and looked down, but without putting the light on. In the dimness he saw a silvery sheen on the plastic, the pale furriness of the blanket and, less comfortably, protruding from it, Harriet's foot.

Not long, though, and he would never have to see it again. No one would see it, ever. He spread newspaper on the floor and set out his tools. The first thing he did was remove the screws on the hinges and take off the door. An ordinary sort of door, consisting of six panels and with a brass handle. Perhaps he could find a use for it. The next stage would take longer. Using his mallet, he set about freeing the architrave from the brickwork and plaster. It was a noisy task, but Orcadia Cottage stood on its own, a road to one side of it, its nearest neighbour twenty feet away and separated from it by a wall and a fence and bushes and trees. There were no Megsie and Nige next door and no common wall for them to bang on.

For all that, the heavy hammer blows made him uneasy, even though he knew that people in London are rarely alerted by building work going on in a neighbour's house. It was different up in Neasden. Almost as disconcerting was the mess he was making, splintered wood lying everywhere and plaster dust making him choke. He realised quite suddenly that he was going to have to make a new skirting board, even perhaps carve it if he couldn't find the right beading to match the existing one.

Once the door frame was off, he could clear up for the night. There would be no more noise. Soon there would be no more cellar. He found a broom, dustpan and brush and a roll of bin-liners, and swept up meticulously. Then the vacuum cleaner came out and he removed the last vestiges of dust.

Should he transport the bricks in preparation for

tomorrow's work? He decided yes. It would have to be done in the morning as he was going on this horrible visit in the afternoon. His anger returned, flickered. Outside in the backyard the night was growing cold, there was frost in the air, reminding him of the night Keith died. He needed a bricklayer's hod but must manage without. His father had been a bricklayer and presumably had had his own hod, but where it was, what had happened to it, Teddy didn't know. He felt an obscure resentment at the disappearance of that hod – along with the absence of so many things which should by rights have been his.

Something he had forgotten, matt white wall paint to match the existing paint. He must buy some on his way in the morning. Bringing bricks into contact with the beautiful velvety carpet or the hardwood floor at the top of the steps pained him. He hunted around until he found a stack of magazines, *Vogue*, *Harper's*, *Hello!*, and spread their glossy pages on the floor before carefully depositing the bricks on them.

It might be best to dispose of the cellar door and door frame splinters at once. He carried them outside to the Edsel. The door would have failed to go into the boot if it had been a centimetre longer. Returning, looking at the manhole cover, he had a thought which made him smile and then laugh. It was another beautiful idea, almost amounting to genius.

Julia worried Francine and made her increasingly uneasy. It was not only that she was like an animal of uncertain temper, which must be constantly placated, but that her behaviour in many small details became more and more bizarre. A lot of this was hidden from Richard, Julia purposely hid it, but Richard was away and in his absence all her strangeness was allowed to show.

At home, for she had nowhere to go without

Teddy, Francine witnessed for the first time Julia's pacing. Up and down, up and down, she could hear it even upstairs in her room, but when she came down Julia stopped and sat stiffly in a chair, as if exasperated, as if obliged to give up for the sake of someone else's whim an essential task. Francine tried to talk to her, asking her what she thought of some item in the morning's newspaper or if she fancied this new film that was so prominently reviewed, but Julia only nodded or shook her head impatiently. Her eyes she kept on the window, staring out into the busy road.

Then, suddenly, without warning, she jumped up and ran out into the hall, snatched a coat off the hall-stand and rushed out of the front door. Francine saw her pause perfunctorily for a lorry to pass, then run across to the island in the middle of the road, pause again before running to the other side. There was someone sitting in the bus shelter and she spoke to him, seemed to harangue him, gesticulating with her hands.

Francine watched her return, said when she came back into the room, 'What was all that about?'

Julia's reply was the disturbed person's gesture of sharply turning away her head like a peevish child. She marched to the other end of the room, wheeled round, came back and sat down heavily on the sofa. She had put on still more weight and when she lowered her body into a chair or settee the springs groaned. Francine wondered if she was a secret eater, bingeing for comfort in some sorrow. But what sorrow?

Julia suddenly began to talk. 'You don't know what men are like, Francine. The decent ones like your father are few and far between, let me tell you. Any boy you are likely to go out with will only want you for one thing, and he'll get as much of that as he

273

can, as much as you give him, and then he'll get tired of you and you won't interest him any more. They are all like that.'

'But you said some are like Dad,' said Francine.

'I've given my life to you, to protecting you and looking after you and trying to make you understand that a special person like you can't go out into this world and mix with filthy creatures; you're not prepared for it; I can't prepare you, though God knows I've tried. I've wished we lived in another age when parents had rights over their children and could compel them to be obedient. The filthy creatures are everywhere out there, there was one of them over in the bus shelter. You know what he was there for, don't you?'

'No, Julia, I don't.' Francine felt a chill in the air, the shiver the unknown brings with it. 'I don't know what you mean.'

'I wish you wouldn't lie to me. I only want you to be honest. You know very well he was waiting for you.'

Francine crossed to the window. The young man was still there, but now he had been joined by another. She was unable to see clearly across that distance, but she thought they had both lit cigarettes.

'I don't know those people, Julia.'

Julia let out a loud derisive snigger. 'You're a barefaced little liar, aren't you?'

She had got to her feet, a tall, heavy woman who carried her increased weight on the front of her, big bolster-like breasts and full stomach without the intervention of a waist. Her face had become jowly, her cheeks cushions and her casque of yellow hair sat on her head like a brass helmet. She took a step and then another, her head threateningly lowered, and Francine remembered that one occasion on which her stepmother had struck her. She refused to retreat and stood her ground.

And Julia's intention was quite different. A weak smile softened her face, made it slack and spongy. She put out her arms in what seemed a pleading gesture, then enfolded Francine in them, holding her, then hugging her suffocatingly tightly.

Francine, when she could tactfully escape from this embrace, laid her hand on Julia's upper arm and stroked it gently. 'Can't we try to be nice to each other, Julia? We used to get on so well when I was little.' Did they? Had they? It seemed best to pretend they had. 'I promise I will be honest with you. I don't mean to deceive. Really. But I'm not meeting that boy over there or his friend, I've never seen either of them before.'

Julia began to cry.

'Please don't cry. Let's go out somewhere together, shall we? I'm not going anywhere, so we could do something together. I'd like to have a look at the Globe theatre, Shakespeare's Globe, wouldn't you? Or we could go shopping, you said you wanted a winter coat.'

'I don't feel like it,' Julia said. 'I'm too ill. You've made me ill.'

After that, Francine felt reluctant to go out anywhere on her own. She went up to her bedroom and sat there thinking about Julia and what was happening and what she might possibly do to change things. The irony was that in those childhood days she had spoken of it was she who had been sent to Julia for psychiatric help, while now she felt it was her function to seek therapy for Julia. The only way, obviously, was to try to talk to her father about Julia's state, persuade him that Julia was having some kind of breakdown. But her father was in Strasbourg.

She picked up her mobile phone and tried to call Teddy, but there was no answer. He was the only person she knew who had no answering machine. But recorded voices weren't much comfort to you, she thought, when she had tried Isabel and Miranda, and Holly's new number only to be told of absence or unavailability.

Teddy's ring, which she had been wearing hung on a ribbon round her neck, she took off and slipped on to her finger. The third finger of her right hand. Perhaps one day, in the distant time to come, when all this with Julia had somehow been made to come right, when she had been to Oxford and was an independent professional woman, when Teddy was a successful artist, then and only then she might move that ring on to her left hand.

He had heard, he couldn't remember where, of slaves sleeping across the doorway of a master's room. And the idea tempted him, though he wasn't a slave and those dead weren't his masters, but to be a guardian of them, a watchdog, to protect them from whoever might come, that was strangely attractive. Until the wall was built and the cellar, to all intents and purposes no longer there.

But no one would come and he wouldn't do it. He bathed, went to bed in Harriet's bed and dreamed he was dismembering furniture, the way he actually had taken apart the dining suite. But when he came to carry the pieces out, daily depositing another segment or joint into a waste bin, he looked into the bag and saw not a carved piece of stained and polished wood, but a severed hand and Harriet's foot in its high-heeled shoe.

Chapter 27

Bricking up the hole in the wall would have been a quick and simple task if there were no question of how the final result looked. If, for instance, a wall of rough, bulging, uneven masonry would serve as well as a smooth one. Teddy wanted to do a proper job. He wanted to make it look beautiful and as if no doorway and no door had ever been there. So he worked slowly and meticulously, laying his courses of bricks in perfect alignment with the existing structure. One surprising discovery he made was that his father's trade was not the child's play he had always believed. There was skill in it, there were techniques and methods which he had never learned. But he managed, with a good deal of trial and error, and by lunch-time when he was due to leave and meet Francine six courses of bricks were in place.

Holly de Marnay's flat was in a street off Kilburn High Road, which the agents described as 'West Hampstead borders'. It was a shabby place of late-Victorian terraced houses, streets which had been tree-lined but were now car-lined as well. Fallen leaves and plastic litter were blown about on the pavements by the wind. Teddy felt a scornful wonder that anyone who had the chance of living where Holly's family did, in a fine big house by Ealing Common, could choose to slum it in this place.

For independence? He had had independence all

his life and it was a precarious, troublesome business. What you want if you can get it, he thought, is a beautiful home with people to look after you, which she had had and rejected. The house where the flat was looked one of the worst-kept in the street, with broken steps going up to the front door and two dilapidated pillars at the foot of them, on one of which sat a headless stone lion and on the other a child's woollen glove, no doubt picked up in the road. He rang the bell that looked as if it might be the right one.

He was expecting Holly to answer it, but it was Francine who came down. She was wearing a dress, a long black dress with a light rose-coloured jacket over it and a long chain of pink beads. Her hair was plaited into a loose braid. She took his hand and led him in, put up her face for a light kiss, but her beauty was too much for him and he took her in his arms in the dark hall, kissing her deeply.

All his vague sensations of disappointment in her were gone. She was perfect. She was his beautiful treasure. Her skin was softer than velvet, smoother than wax. While he had her he could care less than nothing for whoever and whatever awaited him upstairs.

Holly came up to him in her aristocratic manner, holding out her hand and saying, 'Hi, how do you do? We met at that exhibition, do you remember?'

Teddy nodded. Of course he remembered. That was where he had met Francine. The room they were in appalled him. For one thing it was filthy, a great cavernous one-time drawing-room, with folding doors and a ruined hardwood floor, scuffed and stained and pitted, and a hugely high ceiling hung with a grey metal chandelier and, too, with festoons of dusty cobwebs. The smell was a mingling of aromatherapy oils and marijuana.

Christopher was there, reclining on a settee covered in a polyester tiger skin, and there were two girls of the kind Teddy actually disliked letting his eyes rest on. One was fat with curly black hair and silver rings clipped all over her ears and her left eyebrow. The other was a waif-like creature, straw-coloured skin and wispy hair, wearing washed-out blue denim overalls and brown suede knee boots. He didn't catch their names, which hardly mattered since he had no intention of using them.

'I'll show you the rest of it if you like,' Holly said.

'Of course he'd like,' said Francine, linking her arm in his. 'And I'd like. I've been waiting for him to come so that I can see it.'

Was she implying that he was late? He glanced suspiciously at her. He was *never* late. They went out into the hall and through a door into a bedroom. You could see that one big bedroom had been made into three bedrooms and another into two.

'Who put those partitions up?' said Teddy. 'Bodger and Leggett?'

Appreciative laughter greeted his old joke. Perhaps Holly really hadn't heard it before. 'If Francine comes to be our fourth girl you can carry out some much-needed improvements. Be our builder.'

'You didn't tell me,' he said.

She squeezed his arm. 'Because there's nothing to tell. I'm not coming. I can't. They'd never let me.'

Holly laughed. 'Can't you abduct her, Teddy?'

The bedrooms were all the same, ugly cupboards, three of them with mattresses on the floor. When you had to do that it was another story, but to do it from choice . . .! The bathroom had a claw-footed bath, but not the latest fashion kind. This one had been put in when bathrooms were a daring innovation and since then had taken about fifteen coats of paint. Flakes of it, peeling off, disclosed a pattern of black islands in a green sea.

'Occasionally,' said Holly, 'you get out of the bath a most peculiar bruise colour, as if you'd been beaten up.'

She talked like an actress in one of those British films of the forties you sometimes saw on television. He had nothing to say to her or to Christopher. But while they ate their lunch in a pizza place in West End Lane he made the effort for Francine's sake. He told them about the work he was doing, leaving out the part about painting Mrs Trent's house and stressing his cabinet-making. The temptation to talk about Orcadia Cottage was very strong, he hardly knew why, perhaps because, apart from Francine, it was all he thought about at present.

'I've got a contract for a conversion,' he said. 'It's a house in St John's Wood. I'm doing it while the people are away.'

'I wish you'd do a conversion for us,' Holly said. 'Would you? When you've got time? Our landlord's my uncle's friend and I'm positive he'd say yes if I ask him terribly nicely.'

'Yes, we've never actually known anyone who can do this sort of thing, have we, Holl?' said Christopher.

'We have no skills, poor us, and we do tremendously admire someone who has.'

He had an idea they might be sending him up, but afterwards, when he asked Francine, she said no, they really meant it. He mustn't be suspicious of people, lots of people were really nice. Not in his experience, he thought, but he didn't say that.

Holly and Christopher drank a lot, spirits as well as wine, vodka mainly. What was there about that stuff that looked like thick water? He liked to see Francine with a glass of cold white wine in her hand,

280

not so much drinking it as holding the chilly glass, frosted with droplets, her parted lips touched by a gleam of wine. Like a girl in a cover photograph on one of those magazines that were too expensive for him to buy. Like a girl in a foreign film, in Paris maybe or Madrid, sitting outside at a table, waiting for her lover, waiting for him.

The one they went to see wasn't like that and there were few young people in it. Teddy couldn't understand why anyone would want to see a film about Queen Victoria falling in love with an old servant and Francine's enthusiasm he found incomprehensible. For most of the second half of it he kept his eyes shut, dreamed about acquiring ten thousand pounds and taking Francine shopping to expensive clothes shops in Knightsbridge, and buying her black dresses and white dresses made by top designers and floor-length velvet coats with big fur collars.

Back at Holly's, they all wanted him to take them for a ride in the Edsel. It puzzled them that he hadn't mentioned arriving in it. While they had been in the restaurant and the cinema someone, a child probably, had scored the words 'Shit yank car' across the top of the boot with a rusty nail. Christopher was loud in his indignation. He wanted to call the police. Teddy found he cared very little about the damage to the Edsel's bodywork, the sentiment written there was very much his own, and he knew the police would treat such a complaint with incredulity. They had other things to do, especially in this neighbourhood. But he took them all round the block and up and down West End Lane, Holly waving graciously to passers-by like a member of the Royal Family.

It was still only seven when he was able to take Francine away. She gave him an unpleasant surprise when she said she wouldn't come back home with him. He found a place where he could pull in and park and he sat staring at her.

'I'm sorry, Teddy. If I do I'll have to leave again almost immediately. There's no point in my coming back with you if I can't stay.'

'Then why', he said, 'did we waste the whole day with those people?'

'Is that how you saw it, as a waste? They're my friends.'

He picked up her hands. They were exceptionally pretty hands, of a narrowness usually only seen in Asian women, long-fingered, the nails perfect ovals, and creamy white. But what he liked best about them was the pure smoothness of the skin, not a line and scarcely a crease, the veins, instead of root-like, pale-blue shadows under the milky surface. He brought them to his lips, kissing the nails, the knuckles, the delicate membrane between forefinger and thumb. 'It's my place, isn't it? You don't like my place. I don't blame you, I said it was a dump.'

She was amazed and somehow disconcerted. To have her feelings so entirely misunderstood wasn't a new experience for her, but she hadn't expected it from Teddy.

'It's a horrible hole,' he said, 'and it's not fit for you to be in. I know that. I never wanted to take you there, but I didn't have a choice.'

'Teddy, it's not that. I love your house. Haven't I said so over and over? I love it.'

'If you really did you'd come back with me.'

'I can't. Julia's alone. I'm afraid of what she may do.'

'Why do you need these people?' he said. 'These so-called friends? This woman? You have me. I have you and you have me. We don't need other people.'

She said breathlessly, 'Give me back my hands.'

Her face was flushed. She was excited and he had

282

excited her. His heart began beating with steady, heavy thuds. 'You don't ever need to go back. You can stay with me day and night.'

She snatched her hands from him, turned away her face. 'Take me to a tube station. Please.'

He said lifelessly, 'I'll drive you all the way home.'

He couldn't afford it, he couldn't really afford to drive the Edsel at all. But he turned round a roundabout as soon as he could and drove her along the North Circular Road out to Ealing and let her out under the trees where they had parted that first time. She gave him one kiss, and then she jumped out of the car and ran.

The garage was large, but not large enough to accommodate the Edsel. It was a pity as he would have preferred not to leave it out there in the mews, attracting attention as it always did wherever it might be. Not that there was anyone's attention to attract on this evening. There seldom was. On Monday morning he would find a place where they sold spray paint in cans and see if they had a pale primrose one to cover up those incised letters on the boot top.

He entered through the back gate and closed it behind him. It occurred to him then that from the rear the house didn't look like a house at all but like a square bush with eyes in it. They were well into October now – wasn't it time those leaves fell off? Or were they the kind that didn't fall? The street lamp shone in here, but he switched on his torch. He squatted down and examined the manhole cover. A beautiful piece of work, he noticed for the first time: Paulson and Grieve, Ironsmiths of Stoke, and a laurel wreath that someone had designed with considerable skill and taste. He wouldn't junk it, he'd keep it, it was worth keeping.

Somewhere, among all these paving stones, front and back, hidden perhaps or half-hidden by over-hanging plants, must be one of just the right size which he could prise up and fit into the gap removing the cover would leave. Fit in and cement in place. That was a task for another day, for later in the coming week. He had other things to do first.

He let himself into the house by the back door and returned to his courses of brickwork. There he worked steadily, taking it slowly, but growing accustomed to the task and also becoming more expert. To be content only with perfection was his aim. If a brick jutted even a millimetre out of truth he took it down and started again. By the time he had completed a wall to fill the space where the doorway had been it was midnight.

But they were sealed up in there, those two. It was almost as if they no longer existed, as if by creating a doorless tomb for them he had magicked them into the dust he swept up and vacuumed away. Tomor-row he would set about plastering over the brick-work. And when that was done, perhaps even before it was done, he would *bring Francine here*. That was the solution to all their problems. He couldn't rent the elegant apartment he had had in mind, he didn't have the money or the means of raising any, but he had something better and it was free and available.

No one lived here. The owner of the house was gone for ever. In a way it was the Keith situation all over again. Just as he had seen to it that Keith died so that he could occupy Keith's house, so Harriet too had died and left him in possession. Those properties weren't his and, as far as he could see, never would be. But they were more his than they were anyone else's, there was no one to dispute his occupancy and, provided he paid the services bills that must inevitably arrive, no one to evict him.

He would bring Francine here. Tomorrow. He could continue with the work that had to be done. Now the hole in the wall was bricked up she would never guess a door had ever been there, but simply suppose the plaster needed renewing. A plan began taking shape in his mind. He would tell her he had acquired the place in exchange for certain essential work that must be done. It would, of course, be preferable to make her believe that the house was his, but there were too many difficulties in the way of that. Harriet's clothes in the wardrobe, for instance. All the valuable furniture and ornaments and pictures she would know he couldn't have afforded to buy. His lack of familiarity with the workings and arrangements of the house. She must be taught to believe he had taken on some sort of lease . . .

She would love it. It was so exactly suited to her as if it had been designed and built and furnished for her. And once she had seen it all and lain in that gorgeous bed with him, seen herself in those mirrors, felt the soft carpets and the slippery silk hangings, she would forget about having to go home early. She would stop telling him lies about this Julia woman.

And once he had her here he would be able to make love to her. These surroundings were what he needed, he couldn't understand why he hadn't thought of it before. His failure wasn't due to the presence of the Edsel, for the Edsel was clean now and empty, just an ordinary rather big and grotesque car, but to that squalid place where, although they were dead and gone, his parents and Keith remained as ugly and inhibiting presences.

Here everything would be different. He must be the kind of man, and he rather liked the idea of himself in this role, who could only perform the act of love with a beautiful woman in a beautiful environment. The former he had, no one was lovelier than Francine, and now he would place her in the setting fit for her. Then and only then would he find with her complete possession.

He drove home and put the Edsel back in its place in the garden, under the carport.

Chapter 28

Many times Julia wished she had made a note of Jonathan Nicholson's address. All she knew was that he lived somewhere in Fulham, but when she looked in the telephone directory she could find no J. Nicholson in SW6. Perhaps she could find his car again and perhaps that envelope would still be on the dashboard shelf.

She could only go out looking for it while Francine herself was out, for she still adhered to her principle of never allowing the girl to be in the house alone. And the difficulty there was that when Francine was out the car would not, of course, be parked in this vicinity. Francine and Jonathan Nicholson would be out in it somewhere, would probably have gone in it to his house in Fulham. Julia believed that if only she had had a chance to hunt for the car while Francine was at home she would certainly have found it.

Her opportunity came when Richard arrived back in England and took two days off at home. Julia said she was having lunch with Jocelyn and didn't feel it would be right to cancel the engagement. She disliked lying, but told herself that the end justified the means.

She spent two hours searching for the red sports car, walking up and down the parallel streets which radiated from this main road like ribs from a spine, and twice she thought she had found it. Perhaps she had found it, she couldn't be sure. The disappointing thing was that in neither car was there an envelope on the dashboard shelf addressed to Mr Jonathan Nicholson. When she got back Richard said Francine had gone out. She had an interview for a job and afterwards she was seeing a friend. He hadn't liked to ask her who the friend was and where they were going.

'I would have,' said Julia, and then she said, 'What's this about a job?'

He looked unhappy. 'Waitressing, I think it is. In that little coffee and sandwiches place at the other end of the High Street.'

'She can't be a waitress. How could you let her? Why didn't you stop her?'

'I can't stop her, Julia. She's an adult. Besides, she must do something and the job with Noele didn't work out. We've been through all this before.'

'Men will put their filthy hands all over her,' said Julia in a strange high voice. 'Up her skirt and down her blouse. They will slobber over her. They'll *fondle* her. And she won't say no, not she, she won't know how to, she won't want to, she's too highly sexed. The reality is that there's such a thing as nymphomania, you know, even if it's not politically correct to say it. I'd call her a classic case of nymphomania.'

Richard looked at his wife in horror. He thought he could see a shifting in her face, a curious lopsidedness, and the iris of her left eye seemed to loll into the corner of the white. When she had finished speaking her lips wobbled. He could think of nothing to say to her. She stared at him, then wheeled round and left the room.

The ridiculous thought came to him that she couldn't be mentally disturbed because she had been a psychotherapist. As if such people must be exempt from the disorders they treated. But she couldn't be disturbed, she couldn't be, he said over and over to himself. Not Julia, who had always been – he uttered the disloyalty in his mind – so *boringly* sane.

An image of Jennifer came to him. It was the nearest he had ever come to seeing a ghost, this conjuring of his first wife before his eyes. She was in the room and yet she was not, a floater on his retina, a cobweb dangling in his vision. He closed his eyes. He wanted her as a little boy wants his mother. To hold him and hug him. To protect him from mad-women with obscene sexual fantasies.

If, in that last year they had together, he had loved Jennifer as he once had and had awakened love in her, would she ever have died? For instance, he could have got home earlier that evening, just as he could have all those evenings. With him in the house she would have been safe. He couldn't have said how he knew this, for the murderer had come looking for money derived from drug dealing and would have killed anyone who got in his way, but he did know it. By instinct or intuition, he knew.

He opened his eyes and Jennifer's ghost had melted away as swiftly as it had materialised, and when he next saw Julia she was her old calm and rational self. She intended to go up to Oxford again in a few days, she would take Francine with her, and if they settled on a house it might be time to put this one on the market. He was tired, he was perhaps rather overwrought. It must have been his imagina-tion that an insane woman had come in here and harangued him, accusing his sweet and gentle child of sexual hysteria. Or he had dreamed it during the sleep he fell into after his lunch, just as he had dreamed Jennifer's visitation.

'I didn't get the job,' Francine said.

Teddy was relieved. 'You don't want a job like that. It's beneath you.'

'I have to do something. I have to learn about going out to work and earning money. That's part of the point of this gap year. The café didn't think I was tough enough for the job – they didn't quite say that, but it's what they meant.'

'You're not tough enough and you never can be.'

He had met her in the Edsel half a mile up the road. Now he was going to surprise her, if she would let him, if she failed to notice the change from the route he usually took. But her knowledge of London geography was elementary and when he turned off Park Road for Lisson Grove she noticed only the street name.

'Eliza Doolittle came from Lisson Grove,' she said.

'Who?'

'Eliza Doolittle in *Pygmalion*. It's a play by Shaw. She came from this street. Professor Higgins could tell by her accent.'

'Accents matter a lot to you, don't they?'

'What do you mean?'

'Never mind,' he said. 'Forget it.'

A cloud had passed across his pleasure. It hung there, dulling things.

She put her hand on his knee. 'Where are we going, Teddy?'

'You'll see.'

'This isn't the way to your house.'

'It's the way to *a* house.'

From Grove End Road he turned into Melina Place, crossed the mews into Orcadia Place. They would leave the car here, he said, there was a parking space provided for the house. No one would come and clamp it. He handed her out of the car, which was something he had never done before, and they walked round the corner.

When she saw the house the expression on her face was far from what he had expected, or rather, what he had hoped for. She seemed to look warily at its ancient bricks, its latticed windows, the Della Robbia plaque, the curtain of leaves, now crimson and gold. As they came up to the front door and he took the key out of his pocket, took it out with pride as if he really did own this place, a terrible thing happened. In fact, it was an ordinary thing, a nothing, but to his bewilderment it was terrible for her.

A butterfly, a poor bedraggled thing, the last of summer, fluttered from one of the dark-red leaves. Its wings were transparent in places where the velvety dust had worn away, but it was still distinctly a black butterfly with a bright-red and white border to its wings. It half flew, half staggered on the wing to flutter limply against Francine's shoulder. She recoiled with a cry, warding it off with her hands.

'Oh, no, oh, no, please – I can't – no!'

He caught her in his arms, drawing her back. 'What is it? What's wrong?'

'That thing, that's a red admiral. Oh, I'm *sorry*, I'm sorry to be such a fool.'

The butterfly was on the ground, feebly moving its wings. Teddy stamped on it. He thought this decisive action, obviously necessary, would please Francine. It was clearly what she wanted.

She burst into tears. 'You didn't have to kill it, the poor thing, the poor thing!'

He muttered, 'It was going to die anyway. Why do you care so much? It was only an old butterfly,' and he unlocked the front door.

She stepped inside, her head bent and her hands covering her face. It was not an auspicious beginning for their arrival at Orcadia Cottage.

And it took a little while before things became better. Francine's face wore the same wary look when she looked round the hall and was taken by him into the drawing-room, the dining-room, shown the curved white staircase. She had been silent from the moment they entered and he closed the front door behind them. Her face was red and her eyes swollen from crying, and for the time being she was not the beauty he worshipped and loved above everything to gaze at. The perfection of her white skin was spoilt and she sniffed once or twice in a too human way. He had never supposed her capable of sniffing. Added to his dismay at her clothes, the jeans again and a heavy dark sweater, these new doubts half panicked him.

That she was making efforts for his sake escaped him. He didn't see her brace herself. The smile she forced he saw as wholly natural wonderment at the interior of this place.

'Whose house is it, Teddy? Why are we here?'

He had prepared his answer. 'I'm doing a job, plastering, stonework. The woman who owns it has let me live here while that's going on. It's a kind of lease really. She won't be back.'

'But she will be one day?'

He dredged up a phrase he had read or heard somewhere. 'Maybe in the not unforeseeable future.' He laughed. 'Or the *unforeseeable* future. Anyway, it's not our problem. It's ours for now. Come upstairs.'

The house reminded her of the cottage where they had lived and where her mother had died. It was quite different really, not so old for one thing, and inside far more elaborately and expensively furnished. That house had been silent with the quietness of the country, while even inside here you could hear the distant throb of traffic, the hum of London. But she had felt the similarity, some identifying atmosphere, from the first moment she and Teddy had stepped on to the flagstones of that enclosed court that was the front garden. All those leaves, the red and yellow creeper that blanketed the house, they had had one like it on their cottage. Then had come the unpleasant though ridiculous incident of the red admiral, to remind her further, and Teddy's brutal act which for a few moments had seemed utterly to alienate him from her.

She had wept and hoped he would comfort her, but he had only been impatient. She sensed that he was disappointed in her reaction and she did her best to show an enthusiasm she didn't feel. Somehow, in spite of her lack of experience, she understood that because of his failure with her he was under an increasing strain and she sensed that here, in this place he so obviously deeply admired, he would triumph. It was to be, she supposed, in this splendid film star bed, the kind of thing you saw in photographs in glossy house interiors magazines, all white silk draperies and gilding and insertions of classical paintings.

'Do you like it?' he kept saying, and 'What do you think of it?'

She wanted to say, because it was true, that she had liked his house, the way it was done. The word, she imagined, was 'minimalism'. In that case, the expression for this must be 'baroque'. But she said none of it. 'It's lovely.'

'I wanted to see you in this bed. I thought it was made for you, this whole room, this bed. Please.'

A strange feeling took hold of her. It was if she were learning things she couldn't, at her age and with her very limited experience, possibly know. Yet the knowledge was very strong and deeply troubling. For example, an understanding was there that her first love affair shouldn't be conducted in this way, that there was something perilous about it, something damaging to her and to him. And this, too, that she was not a thing of perfect beauty, an icon, an ornament to be adored, but a real and very young woman.

What would he do if he tried and tried but, after everything was the ideal way he wanted it, still failed? What would *she* do? She felt cold and reluctant, but she took off her clothes and got into the bed, expecting him to join her. Instead he stood watching her with an expression of almost cruel concentration. It was late on a November afternoon, dusk almost, and the room was dim and shadowy. She rather liked this twilight that kept some things half secret but now that she was in the bed, positioned by him to face herself in the mirror, the bedclothes drawn from off her so that she was white and naked in that white silk place, he switched on all the lights, making a violent blaze.

She recoiled from it, blinking her eyes. Her hands had closed into fists and in the mirror she saw a frightened girl with huge eyes and a look on her face of appeal, almost a cry for rescue. But she did nothing and said nothing, only let him watch her, drink in his fill of her. For a moment – and she would have hated this – she thought he would fall on his knees like someone before the image of a goddess. Instead, though after a long time, he turned off the brightest of the lights, undressed and came into the bed beside her.

Then followed the gentle kissing and caresses she loved. She had even told him it was enough for her, though this wasn't strictly true. He had told her quite roughly that she was lying, that must be rubbish, she didn't have to be kind to him, only be with him. But it was her nature to be kind and when, now, he tried again and failed again, she held him in her arms with great tenderness and kissed him and stroked his hair.

'Let's go to sleep,' she said, 'just lie here and go to sleep.'

In the late evening when they woke he became more cheerful. He showed her the rest of the house, wanted to know again and again if she liked it, if she *really* liked it. And he seemed resigned to her going home early so long as she promised to come back next day. He walked her to the tube at St John's Wood, it wasn't far, kissed her on the pavement outside the station with all the mastery and power of the successful lover. It was only nine o'clock. She would be home in good time.

It was a new feeling Teddy had. When he was a child, long, long ago, he had known it, but it had passed away with time because it was useless. It saved him from nothing, secured him nothing, brought him no comfort and nothing was changed by it. He couldn't afford to have it, so in his desperate battle to survive it had been cast aside. Or buried deep. But now it had surfaced. The feeling was fear.

He was very afraid. Of himself, mostly. His body which, apart from that mutilated finger, was such a perfect and trouble-free machine, not only obeying him in everything he asked of it, but performing superlative acts beyond what was expected – look how he had lifted Keith's body and how he had moved the stone – now failed lamentably and in an area where at his age and with his strength it should most have gratified him.

For a few moments that afternoon he had come close to hating Francine. It was easy for her, everything was easier for her. His desire for her filled every part of his body and his mind, flooded him with urgency and longing and utter need, so that everything else emptied itself out and drained away.

Why was it, then, that while he looked at her and adored he was erect and strong, a current flowing through his veins, but as soon as they touched and she was in his arms he wilted and shrank like a poisoned tree?

Slowly he walked back to Orcadia Place. He would spend the night there, sleep in that bed. If she had stayed, eventually all would have been well, he thought. He thought it resentfully, though by now he had forgotten his near-dislike of her in the memory of how beautiful she had looked in that room, better even than he had anticipated.

Before meeting her that afternoon he had put the finishing touches to the brickwork. Alone now, in the silent and otherwise dark house, he began the task of plastering. It was far from the simple job he had thought. In fact, try as he would, taking it slowly and methodically, using the tools he had bought, the diamond-shaped plasterer's trowel and the rectangular one, he was unable to achieve an absolutely smooth and regular surface.

It irked him to fail at something which fools like the men his father had worked with did easily every day. But those men had had years of practice and to him it was new. Still, he refused to be content with a botched job and, scraping off the plaster, began again. This time was better. Practice was all. At last the result was close to what he aimed at, acceptable even to a perfectionist like him. Tomorrow he would paint the wall he had made and do it before he went to fetch Francine.

After he had taken a bath in that free-standing claw-footed tub, he found that his mind was still stirred up with a million thoughts and fancies. He was sure he would be a real man, a potent man, if he had more money. At the back of his mind, however much he resisted it, was the fear that Francine despised him. For his class, his accent, his home background and his poverty. How could you make satisfactory love to a woman who felt only contempt for you?

Picking up his clothes from the floor – he would wash them next day in the Orcadia Cottage machine – he felt in his jeans pocket and brought out the small leather-bound address book that had been in Harriet's handbag. Strange, he thought he had thrown it away when he discarded the bag. Returning to the white silk bed where he and Francine had lain that afternoon, he flicked through the pages of the address book, but only one name meant anything to him: Simon Alpheton. He dropped the address book on the floor.

It was two in the morning. Several clocks in the house told him so, but in silence; none of them chimed the hour.

Chapter 29

The woman who accompanied Franklin Merton on his holidays, and who had by this time been his companion on several of these trips, he had met in the Green Park one sunny afternoon in June. Met, that is, meaning encountered, for they had first been introduced to one another some forty-five years earlier.

Franklin was on his way from Green Park tube station down the Queen's Walk to have lunch with a friend at his club in St James's when he saw ahead of him, gambolling on the grass, an Irish setter. As such dogs invariably did, this one reminded him of O'Hara, whom he had been obliged to relinquish to Anthea when he went off with Harriet. In subsequent years he often thought it had been a poor exchange.

The dog came up to him, Franklin put out his hand in a gentle and friendly way, the dog approached, and in that moment a woman appeared, as it seemed, from nowhere. It was Anthea.

He hadn't seen her for eighteen years. In the decade prior to that he had only seen her twice. He knew she had married two years after their divorce, that her husband had been well-off, that he had died and left her a house somewhere in Mayfair. 'Hallo,' he said.

'Hallo.'

'What's the dog called?'

'De Valera.'

She had worn very well, he thought. She must be sixty-five or -six but she looked younger than Harriet. A comfortably plump woman, she had a smooth, unlined round face and her grey hair, untinted, shone like newly polished silver. If she wore make-up it was discreetly applied. The only signs of her wealth were the large diamond rings on both her hands, for the tweed suit she wore, though obviously once expensive, had seen better days. She put out her hand and when the dog came to her, held him by the collar as if to keep him from the cajolements of strangers.

'Come and have a drink,' said Franklin.

'What, now?'

'I know a nice little pub off St James's Square.'

'So do I,' said Anthea. 'Probably the same one. We always had a lot of tastes in common. How's your wife?'

As Franklin returned a rather clipped answer to this question he was thinking that she would refuse his invitation. He found himself quite intensely minding this. 'Do come,' he said.

She put the dog on the lead. In the pub they gave De Valera a bowl of water and there returned to Franklin's mind a similar scene in a pub when he was nearly thirty years younger, but then the woman was Harriet and the dog was O'Hara. He also remembered, rather later, the friend he was meeting and he phoned the club and said he had flu.

After a couple of dry martinis Anthea said, 'I'll just take Dev back to Half Moon Street and then I'd like to give you lunch.'

No woman had ever before paid for any meal eaten by Franklin. It was a novel situation and strangely exciting. When they parted he asked if he could see her again and two months later they went on holiday together to Lugano. That had been five years before.

Now, in a borrowed villa outside San Sebastian, or rather, at that precise moment, sitting on the terrace of a restaurant and looking at the great curved bay and the cresting waves, Franklin said not very romantically, 'Shall we give it another go?'

'I beg your pardon?'

'We don't have to get married unless you're fussy about that. Nobody cares these days. But we do rub along rather well together, don't you think?'

'We always did,' said Anthea, 'until you took up with that red-haired cow.'

'Calling names doesn't help. I think she's got a teenager in tow, very young anyway. I've seen all the signs.'

'She'll take a lot of keeping. From what you say she's an expensive bitch. I could help with that, but I draw the line at someone else's toy boy.' Anthea looked speculatively at him over the rim of her glass. 'You're sure it's me you want and not De Valera?'

Franklin smiled his death's-head grin to take the sting out of what he had to say. 'If we wait much longer the poor old boy will have gone to the Happy Hunting Ground.'

Recalling from somewhere or other that new plaster must be left to dry, for at least a day and perhaps more, Teddy got to work next morning on the backyard. He had woken early, for a few seconds with no idea where he was. Then he remembered. He was up and dressed and outside soon after seven.

It was still dark. The day ahead would be misty and damp. Without too much difficulty he lifted the manhole cover and laid it on the flagstones. A good many solutions to the problem of the open manhole had suggested themselves to him: a flower-bed planted in a fibreglass liner with maybe one tree in it or a rosebush, a birdbath on a plinth or a second marble urn, another paving stone set in cement like the rest of the components of the courtyard. He thought wistfully of creating something beautiful and of transforming this rather dull backyard. What he would have liked best was a statue, a figure, for instance, of Francine in bronze or marble.

That was impracticable, he wasn't a sculptor and the materials in any case would be too expensive. A flagstone inserted in the opening would be the best and safest idea. By the time daylight had come, a pearly cold daylight that seemed to bear no relation to a risen sun, he had found what he was looking for, not in this courtyard but on the edge of the paved area at the front of the house.

The flagstones up against the flower borders on either side were loose and had simply been laid flat on the soil below. However, only one of them was approximately the right shape and size. Teddy realised that he would have to make a wooden frame to insert in the aperture, rest the stone on it and cement it in place. He prised up the stone and watched the woodlice he had disturbed running all directions. A couple of snails adhered to its underside. He brushed them off and when he looked back on the doorstep had the satisfaction of seeing a thrush intent on cracking the shell of one of them, beating it against the flags.

Crumbs of soil and flakes of stone made a trail through the house as he passed. He would clear it up later, have a good clean. It was essential to maintain the house in immaculate condition, in a better state, in fact, than that in which he had found it. The frame he would make of oak, for this was a wood which was practically indestructible, everlasting and undamaged by water, drought or time.

He took measurements, hid the flagstone under the silvery grey shrubs at the side of the courtyard and replaced the manhole cover. His next task would be the purchase of matt white vinyl paint and more ready-mixed cement. A piece of oak he had at home would do for the frame. If not, that would be something else to buy. He washed his hands thoroughly, found a dustpan and brush and the vacuum cleaner, and removed from the floors all traces of the passage of that flagstone through the house. Then he drove home, stopping for the paint and the cement on the way.

Luckily, he had a piece of oak he thought might be big enough. There was no time to waste and he got busy with his saw. He was meeting Francine at three. While he worked he thought about Harriet Oxenholme's bank card. Not the two credit cards, the Diners Club and the American Express, but the Visa Connect card which, from observing the behaviour of other people at cash dispensers, he knew might be used for extracting money from a bank account. How did it work? What did you do?

Half an hour was all the time he needed to complete the drawings for the built-in cupboards in the Highgate house. He put them in an envelope with his estimate, addressed the envelope to Mr Habgood and went out to buy a stamp. The bank next to the Post Office had a cash dispenser beside its front entrance. Teddy eyed it speculatively. He only had to wait a few minutes.

A woman, a young girl really, approached the dispenser and looked over her shoulder to the right and the left before taking a card out of her bag. Trying to be streetwise, Teddy thought. Well, he wasn't going to lay a finger on her. The idea made him shudder, for although she was about the same age as Francine, she was in every way inferior, overweight, spotty and with stubby red hands.

He watched those hands, the fingers with the bitten nails. She put the card into a slot and a lot of green letters came up on to the screen. He got as close behind her as he dared and just made out that the machine was asking for a number. That must be what she punched in. She suddenly looked round sharply and he retreated to be on the safe side, started walking away. Looking back over his shoulder he saw the card reappear and, with a sudden feeling of envy, a wad of cash come out.

So you had to have a number. Just a number the bank gave you? Or your phone number? Your date of birth, if there weren't too many digits? Somehow, he knew Harriet wouldn't have used her date of birth. What would she have used? If he could find that number his worries were over.

All that morning Julia's sufferings had been terrible. She had no belief in Francine's story that Miranda's father might be offering her a job and she was going to see him. Why would a man like that, a tycoon, have a job for an untrained eighteen-year-old anyone could see was emotionally disturbed? She had begun her pacing just after Francine left the house. On one of her marches to the front window she saw a young man sitting in the bus shelter. He was fair-haired and of a heavy build, but that didn't fool Julia. Jonathan Nicholson was clever and would stop at nothing to get Francine. Disguise was an area in which he was an expert and to lighten his hair and flesh out his body was child's play to him.

If he was bent on defying her she was not going to rise to his bait so easily. Instead of going immediately across the road, she opened the window, leaned out and stared at him. He stared back. He had seen her, he knew she was watching him. She moved slowly, in a deceptively casual manner, no manic rushing this time, put on her coat, buttoned it, wrapped a scarf round her neck, opened the front door.

He was still there, but standing up now. She hesitated, thought, suppose he attacks me? Suppose he strikes me, pushes me into the road? It was a risk she had to take. For Francine's sake, to save Francine from him. Nothing he could do to her mattered when it was a question of Francine's safety. She walked briskly across the road to the island. A stream of traffic held her there. The last vehicle in it was the bus.

That was just her luck. To be so near to her quarry and have him get away yet again. She couldn't cross until the bus had gone and he, of course, had gone with it. Or had he? She hadn't seen him get on it, only its arrival, a big red screen before her eyes, and seen its departure wipe him away. He might simply have hidden himself, calculating that she would believe him gone with the bus, while in fact he was hiding behind that fence or in that garden or down that side turning.

Julia searched for some time. She went into several gardens and even lifted the lid off someone's wheelie-bin to see if he was lurking inside. The householder put a head out of an upstairs window and shouted at her. Then she went up and down the street looking for Jonathan Nicholson's car. Of course, she failed to find it because he had been using the bus, hadn't he? His car must be in for a service or perhaps he had sold it, got rid of it because it was such a giveaway and he knew she was on to him.

Eventually she went back home, but an hour or so later she understood that he had been there all the time, for she saw him back in the bus shelter, his hair restored to its natural dark, his extra weight shed. This time he was accompanied by several others. Bodyguards, she thought, heavies was what they called them.

She didn't go back. She found Miranda's number in Francine's address book and called it. A girl who certainly wasn't Miranda answered, thus confirming Julia's worst fears. Julia asked to speak to Miranda's father and the girl said he was at his office and then, hastily and obviously untruthfully, that she'd heard Francine was seeing him about a job. It was just the sort of lie a young girl would tell, confident that by so doing she was serving her friend.

Because she didn't want Jonathan Nicholson to see her go out and thus leave the field clear for him, Julia waited until he and his companions had gone once more into hiding and then she took her shopping bag and went down to the High Street. In the continental patisserie she bought olive ciabatta and date bread and chocolate croissants and several packets of white chocolate finger biscuits. Much of this she ate for her lunch, gorging until she felt sick. When Richard phoned in the late afternoon she put on a bright, sweet manner, telling him everything was fine, it was a lovely day for late November and Francine – imagine – had gone out with Miranda.

'I thought you were going to say, with that boy,' said Richard.

'He'd *like* to. But she's not having any, or that's how I see it. The reality is, he's been watching for her from that bus shelter most of the day.'

'He's what?'

'I'm afraid he does a lot of that. He's quite obsessed.'

'He's not stalking her, is he?'

Julia suddenly felt very frightened. Of course

Jonathan Nicholson was stalking her, but if she admitted that to Richard he would bring the police in, maybe take legal advice. She didn't want interference with her management of Francine, she didn't want busybodies coming in and taking away her control. Her denials poured out. 'Oh, no, no, what an idea! I wouldn't have that, I'd stop that. Let me have a look . . . He's gone now, disappeared. Somehow I have a feeling, an actual gut feeling, darling, that he won't come back.'

'I hope you're right. I should be home by six. Will Francine be home?'

'Oh, yes, quite early. She promised.'

'If you stayed here and slept here and were here all the time it would be all right.' Teddy spoke sullenly, in a grudging, accusing tone. 'I could do it right if you were here with me.'

His grim looks troubled her. He ceased to be handsome or fun or attractive when he drew his black brows together and pushed out his lower lip. Paradoxically, he then looked much younger than his real age, like an overgrown naughty child.

'You won't do what I want,' he said. 'I only want you to do what I want, it's not much to ask, it's simple enough.'

'But I do do what you want, Teddy. I let you wrap me in all those silk things and draperies and whatever, and shine lights on me and put all that jewellery all over me, I do let you, but I can't do it all the time. It makes me feel – well, awkward, I don't know, uneasy. I can do it for a bit, but not for hours and hours.'

'Then what do you want?'

'Maybe go for a walk sometimes, have a meal somewhere, go out in the car, talk. I'd really just like to talk. We never talk.'

They were in Harriet's bedroom, Francine on the bed whose sheets he had changed, putting on the pillows white organza slips he had found in a cupboard. She had been naked at his request, hung only with all the many pearl necklaces he had discovered among Harriet's jewellery, but now, disconcerted by something she didn't know the name of, his obsessive gaze, she had wrapped herself in the white embroidered bedcover.

'I'm sorry, Teddy, I don't want to hurt your feelings, but I don't think it's quite right you dressing me up, or *not* dressing me up really, and staring at me. It's –' she nearly said 'sick' but stopped herself '– not the way it should be.'

Instead of answering he said, 'If we're in the complaints department I'd just like to say that I hate the way you dress. I hate your clothes, jeans and shirts and jackets a guy might wear on a building site. The first time I saw you you had a dress on.'

'I can wear a dress if that's what you want.'

'Find something in the cupboard. Go on. There are plenty. She won't want them. I've got a job to do – remember? I'd best get on with it.'

Left alone, Francine put on her underclothes and opened the wardrobe door. The interior reminded her of Noele's shop. Here hung the dresses and suits of a middle-aged woman of flashy taste, one partial to pearls, sequins and rhinestones. The colours were mostly red, black and white, but one dress of velvet was a startling emerald. Even if she had liked them she wouldn't have wanted to put on any of these garments. They weren't hers and she couldn't believe their owner wouldn't object to her wearing them.

She expected the second wardrobe to contain a more casual line of clothes, but the things inside it were all men's. Suits, sports jackets, trousers, a camel-hair winter coat and the sort of raincoat policemen wear in television serials. A man's clothes, but not a young man's. It was no business of hers, Francine decided, and remembering what Teddy had said about her jeans and her shirt, after some small hesitation she put on a black silk dressing-gown.

Whether Teddy wanted her to be with him while he worked she wasn't sure, but there was nothing else to do in this house. She went downstairs and, guided by the strong and heady smell of paint, found him in a corner of the hall at the back near the kitchen door.

When he saw her he jumped. 'I didn't hear you.'

She laughed. 'Julia would say you had a guilty conscience. Well, she'd more likely say you'd a guilty super-ego.'

He didn't smile. 'Where did you find that dressing-gown?'

'It belongs to your friend – employer, client, whatever she is. Teddy, did you know that other wardrobe is full of men's clothes? You said she lived alone.'

He put down the paint roller. He thought about what she had said. 'They must be Marc Syre's.'

'But he died before either of us was born.'

'I don't know, then. Does it matter?'

She wasn't frightened of him, only puzzled. He followed her up the stairs, switched off the light, went into the kitchen to clean his paint roller and wash his hands.

'What shall we do?' she said, like a child.

'Do?'

'I mean, you've finished working, so what shall we do for the rest of the day?'

Instead of answering, he dried his hands, turned to her and snatched her into his arms. It was like that, a seizing of her, rough and sudden. He pushed the dressing-gown down off her shoulders and kissed her neck and her breasts. He held her waist in his two hands as one might hold a bunch of flowers. 'It'll be all right now,' he kept whispering. 'Come with me now, it'll be fine now.'

Chapter 30

But it was not all right.

Just as he had felt that years-old emotion, long-forgotten, that sense of fear, so now another childhood urge returned. He wanted to cry. In the play-pen he had cried, but never since, not even when he cut his finger with Mr Chance's chisel. He buried his face in her shoulder and heaved with dry sobs.

She held him and told him yet again that it didn't matter, it wasn't important. One day it would come right, if he would stop worrying. She kissed his hands and kissed the mutilated finger, but he hated that, he hated her drawing attention to his one flaw. It would only come right, he said to her peevishly, when she was with him all the time, when she left that old woman, when she wanted him more than that old woman. But he made no physical attempt to stop her going, even drove her part of the way in the Edsel.

And when she was away from him, in a strange way things were better. He could no longer feel she was watching him and wondering, despising him, growing impatient. He could even direct his mind and his actions to the pressing things he had to do in the house. It was no bad thing that she had refused to see him for a few days, for he could spend them finishing the job.

It was a strange feeling, contemplating that wall, on which the white paint was drying, and knowing that behind it was something that maybe no human eye would see again. That was no doubt what those makers of the pyramids thought, when the Pharaoh and his attendants and his artefacts had been laid in the tomb, and they came to seal it up. Of course, they had been wrong, the pyramids had been broken into and the dead discovered, and perhaps his burial chamber would also one day be opened. But no, he thought, no, I have sealed it so that no one will believe anything was ever here.

A little white chamber, a tiny windowless room, lying deep in the earth under London. It was the kind of idea he liked. In a curious way it even cheered him. It took away some of the pain of his inadequacy. In this area, of making death and achieving concealment, he was a king.

No one could enter his secret chamber from the house for there was no entrance to it. From the backyard there would soon be no opening, no hole, no way in, for Paulson and Grieve, Ironsmiths of Stoke, in their laurel wreath, would be hidden in some store-place of his own and where the coal chute had been, a blossoming plant growing in a new flower-bed. Airless it would become inside there and the ill-matched couple slowly decay, return to earth, to dust, to bones. So should all ugliness be concealed and buried . . .

The phone ringing made him jump. Naturally, he wasn't going to answer it. The answering machine cut in. He went upstairs. Francine hadn't made the bed before she left. This omission irritated him. He didn't expect bed-making from her because she was a woman; he would expect it from anyone. She had been on a pinnacle and now she fell a little in his estimation. His grandmother used to say that we can't all be alike and that this was a good thing, but he wasn't so sure. It would be a good idea if everyone were like him, tidy, clean, methodical, circumspect and punctual.

He straightened the bottom sheet and shook out the white silk coverlet. When he plumped up the pillows he saw Harriet's address book lying underneath. Sitting on the bed, he went through it again. One of these phone numbers might be her PIN number. What did PIN stand for, anyway? Personal something? Personal Index Number? No, Personal Identification Number. Perhaps she had used her own phone number. Or Simon Alpheton's. He had an idea that if you kept trying the wrong numbers in one of those machines it would eventually, maybe after three goes, swallow up the card and keep it.

It could be any number. You wouldn't use a friend's phone number for that, though, would you? If you were like him and had no friends it was hard to know. What would he do? Remember it, he thought. But just as few people were as tidy and clean and particular as he, so few had his retentive memory. The time was coming, he had read, when those cash dispensers would work on a fingerprint or a picture of the iris of your eye. But it hadn't come yet. At the moment it still relied on numbers.

Once again he leafed through the address book. Most of the names were of people, but some seemed to be of restaurants and there were a lot for people who performed services, plumbers, electricians, builders of various kinds. To maintain the house in its pristine condition, he supposed. Why would she have all those restaurants?

Rich people ate out a lot, of course. Would she eat out alone? Take a guest with her? He knew so little about that kind of life. He had heard of none of those restaurants: Odette's, the Ivy, Orso's, Odin's, Jason's, La Punaise, L'Artiste Assoiffé, L'Escargot. If they were restaurants.

312

Back at home, he finished making the wooden frame for the flagstone. In Orcadia Cottage he had drawn a section through the skirting board to be sure the moulding was right, and now he set about cutting and planing a suitable piece of deal. It would be possible to buy beading to fit, but he couldn't afford to buy anything. His finances were in a serious state. Francine didn't seem to understand that they couldn't go out driving in the Edsel or eat in even the meanest restaurant because he had no money.

Restaurants. He found the Yellow Pages and looked up all those listed in Harriet's address book. The only one that wasn't there was La Punaise. The exchange was the same as Jason's which meant, according to Jason's address, that it must be somewhere in Maida Vale. The four-digit number was four-one-six-two. He dialled the seven digits and got a woman's voice saying that the number he had called could not be located, whatever that meant.

On the way back to Orcadia Place he found a parking meter off the Finchley Road with fifteen minutes left to run. The space was big enough to accommodate the Edsel, which most were not, so he left the car there and went off to find a cash dispenser.

Nervously – he half expected the machine to carry out immediate retribution of some kind – he inserted Harriet's Connect card and when requested to punch out four digits, used her phone number. *Please Wait*, said the machine. Then it said there was a fault and his order could not be processed. But the card came back. He was afraid to try a second time.

Rage or hysterical joy, Francine was accustomed to one or the other from Julia. But silence was new. To be greeted with an injured stare, head lowered, a frown gathering between those suffering eyes, but not a word uttered, was unprecedented.

Somehow she knew quite well that asking why, what was wrong now, what had she done, what should she do, all those enquiries were useless. Julia was beyond reason. If she had once genuinely feared harm would come to Francine from some external cause or from within herself, this she had long since forgotten. All that now mattered to her was her obsession with keeping Francine there with her, indoors, under her eye day and night. Going upstairs to her room, Francine thought that Julia didn't even want her to have a job, suitable friends, an occupation. She wanted a prisoner she could control.

Her father was at home. She had made up her mind to tell him the truth, that she was meeting Teddy, 'seeing' Teddy, that he was her boyfriend. She was tired of lying, she hated it, the false statements that she was visiting this girl's home or that. But she was unable to be with him without Julia being there and although he would certainly tell Julia, she couldn't bring herself to come out with it all in Julia's presence, face her rage and panic and somehow, too, her triumph. But nor could she say to her father that she would like to speak to him alone. The result was that she said nothing and spent long hours up in her room.

Next day she was due to see Teddy again and she wanted to see him, she wanted to reassure him once more. It was her firm belief that if she could only make him understand it didn't matter and she didn't mind, things would come right. But to go over to Orcadia Place on Thursday would mean directly lying to her father. Making false statements to Julia was one thing, to her father quite another. It would be impossible to bring herself to stand in front of him and say she was going clubbing with Miranda or to the cinema with Holly when in fact she was meeting Teddy. Francine was learning that while it is easy enough to lie to someone who means nothing to you, it is a very different matter with a person for whom you feel love and respect.

She phoned Teddy at home and got no reply. The Orcadia Cottage number she didn't know and she reminded herself to find out what it was. That set her speculating about Orcadia Cottage and worrying a little. Who was this woman who lived there and allowed Teddy to make free with her house? Young as she was, Francine was already an observer of people and she thought that few would behave like that, let someone who was, after all, a builder, move into one's house and sleep in one's bed and bring his girlfriend there.

Teddy's past life remained a mystery, perhaps a secret. She knew only that his parents were dead. It might be that this woman was some relation, an aunt or godmother. There were holes in this theory – who, for instance, did the men's clothes belong to? – but on the whole it satisfied her. She would ask or he would tell her without being asked. When she tried phoning him again, this time in the early evening, he answered.

A sulky response to her excuses for not seeing him was what she expected. She had to listen to indignant protests and a stream of invective directed at Julia.

'I'll see you on Saturday,' she said. 'Don't be cross. Please.'

'I'm not cross with you.' But he sounded it. Then he said, 'Francine?'

'What is it?'

'You know French, don't you? You did it for your A Level.'

'You want me to translate something?'

'What does La Punaise mean? P,u,n,a,i,s,e.'

315

People who don't understand a foreign language that you do always expect you to know every word it contains, to be a complete walking vocabulary. You couldn't be that even in your own language, there would always be some words you had to look up in the dictionary.

'I don't know, Teddy. I've never heard it before. Shall I look it up and call you back?'

At home again, he was working on the skirting board. He didn't mind carving and glass-papering, these were soothing, tranquil activities, but at the same time it irked him to think that if he had had a few pounds at his disposal he could have bought beading to do a job in ten minutes that was taking hours.

There had been no reply from Mr Habgood. No doubt he was impatient, but if that estimate had been accepted, the ten per cent deposit he had asked for should also have come in the envelope. Craftsmen sometimes had to wait weeks, months, to get paid, as he remembered from certain remarks of Mr Chance, complaints that had gone over the head of a small boy but now came back to him.

Francine hadn't called back. He didn't ask himself why not, he could imagine. That old woman had got hold of her and was haranguing her, or her dad had come home and needed her for something or other. Still, you'd think she'd keep a French dictionary in her room. A bell started ringing, but it was the doorbell, not the phone. Nobody ever called, he couldn't imagine who it was unless Nige had come round to make a fuss about the noise the plane made.

It was his grandmother. She had rung the bell – for 'politeness's sake', she said – but immediately let herself in with her key. 'Hallo, stranger,' she said.

He wanted to keep her in the hall, but she came

in, marched into his room and stared at the Edsel, which she evidently hadn't expected to see. But her first remark wasn't about the car. 'This place is like ice. It's colder than outdoors.'

'I can't afford to heat it,' he said.

'Too proud to sign on, are you? Well, it makes a change to find some pride in this family. I'm not stopping, I wouldn't want to take my coat off. The doctor says I'm not to get chilled, I could get that hypothermia they all have nowadays and I don't fancy being wrapped up in cooking foil in an ambulance at my age. I came to say my pal Gladys has done your curtains and what about you painting her outside toilet like you promised.'

The idea of curtains for this house seemed to belong in the distant past. He had a new home now and a warm one. Maybe he could sell Gladys's effort, take it to one of those second-hand curtain places. But meanwhile he would have to paint a freezing-cold backyard privy ...

The phone was ringing. He could see his grandmother brightening up, the way she always did when she had the chance of overhearing someone's private conversation. He picked up the receiver. It was Francine.

'I'm so sorry, Teddy. My dad came home just at that moment. And then Miranda's dad's secretary phoned to say I hadn't got the job.'

He cared nothing about all that. 'Did you find out what La Punaise means?'

'Yes, I did. It means a pin.'

'La Punaise means a pin?'

'That's right.'

'You're wonderful,' he said. 'You're brilliant. I'll call you back.'

He threw his arms into the air and jumped up and

317

down. He burst into peals of laughter. His troubles were over, everything had come right.

'Whatever's got into you?' said Agnes.

Chapter 31

David Stanark had died by his own hand and Richard had failed to be there in his hour of need. He was ignorant of David's troubles because he hadn't bothered to find out, because he had neglected David. An hour of need it must surely have been as, deserted by his wife, no doubt friendless, with no one to whom he could unburden himself, he had hung the rope over a beam in his garage and made a noose, put it round his neck and stepped off the chair.

It was months since Richard had seen him. Their friendship had never been the same after David had said those sententious things about the reason why Pride was one of the Seven Deadly Sins. Richard knew it himself, it was only an echo of his own conclusions, but there are situations in which we dislike those who agree with us. We have confided in them because we want them to deny our humiliating suspicions and too-frank analysis of our own character. Richard could never see David without remembering that little lecture on vanity and learning to live with our own mistakes. So he continued to see him only rarely and then always with his wife Susan, who was Julia's friend.

But now he was dead, David who hadn't deserted him when a friend was needed, David, who, if he hadn't quite saved his life, had at least spared him days or weeks of police interrogation and suspicion

and a calumny that might have stuck. Guilt overwhelmed him. If he had been a true friend David
might be alive now. Again it was that wretched pride
of his intervening to wreck his life and other
people's. All he could do now, and very inadequate
it was, would be what the police asked and go to see
them on his way to Heathrow on Friday.

As soon as her father's back was turned, as it seemed
to Julia, Francine went out. Possibly she said where
she was going, Julia hadn't listened. She was tired of
these attempts to make a fool of her when she knew
the girl was going off to meet Jonathan Nicholson.
  She told herself she was glad to see the back of
Francine. Without her tiresome obstinate presence in
the house she, Julia, could get on with all the tasks
and occupations her conscientiousness had forced
her to neglect for so long. After all, she was an
educated woman with an active mind. There were a
thousand things to do which a tiresome teenager
knew nothing of and should no longer be allowed to
interfere with.
  But when she reviewed these pursuits she found
that they had disappeared or no longer held any
interest for her. That phase of her life was over. She
hadn't had a big lunch, or so it seemed to her now,
three hours later, so she ate up the remains of the
quiche no one had had much of, and all the chocolate
biscuits in the tin and a guava-and-mango yoghurt.
All there was to do was make phone calls. She
phoned Noele, who couldn't talk for long, Friday
being a busy time in the shop, and Jocelyn, whose
answering machine replied, and Laura, who had
time to spare and was quite willing to talk for half an
hour about the outrageousness of the modern adoles-
cent.
  At about six a strange thing happened. She

suddenly understood that all afternoon she had been longing for Francine. It had seemed to her that if the girl had walked in the door all her troubles would be past and she would be happy and serene again, she wouldn't have to gorge herself on unsuitable foods, she wouldn't have to make occupation.

But as it grew dark, and by six it was as dark as midnight, a second desire entered Julia's mind and, although its opposite, existed alongside it, running parallel to it. She longed for Francine and she hoped, perversely, that she wouldn't come, that she would be extravagantly late, as late as midnight, which she had never been. She wanted Francine to be desperately, appallingly late so that she, Julia, could reach a peak of anxiety and terror beyond anything she had known before, a madness of waiting and enduring until, when Francine finally came, she could explode. She could burst like the rainstorm that comes at the end of a day of insufferable heat.

In this frame of mind she watched the clock. Paced and looked at the clock, paced and told herself not to look at the clock again until she had counted a hundred paces. The bus shelter had been empty for hours, she could see into it clearly enough by the street lights, but she was unsurprised by Jonathan Nicholson's absence. Of course he wasn't there, she thought grimly; he was with Francine.

By seven-thirty she was almost happy. She was getting what she wanted. Francine wouldn't come for hours and hours. Huge fantasies of rape and assault and murder could be allowed to fill her mind unchecked. A bulging edifice of tension began to grow. Nine o'clock would become ten and ten eleven, and long before that she would have been sick with dread, actually physically sick, and have eaten to steady herself, perhaps at some point lain on the floor and screamed. She paced and watched the clock, her heart beginning to race.

At nine, or a few minutes after, Francine had come in. Julia couldn't speak. She was stunned with relief and disappointment, both at the same time. She simply looked at Francine, giving her a long, wretched and disgusted glare, and in her misery turned away her head.

Four-one-six-two. Harriet Oxenholme might have had to write it in her address book, masquerading as a restaurant, but he had no need of secret mnemonics. If she had had a memory like his she wouldn't have betrayed herself and opened the door to her bank account, as simply as one might lift the lid of a box of chocolates and offer its contents. What a fool! Probably she thought she was being clever, when all she had had to do was look up 'pin' in a French dictionary.

He walked over to the cash dispenser on the Barclays Bank branch that was on the corner of Circus Road and Wellington Road. Originally, he had meant to wait until he had plastered over his new brickwork, but he found himself unable to bear the suspense any longer. First he checked that the machine would accept Visa Connect. It would. It showed a small picture of a card like Harriet's. Teddy held his breath, told himself not to be stupid and started breathing normally. The card went in. He did it the wrong way up the first time, so had to begin again. This time all was well.

Very carefully, with a finger he would not allow to tremble, he punched out the number, four-one-six-two. There was no explosion, no angry voice, no simple refusal. But this was a slightly different machine from the one he watched the girl operate. Hers required you to say what kind of money you wanted – English, French, US or Spanish – it asked you if you needed a receipt. This one was simpler. He punched the 'enter' key.

'Please Wait', said the machine, then, 'Your order is being processed.' The card came back. He couldn't believe it. He had known it must work, but he still couldn't believe it. The money came out. Not with a squeak or a roll of drums or to the tune of the National Anthem, but slipped out in silence. Eight twenty-pound notes and four ten-pound notes.

It worked. He was in business.

It was a mysterious encounter, this interview with the Detective Superintendent and the Inspector, strangers, for Wallis had retired. Even when it was all over and he was hailing a taxi, Richard had only a scant idea of their purpose in inviting him there. If one concrete fact came out of the meeting it was that Susan Stanark had left her husband back in the summer.

'Is that why he killed himself?' Richard asked.

'Perhaps. Partly. We think there may have been other reasons.'

'You don't want me to – I mean, you haven't asked me here to identify him?'

'No, no. His brother did that. He was related to your present wife, I believe?'

Richard didn't like that 'present', as if he had wives in series. 'Distantly,' he said, surprised. 'A second cousin or something of the sort.'

'You'd known him a long time, I think?'

'Eleven years.'

Richard didn't see why he should go into all that alibi stuff with them. They ought to know about it and if they didn't he wasn't going to assist them. Besides, if you tell a policeman that at one time you needed an alibi he will immediately assume (so reasoned Richard) that you were either guilty or that you engaged in activities that made you a suspect. So he said nothing and the policemen said very little more beyond mysteriously enquiring if he had 'any samples of the late David Stanark's handwriting' in his possession. Richard said he hadn't, they had never written to each other, and then they let him go.

'You are very likely to hear from us again, however,' said the Superintendent, making it sound more like a threat than a guarantee.

When one thing goes well, and it is a big thing, all good things will follow. It is as if that initial success lays a spell over all subsequent enterprises, sheds light on the path towards them. Teddy had had trouble with his plastering of the cellar wall where, as it turned out, it hardly mattered. Up here, beginning the work with caution, he found that he couldn't put a foot wrong – or, rather, make a false move with the diamond-shaped trowel.

The plaster was of precisely the right consistency, neither too dry nor too damp. It went on like cream. His firm, assured movements created a smooth, even surface which, when painted, would be indistinguishable from the original walls of the hall. He set the strip of carved wood he had had to make himself in place and, if anything, he thought, it was an improvement on the existing skirting board.

Now it was finished, though the plaster was still wet, he couldn't keep from laughing out loud. It was going to look as if that wall had been there for ever. He might even hang a picture on it. Why not fetch that Simon Alpheton still life? It deserved a wall to itself, not to be reduced to mediocrity among the other indifferent stuff in the dining-room.

Francine was coming. The golden spell of his success was reaching ahead to her visit as well and he was making plans for it, something almost unprecedented with him. He would be sensible, understand that his failure was due to overwork, to tiredness and anxiety. Today he wouldn't try. Let her make what she liked of that, he wasn't obliged to fall in with all her wishes.

They'd go out for a drive in the Edsel. He was picking her up near where she lived and they would go to the Imperial War Museum and see the exhibition of forties fashion. That was something he longed to see and all girls liked fashion, he thought. Then they'd come back here and he'd show her the new wall and watch her face. Maybe she'd clap her hands, he wouldn't be surprised. She'd expect him to want her to take her clothes off and pose for him all covered in silk and jewels, but he wouldn't ask. Not today.

He'd have wine for her, something expensive, and after that they'd go out to eat. Somewhere or other, it didn't much matter where. Perhaps he'd buy her a dress, white or black. A black velvet dress would be wonderful, with a long skirt cut on the bias and a draped neckline. The Edsel would be full of petrol, so he could drive her all the way home, and if she wanted to be early he wouldn't make a fuss. Tomorrow, Sunday, he'd take the card to the machine again and draw out another two hundred pounds.

Waking hungry at four in the morning, Julia went downstairs and ate two of the white chocolate finger biscuits. Then, because she knew that if she went back to bed on an empty stomach she would only have to come down again, she ate the rest of the packet. Strangely, though she often needed to eat in the night-time she never wanted to pace. She walked languidly from window to window, looking out at

325

nothing, at the empty, light-washed street and the little island in the middle of it with its solitary bollard.

She understood that young girls like to sleep late in the mornings. Miranda's mother had told her that her daughter sometimes lay in bed till two in the afternoon. Julia had never allowed that. Ten was absolutely the latest Francine had been permitted to lie in and that only at the weekends. But she had parted early from Jonathan Nicholson the night before and come home early. This Sunday morning she was up before her stepmother. Julia came downstairs at nine, heavy-eyed from lack of sleep, and found Francine at the kitchen table, eating cornflakes.

'Shall I cook lunch today?' Francine asked. 'You're always cooking for me and I'd like to do it for a change. Shall I?'

'Not if it's going to be mung beans or tofu or anything like that.' Francine was inclined to this sort of food when she prepared it herself. 'You can take some meat out of the freezer or I've got a free-range chicken.'

Francine said she would cook the chicken and bake potatoes. And make what she called her special salad with avocados and peppers. 'You won't have to do a thing. I'll get it ready and clear up and wash up, or at any rate I'll put the stuff in the dishwasher before I go out.'

Only the last part of these remarks really registered with Julia. Francine was going out. Julia got up from the table, cut herself a thick slice of bread, buttered it, spread greengage jam on it and began stuffing it into her mouth, using both hands. She didn't look at Francine so had no idea if the girl was watching her.

Of course, Francine was not going out. She might

think she was, but she was mistaken. Jonathan Nicholson could wait for her over there in that bus shelter for hours, for hours on end, or hide behind the fence or even in someone's dustbin, but Francine wouldn't come. For she, Julia, had had enough. She had borne with Francine's behaviour for months now, for years, going out whenever she pleased, coming home when she liked, using the house as an hotel, and deliberately torturing Julia. It wasn't thoughtlessness or a young girl's ignorance of how to behave, or a disturbed mind, Julia knew that now. It was purposeful malice and wickedness.

But she had done it for the last time. Julia said aloud, her mouth full, 'The worm has turned.'

'I'm sorry, what did you say?'

'Nothing,' said Julia, and liking the sound of it she said it several times more, 'nothing, nothing, nothing . . .'

Francine left the room. She didn't go upstairs. Julia listened to hear what she was doing. Going into the laundry room, by the sound of it, ironing something. Ironing a dress to wear when she went out. Only she wasn't going out. Julia would see to that.

She phoned Noele, she phoned Amy Taylor. Amy had a son of seventeen and a fifteen-year-old daughter and they talked for a while about the problems of living with teenage children. Amy said her daughter had stayed out till two in the morning without any warning, without giving her a sign she meant to do such a thing, and Julia said, how dreadful, and one thing she would say for Francine, she wouldn't *dare* do that.

The conversation cheered her up. She made coffee for herself and Francine, and for once she didn't feel like eating anything, the delicious espresso coffee was enough on its own. Bustling about, tidying the living-room, dusting, she sang to herself the songs of her own adolescence. Francine, in the kitchen, heard the melody of 'Mending Love' and remembered her mother's record that she had broken and being sent to her room and the man coming . . .

Once Julia knew Francine was occupied with preparing lunch, she had seen her tearing lettuce and stripping peel from an avocado, she made her preparations. Carrying a clean bath sheet and a clean bath towel, she took the key out of the laundry-room door and the key out of the cloakroom door and went upstairs. She had calculated that one of them was bound to fit the lock on Francine's bedroom door. It was always so in houses such as this, one key fitted half the locks and the other the rest of them. The key from the cloakroom door slid into the keyhole in Francine's bedroom door and turned smoothly. Julia put the key into her skirt pocket.

Then she opened Francine's door very softly and went into the room. She saw the mobile phone lying on the bedside cabinet. Obviously, she should take that away. As she came out of the bathroom she heard Francine on the stairs so had time to do no more than drop the mobile and push it under the wardrobe with her toe. 'Just putting clean towels in your bathroom,' she said.

Francine had the roast chicken and baked potatoes on the table by just after one. The salad looked very pretty with its slices of pale-green avocado and strips of red pepper against the dark-green cos lettuce in a glass bowl. Julia hadn't intended opening a bottle of wine, but she suddenly felt expansive, she must be *kind* to Francine and it would, after all, be a mercy if she passed part of the afternoon in sleep.

I don't like doing this, said Julia to herself, but I must. Now I know what the Victorians meant when they beat their children and said, this hurts me more than it hurts you.

Francine would only have one glass of wine, but she poured a second one for Julia and then a third. 'Are you going out this afternoon?' she asked. 'Is anyone coming?'

Her guilt was talking, thought Julia. 'I shall be quite alone.'

'I heard you talking to Noele and I thought maybe she was coming over.'

'If you're going to do as you said, Francine,' said Julia, 'and clear up, I wish you'd get on with it. Or do you want to leave it to me?'

'No, I'll do it,' said Francine.

She washed up the roasting pan and the salad bowl. She put the dishes and plates and glasses and cutlery in the dishwasher and the soap powder in, closed the door and switched the machine on. Then she asked Julia if she would like her to make coffee. Julia said, 'I've had quite enough coffee for one day.'

She sat in an armchair and looked at the Sunday paper. There was a scandalous story about an artist called Simon Alpheton turning homosexual and a picture of him with his arm round a young man. Both were smiling. Julia thought how easy life was for some people. As soon as Francine had gone upstairs to change, she ran out into the front garden. Jonathan Nicholson was already there, sitting in the bus shelter with a young woman. He had brought a woman with him to make his appearance seem respectable. There was no end to his craft and deviousness. He had a baseball cap on and big leather boots.

Julia stared at him but he refused to look in her direction. Of course she had no doubt he had seen her. He would soon find out who was in control here. He could wait all afternoon and all evening, too, in that draughty bus shelter and she hoped he got flu for his pains.

She went inside and closed the front door. At the foot of the stairs she stood and listened. When she heard the sound of water running in Francine's shower she went upstairs and paused only for a moment, a few seconds, outside Francine's door in which to take a deep breath and brace herself, before turning the key in the lock.

Chapter 32

The locking of her door passed unheard by Francine.
She was in her bathroom, wrapped in the clean bath
sheet after her shower, with a kd lang CD on rather
loudly. Too loudly for Julia's comfort, she was
thinking, and she stepped across the room to turn
down the volume.

She heard Julia going downstairs. Her tread had
become heavy. Francine went back into her bathroom, plugged in the hair-drier, switched it on to full
power and set about drying her hair. Then she put
on the white dress because Teddy liked it. A coat, or
at any rate her leather jacket, would have to go over
it because, though mild for November, the temperature was no more than ten degrees. To let her hair
hang loose or plait it? In the end she decided on
neither, but twisted it up into a geisha's knot and
fixed it in place with long silver pins.

Teddy was expecting her at three. He would pick
her up two hundred yards down the road as he had
been doing lately. She put on shoes with high heels
because Teddy liked them, decided they were only
possible if no walking was to be done and found
comfortable boots instead. Then she tried the door
handle. The door wouldn't open.

It must be stuck. She turned the handle to the right
and to the left. She pushed and pulled it, but the
door wouldn't budge. For a moment she failed to
understand. There were no keys in the house except

for the one that locked the downstairs cloakroom. No one needed to lock doors, they all respected each other's privacy, or she had thought they did. But if there was no key there was a keyhole. She had never noticed it before, not in all her ten years in this house. A keyhole without a key? She pulled one of the silver pins out of her hair and poked it into the keyhole. No key. If she knelt down and squinted through the hole she could see out to the other side, the landing and a gleam of light from the landing window.

By now she knew what had happened and she was hit by shock. No one had laid a hand on her, but it was as if she had been assaulted. No one had used force on her, but it was as if she had been shackled. Without attempting to find a voice, without even opening her mouth, she thought that the shock had deprived her of the power of speech as it had once before. For a moment she was afraid to try and then she did, she spoke, though not loudly enough to be heard beyond the confines of her room. 'Julia, Julia . . .'

To be able to talk was in itself a huge relief. She asked herself if she should begin shouting, screaming to be let out, please, Julia, please let me out, let me out, please, Julia . . . Her natural dignity held her back from that. Nor would she hammer on the door. She sat down on her bed, she took off her jacket. At least she could phone Teddy. Her mobile phone, which was Julia's gift, was the best present she had ever had. There was an irony there that in other circumstances would have made her smile.

The mobile should have been on the bedside cabinet, but it wasn't. Julia had taken it, of course she had. Francine now recalled her encounter with Julia on the threshold of her bedroom before lunch and Julia saying she had been putting clean towels into her bathroom. That must have been when she

332

removed the mobile to prevent her prisoner phoning anyone. Francine had a quick, sinking sensation of despair. But she got up and went to the window and opened the casement.

People in books got out of windows down ivy obligingly placed at strategic levels or they took the sheets off their beds, knotted them and climbed down the rope thus made. But no one told you what you anchored the rope to at this end or what to do if you had a duvet on your bed and only one sheet. Besides, it was frighteningly far down, Francine couldn't calculate how far, but enough to cause you to break bones if you fell.

In the garden next door but one a woman was working, planting bulbs. Francine knew her as a pleasant but not very sociable neighbour. Certainly she was not numbered among Julia's friends and Francine doubted if she had ever been in the house. Should she call out to her? What would she say? 'My stepmother has locked me in my bedroom and taken away my phone. Could you please ... ?'

Could you please what? Call the police? You don't call the police because someone has locked you in your bedroom. 'My stepmother' sounded like a character in *Grimm's Fairy Tales*. The whole idea of calling for help was humiliating and somehow ridiculous. While Francine was thinking along these lines, still leaning out of the window, the woman brushed earth off her gloved hands, picked up the now empty trug basket in which the bulbs had been and went into her own house.

Francine closed the window. It had begun to rain, a gentle pattering at first, then a downpour. With the rain a good deal of light faded. She switched on a bed lamp. What was she supposed to do about eating and drinking? And how long did Julia intend to keep her here? All day? All *night*?

Because he didn't want Francine to see those words that defaced the Edsel's boot lid, or he didn't want her to see them *again*, Teddy went out on Sunday morning and found a place where they sold him a can of pale-yellow spray paint called Primrose Dawn. On the way back he stopped at a cash dispenser in West End Lane and drew a further two hundred pounds out of Harriet Oxenholme's bank account. A wineshop next door was open. He bought Australian Chardonnay for Francine and a box of liqueur chocolates because he thought she might expect him to give her presents.

Manoeuvring the Edsel into the mews, he saw, standing in the middle of the cobbled area, the woman who had waved to him from a car on the night Harriet died. He recognised her at once. And she, putting the little dog she had been exercising on to its lead, seemed to recognise him.

'Hallo,' she said, and then, rather ominously, 'We meet again.'

'That's right.' What else could he say?

'Harriet well, is she?'

There was no mistaking the note of spite in her voice. What was she getting at? What did she know? Fear flickered through him. 'She's fine,' he said firmly.

'Tell her Mildred said hallo.'

It was a disturbing encounter. He waited until she had gone and then he rubbed down the area of bodywork on the Edsel with emery paper and wiped down the surface. Mildred reappeared at her own gate, carrying a black plastic rubbish bag. She left the gate open, the bag propping it. That must mean the contractors Westminster Council used to collect householders' rubbish would come on Monday morning as well as Thursday morning. He had better

334

put a bag out. Not doing so would only attract attention to himself.

He sprayed on a thin coat of paint. While it was drying he had lifted up the manhole cover and tried slipping his oak frame into place. Here was a setback. The frame was fractionally too small. Any pressure on it – such as the weight of a flagstone – and it would drop through. He asked himself angrily how he had come to make such an easily avoidable mistake. Now he would have to make that frame all over again or find some other way. How about wire netting stretched across to form a kind of basket? That might do it. He would have to buy some wire netting or even a piece of chain-link fencing.

By now it was time to apply a second coat of spray paint to the Edsel. It didn't look too bad, not perfect, but at least those offensive letters were obliterated. Orcadia Cottage was due for a clean. He vacuumed and polished, cleaned the bathroom basin and bath and shower, put out the rubbish bag, made himself some lunch and scrupulously cleaned the kitchen afterwards.

He put a bottle of white wine in the fridge. It wouldn't be right for her to drink too much wine, but he would permit her one glass. A lot of clothes shops would be open, so if he went out in plenty of time he could buy her the black velvet dress on the way to meet her. Then she could wear it when they came back here. He considered postponing the purchase of the dress until she was with him, but dismissed that idea as pointless. He knew her size and it was his taste that counted.

It had begun to rain. He put the manhole cover back.

The DIY place was in a shopping mall. Coming out with his roll of heavy-duty wire netting, he saw the

335

dress in the window of a boutique between the pharmacy and the video rental place. Figured velvet, not black but the darkest of greens, the green of a pine forest, sleeveless, with a scooped neckline cut so that it hung in three folds. It cost eighty pounds, a huge amount, but it was worth every penny, and he imagined Francine wearing it, reclining on the sofa in the Orcadia Cottage drawing-room. She should have Harriet's gold bracelets on her arms and hold a black ostrich feather in her hand.

The rain was coming down in sheets. He ran for cover to the Edsel. By three minutes to three he was at the appointed meeting place. Somewhat abated now, the rain pattered steadily on the car roof. He began making new plans for fixing the flagstone into the manhole. The wire netting would be pinned in initially and act as a kind of sling or hammock . . .

She was often a little late. He couldn't understand anyone being even a minute late, but he accepted it from Francine. Still, today she wasn't a mere minute or even five minutes late. He had been sitting there for nine minutes now. Why say three o'clock if you mean three-fifteen? Rain had emptied the street of people. The dreariness of a wet Sunday afternoon pervaded the place, enough to depress anyone forced to look at those big, semi-detached, thirties-vintage houses, without a light in a single window, the dripping trees, the grey gloom, passing cars sending a spray up out of the gutters.

A quarter of an hour later he was going mad. He, who was always punctual or early, was tortured more than most people by enforced waiting. At twenty to four he drove up to her house, drove past it and round the block. There was no sign of her, no sign of any life, only the rain and the black, glassy puddles lying everywhere. He parked again, on the opposite side of the road.

She had promised, guaranteed, undertaken, to come and she had failed to appear. He knew why and he was covered with shame and bitterness. Whatever she had said – and all those loving words, meant to reassure, came back to him – she despised him. She was contemptuous of his background, his voice, his home and above all, of his failure as a man.

Sitting there in the car, he cursed her under his breath, she was a bitch, a cow, a stupid snob, a liar and a cheat. But by four o'clock he had been swallowed up in the pit of his own pain. A rage and misery disproportionate to the offence she had committed engulfed him. He wanted to destroy things and now he remembered a long-forgotten fact, how in that play-pen he had broken things in a vain bid for attention. A memory of his low-pitched grizzling came back to him and his shouts for one of them to look at him, speak to him. His strong baby's hands had torn the heads off toys and the wheels off toys until there were no more, and no one replaced them.

There was nothing to shatter here and if there had been, if he had been at home or at Orcadia Cottage, he valued things too much to break them. Things were what mattered. He knew he would never see her again. She had chosen this way to leave him. James, or someone like James, who had money and the right voice and the right family, had prevailed with her. Even now, he thought, her slender white body was bared for James. She would never again look in his mirror and see his ring reflected there.

The feelings Teddy had were all new to him. Not the anger, that was usual enough, but the sensation he couldn't define, as of being injured. It was new, yet he could recall distant previous instances, long ago, when he was a small child. Those old feelings of hurt rose up in him now. They had lain there for years, slumbered there, an ancient sore, which Francine's defection awakened. In Francine's broken promise, her failure to come, he felt anew all the pain of his mother's refusal to care for him, talk to him, touch him.

Securing Francine in her bedroom did more for Julia than she had expected. It brought her, temporarily, relief from the raging anxiety that at present governed and dictated everything she did. When she knew Francine must have realised she was locked in, she crept upstairs as quietly as she could – actually crawled up on the thick carpet on all fours – and sitting on the landing, listened outside Francine's door. She heard her open the window, but there was nothing else to hear. No calling for help, no appeals. She had thought Francine might start crying, but if she was she must be stifling the sounds.

Relief. It was all right. She was pleased that there was no protest, no rebellion. Francine had accepted her lot, had recognised Julia's mastery, her right to control, and had bowed to superior authority. Julia sat in the dining-room and drank the rest of the wine she and Francine had had with their lunch. It was a celebration of her victory, her success. When the bottle was empty she poured herself a small brandy.

Nothing stayed the same for long in Julia's always troubled mind. Silence from Francine, which she had taken for acceptance, might only mean she was working on a way of escape. Soon it would be dark. It was raining steadily. Julia put on a raincoat and took an umbrella. She reflected that she had no need to be covert about this, it didn't matter in the least if Francine saw her.

The bus shelter was empty. He had gone. He knew when he was beaten. Julia went through the side gateway. First she looked into the big shed on the

338

left-hand side of the garden. At one time they had kept a ladder, the extending kind, in the shed. Or the builder who had been working on the house had. It was gone now, she was glad to see, and the little pair of steps presented no danger. She went out into the rain, under her umbrella, and looked up at Francine's window. It was closed now. About six feet below the bottom of the window frame a variegated yellow and green ivy grew up against the wall. Julia closed her umbrella, getting wet was of no importance, and began tearing the ivy off the wall. She pulled and wrenched and tore at the tough tendrils and tender shining leaves until the ivy lay in shreds around her feet.

Removing this possible aid to climbing out of the window brought Julia her second phase of relief. It was getting dark now, would soon be night. She went back indoors. The phone was ringing. It would be Jonathan Nicholson, calling to know why Francine hadn't come to meet him in the bus shelter. Julia picked up the receiver and said in her iciest tone, 'She is not coming.'

Richard's voice said, 'What did you say?'

'I'm sorry,' Julia said, 'I thought it was someone else.'

'Who did you think it was?'

Julia had no answer for that and before she could think of one the noise started upstairs. Francine must have heard the phone ringing and begun to hammer on the door, not just with her hands, with some heavy object. She was shouting too – Julia thought she had never heard her shout before – calling, 'Help me, help me!'

Julia put her hand over the mouthpiece, muttered through it, 'This is a very bad line.'

'What's that noise?'

'The builders next door,' said Julia. 'On a Sunday,

too, it's a disgrace.' She knew her voice was slurred and thick with drink. Perhaps he would think that also was due to the bad line. 'We're both fine,' she said. 'The girl is fine. She was going out with Jonathan Nicholson in his red sports car, she was going to his home in Fulham. But she didn't because it's pouring with rain.'

'If I didn't know you better, Julia, I'd say you'd been drinking.'

Julia giggled. 'Francine and I did share a bottle of sauvignon with our lunch.'

When he had rung off she sat down and recovered her composure. The noise from above had stopped. Julia went upstairs again and listened. Not a peep, not a creak. Perhaps she had fallen asleep for want of anything else to pass the time. Julia, too, was very tired. She shouldn't drink brandy, it wore her out. She made her way down again, walking wearily, saw from the hall clock that it was after six-thirty, nearly a quarter to seven. She felt at ease now, tranquil and sleepy, too calm to be in need of food. Francine would be growing hungry and it pained Julia to think of her deprivation. But it couldn't be helped, they must both suffer for her earlier disobedience, her recalcitrance.

Julia walked idly about the house. Pacing was past, she would never pace again. Her legs felt weak and back in the living-room she fell to her knees. Crawling on her hands and knees was a more comfortable way of getting about. She crawled clockwise round the room once, then turned round and crawled round it anti-clockwise. The sofa, over which at some point during the day Francine had draped a woollen throw, looked particularly invit-ing. Julia kicked off her shoes, clambered up on to the sofa and, pulling the throw over her, fell into an exhausted sleep.

Chapter 33

Who had made that phone call Francine didn't know. Her father, possibly, or Noele or Susan or some other of Julia's friends, or Holly or Isabel – or even Teddy. It didn't much matter who it was so long as she could make them hear her prisoner's sounds of pleading to be set free. But of course they didn't hear or else they believed whatever Julia had invented to account for the noise.

To beat on the door she had used the first thing her eye lighted on, her tennis racquet. It had been leaning up against the wall, but now she went to put it back in the place where it was kept, along with a box of tennis balls, her track suit, her running shorts and trainers, in the drawer at the bottom of her wardrobe. As she pushed in the drawer it scraped on something underneath. Francine reached under the drawer with one hand and drew out her mobile phone.

She punched out Teddy's number. She felt a surge of faith in him, trust of him. He would get her out.

Julia's action in locking Francine up and hiding her mobile under the wardrobe had neither shocked nor much surprised Teddy. He expected people to behave bizarrely, madly. In his experience most of them did. A quiet, orderly life of routine and normalcy he had never known. Human beings, in his estimation, were wilder than animals and far uglier.

Only Francine stood apart and she was not quite real, she was too beautiful for reality and too pure.

His resentment and hatred of her were forgotten. She hadn't left him, she hadn't been with James, but locked up in her bedroom by her wicked stepmother. It was what happened to princesses. He drove out to Ealing along the North Circular Road. The Sunday evening traffic was light and the Edsel attracted a lot of attention. He cursed the frequency of traffic lights where he had to stop and endure comments and admiring stares.

On the phone she had told him she would throw her front-door key out of the window. 'I'll do it now,' she had said, 'so that I can tell you where it's fallen.'

He was rather disappointed at such an easy solution to the problem. He had pictured himself breaking into the house or at least climbing up a ladder to fetch Francine down. She had come back to the phone and said the key was on the lawn, not under her window but a bit to the left. 'The side gate won't be locked. You come through that way, but be very quiet and just pick the key up off the grass.'

'Why are you whispering?'

'I don't want Julia to hear,' she said.

The Edsel he parked in a side turning and walked the hundred yards or so to her house. To his surprise it was all in darkness. He felt a certain curiosity. Houses always interested him, all houses. He was looking forward to seeing the inside of this one. The side gate was unlocked, as she had said it would be. He looked up at the rear of the house, where behind an upper window a light was on, but not a very powerful light and the curtains appeared to be drawn.

Half expecting her to be waiting for him, watching for him, her face at that window, he felt a pang of disappointment. But he couldn't call out, he had promised to be very quiet and he would be. Hampered by the darkness, he looked for the key in vain for a while, found it at last hidden by a clump of longer, very wet, grass. It, too, was wet and he wiped it carefully on his sleeve.

The key went very smoothly and almost soundlessly into the front-door lock and the door swung open silently. It was dark inside, but not totally, for from round the corner of a passage a low-wattage lamp shone faintly. It showed him a hallway, all the doors to it closed but one which stood ajar. The floor was carpeted, the walls papered in a showy brocade design he disliked on sight. A large coloured china jar in one corner was full of dried flowers with dusty, fluffy heads.

He set his foot on the lowest tread of the stairs, hesitated and turned back. Francine wouldn't be expecting him immediately, he had got here faster than he had expected. He put out his hand to the door that stood ajar, pushed it a little wider open and went in. Darkness in here, but the curtains were not drawn across and light from the street came in. An ugly room, he thought, the kind of furnishings he most disliked. Suburban, bourgeois, Ideal Home Exhibition. Fitted carpet and rugs on top of it, a fat floral three-piece suite, reproduction tables, a nest of tables, a glass-fronted china cabinet.

The back of the sofa was towards him. He had walked past before he saw that a woman was lying on it, fast asleep. The wicked stepmother. The cause of all Francine's troubles and of his, too, for she kept Francine from him. A strange, but immediately convincing, idea came to him. That it was this woman who caused his impotence, like a witch who sucks out men's strength and seizes their souls and saps their power.

She was fat and pale, with a pallor quite unlike

343

Francine's rose-petal whiteness. The light from the street showed him her plump white hands and the rings set deeply in her flesh. The woollen thing that half covered her reminded him of the shawls his mother used to crochet. It awakened in him a slow, intense surge of anger.

Without thinking much, without pausing or asking himself why, he reached out his hands towards her. But he knew he couldn't bring himself to touch her. His knees would give way or he would be sick if he did. He withdrew his hands and looked around him, around the room. Cushions were everywhere, soft, fat cushions, covered in velvet or silk.

When you have killed twice it is easy to do it a third time. He picked up a big velvet cushion, rectangular and as far as he could tell in this light, red, and held it up a foot from her face. Tightening his grip on the edges of it, he slowly pressed the cushion down on to her face.

She stirred, but otherwise remained immobile. He fetched more cushions, piled them on her, pressed down hard with his hands, leant on the cushions, then knelt on them. Under him and through the mass of silk and feathers, he felt her struggle, heard sounds. Her legs moved and her heels thudded against the sofa arm. With all his strength he kept up the pressure, for more than seconds, for minutes, five minutes, until he knew. Strange how he knew and that he would need to feel no pulse, search for no breath. Life had gone and he felt its departure as plainly as if it had taken wing and flown away through that window.

He had managed it without touching her. You could take life at one remove, by remote control almost. All you had to do was hold the channel changer and at a distance blank out the screen. It was as easy as that. Should he tell Francine? Not yet. One

344

day perhaps, but not yet. He lifted off the cushions, one after another, replacing them on the chairs from which he had taken them. Her face was revealed, the mouth slack, the eyes staring. In the half-dark he thought he detected a blueness about her features, but it was hard to tell. Still without touching her, he drew the woollen cover up to her chin. Then he closed the door and went upstairs to Francine.

'You were so long!' she whispered from behind her door. 'Why were you so long?'

'I came as soon as I could,' he said.

'Have you found a key to my room?'

He had forgotten that, though she had told him. 'Where do you think it is?'

'It might be in the downstairs cloakroom or her bedroom; I don't think there are any other keys in the house. Where's Julia?'

'Downstairs. She's asleep.'

He heard Francine give a little laugh. He took the key out of another bedroom door and the one out of the cloakroom door. That fitted. She came into his arms, hugging him, laughing with relief.

She was wearing the white dress. He pulled the pins out of her hair to let it hang loose. When she was the way he liked her to look, he picked up her suitcase and they crept down the stairs, so as not to wake Julia. He would have liked to tell her that there was no waking Julia and never would be, but he had already decided not to do this, so he went along with the pantomime of tiptoeing and whispering until they were out of the house and crossing the road to where the Edsel was parked.

Then Francine broke into a flood of words. She talked more than he had ever known her to – and if the truth were told, more than he wanted. But he let her continue without interruption, how Julia had seemed to go mad, how she had hidden her mobile,

345

locked her in her room, told ridiculous lies on the phone and apparently invented a boyfriend for Francine called Jonathan Something. That was the only thing that interested Teddy.

'Who is he? Do you know him?'

'Teddy, he doesn't exist. Don't you understand? Julia invented him. Julia's mad.'

He didn't really understand, but he felt calm and free, and very nearly happy. Francine was coming with him, she would stay with him now, there was no other place for her to be. She couldn't go back and she couldn't go anywhere else. She had been Julia's prisoner, but now she was his; he had killed Julia for her.

The first thing she wanted when they got to Orcadia Place was food. It was nine and she hadn't eaten since lunch-time. There were eggs in the fridge and bread and cheese, and she made herself a meal, but she wouldn't drink his wine. He gave her the liqueur chocolates and she ate one that had cherry brandy in it, but she wouldn't have another. All she wanted was to talk, go over and over it: why had Julia done it, what was wrong with Julia? Teddy had no opinion and didn't care. It was the aspect of Francine he liked least, this desire of hers to talk and discuss and speculate and conjecture and wonder.

When he thought she must have talked enough, even for her, he gave her the dress. He wanted her to put it on, but she wouldn't.

'It's beautiful and I love it,' she said, 'but I don't want to wear it now. We're not going anywhere, we're just at home on our own – well, not exactly at home but together and relaxed, it's not the occasion for your lovely dress.'

'I want to see you in it,' he said stonily.

'I'll put it on tomorrow, Teddy. I'm tired now.

346

What I'd really like is to go to bed. I want to go to bed in a place where I'm *free* and no one's locked me in and just sleep and sleep and sleep.'

It was not the way he had envisaged it. All the way here in the car the idea had been growing in his mind with increasing excitement that things would be all right now. He had won, he had succeeded. He had rescued her, done murder for her, and gained possession of her. By these actions, whatever it was that inhibited him and dulled his flesh would be banished. His troubles were over and would never return.

But instead of coming to him, a passive and silent beauty, obedient to his command that she wear his dress, she had talked and talked until he was sick of the sound of 'Julia' and 'Dad' and how awful it had been. A vague, irritable depression settled over him and when he went up to the bedroom he found her, to his disgust, lying in Harriet's bed in a white cotton night-shirt and already asleep.

He lay down beside her, listening to the rain that spattered in the wind against the glass. Desire seemed to come back, a flicker of it, and he put his hands on her, lifted that horrible white cotton garment and felt her warm, sleek flesh. She neither turned towards him nor shuddered away, she was still and heavily asleep, but he was powerless just the same, as dead as a block of wood.

There must be ways. He lay awake thinking of them, of how it might be different if he could silence her, close her eyes, dress her in the dark-green velvet, take that white night-shirt thing away and burn it, or put it out with the rubbish. Hang jewels on her, buy flowers for her and fill her arms with lilies. Now he had money he could do that. Tomorrow he would buy lilies, and maybe peacock's feathers and a length of heavy white silk. He would lay her on the floor on the silk, gathering it up a little, ruffling it, and he would spread out her hair and weave gold chains into it. Paint her eyelids peacock-green and gold, and close them over her eyes like the domed covers of jewel boxes and place a lily in one of her hands and a green plume in the other.

She slept beside him, breathing steadily, and after a while he slept too.

It was eleven before she woke up and then it was the phone ringing that woke her. She picked up the receiver and said hallo and a man's voice asked to speak to Franklin Merton. Francine said she thought he had the wrong number.

Teddy had been up for hours. He took the Edsel up to Cricklewood, filled the tank and used Harriet's Connect card to collect another two hundred pounds. Back at Orcadia Cottage, he carefully rested the flagstone in its wire netting cradle. A lot of space remained around it. He really ought to break the stone into two pieces or find another smaller piece of stone to slip in beside it. The important thing was to avoid an odd appearance, something that would attract attention.

He dabbed cement on to the pins that held the wire in place, then spread on a smooth layer. The rain had held off long enough for him to do the job, but now it began to fall again, a fine but insistent drizzle. He covered up his work with a square of plastic, weighting down the four corners with pebbles. After that he went back into the house and found Francine looking at his new wall where the Alpheton still life now hung.

'I thought there was a door here. I thought I remembered a door to the cellar. Memory playing tricks on me, it must be.'

She had dressed herself in the hideous uniform of jeans and boots and sweater. The effect on him was

348

to make him speak roughly, though the words would please her. 'I'll take you out tonight,' he said. 'We'll go wherever you want. I've got plenty of money.'

'Have you got work, Teddy?'

'As much as I can handle. More. We can go anywhere you like. You can get dressed up and put on her jewellery, anything you want.'

'I must phone my friends,' she said as if he hadn't spoken. 'Phone them and tell where I am.'

They went into the kitchen. She ground coffee, put a filter paper into the coffee machine and poured the coffee in.

'Why must you?' he said. 'Why do you want to do that?'

She didn't answer. 'And phone Julia, too. I can't just vanish into thin air. She'll be frantic with worry about me. When she woke up – just think of how she must have been when she found me gone. She's probably got on to Dad in Germany and been ringing round my friends.'

He stared at her with a kind of despair. What was she talking about? He had got her out of there and she was his now, bound to him, here with him. Then anger drove out his dismay. He took her by the shoulders, gripping the thin flesh, the fine bone, digging in hard fingers. 'You're not making any phone calls, right? Have you got that? You can't just use her phone to call your friends. There's no need for it, d'you understand?'

'Teddy, you're hurting me! Why are you doing that?'

She shrank away from him, but he held on. He moved her backwards and forwards, it was almost but not quite a shaking. 'While you're with me you do as I say, right? No phone calls, no getting on to Julia. We may as well get things straight now. I don't want you knowing people, you don't need friends, you've got me. You're living here with me now and that's how it's going to be, you and me on our own.'

'Please let me go.' She spoke with such calm dignity that it had its effect on him. As his fingers loosened she took his hands and removed them from her shoulders. 'I don't understand what you mean.'

'It's plain enough. I gave you my ring, didn't I? And I saved you. You don't have to see any of them again, not your father or your friends or anyone. You belong to me.'

She was seldom silent and when she was he knew no way of managing her. Impotence extended from his body to his mind and he was filled with a bitter, ragged frustration. She made the coffee, poured a cup for him and pushed it across the table. Her face was stony, beautiful in cold disdain, like a marble statue in a gallery. He wanted to lay down the law – it was his grandmother's phrase, recalled from childhood – tell her he made the rules and what they were, that he was the boss and she must obey. She was to understand the truth of it, that he had made this place possible, had arranged everything, he had the money and the power, she had no right to dispute anything. But the look on her face stopped him. He poured the coffee she had given him down the sink and banged out of the kitchen, slamming the door behind him.

The phone rang and because he evidently wasn't going to answer it, she did. A woman this time, again asking for Franklin Merton, and again she said it was a wrong number, though she was beginning to have her doubts. She dialled Holly's number, then Miranda's, got answering machines both times. Talking to Julia she had postponed, but the time had come to do it. Holly and Miranda being out hadn't really surprised her, but Julia's failure to answer did.

Sitting at the table, sipping her coffee, she began to feel rather miserable. She wanted her father, but she didn't know the name of the hotel where he was staying.

The next time the phone rang she didn't answer it. There seemed no point. After six rings it stopped and the machine took over. Presently she went into the living-room where there were a few books in a glass-fronted bookcase. They weren't her sort of books, but she preferred reading anything to nothing. Teddy came in after half an hour and found her curled up in an armchair with a paperback. He said he was going to work, he was doing a job for a man in Highgate and he'd be back by five.

When he had gone she laid down her book and thought about things. Holly must be out somewhere with Christopher and somehow she knew that it wasn't like this for them. He wasn't a man who thought about nothing but sex and what Holly looked like, he liked talking to her and hearing her talk, and they could laugh and have fun and share things. But I can't go back, she thought, can I? I can't go back to mad Julia and be locked in my bedroom and turned into a sort of Cinderella. What am I going to do?

It was usual for Franklin to phone Harriet a couple of days before he was due home. If she wasn't there he never left a message. After all, he had nothing to say to her except to make sure she'd arranged to have the boiler serviced and had the water meter checked. It struck him as he put down the phone that it mattered very little whether these things were done or not, mattered to him, that is, since he never intended living in Orcadia Cottage again.

'I suppose she'll keep it, will she?' said Anthea.

'Some arrangement will have to be come to.'

'Not the same sort of arrangement as was come to with me, I hope for your sake. I took you to the cleaners, didn't I?'

'What you might call the complete valet service with reproofing,' said Franklin with his skull's smile. 'In the present case all I really want is the furniture. Not that I shall tell her that. That is between you and me.'

Anthea smiled. 'I suppose you'll come back to Half Moon Street with me on Wednesday?'

'We'll pick up De Valera from the kennels on our way.'

Mr Habgood had a wife. Teddy hadn't expected that, for she had never been mentioned. But there she was, a fussy woman, who seemed to think it strange that he had called at the house to find if they were accepting his estimate. Why hadn't he phoned if he was so anxious? No, she couldn't let him in, not if he had no identification. She seemed to expect him to carry a photograph of himself on a chain round his neck.

Keeping him on the doorstep, she relented enough to discuss the cupboard designs with him. She disliked panelled doors and wanted brass fittings. Her husband wouldn't dream of giving him a deposit of fifty per cent, that was out of the question. Ten was more likely. If he would like to phone that evening her husband would be in after seven. But before nine-thirty, please, as they weren't nightbirds.

Teddy couldn't phone that evening. He was taking Francine out. It seemed a more formidable task than making a whole suite of furniture would be. Firstly, he wouldn't be able to wear his usual sort of clothes, jeans and sweat-shirt and zipper jacket. He ought to buy something, but he didn't know where or how.

Women's clothes were easier. He had had no difficulty over Francine's dress. She might know how to go about it, but he wasn't going to lower himself to ask her, she had humiliated him enough already. Then there was the question of where to go. He had never in his life been to that sort of restaurant, let alone taken anyone there, taken a *girl* there.

He wasn't in the habit of asking advice, but he wished he knew someone to ask. Nige? Christopher? Both were impossible. Driving the Edsel home, he remembered Harriet's address book, the real restaurants and the pretend restaurant. He could phone one of those. Or he could get her to phone, she would know what to say.

'Who's Franklin Merton?' she said when he came in and found her reading in the living-room.

'I don't know. Why?'

'People have been phoning for him.'

'Don't answer the phone,' he said. 'I told you. I said not to answer it. The machine will answer it.'

He had written down the names of the restaurants and their phone numbers on a sheet of drawing paper. She said she'd call them if that was what he wanted, of course she would, but he didn't like the look she gave him, as if she were sorry for him or *understood* him. That wasn't possible, but even if it were, he didn't want to be understood.

353

Chapter 34

He went upstairs and opened the door to the wardrobe she said was full of men's clothes. By the look of them it was an old man. Only old men wore tweed suits and check jackets and a thing he thought might be called a tuxedo. Until now he'd only seen them on television. This old man evidently wasn't fat, that at least was something. But could he bring himself to wear someone else's clothes? He shuddered at the thought. Oxfam was one thing, but everything from there could be washed.

One suit only was a possibility. It was sheathed in a clear plastic cover. He took it out on its hanger, slipped off the cover and saw the dry-cleaner's label still attached to neck and waistband with small gold safety-pins. No one had worn it since it was cleaned, a plain dark cloth suit that might fit him. He went into the bathroom and ran a bath, putting in bath essence and aromatherapy oil. Washing himself and washing his hair, he felt he was scrubbing and swilling away all the accumulated dirt of his day, the words of that rude woman in Highgate, Francine's disobedience and contempt, his fear of the new world he was discovering. The towel he used to dry himself had been used before. There was a faint streak of something blue – bath oil, make-up? – on its hem. Tomorrow they must have a big wash . . .

A clean white shirt. He found one in a drawer. It had been beautifully washed and ironed, he couldn't

have done better himself. But still he shrank away a
little from its touch as he put it on and pulled on the
trousers – they were an inch too short – and slipped
his arms into the jacket sleeves. It might have been
dry-cleaned but that wasn't like washing, not a total
immersion, not a complete purification. He found
himself cringing inside his borrowed clothes just as a
man with a sensitive skin shivers at the touch of
wool.

Several times during the course of the afternoon
Francine had tried to phone Julia. Then, when it was
almost too late and everyone would be on the point
of going home, she phoned her father's London
office. They would know the name of the hotel
where he was staying in Hamburg. But all she got
was a voice saying its owner was away from her
desk at present and offering all sorts of numbers,
mobiles and faxes and an e-mail address. Francine
left a message that she wanted the number of her
father's hotel and would call again in the morning.
  A gale was blowing and it was raining hard. She
would have liked to go out, if only for a walk round
a district she barely knew, but outdoors looked
uninviting. When she thought staff would be there,
she booked a table in a restaurant in Primrose Hill.
This was something she had never done before, but
she had heard Julia do it and the woman she spoke
to seemed to understand and made no difficulties.
  The man she met on the stairs as she was going up
to change she barely recognised. Teddy looked
handsome, suave, strange, a different person. He
looked older too and, although she didn't admit this
to herself until she was dressing, somehow rather
frightening. Formal clothes brought out in him a cold
austerity of expression she had never observed while
he wore his jacket and jeans. His mouth seemed

355

tighter, his eyes more hooded. He walked down the stairs in a feline way. He had always seemed graceful, but now there was something more studied and smooth, almost serpentine, in his movements.

She would have liked to say something about the length of his borrowed trousers, not exactly laugh at him but perhaps make the comment that he would have to undo the waistband and slide them a little way down his hips. Something in his face, its awful cold gravity, told her to avoid this.

But when he turned to look at her, to take in her appearance in the dress he had bought her, there was a lightening and a kind of relief in his expression. 'Beautiful,' he said. 'You are so beautiful.'

'It fits. You were clever.'

'Only because you're a perfect size eight.'

She started telling him about Noele and her clients and how angry Noele had been. It seemed funny now, but it had been most unpleasant at the time. Noele had accused her of setting herself up as better-looking than the customers, which she hadn't meant to do and hadn't believed anyway.

He wasn't listening. 'It's time we went,' he said.

The restaurant wasn't the kind she had often been in, but sometimes she had been in places rather like it for lunch with Julia. Teddy was so plainly ill at ease that she took over most of the ordering and asking for things. He wouldn't drink – well, he couldn't really, not with having to drive the Edsel. She felt she drank rather too much, perhaps more than she ever had in her life before. She had to because, otherwise, she wouldn't have been able to get through the evening. It was painful, ugly, a lesson she understood, and understood uncomfortably, that she was learning too early in her life.

He barely spoke. She talked to him about everything she knew, school, her father's marrying Julia, the house she had once lived in that was similar to Orcadia Cottage, the house she lived in now, or had done until the previous day, her friends, the job with Miranda's father that might have been. There was only one thing she didn't talk about.

He reacted to the prospect of a job. She wouldn't need a job. He would keep her, he had money and would soon have more.

'I can't live off you, Teddy.'

'Why not? You lived off your dad.'

'That was different,' she said. 'That's always different. A child is kept by its parents until it earns for itself. Well, *her*self. I ought to keep myself until I go up to Oxford.'

He fell into a mutinous silence. Their bill came. He didn't know what to do with it, made furious impotent faces at her across the table, finally passed notes to her under the cloth. She had to tell him it wasn't enough. It pained and embarrassed her, he looked so aghast, so distressed. She had never seen anyone so engulfed with shame. More notes were passed until she could pay the bill and manage an inadequate tip.

They left without speaking to the waiter or each other, without saying goodbye or thank you. She had forgotten all her exasperation with him, all her dismay at his failure to listen to what she said, all his demands that she should obey him. Everything was swallowed up in a huge pity. It seemed to her that whatever had been done to him in his childhood and youth, what cruelties and deprivations, they had damaged him fearfully, perhaps irrecoverably. She wanted to show him that she too had lost a mother in a dreadful way, that she shared his traumas and his injuries.

The silence was maintained all the way back. She went alone into Orcadia Cottage while he parked the car in the mews. When he came in she was sitting on the ivory satin sofa in her dark-green velvet, her hair loose about her shoulders, clasping her hands, loosening them and laying them in her lap. 'I want to tell you something.'

He nodded. He sat in an armchair, staring at her.

'When I was seven a man came into our house and murdered my mother. I was upstairs, I'd been sent to my room, I'd been naughty, and I heard the doorbell ring and looked out and all I could see was his shoes and the top of his head. My mother came to the door and let him in.'

He was listening. Almost for the first time he was listening with total concentration to something she said. His attention brought strength to her voice and her resolve.

'Our house was a bit like this one, a sort of big cottage with that same plant climbing the wall. Coming here keeps reminding me, but that doesn't matter. I want to tell you, I know how it is. I do know how it is to have something dreadful happen to you when you're young, and how you don't really get over it, how you live it every day. I lost the power of speech, I couldn't speak a word for six months.'

He said hoarsely, 'What happened?'

'You really want to know?'

'What happened?'

'I heard the shot. He shot her. More than once, I think. Twice or three times. The man was looking for drugs or money from the sale of drugs, the police thought he mistook my father's house for a doctor's with the same name. She must have got in his way, have tried to stop him.'

'Why didn't he kill you?'

'You think he would have wanted to? Perhaps. I don't know. I hid in a cupboard in my bedroom and he came in. He went into all the bedrooms, looking

358

for drugs, I suppose. When he'd gone I went downstairs and found my mother.'

He said again, his voice breathless now, 'What happened?'

'There was – blood. A lot of blood. My father came home and found me sitting there covered in my mother's blood. The man had shot her in the chest, one shot had gone into her heart. I couldn't tell them about the man, not for months, I couldn't speak.'

His concentrated gaze alarmed her. She flinched a little. 'Teddy?'

'Someone murdered your mother? Why didn't you tell me?'

'I have told you. Don't look at me like that.'

Something dreadful then. Unbelievable. He got up and came to her, moving as if going in for the attack. His face had gone blank, an empty mask. He was pulling off his clothes as he came, undoing his flies, dropping the too-short trousers, tripping on them, no longer graceful. He made a grab for her, holding her down hard against the shiny slippery sofa. His breathing was as if he had an engine inside him, revving up, spurting. She felt an iron-hard pressure against her stomach and it was something she had never felt before, a rod between her soft flesh and his bones.

His hands had become a workman's tools, sharp, hard, certain. He pulled the dress over her head, but not quite over, leaving enough to wind round her face and mask it. The dress became a blinding hood. The hard rod was out now, no longer separated from her by barriers of clothes. She felt it questing her thighs, seeking entrance, as his hands pressed folds of dark-green velvet into her mouth, her eyes. She kicked him and fought him with her hands. Her shoes might have been a weapon but they flew off. She heard one of them strike against something and break it. The tinkling of china shattering was over-powered by a more brazen sound, the phone ringing.

It was enough momentarily to stay him. Briefly she felt the loosening of his hands. She leapt and pushed him, kicked him as she went, fled across the room, stumbled and fell in the doorway. The phone stopped abruptly, half-way through a ring. She struggled to her feet, certain he would seize her now, that this would be the end for her.

He sat on the floor, half naked, his head in his hands. She saw his shoulders shake. He was crying. For a moment she simply didn't know what to do. The shock of what he had attempted was making her heart drum heavily. Her mouth had dried, her hands were shaking. A voice, her own voice, inside her head kept saying over and over, 'How could he? How could I? Why did I? Why did I?'

To touch him now, comfort him with her hand on his shoulder, perhaps stroke his hair, take his hand, all this was impossible. Hardly knowing what she was doing, she dragged herself out of the room and upstairs, hanging on to the banisters. There was another bedroom with another bed in it, an ordinary, rather pretty brass bedstead. A key was in the lock. She went inside and locked herself in. The irony of it struck her after a few minutes, that here was she, who had been forcibly imprisoned in a bedroom, now voluntarily locking herself in another, to protect herself from the man who had rescued her.

In the morning she came into the big white bedroom to find her clothes. He watched her in silence. For the first time for a long while he wasn't up at first light. He lay there in misery because he had nowhere to go and nothing to do.

The rain had come back. It was pouring. She still had the velvet dress on. In the grey water-washed light he watched her taking jeans, a shirt, a sweater out of the suitcase she had brought with her. She wouldn't put on her clothes in front of him. He watched her go into the bathroom, carrying her clothes, he heard her bolt the door, then the shower running.

When she came back she was dressed the way he hated, but he scarcely noticed that now. She went to the dressing-table and began braiding her hair, winding the plait on to the back of her head. On her right hand she still wore his ring.

He said, 'I thought you'd gone away.'

It was the nearest he could get to an apology. She made no reply. She opened the wardrobe and he supposed she was looking for her coat.

'Don't go,' he said.

The words were wrenched out of him. It was like the squeezing of a nearly empty tube. His voice was dry and hoarse. She turned round and came to sit on the end of the bed.

'You're going.'

She shook her head. 'I don't know what to say. I was frightened last night. You tried to rape me.'

That shocked him. 'Me? How could I rape you? You're mine, we're together.'

'Rape', she said, 'isn't only when the girl's someone you give a lift to or meet in a street at night.'

'Anyway,' he said, 'I didn't mean it. Not that.'

'Why did you, Teddy? Why did you want to?'

He shrugged, swung his legs over to the other side and got out of bed. 'Don't go,' he said again, biting on the words as if they hurt him.

She was in the kitchen when he got downstairs, drinking coffee, making toast. It was raining so hard that the room was dark and the windows misted over. She shocked him by talking of something quite different, almost social small-talk. Her voice was

361

neutral, polite, distant. 'I keep trying to phone Julia, but I'm not getting an answer.'

And you won't. But he didn't say so.

'I'll get hold of my dad today. I shouldn't be here and no one knows where I am. I'll feel better if I can speak to my dad in Hamburg.'

'It's too wet to go out,' he said. 'You'll have to stay here today.'

'Teddy,' she said, her tone very serious, 'if I go out I promise I will come back. I know you're worrying I won't come back, but I will. I wouldn't just leave you.'

After that he had to pretend he didn't care. And of course she'd come back – where else did she have to go to? He drank some coffee, went into the living-room and picked up the pieces of the blue-and-white china figurine her flying shoe had broken the previous evening. On a fragment were printed a crown and the words Royal Copenhagen. It had been beautiful, that child in pastel porcelain, and he hated to see it broken by careless indifference. Could he get it mended? And how much would that cost? Wanton destruction of something so lovely made him feel sick with dislike of humanity.

Moodily, he cleared a space in the mist on the window and looked out into the yard. Everywhere was wet, the flagstones darkened by rain and water lying in puddles. The protective plastic over his wire netting and cement structure flapped in the wind.

So much had happened, so many disturbing things, that he had forgotten all about the manhole, that it had been open, covered only by that thin membrane, for hours. It had been raining all night and water must have got into the hole, down there, with what lay down there ...

He went outside, picked up the plastic and the stones and replaced the manhole cover. The rain was heavy enough to have soaked his hair and made sodden patches on his jeans in the few minutes he was out there. He shivered. The Edsel's tank was nearly empty and he needed more money. Apart from that, he had to go home, check on his post, see if anything had come from Habgood, perhaps go and see his grandmother's friend Gladys. The bill in the restaurant had been an almost greater shock to him than Francine's rejection of him. He didn't know food could cost so much. He had barely fifty pounds left and of that thirty could easily go on petrol.

Francine had gone into the living-room and was phoning someone. That Holly, it sounded like.

'I'm going out,' he said. 'I'll have another key cut for you, shall I?'

If she said yes, everything would be all right. She covered the mouthpiece with her hand. 'Yes, fine. Do that. If I do go out I promise I'll be back.'

'You can have the front-door key and I'll take the back-door key.'

A thought struck her. 'Do you want to know exactly when?'

He nodded.

'Then I'll be back exactly at six.'

He wasn't much of a student of facial expression or tones of voice, but even he could tell that she was making an effort to be kind to him. 'Humouring' was what they called it, he thought. But she would come back at six. He began thinking of ways to keep her, but so that she couldn't get away, so that there was no escape.

Enough petrol remained in the tank to get him to the nearest pump. When he had paid for it, he drove to his favourite cash dispenser, the one on the corner of Wellington Road. He put the card in, punched out the number, asked for two hundred pounds and

363

waited. Even before any more digits or words had appeared on the screen he knew something was wrong. Then green letters displayed: Your order cannot be processed. Please collect your card. Puzzled, he took it. Should he try again, maybe in the Edgware Road?

He found a dispenser at the NatWest Bank on the corner of Aberdeen Place. It was the kind that wanted to know if he required English money. He punched out 'yes' to that and 'no' to a receipt and, just as his hopes were rising, the refusal came again. There was a fault. His order couldn't be carried out and he was to collect his card.

Then he knew, or guessed. Harriet's money had dried up. He had drawn out so much that no funds remained in her current account.

Chapter 35

Richard read the fax from London with some bewilderment. His daughter had been trying to get in touch with him but had left no contact number. Why should she leave a number? Her number was his home phone.

Since speaking to Julia on Sunday afternoon he had made no more calls to her. This was normal. He had never got into the habit of phoning every day. But now a phone call must be made. Francine had never before tried to get in touch with him while he was away, therefore if she had tried this time there had to be something seriously wrong.

So, at eleven at night – only ten in London – he had tried to phone. No answer and the answering machine switched off. He thought of the man who stalked her. Jonathan Nicholson. Was she trying to contact her father because of some outrage perpetrated against her by Nicholson? Had Julia unplugged the phone because of harassing calls from Nicholson? In that case, a ringing tone would still be heard by a caller. He went to bed, but slept badly.

At nine in the morning, eight in London, he tried again. Julia might be up, Francine hardly would be. Still, he would be sure of getting one of them. He punched out the number and, when there was no reply, tried again through the hotel switchboard. Still no answer. If, as he thought, they had unplugged the phone, could they have forgotten to reconnect it?

He could phone a neighbour. He felt the same reluctance to do this as Francine had felt about calling for help when locked in her room. Holly's mother was the only other contact he could think of. She answered, couldn't help, but gave him the number of Holly's flat. Again he got through, but the answering machine replied.

In half an hour's time he was due to give a lecture, the last one of the conference. He had intended to stay on till the next morning, visiting the chief executive of a new company of software manufacturers, but now he decided to abandon this plan and go home on the afternoon flight.

The silk curtains in a shade of pale autumn leaf were as beautiful as he could have wished, but now he had no use for them. He saw himself as living, if not permanently in Orcadia Cottage, then for years. Provided he paid the services bills, what or who was there to stop him? They could come and turn off the water and the power in his old home for all he cared, he was determined never to return.

The old woman who had made the curtains was clamouring for him to paint the smelly hole at the back of her house. Agnes, who had come with him, backed her up. He could start any time, she insisted, he didn't know what to do with his time, hadn't got a regular job. If his source of supply hadn't dried up he would have paid her for her work and so got out of a hated task. Now he bitterly regretted that expensive meal. It wasn't as if there had been any pleasure involved. All that money had been wasted.

'He'll start tomorrow,' said Agnes, appointing herself his spokeswoman.

'I'll start on Friday,' Teddy said.

Anything could happen before Friday. For all he knew, that bank account might fill up again, might automatically do so in, say, the third week of the month, and sets of two hundred pounds in series once more be available. He drove home – what else could he call it? – with Agnes in the passenger seat. She had no objection to him as driver now he had a full licence.

Suddenly she asked, 'Has Keith given you this car?'

He didn't answer. He was listening to a new sound the engine was making, a knocking. A vague memory came to him of Keith taking it to bits and reassembling it. Should a car be regularly serviced and if so, how often? One thing was for sure, no one had looked at this engine for nine months.

'He hasn't given it to me,' he said slowly, and then, 'He wants it back.'

'Of course he does.' Agnes always took a triumphant pleasure in other people's regrets and resignation. 'He'll be after you if you've not taken care of it properly. He'll want compensation.'

This was too stupid and, considering Keith's fate, nasty, to get a reply. Teddy went into the house with the curtains. There was a letter on the doormat for him. He ripped open the envelope on which the postmark showed the evening before. The letter was from Mr Habgood to say that his wife wasn't happy with the designs and not at all pleased with the estimated cost, so in the circumstances they wouldn't proceed further. A tiny thread of panic flickered in Teddy's chest. It seemed that he had gone from riches to rags in a matter of days.

He went into the room that he had always thought of, and still did think of, as his own and unhooked the mirror from the wall. When she came back at six she'd be glad to see it and she'd forget all the stupid accusations she'd made. He took a blanket off his bed, wrapped the mirror in it and carried it back to the car. Still in the passenger seat, Agnes was talking to Megsie through the window.

'Hallo, stranger,' said Megsie. 'You ought to tell us when you're going away, you know, on account of keeping a look-out for intruders.'

'I've moved,' he said recklessly. 'I'm living down in St John's Wood.'

His grandmother said it was the first she had heard of it and it would be fifty pee to speak to him now.

'We quite miss this lovely old car,' said Megsie. 'It was only yesterday Nige said to me, the place isn't the same without that lovely old Elvis.'

'Edsel,' said Teddy, and then, because it was true, it was his intention, the decision he had suddenly come to, 'I'm going to drive it down to Liphook, to Keith. Later in the week.'

Quick as a flash Agnes said, 'Not Friday you're not. Friday you're painting Gladys's toilet.'

'Won't Keith be happy to see it,' Megsie gushed. 'I bet you he'll feel just like he's got his beloved pet out of quarantine. And you have kept it nice, Teddy, not a speck on it.'

He drove his grandmother home. Why later in the week, he thought. Why not now? He had nothing else to do. He would drive to Liphook and just abandon the Edsel, leave it in the street somewhere. They'd tow it away eventually, but if they got on to him all he had to do was say it was his uncle's and his uncle lived down there somewhere. Anyone they spoke to would confirm that Keith lived in Liphook. And he would be rid of it and the cost and worry of it.

After she had gone inside, he sat in the car for a while just looking at his grandmother's house. It *was* her house, no doubt about it, not rented, not on a life interest, but hers to do as she liked with. Or hers to do nothing with, just to die and leave him to inherit. A house that would be his that he could sell, not one that had come vaguely into his possession for him to occupy but not own.

He drove back to Orcadia Cottage. It was empty. Francine had gone out. He expected that, she had said she might go out and had promised to be back by six. That reminded him he had said he would get her a key. It wasn't worth taking the Edsel, it hardly ever was worth taking it. He walked across Hamilton Terrace to Maida Vale and down the Edgware Road where there were shops where keys could be cut. She wouldn't have let him go to the bother of having a key cut if she hadn't meant to stay.

They looked at the key and said they couldn't copy it. That was the point of keys like that. You had to apply for copies to the manufacturer locksmiths. He tried two more places, but they said the same thing. He didn't feel bad about it, it scarcely mattered, he and Francine had a key each. The main thing was that she wanted a key because she meant to come back.

The shop next door was a place where 'nearly new' clothes were sold. He remembered Noele's and the day he had called there in search of Francine. But Noele's place was a lot more up-market than this one. You wouldn't expect even second-hand designer clothes on sale in the Edgware Road, but in smarter, more fashionable parts of London there must be plenty of places. And they had to buy before they could sell.

The wind had got up as he was walking back, bringing squally rain with it. As soon as it let up he lifted his mirror out of the boot of the Edsel and carried it across the yard into the house. Why not hang it where the Alpheton still life used to be? The hook was still there, a strong double-pronged hook screwed, not pinned, to the wall. He hung up the mirror, straightened it precisely – crooked mirrors and pictures were among his hates – and studied the effect. It looked good. He had feared it would be too modern for the room, too great a contrast with the rest of the furniture, but it fitted in very well. It reflected the paintings that faced it and the trailing plant in a wall vase.

He went upstairs and into the bedroom. No wonder Francine hadn't been able to find anything to wear in that wardrobe. What horrible clothes Harriet had had! Just the same, you could see that they had been very expensive. A bright pink and black suit carried a Lacroix label. There was a fur coat, a sort of speckled yellow thing, that felt real, and an evening gown with a top like a corset encrusted with blue and red and yellow jewels.

It wouldn't do for Mildred or any of the neighbours to see him coming out with an armful of Harriet's clothes. He searched for suitcases and finally found one in a landing cupboard. If anyone saw him carrying that they would simply think he had been staying at Orcadia Cottage and was going home.

The wind had become a gale, blowing leaves from the trees and whirling them high into the air. The rain that came with it brought a premature dusk. Other cars had their lights on so he turned on the Edsel's. Driving south-westwards, he and the Edsel entered the procession of vehicles that moved with grinding slowness through the wet grey mist of a winter's afternoon. Leaves were blown on to the bonnet and a red plastic bag, bright as a tropical bird, flew down to catch itself on his windscreen wipers.

'And Teddy rescued you?' Holly said. 'How awfully romantic! Don't you think that's romantic, Chris?'

'I'd do the same in the unlikely circumstances of your mum locking you up.'

'You'll never have the chance. Teddy actually did it.'

Francine was in Holly's flat in Kilburn where she had arrived ten minutes before. Its chaos, its scents of joss sticks and aromatherapy oils and cigarettes, the empty but far from clean cups and plates which stood about, were all immensely comforting. She sat on the floor, on a heap of cushions and shawls and bedcovers, and thought how nice sitting on the floor was and asked herself how she had missed out on this pleasant and comfortable way of relaxing.

As if reading her thoughts, Holly said, 'You've missed out on a hell of a lot of things, haven't you? I just hope you've put a stop to that.'

It wasn't so easy. Holly always made everything sound so simple. Francine hadn't said anything about what had happened the night before and she wasn't going to. It hadn't, after all, been rape. It hadn't come to that and therefore could be forgotten, put behind her. She had thought of telling Holly and Christopher and James, who had just come in with a bottle of champagne, about Orcadia Cottage and its being lent to Teddy and the work he was doing there, but she decided against it. It was probably ridiculously suspicious and middle-class of her but she felt uneasy about Orcadia Cottage. She thought they, or at any rate she, ought not to be there.

James poured the champagne. He seemed used to opening bottles like this one because he didn't spill a drop. 'It's to celebrate your escape,' he said.

They all drank a toast to her and to Teddy who Holly said ought to be dressed in armour and on a white horse. Where was he anyway? Why hadn't he come with her? Francine said he was working.

'It's actually quite funny Julia hasn't given us a

bell,' said Christopher. 'I mean, you'd have expected that, wouldn't you, Holl?'

Holly nodded. 'She doesn't know Teddy rescued you. She must think you got out on your own. Or, no, it's most likely she thinks you phoned me and I came and you threw the key out to me. So why hasn't she called?'

'Because she's afraid of admitting to anyone', said James, 'that at the end of the twentieth century she locked her stepdaughter up in a bedroom. It makes her look cruel and very very foolish.'

'It makes her look draconian.'

'Bloody-minded.'

'Mad.'

'She is a bit mad,' said Francine. 'I've thought so for a long time. But you can't tell a psychotherapist she's crazy, any more than you can tell a doctor she's got – well, chicken-pox.'

They all laughed at that. Francine felt better by the minute. She asked if she could phone her father's office, but when she did she once more got the woman's voice saying she was away from her desk. Holly said that now the champagne was finished why didn't they all go down to the pub and celebrate some more and then buy some deep-pan pizzas at the Safeway. It used to be an Irish pub, but now it was full of very good-looking fierce Somalis all living on the benefit.

'Racist,' said James.

His brother said, 'Holly thinks that if she says they're handsome that makes it PC.'

It was a different world. Francine thought wistfully that she liked it. The pub was smoky and noisy, and the people looked rough, but she liked that too. Holly cooked the pizzas and after lunch Christopher and James, who both had jobs, had to go off to work. Holly's work was finished, she was off in a week's time to join a study group conserving coral on the Banggai Islands of Sulawesi.

'You ought to come. Well, I think it's all booked, but I could see. Or you could get on this Earthwatch thing I'm doing in the spring.'

'Could I?'

'You've escaped – remember? It's studying Trinidadian land crabs. Don't laugh, it's really worthwhile.'

'I wasn't going to laugh, Holly. I was thinking I'd better go home and confront Julia.' Holly's look of horror did make her laugh. 'My dad'll be home tomorrow. I can't just desert him. I won't stay, don't think that, I've promised Teddy I'll be back by six . . .'

Holly said very seriously, 'France, don't get into that again. Not even with Teddy. Not with anyone.'

'Into what?'

'Promising you'll be home. You'll be home at six or whatever. Don't do it. You've had it all your life, you'll never be free at this rate. Get out of it now.' Holly added as if she were middle-aged, 'While you're young.'

'All right. I'll try not to. I'll try to change. But I do have to go and see Julia and – and tell her things.'

'Do you want me to come with you?'

'No. No, thanks. I mean, I'd really like you to come, it's a long way, it'd be nice to have you there, but I have to go alone. I have to face her on my own. It's better that way. It's better even without my dad there. You do see, don't you?'

The shop Teddy found was in Notting Hill Gate. It was called Designers Please and claimed to buy and sell only first-quality second-hand clothes. This part of London was unknown to him. He couldn't remember ever having been there before. He drove around in the gloom, his lights on, looking for a parking space.

Every metered space in the neighbourhood seemed to be occupied. He knew it would be risky parking on a double yellow line, or even a single yellow line, at this hour, but in a side-street off the back of Kensington Church Street he found areas demarcated on the roadway with white lines. All but one of these was occupied and it was just large enough to take the Edsel.

While there, he decided he might as well make another attempt on a cash dispenser. He tried, failed once more and went back to the car. Carrying the suitcase, he made his way up Kensington Church Street. He had been obliged to park the car at such a distance that Designers Please was nearly half a mile away. A woman who wasn't in the least like Noele, being overweight, dark and multi-chinned, was attending to a customer and it was another ten minutes before she asked how she could help him. He fidgeted and paced, and looked at his watch. He was beginning to realise that if he wanted to spend the evening with Francine he was not going to make it to Liphook that day.

The woman scarcely glanced at the clothes in the suitcase, but said she couldn't consider anything that hadn't been dry-cleaned. Swallowing his anger, Teddy asked her just to take a look and tell him if she'd be interested in the event of his having the clothes cleaned. Her contemptuous expression changed when she saw the Lacroix label and the Givenchy. It seemed as if he had some very high-quality garments there, she said, but he'd have to have everything dry-cleaned – he did understand that, didn't he?

There was a cleaners a few doors up the street. The unremitting wind blew him along, once stopped him

374

in his tracks, it was so fierce. He opened the suitcase once more, piled Harriet's suits and dresses on the counter and was told they would be ready by Thursday. While he was putting the suitcase back in the Edsel's boot he saw a sign he hadn't noticed before which seemed to be explaining that this was residents' parking and available only to permit holders.

The relief he felt was premature. He got into the driver's seat and switched on the ignition, but the engine wouldn't start. Nothing like this had ever happened before. He tried again and again, urging the engine to fire but hearing only that monotonous and maddening chug-chug-chug. Another ten minutes had passed before he noticed his lights were on and simultaneously understood that this was why the car failed to start. The battery. He had run the battery flat.

Keith would have known what to do, Nige would know, that Christopher would know, but he didn't. The words 'jump leads' he distantly remembered Keith uttering in connection with a flat battery, but what these things were he had no idea. The only thing would be to find a garage and get the people there to restart the car.

Although not yet four, it was dark. The wind tore the air, carrying with it spitting rain. The Edsel's windscreen was patterned with huge splashes and thin trickles. People battled through the wind, heads lowered, coats clutched about them. A woman brandished a black umbrella, blown inside out. Teddy sat in the car and counted his money, all he had in the world. Twenty-four pounds and some loose change. Suppose the garage people charged him twenty pounds for starting the car? They might. Equally they might charge him five or forty. He had no idea.

The only thing to do was leave the Edsel, go home and think. Come back tomorrow. Meanwhile, think how to get his hands on money. Could he sell some of Harriet's silverware or glass? Her jewellery? It wouldn't be stolen – or not until he stole it – so the jeweller wouldn't have it on any stolen-property list. Leave the suitcase in the boot. There was no point in being lumbered with that. He had to fight the wind in order to get out of the car, battle with it and push himself on to the pavement.

Getting up to St John's Wood took a long time and then there was the walk home, struggling against the wind. The front garden of Orcadia Cottage was lost under a carpet of fallen Virginia creeper leaves, red and purple and yellow-green and gold, by now a sodden, slippery mass. He went out again and in by the back way. He had to. Francine had the front-door key.

376

Chapter 36

A wise move would be to collect up the silverware and jewellery immediately, before Francine came back. She wouldn't believe any explanation he might give her as to why he was selling Harriet's property. The future, which he seldom thought about for long, now presented itself to him as a blank, a mystery. It had to be filled – with money, with work and above all with Francine.

Speculating about people, their motives, their wishes, hopes and fears, came very hard to him. He had never done it before, he had never cared. He cared now. He struggled to understand her, to know what she wanted. Money, of course. A girl brought up like that, with those parents, going to that school, needed a constant supply of money. Not for a moment had he believed that stuff about not wanting him to support her. She had liked the ring and the dress and that restaurant, being taken about by car, drinking wine. If he wanted to keep her, and he desperately did, he had to have, find, make, money.

He went upstairs and into the bedroom. Harriet's jewellery was already familiar to him. Often enough he had draped these pearls and ropes of shining stones round Francine's neck and put these bracelets on her arms. He put a handful into each pocket of his jacket. A small silver bowl, a silver-backed hairbrush and silver-bound comb also looked saleable. He would take a necklace to one jeweller's and a bracelet to another, the hairbrush to a third. It would take a long time, but he might realise a thousand pounds out of it.

Francine would want clothes and a car to go about in, more of those restaurants and maybe books. She seemed keen on books. Could he let the Neasden house? Hard to imagine anyone wanting to live in the neighbourhood, pay rent for such a house, but Megsie and Nige liked it, they had bought next door. Or maybe he could even rent out this place? It was a daring thought.

During the long slow journey by tube, Francine reflected that this was the first time in her life she was going home without, so to speak, an appointment; going to where Julia was without a pre-arrangement to be there by seven or nine or ten.

On all those previous occasions, hundreds of them, she had been apprehensive as to how Julia would greet her. Even if she were early or on time. Tears or rage or happy smiles, reproaches or gratified approval, it was bound to have been one of these. Never had Julia simply acknowledged her arrival with a nod or a simple 'hallo'. She realised, looking back, how terribly it had plagued her life. How she would have loved a casual, laid-back or light-hearted companion, someone who took things easy. But it was over now, the end had come on Sunday and she was no longer in the least afraid of Julia's reception of her.

She emerged from the station to find the rain coming down harder than ever and the wind blowing it in horizontal sheets. It was also growing dark and she saw that she had left her departure from Holly's till rather too late, for now it was past four. Getting back to Orcadia Place by six would be difficult, but as that thought came to her she remembered Holly's words. 'France, don't get into that again. Not with Teddy, not with anyone.' She could phone him from home, she could tell him she'd be back late.

All the taxis were taken. They always were when it was raining. She could walk, it would take a quarter of an hour, that was all, and if she got wet through she had plenty of clothes there to change into.

Walking – even walking in a gale and a downpour – was a good activity for thinking and clearing the mind. She had often noticed this. Things fell into place more logically and reasonably than when one tried to concentrate before going to sleep at night. She thought about Teddy and she knew suddenly and regretfully that it wouldn't work. He wasn't for her and never could be. They had nothing in common and they looked at life quite differently. Probably she would never have gone out with him, never had secret meetings with him, if Julia hadn't put the pressure on and her father been so moralistic.

That didn't mean she wouldn't go back. Of course she would, and tonight as she had undertaken to do. She'd even stay a few days and she'd explain and make him listen and try to show him they weren't suited to each other. At the time, at each time, she had felt very frustrated and somehow deprived of a right, but now she was glad they had never had sex. Well, never had real sex, proper sex. She would have felt more committed to him if they had.

She hadn't liked the way he wanted her to dress up and pose and be stared at. It was – she searched for and found the unfamiliar word – voyeuristic. It was like a striptease in reverse. She had felt uncomfortable all the time during those sessions and bored too. How anyone could bear to be a model she couldn't imagine. But worse than any of that had been his behaviour of the night before. She hadn't told Holly, she couldn't have told anyone, but she knew now, if she hadn't then, that he had wanted to have sex with her, had almost been *able* to have sex, because her mother had been murdered and she had talked about murder. It had been a sort of trigger to excite him and she couldn't bear that. That had been the end, the final thing.

His ring slid on her finger in the wet. She brought her hand up in front of her face and looked at the blue stones and the diamond. He must have it back. Books had taught her that you gave a man back his ring, even if it wasn't ever an engagement ring.

It was a joyous reunion. They collected De Valera from the kennels on their way home from Heathrow. The Irish setter gave the same welcome, it seemed, to each of them, favouring Franklin equally with Anthea in bestowing licks and uttering whimpers of happiness.

'With luck,' said Anthea, 'they'll put an end to this ghastly quarantine and we'll be able to take him with us next time.'

They had firmly become 'us' and their future a joint affair. If there was a problem it was only that Franklin, being without a resident's parking permit in the City of Westminster, had to put the BMW in an underground car-park. He and Anthea ordered Thai food over the phone. They disliked the idea of going out and leaving De Valera again.

'Are you going to phone Harriet?' Anthea said.

'I've thought about that and I can't see why I should. I never do, normally. She expects me back tomorrow and tomorrow I shall go back – for half an hour.'

'It had better not be more than half an hour,' said Anthea, who was beginning to exhibit her old signs of possessiveness.

Franklin rather liked it. For one thing, he hadn't seen much of it for nearly thirty years and for another, it brought back tender memories of his youth. 'I shall stay long enough to tell her what has happened and that I am leaving her. I shall pack some of my clothes into a suitcase and come away.'

'Mind you don't weaken.'

'I never weaken, you know that,' said Franklin with one of his awful smiles.

It was true. He always did exactly what he wanted, whatever the cost in money and trouble. He had wanted Harriet, so had got rid of Anthea, though it took him five years and cost, until she married again, something in the region of half a million. Now he wanted her again and was getting rid of Harriet. Probably it would take another five years and cost three or four times that. But he would do it.

She supposed she must love him. It was very hard to know quite what that meant when you got to her age. Certainly there were things about him she loved and had missed. The way he threw cushions on the floor before sitting down in an armchair. The way he had of emptying his pockets on the dressing-table each night before he went to bed, a crumpled handkerchief, his keys, his wallet, his loose change tipped into a little glass powder bowl. She had always found it touching and when she saw him go through those endearing manoeuvres the first night they had spent together in Half Moon Street after so many years, tears came into her eyes.

'What are the waterworks in aid of?' he had asked and turned on her his skull grin, so that for a moment it was Father Time she saw standing there, the Grim Reaper. And then he came to her.

The newspapers were still in the letter-box. That was

the first thing she noticed when she came up to the gate. Could Julia have gone away? She closed the gate behind her. It was dark now, but no lights were on. Yet as she came up the path to the door her past experiences warned her that Julia could be waiting behind it. A split second before her key went into the lock Julia would open the door.

Julia didn't. Francine had a very strong sense by now that Julia wasn't there. She unlocked the door and went inside. The hall was dark, the whole house seemed to be in darkness. It felt stuffy, oppressive, as if unaired for days. Plainly, no one was at home. She put on the hall and landing lights, went upstairs and into her own room, took off her wet clothes and laid them over the edge of the bath. There was no point in packing another suitcase, for she would be back in two or three days. The idea of coming back wasn't pleasant, but where else could she go?

If Holly could get her on this Trinidadian trip or even on the coral reef study . . . Would her father let her? He might. He would be incensed about what Julia had done and so in the mood to make great concessions. She dried her hair on a towel, put on fresh jeans, a T-shirt and sweater, boots that would keep water out. Teddy would hate every item of that costume, but worrying about what Teddy wanted and thought was also soon to be a thing of the past. She put her mobile into her bag and went downstairs.

It was rare for the living-room door to be closed. She had noticed when she first came in, but the fact of it hadn't really registered. She hesitated and then she opened the door. It was dark inside, but with a twilight sort of darkness, grey, shadowy, a blaze of light suddenly flaring across wall and ceiling from a passing car's headlights. On the carpet, by the end of the sofa, was a shoe.

Last night, in the struggle with Teddy, she had kicked off a shoe and it had flown across the room, breaking a china statuette. This was Julia's shoe, she recognised it, a suede pump with a highish heel. Blue, she thought it was, but she couldn't see colours in the dimness. Why had Julia left her shoe in the middle of the living-room floor?

The back of the sofa was towards her. She went into the room without turning on a light. Before, just immediately before, rounding the sofa and looking down on to it, she realised that it was fear of what she might see which had stopped her switching on the light. She didn't want to see it, whatever it was.

But there was no help for that. Julia's face, white as bone, white as pearl, gleamed in the dusk. Her eyes fixed on the girl who looked fearfully at her accusing gaze. One hand hung at an unnatural angle, looking stiff, controlled, but when Francine touched it, subsided with a faint rustle, weak as thread. Icy cold, the touch of that skin had been. The face was like a waxwork's mask, dewy, gleaming, unlined, as if it had never been alive. Francine sank on to the floor and broke into silent dry sobs.

Richard found her there when he came into the house at just after six. Light flooding the room showed him his dead wife on the sofa and his daughter sitting on the floor beside her. There was no blood this time and Francine was a dozen years older, but that seemed to him the only difference.

She was conscious. When he lifted her up she came thankfully into his arms. But she could tell him nothing. She had no words, once more she was dumb.

Chapter 37

Splitting the paving stone in two was easier than he had expected. He placed the pieces on the wire base and immediately realised it wasn't going to work. The cement would slide through the wire, the wire would bear only the lightest of weights. The proper way to fill in a hole is to fill it from the bottom or provide an adequate lid. He was learning that now. The lid was there, but the whole point of the exercise was to dispense with it. The idea of filling in from the bottom upwards appealed to him – but fill it with what? Stones, ideally, rubble. There were too many difficulties in the way of that. No doubt he could get a delivery of hardcore but it would cost him and he had no money.

He fetched his wire cutters and clipped away the wire netting. It would have stopped the manhole cover fitting properly and now it looked as if he might have to settle for simply putting the cover back. But not yet. He'd give it some thought, try and work out an alternative. The flower-bed in the fibreglass container? It had always been the most attractive idea.

The rain had stopped, though water lay in pools. Out in the mews the plane trees had shed their leaves, their fall hastened by the gale, but space in here was reserved for the Virginia creeper whose foliage, rose-pink, crimson, purple, almost black as well as yellow and gold, lay thick on the paving of the yard, floating in puddles or pasted to the stones. Strange that the now multicoloured leafy wall seemed as dense as ever, though tens of thousands of leaves had been shed. In the morning he would have a sweep-up. He opened the gate and looked into the mews just in time to see a woman, not Mildred but also out with a dog, slip on the wet leaves, slide forward and fall flat on her back.

The time was approaching six. Exactly at six was what she had said. He returned to the house. Food never interested him much, but there was meat in the freezer, eggs in the fridge and plenty of cans. The untouched wine was still in there too. After being out with her friends all day she would be in a happy, compliant mood and, once she had eaten, would agree to wear his dress, pose for him. The house was full of cushions. He gathered them up, silk and velvet, plain and quilted, patchwork and brocade, and piled them on the living-room floor. The black plume he had promised himself should be part of the picture he hadn't been able to find in the house. There must be something that would serve as a substitute. He went upstairs and searched through Harriet's things, shawls, scarves, gloves, stoles, and there at the back of a drawer found a blood-red feather boa.

The sight of it made him shiver. It was like a dead bird or a plumed snake. It smelt of a heavy cloying perfume, gone stale with time. He imagined it held in Francine's white hand, its fronds brushing her pale cheek. Bracelets on her arms, her legs bare, the skirt of the green figured velvet pulled up about her thighs, dark-green shoes on her feet with heels sharp as knives. His body rose, yearning to the fantasy, he was erect and hard, just thinking of it. He closed his eyes, sighed, held himself for a moment. Then he started searching the room again, this time for green shoes, any shoes that were suitable. These clothes, this pose, especially that red snaky boa, would do the trick, he knew it.

Julia had passed from his mind. He had scarcely thought of her at all since he had killed her, nor of that act of killing which had been so easy, had met with such little resistance. He had almost forgotten her, as he had forgotten Francine's tale of her mother's murder. It returned to him now, but he dismissed it as unbelievable. For reasons of her own, she had been trying to make an impression on him and it had worked, or almost worked.

The phone was unplugged in the bedroom, but he heard it ringing downstairs. He never answered it and he hoped he had stopped Francine answering it. After half a dozen rings the machine cut in. It might have been Francine to explain why she was so late. He smiled to himself. She so often was late, punctuality meant nothing to her, that he wasn't much concerned. She would come, she had promised.

It seemed like a near-miracle actually finding a pair of high-heeled dark-green suede shoes. They would be too small for Francine, but that hardly mattered since she wasn't going to walk about in them. Tonight was going to be *the* night, he knew it, he was convinced. Perhaps he would ask her to tell that story of her mother's murder again while she lay on the cushions and held the red boa close to her face. True or false, it didn't matter, he just had to hear it in the right place and at the right time.

For a long time, when she didn't come and it got to seven, to eight, to eight-thirty, he lay on the floor, on the cushions, thinking of how he would cure her of unpunctuality, change her and make her more like himself. But this was a refuge that could last only so long and when it got to nine he was desperate and enraged by turns. He couldn't phone Holly, he didn't know her number. Once she was back with him, he would cure her of Holly too, root the woman out, rid Francine and himself of her, as he had rid them of Julia.

But he was angry now. If she had come then he would have hit her, struck her in such a way as to leave no mark, or no mark ordinary acquaintances might see. He would see and she would and be taught. He ran his tongue across his lips, then sat, sullen, thinking how easy it was, really, how simple. He could be gratified and successful and even proficient, if only a silly unthinking girl would do as he asked. And it wasn't much to ask. Any other woman would have done it, he was sure of that.

That might have been Francine on the phone. He did what he had never done before and played back Harriet's messages. There were a great many, two from a man who didn't leave his name, who was evidently too familiar to her for that, several from different women, one from Simon Alpheton, to which Teddy listened in wonder and near-disbelief. He found a way to switch the machine off and did so. Now if Francine phoned . . .

He tried to make himself think of other things, the Edsel abandoned in the street in Notting Hill, Harriet's clothes which must be collected from the cleaners, suitable jeweller's shops where they would buy those necklaces and bracelets and rings without asking awkward questions. When it got to nine-thirty he ate some bread and cheese, and drank a glass of milk. It made him feel sick, for he knew by then that she wasn't coming.

Because he couldn't give her what she wanted. It wasn't important, what she wanted, not like being with someone was and giving them your support and having respect for them and backing them up in what they did. Those were the things that counted. But women wanted sex, they always did, he knew that from the way those girls had looked at him and talked to him at college. It was easy for them, they only had to lie there and wait for it. They didn't understand what a strain it was for a man, the pressures on him, how fragile it was, all this preparing oneself and concentrating and keeping going. No wonder he couldn't succeed with all he had on his mind, but she didn't understand that, she only knew she wasn't getting what she wanted and so she hadn't come back.

Her promises meant nothing. Maybe they had meant something when she made them, but she had talked to her friends since then and they had laughed and told her not to bother with him. She would be there with them now. If he had still had the Edsel he would have driven up to Kilburn and fetched her away by force. But she wouldn't be in the house, she'd be out with them, out with James, most likely.

She had his front-door key. Keeping that and not coming back would be stealing. He went to the front of the house and looked out of the window, as if looking for her would bring her. Nothing could be seen beyond the confines of the enclosed front garden. The paving lay buried under a sea of leaves, calm now the wind had dropped, dark and shining in the yellow light. The tubs and troughs emerged like islands out of this still and waveless sea, and they too were draped and hung with leaves.

Even if she came now he wouldn't see her until a hand appeared, lifting the latch on the gate. He felt a need of air and, returning to the back of the house, went out into the courtyard. It was darker there, lit only by what light was shed from the kitchen and from a table lamp inside the french windows. Instead of a sea, here was a thick, slimy mat of leaves, due no doubt to the water having lain about in pools before the bulk of them were blown down. If he lived here permanently, if this were really his house, he'd chop down that creeper. Never mind Alpheton putting it in his most famous painting, it was a nuisance. No one ought to have to cope with all this mess each autumn.

He unbolted the gate and went out into the mews. Mildred and a man were getting out of a car. If he had been able to see over the wall he wouldn't have gone out there, if he had checked by looking through a knothole in the gate, but he hadn't and it was too late now. The man said good-evening and Mildred said hi.

'Where's your amazing car?' Mildred asked.

For a moment he thought she must know what had happened that day, must have followed him, spied on him, or with witchlike insight read his mind. But of course it wasn't any of that. They had simply got used to seeing the Edsel outside, to seeing it wherever he was, just as their dog, which now jumped out of the back of the car, was wherever they were.

'In for a service,' he said, using Keith's phrase.

'Harriet OK?'

He nodded, not much liking her knowing look.

'These leaves are just as much litter as old paper and cans, in my opinion. Paula slipped on them and broke her leg. Tell Harriet if she doesn't know, Paula at number eleven. My father poisoned a tree in the next-door garden when his neighbours refused to cut it down. He couldn't stand the leaves any longer.'

'Poisoned it?' said Teddy.

'It was right up against his fence. In the dark, in the middle of the night actually, he drilled a hole in the trunk with a Black & Decker and poured in rat poison. Really, I kid you not.'

'Now, come on, Mildred,' the man said. 'Harriet's friend will think you're a criminal, won't you, Mr er –?'

'Hill,' said Teddy. 'Keith Hill.'

The man said soothingly, 'The council will come in the morning and sweep up. They're pretty good about that.'

Teddy didn't believe the story about the poisoned tree, he never believed any of these crazy tales women told. It was Francine's mother getting herself murdered all over again. But still he had to ask. 'Did it die? The tree, I mean.'

'It died all right. It fell over into Daddy's garden and it cost him a packet getting it taken away. Goodnight. Give my love to Harriet.'

The night was clear and cold, the sky overspread by a purplish mist. He looked up and down the mews, for no special reason. She wouldn't come that way. The hours ahead loomed as a horrible prospect, a night of misery and rage. He couldn't just go to bed, he needed to do something, take some powerful and perhaps violent action. In that moment he decided to go to Kilburn and fetch her away.

He had done it before, rescued her and brought her here. For all he knew, Holly and Christopher and James were also keeping her by force. This time he might have to storm the place, break in, smash down doors. He felt ready for it. Of course he no longer had a car, but it didn't seem important. There were taxis, buses, trains, and it wasn't even very far away.

Once he had got her he wouldn't let her go again. He should never have allowed her out on her own. Others imprisoned her and so would he, only he had the most right. She was his to do as he liked with.

The chill of the night penetrated his thin jacket. He felt the weight of Harriet's jewels in the pockets and they comforted him. They were like heavy money, coinage, to keep him safe, shored up, protected. He would need a sweater, maybe a thicker coat from that wardrobe of men's clothes.

He closed the gate and bolted it, had taken a step across the courtyard when the phone began ringing inside the house, loud and shrill and insistent. At this hour it must be Francine, it had to be. No one else would phone at ten-thirty, no one ever did. He ran for the door, but never reached it. The thick, slimy paste of leaves acted as a slide, more slippery than ice. His legs buckled as he slid. He lost all orientation, and reaching out for something to catch hold of, felt his hands slither too, as he sledged forward across the greasy sludge and dropped down the hole.

It wasn't a free uninterrupted fall. He clutched at the rim as he went down and hung there, his fingertips sliding on the leafy slime. But the pain of the newly cut wire piercing his palms forced him to let go and drop the eight feet or so into the coal-hole, on to a paste of wet coal-dust.

He closed his eyes and made himself take slow, deep breaths. The disadvantage of that was that on the inhalations came the stench of decay. It came through the boards of the door and the hatch. But he had to bear that, he had to *discount* that, take no notice of it. However you looked at it, that was the last thing he had to worry about. Nor was there much point in putting the clock back five minutes and not running, not sliding, *remembering* that the leaves were there, that they were slippery. He couldn't go back, he had to accept what had happened. He was in no real danger, that was the thing to hold on to.

It couldn't have been more than ten minutes since he had been talking to Mildred and the man with her. If he shouted they would probably hear, or someone would. They would come and get him out. Probably a couple of hands extended down into the hole would be sufficient for him to pull himself up. A rope tied to the gatepost or a pair of steps lowered.

But whoever came near would smell the smell. Perhaps not, if they just stood in the courtyard, but they would if they bent over to help him out of the hole. And they wouldn't just make some comment about drains, they would fetch someone to do something about it.

The manhole opening appeared to him from below as a rectangular aperture like a window. It was filled with reddish-purple sky. He stretched upwards as far as he could, but found that even so, his fingertips were a good six inches from the opening.

Although he knew it was stupid and pointless to have regrets, he couldn't help cursing himself for not having left that chair in the coal-hole. With that to stand on he would have had no difficulties. It would have elevated him enough to climb out of the hole with ease. More stupid regrets, for no one in his circumstances would have left that chair in here. Strange that he could hear the phone again. Through the house, perhaps, or across the courtyard. If she got no reply would she come? A wished-for scenario presented itself to his eyes, Francine letting herself in the front door, calling him, looking for him, coming out to the back, to the mews, to see if the Edsel was there . . .

No one died from being down an eight-foot-deep pit in the middle of London. Then he remembered he had bolted the gate on the inside after he came back from the mews. Probably it didn't matter, probably it wasn't important, but he couldn't help thinking things would be easier for him if that gate were unlocked.

He knelt down on the floor in front of the door into the cellar and tried to raise the hatch from the inside. To his surprise it was an easy task. The smell that came from the cellar was horrible and he recoiled from it, sitting back on his haunches. Would you ever get used to that smell? Would there ever come a time when you got accustomed to it? He remembered how he had wondered what dead bodies smelt like. He knew now. You could plug up your ears, cover your eyes, but no way existed to blocking your nose if you wanted to be able to breathe. No one died from a bad smell, though. He must hold on to that.

His arm went in round the framework of the hatch and he felt about for the bolt. He had been pretty sure he could reach it and he could. The door swung open and he stepped into the burial chamber. Once there, he couldn't help remembering those thoughts he had had about Egyptian Pharaohs and rooms in the earth no human eye saw for thousands of years. This human eye was seeing it, he thought grimly, or rather feeling it, for removed from the dim light that came through the manhole opening, in here it was nearly pitch dark.

He dreaded touching or even brushing against the bodies on the floor, so he made his way to the stairs by feeling his way along the wall. Even so, he tripped over something on the floor. It was the pole with a hook on one end that Harriet had been carrying. At the stairs he crouched down and went up on all fours. The space in front of the new wall seemed very narrow, no more than a foot or so in depth. He felt the rough brickwork with his finger-tips, pulled himself up so that he was pressed close to the wall.

For the first time in his life he was regretting being so thorough, such a perfectionist, always doing everything as *beautifully* as he could. If he had skimped on the mortar, left gaps in the brickwork, made the plaster thinner ... But he tried just the same. In the dark he pushed and kicked at that wall, pounded on it with his fists and beat on it with the pole. It was as solid as if it had been built as part of the original house. There was no sense of yielding at all. He doubted if the Alpheton painting on the other side even trembled.

But increasing panic, a very real fear that things might be worse than he had at first thought, worse than he could imagine, made him keep on pounding, made him stamp against the wall with the sole of his right foot. And it was this, for he had nothing to hold on to, which made him lose his footing and tumble backwards down the stairs.

Like Harriet, he landed on the cellar floor and, like her, he lost consciousness.

Chapter 38

The police knew Francine's history and made no attempt to harass her. In the morning, of her own volition, she wrote down where she had been since Sunday, what she had done and when she had returned to the house. Staying with friends, she wrote, giving Holly's address. Why involve Teddy? Especially as he might get into trouble over Orcadia Cottage. Julia had been asleep when she left the house on Sunday, she was sure of that, but she went into no details. She didn't want them to know that her stepmother had locked her up. To go into all that would have seemed like speaking ill of the dead.

She tried to remember how it had been before, the first time she had lost her voice. But she couldn't, only that it had been like it was now, the words there and the desire to speak, but the inability to enunciate. It was the ultimate frustration for her and she thought of Teddy, who had been unable to function as a virile man. I will tell them nothing about him, she thought, for he has done nothing, only been here and been with me and tried to love me.

They got more help from Richard. Or so it seemed at first. 'There's a man called Jonathan Nicholson. He's been harassing my daughter. Stalking her.'

Of course they wanted to know why Richard and Julia had never reported this, and Richard could only say he meant to, he intended to, when he got home. By that time, their faces told him, it was too late. A new guilt replaced the old one in Richard's mind. If he had gone to the police about Jonathan Nicholson, if he had only phoned them from Germany, would Julia be alive now? Would his dear girl, his sweet daughter, have the power of speech?

She sat silent and strangely tranquil, though once or twice tears slid out of her eyes and fell down her cheeks. He was reminded of that other time, after Jennifer died. She was too old now for him to read to her and buying her a kitten wasn't the answer. Instead, he bought her books. She wrote out a list for him and he bought them all.

The police were interested in Jonathan Nicholson and instituted a search for him. From Richard they knew that he was young, dark-haired, had a red sports car and lived in Fulham. It wouldn't take them long to find him.

For a moment, when he regained consciousness, Teddy didn't know where he was. Then, as he awoke and his sight came back and his sense of smell, he experienced a long spasm of pure terror. He was more afraid than he had ever been in all his life. He wanted to scream and cry, and beat with his hands on these rough stone walls.

Instead, he held both hands hard across his mouth until the need began to pass. Slowly he knelt up, but his head hurt and throbbed. There seemed no point in struggling to stand. He sat down, facing the wall, with his back against the thick folds of plastic. It was as if a pulse beat in his head where no pulse had been before.

It was lighter inside the cellar and he saw why. Very little time had passed, a matter only of minutes, but a misty yellow moon had swum across the red-lit rectangle that was the manhole opening. The light it shed illuminated the cobwebbed sides of the hole, the glimmering plastic, and worse things. It was to avoid seeing them that he sat with his face to the wall. Later on, he thought, when the drumming in his head stopped and also perhaps when the moon-light had passed, he would make an attempt to lever himself up out of the hole.

Inside there, eight feet down in the earth, it had grown very cold. His hands were icy and goose-flesh stood on his arms under the thin jacket. The moon-light made it possible for him to see the hands on his watch. It was only just after eleven. Maybe Francine would still come. Would he hear a taxi down here? He re-created in his mind the throb of a diesel engine, but the longed-for sound didn't come. He shut his eyes and tried to think.

If the worst came to the worst, if the unthinkable happened and he was here all night, Westminster Council's contractors would be here in the morning to clear away the leaves. Mildred's friend or what-ever he was had said so. Not in here, of course. But if when he heard them come he shouted and called for help, would they get him out with no questions asked? Would they just respond by coming in here and throwing down a rope or a pair of steps? He fancied those people always had ropes and pairs of steps on board their lorry. But he had bolted the gate on the inside.

Another idea he had was almost too terrible to contemplate. He could drag those bodies into the hole, pile one on top of the other and, standing on them, reach the opening. Perhaps. Just about. His heart quailed, he couldn't do it, he couldn't touch them. But he had to contemplate it, he had to think of everything. If he forced his feet into Harriet's high-heeled shoes and then those into Keith's it would raise him maybe four inches. Then standing on the bodies, he would be able to grip the edges of the hole that much more easily. He might even be able to scrape away with his fingers the sticky crust of leaves on the flagstones, on the rim of the hole.

He waited a while before beginning. He couldn't help himself. The shivering which galvanised him had to be got under control. When the moon disappeared and semi-darkness returned it became easier. Even so, he closed his eyes before reaching for Harriet's feet. He expected stiffness, but they were limp and slack. The shoes she was wearing had higher heels than he remembered, these must be four inches high, and he felt something unexpected, a small surge of excitement, as he held them in his hands. These shoes would save him, they would lift him up and get him out, without the need of anyone else's intervention.

They wouldn't go on. He pushed and thrust and squeezed his feet into the pointed toes, took off his socks even though he was freezing. His heels wouldn't go in. The shoes were five sizes too small, at least. Still, he must try without them. He stepped on to the two bodies, trod on them sickeningly, pretended he was somewhere else, pushed away reality and reached up for the mouth of the opening. His hands were very sore from the wire and from scraping on the stone, and it was no less slippery out there. Something had happened to him too when he fell, concussion perhaps, he didn't know, but it had been enough to weaken him and take the strength from his shoulders and his arm muscles. He felt his fingers slide helplessly back across the greasy surface. He scrabbled with his nails, prayed for a grip, a purchase, but his sticky, weak fingers slithered and slid, and the point came where they lost their hold and he slipped back, half dropping, half falling, to the bottom of the shaft.

This time he didn't hurt himself much. The worst

part was falling on the bodies of Keith and Harriet. There was something terrible about it, as if they, the dead, were pulling him down into their awful ugliness and decay, he was drowning in their putrefaction. He shrank away from them and huddled up against the wall. For some minutes he remained pressed against the cold brickwork as if, by pushing hard enough, it would yield and absorb him. But he knew what he must do if he were to survive the night: drag them back into the cellar and keep the coal-hole to himself, pass the night there as best he could, alone, isolated, committed to thoughts of how to get out. Cold too. He was suddenly aware of how terribly cold it was in the hole.

In this respect, too, he knew what he had to do. But it took him a long time to prepare himself. He had expected never to see the occupants of the cellar again, still less to have to touch them. Growing stiff with cold, his teeth chattering and the goose-flesh on his arms like a rash, he told himself in a low mutter that he must, he had to do it. Otherwise he might die of hypothermia. 'Just do it,' he said, fully out loud this time, 'just do it.'

Turning away his face, he reached for the blanket in which Harriet's body was rolled up, got hold of one side of it and tugged. It came away easily enough, but the sliding and bumping of what it had contained as it slumped on to the floor made his throat close up and rise. The blanket smelt, but not badly. Strangely, rather, of exotic perfume and luxury, and something sweet-sour and fierce and indefinable, which he felt would swiftly become, maybe tomorrow, appalling.

It took him as long again to put the blanket to the use for which he intended it. One thing to touch the edges of it with his hands, quite another to wrap himself in it. Yet it was a beautiful object. He remembered that from when he had fetched it out of the cupboard, soft, thick, baby-blue, with satin binding. In the dim light from above he could see that it was smeared all over with coal-dust and this troubled him. He felt ashamed of himself for dirtying this lovely, clean, expensive wool, for doing something so alien to his nature. Gently, for a while, he stroked it with his fingertips. Then, familiar with it by now, easing himself away from the use to which it had been put, he wrapped himself in it and curled up on the floor.

Tears ran down his face, hot as water from a tap. He stroked them away with his fingers. Inside the blanket's pastel-blue fluffy folds it was warm, and more than that. It was like being a child again, though not the kind of child he had ever been.

But he couldn't sleep. He covered up his face with the blanket, huddled more and more deeply inside it, pulling a fold of it over his head so that he was cocooned. Back inside Eileen's womb, warm and dark, he tried to sleep and failed. Who knows if a foetus sleeps?

Anthea surprised herself. She never thought it would fall to her lot to urge Franklin to go home and speak to Harriet. Her hope would have been for Franklin simply to leave well, or ill, alone. But suddenly she wanted clarification, all things made smooth, everything brought out into the open. 'Just go,' she said. 'Explain. Promise nothing, but hint that all things are possible.'

Sometimes, though without empathy, Franklin had wondered how Harriet got on during his absences without him to bring her tea in the morning. Without him, come to that, to clean for, run a household for and to run back and forth to the cleaners with his clothes. Enjoyed herself, perhaps, or

400

went to pieces. At any rate, now she had to get her own tea, but whether that got her up earlier or kept her in bed later he couldn't tell. But he was pretty sure she would still be in the house and probably titivating herself after her morning shower at ten-past nine, which was the time he calculated getting to Orcadia Cottage.

The traffic was heavy and it made him a little later than that. He parked the car in the mews and waved to Mildred, who was out with her dog. She waved back, managed a half-smile and it was probably his imagination that she looked embarrassed. As if she hadn't expected to see him or he were in the wrong place at the wrong time. Imagination, no doubt. There was a chance the back gate might have been left unbolted, for Harriet was careless about such things, but she hadn't been this time and he couldn't get in that way.

He walked round the corner and opened the gate into the front garden. The Virginia creeper had shed half its leaves, they were so thick you couldn't see the paving stones. Harriet never did a stroke of gardening, of course, but surely she could have swept up. He reminded himself that it need no longer matter to him what she did or failed to do, or even how the place looked, and he put his key into the front-door lock and entered the house.

To be fair to her, she had always kept it clean. And it was like that now, even, it seemed to Franklin's keen eye, cleaner and tidier than usual. He called out, 'Hallo. It's me.'

The answer should have been a shriek of astonishment. He had never before arrived home from a holiday at this sort of time. There was no answer. Franklin went upstairs. The bed was made and looking exquisite. It was apparent that no one had slept in it the night before, or used the room or the

401

bathroom. The shower cabinet would have been wet, but it was dry and the ivory-coloured towels on the rack were dry too.

He went back downstairs and had a look round. The place was so clean it looked as if a bevy of maids had been in, dusting and vacuuming and polishing. Harriet must have been spring-cleaning in November. The one incongruity, apart from the lights she'd left on, was the pile of cushions on the living-room floor. Every cushion from the chairs and the two sofas had found its way there, and draped across the top of the heap was Harriet's scarlet feather boa.

Reserving his judgement, Franklin went into the kitchen. Everything was normal there, if gleaming glass and polished surfaces could be called normal. There was something different about the dining-room, though it took him a moment or two to decide what. The mirror, it must be, the new mirror. Harriet, who never bought anything for the house, who spent all her money on clothes and beauty treatments, had in his absence bought this beautiful mirror. It was rather too modern for his own taste, but he recognised the exquisite craftsmanship, the delicate balance of colours.

But what, then, had become of the Alpheton still life? If she has sold it, thought Franklin, I will punish her till she squeals. But she hadn't sold it, it was hanging on the wall at the end of the passage, a most unsuitable place for such a delightful and, incidentally, valuable painting. It was a funny thing to think of about one's own house, but this was a part of it, an obscure corner, never much visited by him. He couldn't remember when he had last turned this corner into the passage, which was surely why he remembered it differently, why he thought there had been another door here somewhere, or a window.

Where was she? Where and why had she gone?

Once more he went upstairs. If she had gone away some of her clothes would be missing and a suitcase. He opened the wardrobe doors and saw that half her clothes were gone, the newest and showiest, he noted. The biggest of their suitcases was missing from the landing cupboard. But it was something else which aroused a hope that seemed almost too good to be true, that she hadn't simply gone away but had left him, and that was the absence of the best of her jewellery. He looked in the various boxes and drawstring bags in the drawer and in the two jewel cases, and found the pearls gone, the diamond-and-sapphire necklace gone, the two gold bracelets gone.

The trashy bits on the ear-ring tree she hadn't bothered with, nor the obvious costume stuff. If she had just taken herself off in advance of the arrangements made for her holiday, she wouldn't have taken the pearls and the necklace and all those rings. No, it was clear that she had left for good. Franklin did one of his little dances round the bedroom, thought of phoning Anthea to tell her the glad news, decided to tell her in person, waltzed across the spare bedroom and looked out of the window.

Leaves were as thickly scattered out there as in the front and someone had left the manhole cover off. Downstairs again, he contemplated the pile of cushions decorated with that red boa. Now he had seen other evidence of Harriet's departure he thought he could interpret this strange arrangement as some kind of sign from her of defiance or simple farewell. She had, he remembered, always disliked his habit of tossing cushions on to the floor when he sat down. As for the boa, he recalled laughing when first she bought it and saying she was some thirty-five years too old to wear it. A sign, then, where another woman would have left a note.

He unhooked the Alpheton from the wall he

couldn't remember being there and rested it against the hall wall. That was something he would take with him.

The sweeping up had begun at eight. He had been listening for it from first light, the first glimmer of dawn to show itself through that distant window to the world. By the time it began enough light showed for him to see the time by his watch.

He was neither hungry nor thirsty and this obscurely troubled him, the fact that he thought about it, for it seemed an indication that soon he would be very very thirsty. The prospect of hunger seemed to matter less. Perhaps, if it rained, he could catch the drops on his tongue. But what was he thinking of? He wouldn't be down here long enough for that.

The street cleaner announced its arrival with a clatter followed by a roaring sucking sound. This was accompanied by a siren-like moaning, which rose and fell, and he realised that instead of brooms and brushes a giant vacuum cleaner was at work up there. Only one man would be using that, he calculated, and he wouldn't have steps with him or a rope. He stood up and started shouting just the same, calling out hallo the first few times, then, 'Help me! Help me!'

He soon understood that he wasn't able to make himself heard above the roar and whine of the vacuum cleaner, and after a little while the sound of it began to fade, as it made its slow progress along the mews. He went on calling out and hammered on the wall with his fists and the skylight pole.

Nothing happened. No one came. Until now he had never thought about the house next door, number seven Orcadia Place, had scarcely glanced at it in his comings and goings, but gradually, as the moan of the vacuum cleaner dwindled into silence, the conviction came to him that it must be mostly empty, that its occupants perhaps had a country home as well and generally lived there. Lights came on in it in the evenings, but that meant only that a timer regulated them at prescribed hours, as one did in Harriet's house.

Other people would come, surely, sooner or later. Delivery men, a milkman, someone bringing newspapers? But not this way, not this back way. And, in any case, he had bolted the gate on the inside. He knew what he must do. At all costs he had to survive. If his rescuers smelt the smell and found the two who were down here with him, so be it. Maybe he could deny knowing anything about them, maybe they wouldn't find out his connection with Keith, or even discover who Keith was. And if they did and the worst came to the worst, prison was preferable to death.

He moved back into the coal-hole, closing the door behind him. In this narrow cell the air was fresher and sweeter. Just being able to see the light of day was comforting, a pale, flickering sunshine that made a little spot of light on the brick wall.

Sooner or later, perhaps not till nearly lunch-time, someone would come into the mews to fetch a car. He would hear their footsteps. And then he would begin shouting for help. He would start yelling as loud as he could and beating on the wall with the pole. The vacuum cleaner man hadn't heard him because of the noise the machine made. But in the silence he would be heard. Now that he had decided to risk the discovery of those two it was only a matter of waiting till someone came.

Wrapping himself in the blanket once more, he sat on the floor with his back towards the wall. Resting his head on it, he began thinking up a story which would be a defence against any accusations that might be brought. Doing a job for Harriet, that was how he would account for being there. She couldn't deny it, she was dead. He had slipped and fallen down the hole. Cellar? He didn't even know there was a cellar. This coal-hole was all he knew.

These thoughts were soothing and they sent him to sleep. He hadn't slept all night, but he could sleep now, secure in the knowledge that he would soon get out of here, be free, an innocent victim of a trap made from wet leaves.

The expression on Mildred's face had remained with Franklin while he explored the house. There was no doubt she knew something. He re-examined the pile of cushions, studied the feather boa as if there might be a clue among its scarlet fronds and, giving up further speculation, went out to call on Mildred.

They had not been friends, never more than neighbours passing the time of day, though he believed she had once been in the house for coffee with Harriet – a drink, more likely, knowing Harriet – but she welcomed him with open arms.

'I'm not at all surprised,' she said when he told her of his wife's absence, and she repeated it three times more. She gave him a coy sideways glance. 'Her young friend has been here with her for – oh, at least two weeks.'

'Her young friend?' said Franklin, barely able to keep from smiling.

'Keith Hill, he's called. Very good-looking. He has this amazing old American car and when that disappeared from the mews I thought – well, I couldn't help thinking ...'

'That he and Harriet had done a moonlight flit,' said Franklin, grinning.

Mildred thought smiling inappropriate. She was

almost shocked. 'Tony and I saw him here last night. I expect they were just about to leave. Surely she left you a note?'

'Just a feather boa,' said Franklin.

He walked back to Orcadia Cottage, for he had one task left to perform before taking the glad news to Anthea. For the first time he noticed that the back door was unlocked and the key missing. That sort of carelessness was typical of Harriet. It might be wise for him to have the locks changed.

Out in the yard, walking with care to avoid slipping on the sticky paste the leaves made, Franklin lifted up the manhole cover. He was strong for his age and it presented him with no problem to lug it the necessary couple of feet and insert it quietly into the opening. Then he trod on it a couple of times to make sure it was airtight and watertight.

Teddy slept. He dreamt of the wooden mansion, but this time he was inside it, making his way through its timbered chambers, smelling its aromatic resinous scent. He must have grown very small, for this, after all, was the sideboard he had dismembered. The towers he stood beneath, looking up through their hollow spires, were the finials that ornamented its shelves, and the galleries he climbed so laboriously, its drawers. Its pillars had become flying buttresses and now he emerged into a high, dark cloister, which was the double row of railings that ran round its table top.

The cloister ended at something like a cliff edge. He stood on the dark, shiny ridge looking down an immense distance into a darkness in which paler vapours swirled. For some reason he expected an emergence from those depths, not Francine, but someone from the distant past. Mr Chance, perhaps. As he stood there, gazing, longing for a sign, a glimmer of life and light, it came to him that of all the people he had ever known – Francine didn't count, Francine was different – Mr Chance was the only one he had really liked.

But he turned away, knowing he was to be disappointed, and walked back the way he had come, along the wooden passages, through the wooden chambers, into the heart of the sideboard mansion, until he found himself in a tiny dark cell. With the closing of the door behind him he woke up.

Rather, he was unsure whether he woke or still slept. He had been in a cell and was now in another and in an even deeper darkness. Blackness was absolute, dense as the inside of a cloth bag. And his breathing was shallow, the air – or some scarcely breathable atmosphere – pressed around him, thick and foul-smelling. There was too little of it to permit of struggling or thought or activity, so he pulled the blanket over his head once more and fell back into sleep.

The sleep from which there's no awakening.

Chapter 39

Jonathan Nicholson was a fifty-five-year-old civil servant who lived in Dawes Road, Fulham, with a wife and three teenage children. It was his wife's nephew, not he, who was the owner of a red sports car. The nephew was called Darren Curlew, he lived in Chiswick and had a girlfriend in Ealing. Darren Curlew was taken to the police station at five in the morning and was still there when the sun rose, the light came and the day's business began.

Silenced and retreating into her inner world, Francine was not unhappy. She had a sense of the bad things in her life all being past, that soon there would be a new beginning. Her speechlessness troubled her chiefly because it brought her father so much distress and because she couldn't phone Teddy. Something told her, some deep certainty and faith in herself, that if she remained calm and tranquil – and she had no inclination to be otherwise – the power of speech would come back to her and never depart again.

To Teddy she wrote several letters, not to Orcadia Cottage, where she was increasingly sure he should never have been, but to his own home. No answers came, though she had told him he could phone her and her father would speak for her. He was angry with her, she thought rather sadly, for not going back to him when she had promised. But his silence was really only what she had expected and it brought her nothing more than ruefulness. Things would never have worked out for them, they were quite wrong for each other, and had been drawn together in the first place only by their youth and their looks.

She slept a lot, she read, she thought about the past. Holly, back from Sulawesi, came to see her and talked for hours, expecting no answers. Miranda came back from Apia and Isabel down from Cambridge and they sat with her and told her of their adventurous lives. She and her father spent Christmas quietly at home, and Flora came to see them with her new husband and their little boy aged two.

A silent woman, yet one who was able to ride on the tube and use a ticket machine – if she was spoken to and made no reply, the enquirer took her for a foreign tourist – she went in the first week of January up to Teddy's house in Neasden. With her she took the diamond-and-sapphire ring, wrapped in a tissue and sealed in an envelope. Before leaving home she had dialled his number, unable to speak to him, but just for an indication as to whether he was at home or not. There had been no reply.

And there was no reply when she rang his doorbell. That was a relief, for she couldn't explain, she couldn't defend herself, she could only be passive and silent. So she put the envelope through the letter-box and made her way home again.

Victor in the second contest between herself and Harriet, Anthea could afford to be generous. In her opinion Franklin should do his best to find his wife, even though she might be living happily somewhere with Keith Hill. Franklin said she would find him soon enough. As soon as she was in need, and that wouldn't be long delayed, she would be in touch. Meanwhile, he put Orcadia Cottage on the market. After all, it belonged to him. He bought a house in

South Kensington because Anthea had always wanted to live there. Considering its location, it had quite a large garden, which he could tend and De Valera run about in. Even before contracts were exchanged he moved the best of the furniture out of Orcadia Cottage, including the four-poster bed and the new mirror.

Darren Curlew and Jonathan Nicholson were soon dismissed from the police enquiries and they were no further in finding who was responsible for Julia's death. Her funeral took place at last, in the second week of January.

The Edsel was first clamped, then removed. Eventually its ownership was traced to Keith Grex. But, according to Nigel Hewlett and Marguerite Palmer, occupants of the house next door, he hadn't lived there for months, nearly a year by now. They told the police he had moved to Liphook, though they had no address for him. Teddy, his nephew, would know. Teddy had shared the house with him, but he too had not been seen for a long time.

'October, wasn't it, Nige?' said Marguerite Palmer. 'No, I tell a lie, it was November. The twentieth, your mum's birthday, because she was over here and she said, "Where's that car then," and I said he'd taken it out the night before and not been back.'

'And he never came back,' said Nigel Hewlett. 'His grandma's been in and out, but it's no good you asking her, she doesn't know his whereabouts either.'

The dry-cleaners in Notting Hill Gate pursued their usual policy with uncollected cleaning, kept it for three months, then put it on sale. Harriet's Versace and Lacroix hung on a clothes rack out on the pavement alongside blouses from C & A and trousers from Littlewoods. The only concession the

411

shop made was to offer her suits at five pounds apiece instead of the usual one pound fifty. Even at the higher price they were soon snapped up.

Immersed in his new troubles, Richard had almost forgotten that strange interview he had had with a Detective Superintendent and a Detective Inspector a few days before Julia's death. He might never have reverted to it but for the idea that came into his head one midnight when, as was often the case with him, he couldn't sleep. Suppose the same man had killed both his wives? Suppose the murderer was someone not primarily intent on destroying them but himself?

It was a dreadful thought, yet there was a gleam of light in that darkness. For if personal hatred of him had been the motive, it could not have been confusion between the two Dr Hills which had brought the killer to the house.

In the morning he phoned the police. They said, not with contempt but with patience, that this theory had early on occurred to them. But they had almost immediately dismissed it.

'Why?' Richard asked.

'We'd like to see you, Dr Hill.' He winced at that 'Dr', as he always did, yet they were only trying to be polite. The policeman mentioned the Inspector Richard had talked to before. 'He's got something to tell you. We were about to give you a ring.'

'Why?' Richard asked again when he was sitting in the Inspector's office. 'Since you haven't found anyone for either of these murders how can you be so sure the same man wasn't responsible for both?'

'We have found someone for the murder of Mrs Jennifer Hill.'

We often react very differently to such revelations from the way we think we will. Richard didn't know why he should blush when told his first wife's killer

412

had been found; he would have expected to shiver. But the hot blood poured into his face and he felt a sprinkling of sweat on his upper lip. 'You've made an arrest?' he said.

A shake of the head, a mildly embarrassed look – was he imagining it? 'There have been considerable advances in techniques of DNA testing since your wife's death, Dr Hill. Had these been available to the investigation at the time, the perpetrator would have been found within days of the murder. There is no doubt about that.'

Bewildered, Richard said nothing.

'These things are painful to talk about, even after so long, I know that. Hairs were found on your wife's clothing, apart from her own, short, light-brown hairs. The DNA in them has now been matched.'

'But why? How?'

'Dr Hill . . .'

'For God's sake don't call me that!' Richard had never explained his feelings to the police, had spoken of them only to David Stanark and to Julia, but now he did. 'It is because I called myself "Doctor" in the phone book that my wife was killed. My house was mistaken for the home of another Dr Hill.'

'No, no, that's not the case. That was the view taken at the time, but it was mistaken. I am sorry to have to tell you this, Dr – er, Mr Hill, but your wife was involved with another man and it was he who killed her. He killed her because she wanted to end the relationship. After he had shot her he went upstairs to look for the letters he had written her, and presumably he found them, because we never did.'

And now Richard began to react as he had anticipated in dreams and fantasies; he shivered and his hands trembled. But he found a voice and

413

managed questions. 'Why now? How do you know all this now? Out of the blue . . .'

'Because the man is dead. He confessed some of this to his wife before he died. It was too much for her to take and she left him. I think, if it is any consolation to you, that his remorse was very great for many years. And not only for the murder . . .'

'I don't understand.'

'Let's say for deceiving you, not just with your wife, but afterwards, for giving himself an alibi by providing you with one. For establishing himself as your friend – for presuming to – well, counsel you.'

'I don't believe it,' Richard said, meaning as people often do when they say this, that they believe it all too well.

'Your daughter recognised the top of his head when he came to the door.'

'My daughter recognised, or thought she recognised, the tops of several men's heads when they came to the door.'

'In the case of David Stanark', said the Inspector, 'she was right.'

The shock of knowing the truth brought back Francine's voice. Richard had hesitated about telling her, but at last he reasoned that it would be wrong to keep the truth from her. It would have been a different matter if she had not been in the house at the time, not taken to that identity parade, not made to suffer so long for the consequences of the crime, as he too had been.

One load of guilt had been shed. The last thing he wanted was to assume another, that of deceiving Francine and keeping up the deception for the rest of his life.

She astounded him. 'I found the letters,' she said.

414

'They were in the wig cupboard. I brought them here and hid them.'

He felt a pang as if someone had struck him in the chest. His voice was hoarse. 'Did you read them?'

'I couldn't read joined-up writing.' She managed a smile. 'Cursive script. By the time I could I was afraid to read them. I think that even then I knew they were things no one should read.'

'You kept them?'

'I threw them away. In the bin in the school playground.'

They said no more about it. Richard felt it improper and humiliating to discuss with his eighteen-year-old daughter her mother's love affair; Francine thought humbly that as yet she knew too little about love and sex to make judgements or even to comment. Perhaps, if she had shown the letters to her father her life would have been very different. On the other hand, poor Julia had been a woman who in any circumstances would have found some pretext for imprisoning and protecting her.

But she did use the advantage she seemed to have gained to ask her father if she could go with Holly on the trip charting the progress of Trinidadian land crabs and when they returned, share her flat until they both went up to Oxford. Asking was perhaps not quite what she did; she told him of her intention, though so gently that he believed she was asking permission. He gave it gladly.

Junk mail was mostly what came through the letter-box, flyers from restaurants and car-hire companies, carpet cleaners and plumbers. Coals to Newcastle, this last, in the opinion of Agnes Tawton, though no plumber lived there now. She had taken to popping in once a week, picking up the post and looking for unconsidered trifles.

A cheque for a hundred pounds from a Marjorie J. Trent and made out to T. Grex was useless to her. She had no bank account. The only other item of interest was a ring in an envelope. Agnes recognised it as her daughter's engagement ring, though she hadn't seen it for many years.

The proper thing to do with a ring is put it on one's finger and this Agnes did, the little finger of her left hand, all the others being too big for it. Of her son-in-law she had always had a low opinion, so she doubted if the ring could be worth much – he had probably picked it up in Wembley market for a couple of quid.

But she kept it on. Her friend Gladys said it was 'dressy', so she wore it on the Over-Sixties spring outing to Felixstowe. After tea in a restaurant on the front she went into the ladies' cloakroom to powder her nose and wash her hands. Agnes had never had an engagement ring of her own and now, so late in her life, it gave her a thrill to take off the ring and lay it on the side of the basin like all the other ladies lined up at all the other basins.

There were no towels, only those hand driers that blew out hot air, and blew it slowly. One alone was in working order and Agnes had to queue up. By the time her hands were dry Gladys was calling to her to hurry up, the coach was going, and she trotted off, rather flustered, leaving the ring on the side of the basin.

In their advertisements the estate agents described Orcadia Cottage as 'the bijou home immortalised in the internationally acclaimed artwork of Simon Alpheton', though the photograph they took looked nothing like the painting. In the depths of winter Orcadia Cottage displayed its true self, its shape and proportions. The cherry-coloured brickwork, usually concealed under festoons of green or gold or crimson leaves, was now veiled only by a network of fine ginger-coloured tendrils like cobwebs made by a red spider. Anthea, who understandably had always disliked the place, said it looked as if it had taken its clothes off and stood revealed in its dirty underwear.

But Franklin soon got an offer. The purchasers, an American businessman and his wife, wanted to move in quickly. When Franklin offered them the report his surveyors had made thirty years before they were happy to dispense with a survey.

After all, the house had been there for two hundred years and wasn't likely to fall down now.

The Rottweiler

Ruth Rendell

The first girl had a bite mark on her neck but they traced the DNA to her boyfriend. But the tabloids got hold of the story and called the killer 'The Rottweiler' and the name stuck.

The latest murder takes place very near Inez Ferry's antique shop in Marylebone. Someone saw a shadowy figure running away past the station, but the only other clues are that the murderer usually strangles his victims and removes something personal – like a cigarette lighter or a necklace . . .

SInce her husband died, too soon in their relationship, Inez has supplemented her income by taking in tenants. The murderous activities of the sinister 'Rottweiler' will exert a profound influence on the lives of this heterogeneous little community, especially when the suspicion emerges that one of them may be a homicidal maniac.

'In the world of contemporary crime fiction, Rendell really is top dog'
Sunday Times

'In Rendell's expert hands, you'll want to keep reading until dawn – without the light on'
Red

'Rendell skilfully crafts her characters and they breathe feverishly through her imagination'
The Times

arrow books

Road Rage

Ruth Rendell

A by-pass is planned in Knightsbridge that will destroy its peace and natural habitat for ever. Dora Wexford joins the protest, but the Chief Inspector must be more circumspect: trouble is expected.

As the protesters begin to make their presence felt, a young woman's badly decomposed body is unearthed. Burden believes he knows the murderer's identity but Wexford is not convinced. Furthermore, having just become a grandfather, he is struggling to put aside his familial responsibilities and emotions in order to do his job.

The case progresses, the protest escalates. And alarmingly, a number of people begin to disappear, including Dora Wexford . . .

'One of the greatest novelists presently at work in our language . . . a writer whose work should be read by anyone who either enjoys a brilliant mystery – or distinguished literature'
Scott Turow

arrow books

Adam and Eve and Pinch Me

Ruth Rendell

'Adam and Eve and Pinch Me went down to the river to bathe Adam and Eve were drowned. Who was saved?'

This old nursery rhyme is a favourite of Jerry Leach (if that is the name he is using at the time), a handsome ne're do well, who sponges off women.

Five women, unknown to each other, are his willing victims. One he even married once and abandoned, while promising to marry another. But, with the cruel irony he would be the first to recognise in that nursery rhyme, Jerry, almost accidentally, becomes the victim of one of his female prey.

'It is not only her rate of productivity which is startling. It is also ability . . . to tap into registers of feeling which range from the commonplace to the psychopathic. She is to be treasured.'
Anita Brookner, *Spectator*

'Rendell is not only irresistible because of the brilliance of her descriptions of contemporary life and the sad truth of her characters. She is a great storyteller who knows how to make sure that the reader has to turn the pages out of a desperate need to find out what is going to happen next.'
John Mortimer, *Sunday Times*

'Unequalled ability to build and sustain suspense'
Peter Guttridge, *Observer*

arrow books

The Babes in the Wood
Ruth Rendell

A Chief Inspector Wexford Novel

Thee hadn't been anything like this kind of rain in living memory. The River Brede had burst its banks, and not a single house in the valley had escaped the flooding. In the midst of all this, two teenagers – Giles and Sophie Dade – and Joanna Tray, the women who had been looking after them, have vanished. The Subaqua Task Force could find no trace of them, but Mrs Dade was still convinced her children were dead.

The investigation would call into question many of Wexford's assumptions about the way people behaved, including his own family . . .

'A complex saga of family relationships, remorselessly exposing neurotic inner lives'
Scotland on Sunday

'Superb plotting and psychological insight make this another Rendell gripper'
Woman & Home

'*The Babes in the Wood* extends the conventions of the who-dunit, going beyond a cool analysis of how and why a crime was committed, and building into a convincing, often troubling exploration of the way violence infects and damages everyone it touches'
Sunday Times

arrow books

The Bridesmaid

Ruth Rendell

Philip hated violence in any form. He loved beautiful things – like Flora, the stone statue in his mother's garden and Senta, his sister's bridesmaid.

White-skinned, delicate Senta of the silver hair, who looked just like Flora. The passionate, fascinating Senta who begged Philip to prove his love for her by killing someone . . .

'Every sentence is appallingly, shockingly convincing'
The Times

'To read her at her best – and *The Bridesmaid* is perhaps her best book – is like stepping onto a trundling country bus and feeling it turn into a roller coaster'
Sunday Times

arrow books

A Demon In My View

Ruth Rendell

Her white face, beautiful, unmarked by any flaw of skin or feature, stared blankly back at him. He fancied that she had cringed, her slim body pressing further into the wall behind her.

He didn't speak. He had never known how to talk to women. There was only one thing he had ever been able to do to women and, advancing now, smiling, he did it.

Then, when it was all over, he straightened her against the wall so that she would be ready to die for him again. It was the best thing in his life, just knowing she was there, waiting till the next time . . .

But one day she wasn't waiting, wasn't there . . .

'A major talent'
The Sun

'A distinguished storyteller at the very height of her powers'
Sunday Express

arrow books